CRITICAL ACC[...]
J. NEIL SCHU[...]

THE RAINBOW CADENZA

"Particular praise is due Schulman for the detailed working out of the heroine's profession of laser-graphics composer. Future art forms are seldom handled with the intelligence and vividness seen here."

Booklist

"A highly recommended feast of invention and serious speculation"

Library Journal

"A thoughtful, unusually well written book that raises the most important questions about life and art"

Michael Medved, author of *Hospital*

"Intensely interesting...Mr. Schulman is a remarkably gifted author."

Nathaniel Branden, Ph.D., author of
The Psychology of Self-Esteem

"An impassioned plea for individual liberty...A feast of clones, underground ministers, witchcraft, and politics. This is an entertaining and challenging book."

The Sacramento Bee

"Engrossingly suspenseful...wickedly funny and chilling at the same time"

Publishers Weekly

THE RAINBOW CADENZA

CADENZA

A Novel in Vistata Form

J. NEIL SCHULMAN

AVON
PUBLISHERS OF BARD, CAMELOT, DISCUS AND FLARE BOOKS

This novel is a work of fiction. Names, characters, places, and incidents either are the product of the author's imagination or are used fictitiously. Any resemblance to actual events or locales or persons, living or dead, is entirely coincidental.

AVON BOOKS
A division of
The Hearst Corporation
1790 Broadway
New York, New York 10019

Library of Congress Cataloging in Publication Data

Schulman, J. Neil (Joseph Neil).
   The rainbow cadenza.

   I. Title.
PS3569.C539R3   1983   813'.54   82-19680

First Avon Printing: November 1986

AVON TRADEMARK REG. U.S. PAT. OFF. AND IN OTHER COUNTRIES, MARCA REGISTRADA, HECHO EN U.S.A.

Printed in the U.S.A.

K-R 10 9 8 7 6 5 4 3 2 1

AUTHOR'S NOTE

The Wiccen rituals portrayed in this novel have been adapted from rituals described in *The Book of Shadows* by Lady Sheba (Llewellyn Publications, 1973) and from *The Feminist Book of Lights and Shadows* by Zsuzanna E. Budapest (Luna Publications, 1976). I have, however, seen fit to adapt, edit, and rewrite the entire universe to fit the needs of my story, and these rituals are no exception; they should not be taken as authentic by serious students of the Craft, whom I refer to these two volumes.

The only actual location in this book is the Villa Olga, a resort hotel in Charlotte Amalie, St. Thomas, where I spent a pleasant three weeks in 1972 playing chess with its owner and drinking piña coladas. Since I have not been back since, I have no idea of its current status as of this writing, and references should not be taken as literal.

Except for philosophers, authors, and artists mentioned for literary purpose, no names, events, characters, customs or institutions should be taken as referring to actual events, people, customs, or institutions, past or present. For the record, Clive Staples Lewis has not been canonized—yet.

LASERIUM is a registered trademark of Laser Images, Inc., of Van Nuys, California, for laser concerts of the kind described in this novel. The use of laserium as a lower-case generic term for the place where such concerts would be performed in the distant future—presumably when such a trademark had normally expired—is a device common to futuristic fiction, and should not be held to deny, weaken, or otherwise louse up Laser Images, Inc.'s, use of the LASERIUM trademark.

The opinions and lifestyles of the characters in this book should not be taken as being the author's own, or those of any real person. If there's anything I want to pin myself down on, I'll do it in my own voice.

J. N. S.

To My Father
The Lord High Violinist
and to My Mother
The Lord High Everything Else

THE RAINBOW CADENZA

THE SCALE

I.

λ3800Å to 4100Å

SHE LOVED the lights.

She watched as they circled around her, a merry waltz of blue sparks and red. She watched as one of the red sparks quite suddenly turned bright gold. She watched as the other lights began dancing around the gold, teasing it, then finally chased it away from the waltzes of red and blue, to dance alone.

She watched the dances of red and blue as they rose and fell, advanced and retreated, changed size and form then changed back again, burned brightly, then, one spark by one, winked out. She watched the single, golden spark begin a new dance by itself, dancing until it exploded into hundreds and hundreds of other sparks: golds and oranges, oranges and reds, reds and violets, violets and indigos, indigos and blues, blues and greens, greens and more sparks of gold.

She watched thousands of sparks dance wildly, ecstatically, for a few minutes, then, beginning slowly, race around her faster and faster and faster until she was surrounded by an immense spiral rainbow.

When the dance was over, she did not understand what, or how, or why, but she knew the lights were telling her something, if only she could understand them. She knew she had to find out what the lights were telling her, and more: though she was not yet five years old, Joan Seymour Darris made a promise to herself that someday she also would tell the colors how to make a rainbow.

THE PYRADOME sits on Manhattan Boulevard in midtown Newer York, about where Saint Patrick's used to be, a thirty-story-high pyramid whose dome, bulging out the sides, makes it look pregnant. Indeed, as one watches it—an immense jewel pulsating in kaleidoscopic colors under the noontide sun—one can easily believe that this is not a building but a huge, primordial creature about to give birth.

Give birth it did, almost precisely at noon, as five thousand children, teachers, and very harried mothers swarmed out the apex of the McDanald Media Temple onto the escalators descending the outside of the pyradome. Well into the maternal category, but looking spectacularly composed in spite of the four children she was herding, Eleanor Delaney Darris paused on the pyradome's middle landing long enough to light a desperately needed joynette, then exhaled in time to tell six-year-old Nick for the third and *last* time to stop calling his twin brother, Vic, a dirty Touchable.

The twins had been just impossible for the hour-long children's concert. The boys'-section usher had reported to Eleanor afterward that he had shushed them twice during the performance, and Eleanor had promised them a spanking from their father when they got home, though this was an idle threat meant only to settle them down. Eleanor did not blame six-year-olds for having the attention spans of, well, *six-year-olds* . . . not anymore. Thank the Lady, that was one mistake she wasn't making this time. She blamed herself, instead, for not sitting with her children in a family box, where she could have explained things a bit, but of course this possibility was excluded by the very reason she had taken them to this concert on an impossibly busy day.

She was there as head of the Darris Foundation to introduce the morning's two solo performers: the elderly lasemeister, Wolfgang Jaeger, and a twelve-year-old prodigy whom the Foundation was sponsoring to study under the semiretired virtuoso at the conservatory Jaeger now headed in Ad Astra. So Eleanor consoled herself that at least eight-year-old Mark had behaved, and was delightfully surprised when the pyradome patron had reported to her that four-year-old Joanie—who'd had a couch all to herself in the girls' section—had been completely entranced by her first lasegraphy concert.

She glanced down at Joanie, who was staring back at the pyradome's changing colors. Was there any possibility . . . ? But no. Eleanor's first daughter, Vera, had taught her not to make that mistake again either. Don't fool yourself into believing it, she cautioned herself. Whatever seeds you plant here, the harvest will not be your own.

She told Mark to grab on to his sister's hand, then guided the children back down the escalator. Eleanor was no longer inclined to let worries about children mar her enjoyment of an April day such as this. When they reached the promenade level, transferring onto a slidewalk to the parking zone, she leaned into the wind, allowing it to ripple her ash-blond hair. Eleanor inhaled deeply. The promenade smelled of marigolds and freshly cut grass, here and there mixed with confectionery odors from hovercart vendors. Taking a final toke from her joynette, she hurried her children past a red-cloaked woman selling hoop dogs on bagels. She reassured herself that she had nothing against Touchables—what enlightened person did?—but merely wanted to avoid the twins' wheedling her for something to spoil their lunch.

Visits to the city were a rare luxury for Eleanor these days, what with taking care of a husband and five children, and another pregnancy—another *boy*—planned for next year. If one added in her chair duties for the Darris Foundation, her administrative responsibilities for her family circle, and her U.S.O. volunteer work, a trip to town for a concert was near priceless, even if she *did* have to emcee the concert.

Eleanor felt a proprietorship over spring in Newer York. She had been born on this island, grown up here, gone to school here, and—except for nine years immediately following the Colonial War—had spent the better part of her sixty-three years living here. When she was nine, on a school field trip to Staten Island, she had watched a rain of meteors kill Manhattan, orphaning her, but she did not often think about the War, and she did not think about it now. Spring was a time for rebirth, not for mourning a long-dead past. So, rather, she thought of this Newer York's resurrection, a city designed as a single work of art. She knew this city's rhythms and its seasons as well as she knew her own, and she felt in this particular spring a promise of great things about to happen.

But there was no time to spend admiring the season; she keyed her wristphone, then ordered her limousine to wait for them at passenger loading. Eleanor had promised Mr. McIntosh that she would take back two-year-old Zack by one o'clock, giving the governor his afternoon off before taking charge of visiting children during the ball that evening. Vera's coming-out ball, Eleanor reminded herself again; the thought caused a point of light inside her to flare, as if she'd touched a fire gem. Tonight, Vera was returning home after her three years in the service.

It was not that Eleanor was particularly patriotic, as one might naturally have assumed. She was not *particularly* patriotic—no more than anybody else, and no more than she had to be. Eleanor had been thirty-four when the first women's draft lottery had been held—just under the age limit—and she had accepted her own term of service with neither pride nor resentment. It was just something she was being made to do. But Eleanor had wanted to be proud of her twin-daughter for so long, and Vera had provided Eleanor with so little opportunity to be. While a good term of service was not quite the same thing as the premiere at the pyradome Eleanor had once wished for Vera, still, it was something.

If the cliché was true that twinning yourself only doubled your problems, then Eleanor had found in Vera the classic twin. Eleanor had self-conceived right after her own term of service had ended, twenty-six years before, by what was poetically called virgin birth— poetic since Eleanor had by no means been untouched by men. Three years of serving under men, day in and day out, had seemed enough for a while, and a daughter who was all her own was to be Eleanor's claim to her own destiny again, after the regimentation of service life.

A parthenogenic daughter, with all forty-six chromosomes taken from her mother, would be virtually a genetic duplicate of Eleanor. Eleanor decided to call her Vera, since she would breed true. Vera was to be a creative extension of Eleanor, in a way no child born of both mother and father could be, because not only would she be a twin of her mother, but also she would be raised according to her mother's beliefs alone. Her upbringing would not subject her to the male-centered channeling by which a little girl was programmed, before she could consciously question it, that being female meant being the passive and the inferior.

That had been her own lifelong barrier, Eleanor thought, which prevented her from attaining what she could only call "something of my own." It wasn't possessions, it wasn't a home, it wasn't friends, it wasn't lovers, it wasn't a husband, it wasn't wealth or power, it wasn't any job she had ever had, it wasn't—she had found out the hard way—a twin daughter. She had traveled the world looking for it. She had searched through libraries and museums, universities and cathedrals. She had explored her soul, self, and psyche through dozens of techniques, with dozens of masters. But what she was looking for was not to be found in this way. She had always known there was something—there had to be something—that she could do in a way nobody else could, and it would be doing this particular thing that would be her existence and her joy. But she had never found it, and her inability to find it was a mystery to her and an open wound.

She tried to think what events in her childhood had done this to her, but she had only a dim recollection of her parents during her formative years before the Colonial War. When her parents and younger brothers had been killed, Eleanor was sent to live with her mother's parents in Kentucky, while her three older brothers remained at boarding schools.

Grandma and Grandpa Collier were strict Southern Baptists who had raised Eleanor's mother, then Eleanor, on their marijuana farm. Grandpa Collier had been one of the first subsidized male babies in the thirty-year-long Brushfire War, and when he got out of the army he bought the marijuana farm with G.I. loans. Soon he had earned a fortune large enough to win Grandma's hand in marriage, as he phrased it. This was no small feat, considering that as a result of militarists' paying families to produce extra male babies for a generation, at the end of the Brushfire War there were already four men for every woman.

The Colliers had a typical Brushfire War mentality and even forty-five years later Eleanor found it difficult to break free of it entirely. Men were supposed to work, fight, and achieve; women were supposed to keep their country strong by having lots of male babies.

But men were dangerous creatures who had no compunction about using force to have a woman, just as they'd used force to have enemy women in the Brushfire War they'd just fought. Even today, one war later, forty years into the World Federation, and three decades after the women's service had solved the rape problem—as popular history had it—Eleanor felt nervous walking out alone at night, after Grandma's incessant warnings. How many times had she had to listen to Grandma's story about how she'd been raped the one night she'd gone out having forgotten to wear her chastity electrobelt?

Eleanor had rebelled against these hopelessly old-fashioned attitudes, and at eighteen had broken free from her grandparents to return to what was now Newer York. There she had lived alone and with a number of lovers of both sexes. Her father's fortune had been wiped out with Wall Street, and her grandparents could send her no money because they'd traded in their farm for a condominium in the first postwar colony, St. Clive, but Eleanor never had to worry where her rent money was coming from. With six men for every woman on Earth such things were not a problem for an attractive girl who frequented the mocha houses in those days—even without outright prostitution, which was still legal then.

It was after sixteen years of living the free-spirited life of a *boh*— consorting with the coca drinkers and roga players, doing what she wanted, when she wanted, where she wanted—that the Federation had begun Universal Service and Eleanor had been drafted into its Peace Corps.

Vera was to have been Eleanor's reply both to her grandparents—now living in the colonies—and to her own society. Eleanor had given Vera the opportunity and the encouragement to sample the world's culture—to choose an ascending path for herself—and to demonstrate to the world that a mind and a spirit in a female body could equal or better any accomplishment a mind and a spirit in a male body could achieve.

It had not quite worked out that way. Though Vera had proved to be neither passive nor inferior, she directed her talents in ways that her mother could interpret only as perverse. Eleanor had wanted to dress her daughter to emphasize her individuality; Vera had been more interested in identical mother-daughter outfits. Eleanor had given her daughter toys and games designed to encourage her intellectual development. These remained in the toy chest while Vera played Mommy endlessly to a doll her great-grandparents had sent her: a lifelike re-creation, taken from holograms, of Eleanor as a baby.

Later on, Eleanor wanted her daughter to experience the great cultural treasures of the world. Vera sat in the Louvre, in the Kremlin, and on the steps of Chichén Itzá playing trashy storydiscs. Eleanor was left to experience the great cultural treasures of the world.

In school, Vera's teachers acknowledged that she was capable of brilliant work, but her grades never seemed to reflect it. Eleanor heard variations on the same theme over and over again: Vera's test had been perfect, but she had allowed another student to copy from her, failing both of them. Vera's essay had been brilliant, but the teacher was sure she had plagiarized it, even though the original source couldn't be located. Vera's homework assignments had proved she knew the material cold, but mysteriously she still managed to fail the final.

Eleanor's worst disappointment with Vera, however, was caused by their one mutual love: lasegraphy. Eleanor had started Vera on lessons when she was four—the same age at which Eleanor's mother had started her on the console. Vera's teacher, Jack Malcolm, had told Eleanor that her daughter showed an unusual grasp of sequential logic, as well as having a formidable sense of color, motion, and form. She continued her lessons for eleven years—developing a brilliant console technique along the way—and performed remarkably in student competitions.

When Vera was fifteen, Malcolm arranged financial backing through the Darris Foundation (and in doing so introduced Eleanor to her future husband) for Vera to give a premiere recital at the pyradome. Several of Newer York's most influential lasegraphic critics had promised to attend. Vera was to perform Geoffrey Moulton's *Vistata No. 3*, several rather pyrotechnic *Konzertstücke* by Wolfgang Jaeger, and a new composition of her own, *Fugue in Blue*.

Fugue in Blue was never premiered. Three hours before her recital, Vera went into convulsions and was rushed to Golden-Sky General Hospital. She stayed there five days while doctors ran every conceivable test on her. And though they reported that her convulsions had been genuine, they were never able to detect any physiological cause.

Vera refused ever to return to the console, and she refused to give her reasons to anyone. For years afterward, she even refused to remain in the same room where a lasegraphic recording was being played. It was only in her senior year of university, where she maintained above-mediocre work in a political-science major, that Vera relaxed enough to begin participating in lasegraphy again, but solely as a viewer. She began attending concerts and playing recordings, but she never again allowed it any importance in her life.

She entered into the service immediately after her university graduation, as soon as her student draft deferment was up. From all accounts her mother had been able to receive, Vera's service record was consistently excellent. Although this was the only consistent excellence Vera had shown since abandoning the console, Eleanor wondered why this knowledge now filled her with a dread that wiped out the warm tingle she'd felt a few minutes before. The apprehension lasted just an instant, but when it was gone it took the warmth with it, leaving only the chill of someone's death.

Eleanor tried putting this out of her mind as she marched her second daughter and three of her four sons—all conceived in the usual way—into the pyradome parking zone. Soon she was aided in her attempt by the slidewalk, as it merged them into the crush of departing passengers. Her limousine phoned her back to let her know that it was waiting for them at Platform Green. She struggled to keep her children together as they passed through red, orange, and yellow platforms, where schoolmasters were shepherding uniformed boys back onto the airbuses they'd arrived in. When the family reached Platform Green, Eleanor did some quick shepherding of her own, until they reached a queue of private skymobiles. Past a Schwinn station wagon, past a Cadillac de Sade, past a Mao miniflyer, a powder-blue Astarte limousine was hovering.

Eleanor's skymobile was a brand-new bubble-top model and there was the usual argument with the children about which one would get the prized seat up top. She awarded it to Mark, this time, for his good behavior at the concert. As soon as everyone was strapped in, she told the computer to fly them directly home.

"Home," to both the Darris family and the onboard computer pilot, was an estate in upper Hudson Parish about 160 kilometers north of Manhattan via the Hudson River Air Corridor—in Kingston, to be exact. Traffic control cleared them for takeoff, only to stick them into a holding circle at 1,000 meters for nine minutes. Eleanor smoked another joynette and allowed Joanie to join Mark in the bubble for aerial views of the pyradome and the Rainborough Bridge. Nick, feeling left out, started complaining that he had to go to the bathroom. Not to be outdone by his twin brother,

Vic immediately chimed in. Eleanor told them they should have thought of that back at the pyradome, thinking herself that the little monsters deserved to wet themselves.

Joanie was already rebelted into her seat by the time traffic control routed them through Newark—the wrong direction, but avoiding the worst of noon traffic—and when they were eventually into the Hudson Corridor they were assigned a 5,000-meter cruising altitude. Eight minutes later, they dropped out of the corridor at Poughkeepsie, circled Port Ewen, and in another few minutes were into a final descent over the Darris apple orchards. A quick pass over their squatball course, their horse stables, and Lake Kingston brought them to the landing strip on the Darris estate, Helix Vista.

Suddenly, the computer sounded collision alarm. All of them were shoved back into their seats as the craft accelerated into a steep, banked climb. What the rape is going on? Eleanor wondered. Then they were hit by the airwash of another skymobile cutting only meters under them, and were violently rocked back and forth several times until the computer managed to compensate. All three boys started crying.

As suddenly as it started, the alarm stopped. The computer brought them around again in preparation for their landing. Eleanor could see a silvered craft on the Darris strip just ahead of them, taxiing across the lawn to their house, but it was too far off to recognize.

They came into the landing strip again and slowed to a hover. Eleanor manually taxied them off the runway before she cut out the impellents. Only after she had checked to make sure her children were all right, and had quieted down the boys, did Eleanor notice her own galloping pulse rate. No computer would have cut it that close. That other skymobile had been on manual. She was going to have that cloneraping pilot's heart for lunch.

Eleanor let Mark and Joanie out—her little girl amazingly serene, as if nothing unusual had happened—then turned around to let the twins out. "Oh, scat," she said.

The twins had wet the seat.

3

THAT CLONERAPING PILOT was, of course, Vera.

Eleanor marched across the lawn, her cubs in tow, a lioness preparing to make cat food out of the brainwiped lout who had dared to frighten her children. When she approached her house, though, she saw not a delivery boy's craft but a stiletto-shaped Phaethon sportster. The sportster's trunk was open, so she did not immediately see the jump-suited woman who was pulling out a general-issue Kevlar valise. When the bonnet was slammed shut, allowing her to see Vera, Eleanor was stunned.

Vera was not supposed to be home until that evening, arriving by suborbital shuttle; Stanton Darris—Eleanor's husband and Vera's stepfather—was supposed to pick up Vera at Soleri Skyport on his way home from work. Moreover, when Eleanor had seen her daughter on the last holiday leave Vera had used to come home— Beltane, almost a year ago—Vera had not even owned a skymobile.

So when, somewhat uncharacteristically, Vera shouted, "Mother!" and dropped her valise to throw her arms around Eleanor, it may be understandable why, in the spirit of the moment, Eleanor decided to forget the incident.

When lunch was served up, Vera was at the table, not on it.

Corporal Vera Delaney had been stationed in Honolulu. The night before her discharge, she had gone out to celebrate with several of her messmates; as usual the women went to the casinos on Molokai. They'd had a few tokes in the cannabistro, spent some time at the blackjack tables, and eventually lost all their money gambling. They were about to head back to their quarters when they passed by a velletrom table just as a player started a psychokinetic winning streak. Vera stopped for a moment to look, the man immediately associated his sudden streak of velleity with Vera's presence, and he asked her to stick around.

He kept pulling threes. And sixes. And twelves.

He'd just read a disc called *Velletrom: Free Will Can Pay Big!*

He owned a local skymobile dealership.

It was, of course, against regulations for a civilian to give a gift to a corporal in the Federation Peace Corps while she was on active duty. So he told Vera to drop by his dealership as soon as she was officially a civilian again. The silver Phaethon was a demonstrator.

"He didn't even want to fuck me," Vera told her mother.

"Lavender," Eleanor said.

Vera shook her head. "Would I have brought this up if he wasn't wearing blue? Uh-uh. He said if we fucked it wouldn't be a gift. Then where would he be the next time he wanted the Lady to bring him kinesis?"

"Gamblers and their superstitions," Eleanor said. She had been put off by her grandparents' religious fanaticism and believed in neither God nor Goddess.

Rather than have her new toy freighted home, Vera had decided to fly the craft herself, leaving that evening. From Honolulu to Newer York, 8,000 kilometers. Ten hours' flying time, with a two-hour rest stop in Pacifica and nothing to keep her going but a reservoir of hot coca mocha. And, of course, the Phaethon being a sport-ster, it was manual control all the way.

Aside from an hour's nap she'd caught in the parking zone of a Quiche & Knish in Los Angeles, Vera had been up since 9 A.M., Honolulu time, the previous day. Eleanor could well appreciate why Vera might have been a little bleary-eyed by the time she came into Helix Vista for a landing.

"But why didn't you phone me last night, to let us know your change of plans?"

"I thought I'd surprise you," Vera said.

"You did," Eleanor replied. She didn't add that she'd just as soon pass up such surprises. "But I'll get even tonight," she told her daughter. "I've managed to work up a little surprise of my own."

Vera went up to get some sleep before her ball. Eleanor made a quick call to Stanton's office, letting his secretary know that Stanton no longer needed to pick Vera up, then went to the kitchen to check on preparations. One of the robots brought her a bowl of dip to taste. She dipped her finger into it, then scowled. "Much too much garlic. Throw this away and start again." The robot threw the dip into the scintillator and made more dip while she checked on the caviar. This time she gave her okay.

She was just about to head into the children's den, to relieve Mr. McIntosh, when the repairman for the lawn dome and the champagne delivery arrived simultaneously. This day was becoming more impossible by the minute.

When Eleanor stopped into the children's den, Mr. McIntosh and the children had finished lunch, and the boys were on the floor with him playing a round-robin game; two-year-old Zack was perched on the governor's lap. Joan was sitting Indian-style in a big old beat-up armchair, drawing on rainbow paper with thermocrayons.

Mr. McIntosh was the youngest, and the best, governor Eleanor had ever hired; the slim, light-brown-haired boy had been nineteen when he had come to work for the Darris family three years before. His gentleness, endless patience, and easygoing intelligence ensured his rapport with the children. Eleanor just couldn't understand how some families could trust their children to a robot. A robot couldn't make a sulking child laugh, no matter how flexible its programming was supposed to be.

Eleanor sighed. "Mac . . ."

"I'll stay," the governor said. His rapport seemed almost magical at times. "Your turn, Mark."

"Onions," said Mark.

"But your afternoon," Eleanor said. "I promised."

"Nothing I can't put off," Mr. McIntosh said. "Very good, Mark. Vic?"

"Oranges."

"Sorry, Nick said oranges already. Try again." He turned to Eleanor again. "You can make it up to me next week."

"He did not! Go ick yourself!"

"I did too! You go ick *your*self!"

"You're a sweetheart," Eleanor said.

Mr. McIntosh smiled. "Let me prove it sometime."

Eleanor smiled slightly. "I'll take my word for it." The young man grinned again, then was immediately busy mediating between the twins.

She decided to put off her duties for another minute and walked over to Joan. Her daughter had drawn a big yellow dot with a multicolored spiral shooting out of it. It changed color with each orbit: yellow to orange, orange to red, red to violet, violet to indigo, indigo to blue, blue to green, green and circling back into the yellow again. A rainbow helix, of sorts.

"What have you got there, darling?"

Joan held up the paper to her mother. "See? I'm telling the lights."

" 'Telling the lights'?"

"Telling them, like this morning. They're dancing for me."

Eleanor crouched to examine the paper more closely. It was true. Joan had exactly remembered a spectral sequence from the children's concert—the finale to the last movement of Wolfgang Jaeger's *Resurrection Vistata*. She had drawn the correct sequence for a color scale.

For just a moment, Eleanor let her hopes sweep away her doubts. But once burned by Vera, Eleanor was shy of the fire. She believed it was her stage-mothering that had pressured her first daughter into a nervous collapse.

"Honey, can I have this when you're through with it? I want to keep it."

Joan handed it to her mother. "I'm gonna do another one."

Eleanor kissed Joan on her cheek, then rolled up the drawing, deciding to hang it in the kitchen. When she left to supervise unloading of the champagne, she began singing to herself, happily.

In the year Joan Seymour Darris turned five, there lived seven men for every woman on Earth.

A century earlier, cynics had commented that given an opportunity to create an advantage, the human race inevitably turned it into a disadvantage. Ecologists had said that given the possibility of destroying the natural balance, the "Cancer of the Planet" just naturally chose the unnatural. Clergy had found the chance to preach that once men and women turned from God's ordained plans, nothing but evil could result.

Only one thing was certain. Repeatedly given the choice between self-control and its opposites, tyranny and dissipation, too many of the race forswore self-control.

On February 15, 1979, following up on a technique developed by Dr. Ronald Ericsson of Sausalito, California, Dr. W. Paul Dmowski of Chicago announced his successful demonstration of a procedure whereby androsperm—those spermatozoa producing male offspring—could be concentrated to increase the probability of male children. The technique, however, would not work with female-producing gynosperm, and could therefore be used only to help create male babies. But the procedure was expensive, and there was no noticeable effect on population demographics.

Some years later, Dr. Bowie Golden-Sky of Los Angeles perfected a drug that, taken by a man the day before sexual intercourse, would deactivate his gynosperm entirely, thus ensuring that any offspring resulting from such a union would be male. There

23

was nothing at the time that a woman could take to change this. The most she could manage was the null result of no offspring at all.

After laboratory testing, Upjohnson Pharmaceuticals began marketing the drug worldwide under the commercial name Adamine.

Oddly or not, Adamine encountered little political opposition. Perhaps the pro-abortion arguments feminists had used regarding absolute control over their own bodies restrained them from telling men what they, in turn, could put into theirs.

It did not take long for the statisticians to notice that just about twice as many male babies were being born as female babies. Patriarchal cultures, particularly in the Middle and Far East, demonstrated a preference for male offspring. By the time the demographics became obvious to all, the Brushfire War had started. Male military leaders saw advantages to a surplus of males in a conventional war that looked bound to drag on. Politicians saw their advantage in victory from the cradle.

Manpower—specifically male—was demanded. In totalitarian countries, men were simply ordered to produce male babies. Those families not producing the desired surplus were punished. That women played a less-than-peripheral role in producing babies was a minor point that male political rulers never seemed to notice.

For the United States, it was another generation of young American men being chewed up in remote jungles, deserts, and ice floes. A long war seemed inevitable, but the constant drain on the country's supply of young men was making the war uneconomic and unpopular. Two solutions were arrived at.

In the short term, the United States persuaded Canada, Mexico, and its new ally Cuba to combine with it—on the models of NATO and the European Common Market—to form the North American Concord.

In the long term, the Concord parliament passed an act granting progressive tax rebates to families producing healthy male babies. Female babies were still allowed, of course, but were not subsidized.

It was a popular law. For many families, the tax rebates were the difference between soyaburgers and beefalo steaks—with enough, perhaps, left over for a new holovision set. In Cuba and Mexico, the rebates were for many families the difference between squalor and the much higher level of American squalor.

The Concord eventually won its war but by the time the Brush-

24

fire War ended, males under twenty-six years old outnumbered females by four to one. The subsidies were repealed, but it was much too late.

With a shortage of young women, the overall birthrate was dropping rapidly. Illegal prostitution thrived, then was legalized to be inspected and taxed. Men who had learned how to rape the wives and daughters of their enemies brought this lesson home with them. The ratio of men to women made rape epidemic. As in prisons and boarding schools for centuries earlier, men turned to—and on—other men.

New and inexpensive technologies perfected during the war provided at least the hope of an exit for the surplus of men: outer space. A permanent lunar-exploration outpost was established. Laser launching systems and, later, continuous-boost thermonuclear spaceships provided access to the entire solar system. Scientific footholds were made on Mars, on several of Jupiter's moons, and even on Venus.

Several free-space habitats—huge orbiting cities envisioned the previous century by such pioneers as Gerard K. O'Neill of Princeton—were constructed, each housing thousands of colonists. Permanent mining operations on the moon, and later in the asteroid belt, combined with near-free solar energy to make such efforts both technologically and economically possible.

Second- and third-generation O'Neill colonies—massive cylindrical habitats, each with a population capacity in the millions—included the Concord's Ad Astra, the Chinese Confucius, and the Soviet Lenin. O'Neill, Kibbutz, Uhuru, and Rising Sun soon followed.

Nonetheless, only a small fraction of the surplus male population was able to leave. Political measures throughout the world tried to control the marauding young men.

In the North American Concord—using the precedent of minimum-wage laws—a minimum-sex law was passed. All healthy, adult females were legally required to have sex at least three times a week.

The only trouble was that only those men who were getting any in the first place got any more.

The marauding young men were still marauding.

An equalization-of-sex-opportunity law was passed. Women were now issued what were euphemistically called dance cards. New partners from the "sexually deprived" had to be accommodated.

A huge black market in false dance-card signatures arose.

The marauding young men were older, but still marauding.

Again, science came to the rescue. A new drug was born that, when taken by a woman, reactivated Adamine-inhibited gynosperm, at the same time sterilizing male-producing androsperm. It was developed in Ad Astra—its manufacture requiring elaborate facilities for zero-gravity mixing—and was commercially marketed to Earth under the name Eveline.

Its sole manufacturer—by exclusive license from its inventors—was a young asteroid miner who had risked venture capital on the drug's testing. The young miner was named Zachary Armstrong Darris. He returned to Earth to set up a marketing network for the new drug.

More years passed, with the ratio of male-to-female births dropping back to the pre–Brushfire War level of only two-to-one again.

Aside from the still serious, but now lessened, sexual imbalance, the world was enjoying one of its freest and most prosperous periods in history. Gone were oil shortages and pollution as cheap solar energy was collected by orbiting "powersats" and beamed down by laser beams to Earth-based distribution stations. Space manufacturing revolutionized industry after industry with miraculous new, and miraculously cheap, products. Laissez-faire was becoming the worldwide watchword in both economics and personal lifestyle. Even the Soviet Union found affluence easing its political grip. The problems of inflation, soaring taxation, energy shortage, unemployment, the destructive business cycle, and poverty itself began disappearing.

New advances in gerontology lowered the deathrate to match the lowered birthrate: the average human lifespan more than doubled, with fertility and youth continuing in both sexes well past a century. Gone were cancer, tooth decay, the common cold, and venereal disease.

Then came the War of Colonial Secession.

Stanton Darris, like his father the asteroid miner, viewed the Colonial War as a personal attack on his family. It was a rather parochial view concerning a war that had killed five million in the colonies and thirteen million on Earth. Nevertheless, there was some truth to it. It was true that the War had cut off all trade between the colonies and Earth for two decades, to the personal gain of certain Earth-bound manufacturers who had been unable to compete with free-space factories, several of these latter being Darris-owned. It was also true that the War effectively halted the sale of Eveline on

Earth, and by the time colonial–Earth trade had resumed, sociological and political changes on Earth had shifted the balance of power so far that the new Federation succeeded in passing laws banning Eveline from the planet permanently.

But it was ridiculous to suppose that the generals of the North American Concord had these results mapped out when they launched the preemptive first strike destroying the free-space habitat O'Neill.

Regardless of why it had started, half a century later Stanton Darris was still dealing on a daily basis with business problems that resulted directly from the War.

Today the problem was ferrofoam futures.

Ferrofoam—a steel product that, in terms of industrial usefulness, was to steel as steel had been to iron—could for all practical purposes be manufactured only in the colonies. Its production required the free-fall injection of microscopic gas bubbles into molten steel, then cooling it to produce a metal that was lighter than steel but could surpass it in a number of ways.

Both before and after the War, except for the embargo just after it, ferrofoam was one of the chief exports of the free-space colonies to Earth. One of the main causes of the colonial secessionist movement had been a difference of opinion between colonial residents and absentee owners back on Earth with respect to profit sharing and *who* could do without *whom* when push came to shove. On this issue the colonists won.

Ferrofoam, thought Stanton Darris. Fifty-four years postbellum and taking a futures contract on the financially volatile metal still made his stomach churn, as if the gas bubbles being pumped into the molten steel were ending up in his belly instead.

He was seventy-seven years old, with smooth skin, a body he kept athletically trim, craggy features, and bright-red hair. Of his children, only four-year-old Joanie had inherited the red hair intact; all four of his sons had strawberry-blond hair that more-or-less favored his wife. He wondered whether a redhead would show up in the next three sons he and Eleanor planned as a tax shelter—the Federation levied stiff progressive taxes on second and further female babies, with progresssive tax rebates for male babies. A redheaded son, however, would be something he could enjoy for his own sake—his father had been redheaded too.

Ferrofoam, thought Stanton Darris. He sat facing a video price listing and longed for the days of his great-grandfather, when the price of structural shapes was stable enough that there was no need

27

for a futures market at all. His office was in the penthouse of the 150-story-high Darris Tower, his father's phallic reply to the society he felt had given him the bird. The building had been sold soon after completion to pay off debts caused by the embargo, but Darris Investment Corporation still held the top dozen floors.

Far below him, Stanton could see Harlem Lake, where a neighborhood by that name had once been. Family history said that his father's paternal grandfather had lived in that neighborhood, but the closest the man had ever come to knowing anything about structural shapes of steel was the searing pain of the stiletto that had murdered him.

The video terminal finally displayed the information Stanton was awaiting. He spoke to it. "Offered," he said, "on one hundred kilotons of March ferrofoam, Au 2,730 grams."

The terminal printed out the bid on its display and said, "Please confirm."

"Confirmed. Transmit."

TRANSMITTING appeared on the display, and "Transmitting," the terminal said aloud. Stanton turned back to the window and began tapping his fingertips together rhythmically.

Racists might have said this sense of rhythm had come from that black man in Harlem—Neil Armstrong Darris, born July 20, 1969, dead of knife wounds received thirty-two years later while defending his pregnant wife from bread rioters during the monetary collapse. His wife, the former Mary O'Hare—a third-generation Irish Bostonian—survived; seven of the rioters did not. The family name and the beginnings of a tradition were passed on.

Their only son, a light-skinned mulatto whom she named Louis Armstrong Darris, was born fourteen weeks after his father's death. Louis Darris enlisted in the Aerospace Force on his eighteenth birthday, in the ninth year of the Brushfire War, rose to shuttle pilot, and was disabled out with a back injury, sustained during reentry, in the war's twentieth year. He lived on his benefits until the war was over, got a pilot's job with Trans European Skylines, and married a blond, blue-eyed copilot named Candice Bach.

Candice's fourth child, Zachary Armstrong Darris, shipped out to the asteroid belt at sixteen, using a false birth-record printout, after flunking out of prep school. After making his first 100,000 grams of gold, Zachary bought himself a seat on the board of trustees of that school, solely for the pleasure of bringing about the firing of a particular math teacher, who he felt had ruined him for the scientific career he'd wanted.

28

He considered the firing of that teacher as the most fun he'd had out of bed, where he spent much of his spare time to the day he died, at the age of ninety-one, shot by a jealous husband.

The life of Zachary Armstrong Darris had been one filled with fortunes made and lost, fame—or infamy, depending on whom one talked to—and three marriages in an age when most men couldn't enter even one. Three marriages produced three offspring, two sons from his first wife—a platinum-blond nightclub singer named Kate Seymour—and a daughter from his last marriage.

Stanton Armstrong Darris always felt he'd been a disappointment to his father. He felt he wasn't cast from the same mold as his ancestors. He just wasn't the sort to face off rioters, or fly combat missions, or blast a fortune out of worthless rock a few hundred million kilometers away from Earth. Maybe he'd inherited some of his father's business ability, but he felt he'd missed out on the ancestral guts. The only thing Stanton felt sure he'd inherited from his father was the red hair.

The terminal spoke to Stanton again: "Bid accepted. Carlisle, St. Clive, D.H. Transaction on display."

Stanton stood up, not bothering to look at the screen. "Just store it," he told the terminal. "Notify me if trading on March ferrofoam goes plus or minus this transaction 15 percent or greater. I'm going home."

"I will, I will, I hear you," the computer said.

Stanton looked across the office to a portrait of his father—one of those damnable holographic atrocities in which the eyes followed you wherever you went in the room. As usual, the eyes were looking right through him, mocking and critical. Even thirteen years after his death, his father was still disapproving. "You bastard," Stanton told the portrait.

He called his secretary, Larry, to say good night, and put on a jacket. Then he took his personal lift up one level to the roof of the 150-story-high Darris Tower, and after taking just a minute to prepare himself, Stanton Armstrong Darris jumped off.

4

HELIX VISTA was lit up like a Solstice tree.

Approaching it by air, soon after nightfall, he first saw the squat-ball course, floodlighted although it was deserted this evening. Receiving approach instructions from the estate's domestic computer, he circled around the perimeter of the stables to avoid having his engine noise frighten the horses. He skimmed low over Lake Kingston, enjoying the spray caused by his airwash, watching his path alternating red and blue, red and blue under his anticollison beacons.

Helix Vista reached to touch the sky, a staircase of seven ovals spiraling upward to heaven, each level lighted a proper color in the spectral sequence of a rainbow. Topping each level was a garden, and on the uppermost oval there was an open-air terrace from which one could oversee the entire estate.

Few guests had arrived at a quarter to seven, so there was no one but serving robots to watch what would have made a spectacular entrance. But he could see, during his approach, that there was an open, lighted window with a small, red-haired girl waving to him, so he decided to make his descent to please her.

Like Peter Pan flying up to Wendy's window, Stanton Darris guided his General Electric Joob flying belt to the garden on the fourth oval of Helix Vista, next to his daughter's fifth-story bedroom, then dropped into it for a landing.

No father had ever had a more appreciative audience.

Joan was squealing with delight as he slipped out of harness, removed headpiece and leather jacket, then climbed in through the window. "Daddy, Daddy!" Joan shouted as she ran toward him.

The run ended with a flying leap. Stanton caught her and accepted a sloppy, wet kiss. He returned it. "How's my little tangerine-top?" he asked her. "And how come you're not in your pajamas yet?"

"Mr. Mac is helping Cousin 'lizabeth get into hers first. Daddy, can I stay up and come to the party?"

"I'm sorry, honey, but it starts way past your bedtime. You wouldn't be able to keep your eyes open."

"I would, I promise!"

"Darling, you'd be so bored you'd fall right asleep. There won't

30

be anyone your own age there to play with, and all the grown-ups will be too busy doing grown-up things to spend any time with you. Besides, aren't you having a party of your own next week for your birthday?"

Joan nodded. "I'm gonna be five."

"Well, parties for five-year-olds are lots more fun, I promise you. Now tell me what you did today."

"Mommy took us all to the peera—peera—"

"Pyradome."

"Peeradome, and she got into a hole in the center with a boy and an old man and Mommy talked to everybody. Then it got all dark and the colors did a dance in the sky. Daddy, who tells the colors how to dance?"

"Well, it's a hard word to say, honey. They're called lasegraphers."

Joan looked crestfallen. "Can't people tell the lights?"

"Eh? Of course they can, darling. Why do you ask?"

"Well, if people can tell the colors how to dance, then why do they use lazy gophers?"

Stanton received a clear image of a shiftless furry rodent in a hole, communing with the heavens. "Uh, sweetheart, it's not 'lazy gophers.' It's 'lasegraphers'—a funny word that means something else."

"I didn't *think* gophers were that smart," Joan said.

Stanton smiled. "No. Lasegraphers are people who study for a long time until they learn how to draw dancing pictures with lights, like you saw today at the pyradome. In fact, your sister Vera used to be a lasegrapher."

Joan's eyes widened. "She *was?*"

"Mmm-hmm."

"Could I draw with lights? Real lights, not pretending?"

"Darling, if you really want to, and you're willing to spend enough time learning how to do it, I'm sure you can. Now can you get into your pajamas, like a big five-year-old?"

"Uh-huh." Joan went to the pajamas dispenser and pulled out a plastisealed package. "Daddy, will you sing me a song, like Mr. McIntosh does?"

"Uh, I don't know a lot of songs, sweetheart."

"Please?"

"Well, get into your pajamas while I try to remember one."

Joan spent the next few minutes getting out of her play dress, throwing it away, then changing into her pajamas. Her father

31

helped her only in breaking the plastic seal on the package. Stanton tucked Joanie into bed, then started a song his mother had recorded when she began singing professionally again, about the time his father had married for the third time.

> "As I was going to St. Clive
> I met a man one-hundred-five
> Who's with his ma, one-hundred-thirty,
> Who's with her pa, one-hundred-sixty.
> Sixty, thirty, hundred-five—
> I hear they're living in St. Clive,
> But how long can they stay alive?"

Stanton paused. Joanie asked, "How does the rest of it go?"

"Those are all the words, honey. It just keeps on over and over, going faster each time."

"Will you sing it again? As fast as you can?"

"Well, all right. But then you'll go right to sleep."

Stanton sang the song again, this time running the words together so quickly he thought he'd surely trip over them. Amazing himself, but not his daughter, he got through it perfectly.

When he finished, Joan asked, "Daddy, will you teach it to me?"

"I'll tell you what, sweetheart. Grandma is staying over tonight, and she taught it to me. Suppose I ask her to teach it to you tomorrow?"

"Okay."

"Now give me another kiss, then go to sleep."

She kissed her father and slid back under the covers. "Good night, Daddy."

"Sweet dreams, carrot-top."

He dimmed the lights on his way out. Reflections from the lawn dome, still being tested, projected in through the window, flickering colors onto the bedroom wall. "Daddy?"

"Hmm?"

"You sing much better than Mr. McIntosh."

"Thank you, honey."

Stanton went out. He decided that maybe he didn't need a red-headed son after all.

Colors in motion, thought His Gaylordship Wendell Darris; that was the essence of a ball. That, at least, was all he could discern of the swirling rooftop dancers as his official Federation limousine came into Helix Vista that night. It felt good coming home again, even if there was a slight bittersweet flavor. Stanton was the only

32

Darris heir who lived here nowadays, and it was almost a year and a half since Wendell had visited his brother at home.

His last visit, the family circle's traditional Hallowmas feast, had been during happier times, before Wendell's adoption of Marion had gone sour, before the two of them had separated. Their upcoming divorce was still a closely held secret, with Wendell's seat in the House of Gentry coming up for election this June, but for all his sexual infidelities, Marion was a Libertarian Party loyalist who had no desire to see the North American Concord's lavender seat in the Upper Manor lost to the Chauvinists. Wendell wished Marion had accompanied him tonight.

Colors in motion, Gaylord Darris thought, as he entered onto the terrace and saw the ball close up: the improvisational lasegraphy of the roga player, backed up by the hard-driving music of the Ramon Raquello Orchestra. Wendell's escort of sky marshals had discarded their flying belts and now discreetly preceded him onto the terrace, where they took up guard posts. Wendell did not see his brother and sister-in-law right off and used his few free minutes before he was recognized to look around.

Eleanor was an expert hostess when it came to keeping the proper proportions at a party, he observed. There were just the right number of gaily plumed commen, carefully selected to try for the attentions of the equal number of invited single women. An equivalent number of andromen couples—mostly husbands and wards—were more drably attired in their lavender capotes; Wendell gave thanks that hoods were no longer required on cloaks for full dress. Just the correct number of society witches were towing their husbands around the dance floor, here to pass judgment on the newest postulant to their order. And just the suitable dash of clones were here to prove the Darrises had compassion—a few too many to be considered tokens, but not enough to create a scandal. Wendell smiled as he thought he could use Eleanor's expertise the next time he had to assemble just the right mix of gaylords, ladies, and commen in a joint-Manor conference committee.

At five to nine, a stunning woman with ash-blond hair, sky-blue eyes, and a figure that was an exercise in lightness ascended onto the terrace. As did every veteran at this ball, she wore the white dress uniform of the Federation Peace Corps: a gown that revealed nothing but promised it all.

A tall, black-skinned, and handsome comman walked up to her, presenting his dance card. "Mademoiselle," he said with a slight *québecois* accent, "may I escort you until our first dance?"

For a moment she looked no older than sixteen, and she laughed. "Thank you, but I believe my husband might object."

The young comman was even more taken aback when Stanton Darris walked up and led Eleanor away, winding their way across the roga imagery reflected from the gossamer canopy onto the dance floor.

The comman was not to be blamed for his mistake. What biological distinctions there were between Eleanor Darris and her parthenogenic daughter would have shown up only in a medical or Federation Monitor laboratory—assuming their brainprints hadn't already been scanned.

The comman stood watching after them as Eleanor and Stanton reached the cannabistro, where they approached a tall, somewhat stout, and curly-haired androman the comman recognized from holovision as His Gaylordship Wendell Darris.

Wendell stood at the cannabistro, loading his pipe with a marijuana blend Darris Investments imported from the Lenin colony—Colombian seeds grown in lunar soil. "A fine welcome," Gaylord Darris said to his brother before Stanton could open his mouth. "No balloons, no pretty boys waving placards, no holy reporters. And in an election year."

Stanton shook his brother's hand. "There's a kid here from the *Harvard Crimson,*" he said. "You want me to get him?"

"Lady, no," Wendell said. "He might win the Murdoch Prize for the interview and I'd be thrown out of the Yale Alumni Association. Hello, Eleanor. You can still fit into the uniform, I see."

"And you're looking particularly effete tonight," she said.

"Thanks, but you can save the compliments. If I look at all the way I feel, I must look like scat. Has our surprise arrived yet?"

"Not till ten."

Wendell nodded and turned back to his brother. "I haven't seen Mom yet."

"She's still vesting, and burning mad that we allowed the party to start before she gave the service."

"You know how traditionalist she can be."

"Wendy, where's Marion hiding?" Eleanor asked. "I'd like to say hello before I have to start playing hostess again."

Wendell paused just a moment, to underscore a warning. "Marion sends his regrets. A last-minute stomach-ache, I'm afraid."

Eleanor caught his tone. "That's dreadful. Was it something he ate?"

"Probably," Wendell replied, tamping down his pipe. "Marion seems never to have learned what not to swallow."

Precisely at nine, a stunning woman with ash-blond hair, sky-blue eyes, and a figure that was an exercise in lightness ascended onto the terrace. As did every veteran at this ball, she wore the white dress uniform of the Federation Peace Corps: a gown that revealed nothing but promised it all.

A tall, black-skinned, and handsome comman walked up to her, again presenting his dance card. This time, Vera Collier Delaney nodded to him, but she told him to wait.

Right behind Vera, a silver-haired woman in flowing emerald robes, a regal strength belying her one hundred years, ascended onto the floor. Though she no longer wore the vernal beauty of her daughter-in-law and adopted granddaughter, Kate Seymour could still command every set of eyes on the terrace. The High Priestess of the Darris family circle moved in front of Vera and—with years of nightclub experience—took her stage. The crowd naturally made a pathway as she led Vera up to the bandstand. As Kate Seymour stepped onto it, the orchestra immediately shifted into an ancient and rhythmic strain. All lights went out.

The High Priestess lit two white candles on the bandstand, then removed a short sword from her emerald robes. She traced a nine-foot circle, east to east, around her, and as she traced, it appeared in glowing light on the floor—courtesy of the roga player.

Then she took her sword and pointed it at Vera, who was suddenly bathed in white light. By stage magic, there stood Vera just outside the circle, naked and blindfolded.

The High Priestess drew next to her and pointed the sword directly at Vera's heart. "O you who stand on the threshold of initiation, the world of men, and the domains of the Dread Lords of the outer spaces, do you have the courage to undergo the trial?"

"I do," Vera replied. "I have two passwords."

"Speak them."

"Perfect love and perfect peace."

Kate Seymour dropped her sword; the clatter echoed across the terrace. "All who bring such words are doubly welcome." She drew Vera into the circle with her. "I give you a third password—a kiss." She kissed Vera on the lips. "This is the way all are first brought into the circle."

For the next ten minutes, Vera was subjected to ancient rituals of consecration, bondage, and scourging. Vows were made and presents given. Finally, Vera stood before her grandmother, without blindfold and again in uniform, as the old High Priestess completed her last service. "Listen, O Mighty Ones! Vera Collier Delaney has been consecrated a High Priestess of the Art and a Sister of the Wicce."

Kate Seymour left the bandstand and walked off the terrace.

Vera waited for silence, then spoke. "Listen now to the words of the Great Mother:

" 'I who am the beauty of the Green Earth, and the White Moon among the stars, I call unto your soul to arise and come to me. Rejoice, for all acts of love and pleasure are my rituals. Let there be beauty and strength, power and compassion, honor and humility, mirth and reverence—within you. And you who think to search for me, behold—I have been with you from the beginning, and I am that which is attained at the end of all desire.' "

"So be it ordained," the crowd intoned.

"Blessed be," said Vera. "Let the festivities resume."

The lights came back on. Vera signaled to the roga player to begin again, then led the young comman, whose dance card she had signed first, onto the floor.

A few minutes later, the party was in full swing again. Even Kate Seymour, who had changed from her emerald robes into an evening formal, had dragged Stanton onto the dance floor.

Over at the cannabistro, Gaylord Darris was holding court, surrounded by Eleanor and a dozen of her guests. At the moment, Wendell was trying to stump—with a 1-centigram bet on the line— a commerical envoy from Lenin. *"So,"* he said, speaking in Russian, *"the Minister of Ecology says to the waiter, 'Waiter, there's a fly in my soup.' "*

The envoy smiled. *"And the waiter says, 'Don't worry,* tovarishch, *it won't drink much.' "*

Several of the guests understood Russian and laughed. "Rapier," Wendell said, blunting the tip of his profanity at the last instant. He withdrew an aurafoam coin from his capote and dropped it into the envoy's hand. "I could have sworn that one was new."

The envoy shook his head. I heard it in Daedalus more than six months ago."

A puzzled matron asked, "But I thought they didn't import any flies to the habitats."

"We don't, madam," the envoy said. "That's what makes it so funny."

"Vladimir!" a woman's voice called.

"My wife wishes to dance," the envoy said, bowing to Gaylord Darris, then withdrawing.

Wendell and Eleanor spent the next few mintues discussing classical lasegraphy, and their joint work for the Darris Foundation.

After the first dance, Vera took the young comman over to the cannabistro to meet Eleanor; the crowd around Wendell began dispersing, allowing some privacy, as robots began handing out glasses of champagne. "Mother and Wendell," Vera said, "may I introduce François Duroux. François, my mother, Eleanor Darris, and her brother-in-law, Gaylord Darris."

"How do you do?" Duroux freed his right hand from a champagne glass so he could shake hands with them. "Madame," he said to Eleanor, "I apologize for my confusion earlier tonight. I hope I did not cause you and your husband embarrassment."

Eleanor smiled pleasantly. "Please don't give it a second thought."

"Certainly not," Vera said, somewhat acidly. "My mother has always played our resemblance for all it's worth."

The remark stung Eleanor, though it didn't surprise her. Eleanor was about to comment when she saw Wendell quickly shake his head once at her, so she said nothing.

Duroux carefully tried to disappear into his champagne glass for a moment.

Vera changed the subject. "François wants to recruit me for his mother's judiciary firm in Montreal."

"That is not quite right," Duroux corrected her. "*Maman* wishes Vera to work for her. I merely convey the offer as her employee."

"You do have your own desires, though?" Eleanor asked.

"But of course."

"Then I assume you met my daughter in the Hawaiian dicteriat?"

"Mother!" Vera said, scandalized.

But Duroux was quite used to overprotective parents, so he rolled with the punch. "Madame, the judiciary profession is much too sensitive to public opinion for a firm to risk—shall we say—so *intimate* a channel. No. Vera and I met several months ago at our corporate offices in Montreal."

"I used a leave to take their company's entrance exams," said Vera.

"I apologize," Eleanor said. "But getting back to your mother's offer—which firm is this?"

"Legos, Limited."

"Legos would sponsor her law training?"

"To a Doctor of Jurisprudence degree—three years. Then another year of internship as my mother's law clerk before *Maman* would give Vera a bench of her own."

"Your mother is *Claudine* Duroux?" Gaylord Darris asked. The young comman nodded. "I met her when she ovafied before the Select Committee on the Touchable Riots last session—something about cost overruns?"

Duroux nodded again. "I don't know what was more costly, sentencing Touchables to the microwaves—capital cases just drag on—or fining the Marnies for daylight venery. The costliest was the trial of the Marnies who had icarated about a dozen Touchables. By the way, Your Gaylordship, do you hunt?

Wendell shook his head. "Barbaric practice."

"Chacun à son goût," Duroux said, abandoning the idea of inviting His Gaylordship along on his next nightstalk. "Regardless, all this backed up our court dockets for almost a year. I should know. Scheduling of trials is my primary responsibility for Legos."

"I also recall your mother's appearance before my Ways and Means Committee, several months later. . . ."

"Maman spoke of it. Painfully."

Wendell laughed. "I'll just bet Her Honor did; I'll just bet. Gaylord Chung and Lady Weinstein were batting her back and forth at the hearing like a squatball in the fifth down. If I hadn't stepped in, I think they'd have stuffed her up the net too."

Duroux smiled. "She remembers, and has told me she will support your ticket this June, even though she dislikes your running mate."

"Tell her not to worry. A first-term lady doesn't have seniority to get anywhere near the Judiciary Committee. You will understand why I can't comment more explicitly."

"Of course."

"A toast," said Stanton Darris from the bandstand, where he addressed the assemblage. "Vera, come on up here where people can see you."

5

ELEANOR AND WENDELL's surprise for Vera arrived on schedule at
ten o'clock. Colors in motion, observed Wolfgang Jaeger as he was
flown in by taxi to Helix Vista. But it was by no means an infre-
quent perception for him, since he saw colors in motion wherever
he looked, in much the same way that a sculptor can't help noticing
passing faces. For Jaeger, colors in motion weren't only the essence
of a ball, they were the essence of his life—the essence of everything.

A sculptor looking at Jaeger's face would have seen it lined with
age and pain. He was one hundred fifty-five years old, and this was
his last night on Earth. He was not sorry to be leaving. His bones
ached from too much sustained gravity, his neck still ached from
the identity transponder implanted at Federation customs, his mind
ached from too many remembrances, his eyes ached from having
seen much too much.

Though he was one of the last children of the old millennium,
virtually his entire life had been in the new one. The art form of
which he was, and had been for the last century, the uncontested
master had barely reached its puberty when he'd reached his own.
Under his tutelage, lasegraphy had grown to rival music as the essential expression of the human soul.

Such growth had not come automatically. A lover had said to
him half a lifetime ago, "Wolf, you treat yourself like a hothouse
plant." It was true. But for a tropical plant in a northern climate, a
hothouse was what it took to survive. He had told her, "If you want
lushness, you pay for it."

She had left him soon thereafter.

He was often unspeakably alone. Everyone was perfectly willing
to stand up after his recitals, applauding wildly for his finished
masterpieces, but no audience had ever wanted to know the pain
he'd had to endure to make the masterpieces possible. He heard
backstage and during interviews phrases such as "the nobility of artistic suffering," but these had only been words. He saw nothing
noble in his own pain. It just existed, silently, like a star exploding
in a vacuum.

So he had paced and he had worried; he had debased himself before the backers, booking agents, and promoters; he had waited for

them to get back to him. Then he would wonder why he didn't have enough energy left to sit down at the console. He wondered why the lights wouldn't dance, why the dreams had stopped. He was spiritually dead, and he haunted anyone who came to visit his grave.

He ranted and he raved, he cursed the universe and he cursed himself, he drove away anyone who'd had the misfortune to love him. But no one understood—*could* understand. Only someone whose mind took the same odd turns his mind took could have understood. Others tried, they made mighty and worthy efforts, but they had never been up against the chromatic laser and a cathedral of empty night.

One night, when the pain became too much to take, he returned to the console.

And, my God, the lights began to dance. The pain began flowing out of his fingers and slashing through the dark. Dreams of wandering and speaking, trial and suffering, death and rebirth were translated into colors and motion, patterns in cadence.

When his fingers had stopped moving, he had finished a composition that had eluded him for six years. When he played it once all the way through, and shut off his instrument, he felt he had returned to God the rainbow He had given Noah after the flood.

Vistata No. 7: "The Resurrection" had premiered in New York the next spring. He had come back to Newer York now to celebrate the centennial of that premiere.

It had not been an easy decision to come back to Earth. In the two catastrophic wars his long life had driven him through, he had seen human beings needlessly set against each other. He had seen the Brushfire War set East against West, and its aftermath set men against women. In this war he had refused to become a partisan. He had seen the War of Colonial Secession set Earth against the heavens. But in this war he had sided with the heavens. This was his only return trip to his native world since.

A thought struck him and he laughed. Here he was, on the last night of his only trip to Earth since he had moved to Ad Astra sixty years ago, and he was spending it playing at a witch's *bat mitzvah*. At age eleven, he had started his career by playing at a *bat mitzvah* of the original sort. It was an appropriate goodbye.

After the taxi had landed, Jaeger paid its computer with a credit card, telling it to have dispatch send another taxi for him at 1 A.M. Then he took a tall, flat ferrofoam case—bulging at one end—from the seat beside him and climbed out of the taxi with some difficulty. A robot butler met him at the house, took his coat, and directed him to a lift which took him directly to the terrace. When he had ascended onto it, he set his instrument between his feet and looked around.

It was a celebration like so many other celebrations he'd attended in a long life. The details never seemed to change. There was loud music, that horrible roga—people dancing, eating, drinking, smoking. Clusters of people talked about things that didn't matter to them. For a moment, Jaeger forgot that this was the world he was born on and felt himself completely an alien. Why, he wondered, was doing *this* considered celebrating? What did these people do with their lives that this was their most prized way of marking it? For him, his best moments were spent alone at the console, with no one watching, and what he found there needed no external celebration. And if he felt, when the hunting was particularly good, that he wished to celebrate it further, the celebration came in sharing what he had found with others. But what were these people sharing with each other that this mindless chaos was the result? Give me even one person who sees the things I see, Jaeger thought, and you can keep all the champagne and caviar on Earth.

He did not have long to dwell on these thoughts; he spotted his hostess on the way to greet him. For just an instant, Jaeger thought he was having a stroke—wasn't seeing double one of the symptoms? But the two women weren't moving together, and there were two men with them who shared only a familial resemblance, so he decided he wasn't done for yet.

Eleanor relieved his confusion by stepping forward. "Maestro Jaeger, thank you so much for coming tonight. May I introduce my daughter, Vera; my husband, Stanton; and His Gaylordship Wendell Darris."

"Delighted to meet each of you." Jaeger shook their hands in turn, carefully extending his index finger to apply counterpressure in case of too crushing a grip.

Vera said, "I'm so honored you've decided to play for us, Maestro. This is a greater surprise than I could have possibly imagined."

Eleanor wondered just exactly how Vera meant that.

"The honor is all mine, young lady." Jaeger looked back and forth between Eleanor and Vera. "Excuse an old man for staring, but I can't help studying your remarkable resemblance to your mother. We don't have very many clones in the habitats. Different eugenic goals, you know."

Vera concealed her annoyance; she knew the word "clone" was used less precisely in the colonies—the "habitats," she must remember to say around Jaeger, if she didn't want to provoke war. "I'm my mother's *twin*," she told Jaeger, "by parthenogenesis. The process doesn't produce the various inadequacies that clones suffer from."

"Forgive me my error," Jaeger said. "I didn't mean to insult you. But I must say it was rather my impression that such 'inadequacies' resulted from nurture rather than nature."

"Hear, hear," Wendell said.

Vera flushed deeply but avoided looking at Wendell. "Some people," she told Jaeger, "reject any scientific conclusion that doesn't happen to support their convictions."

"Some people do indeed," Wendell said.

"Maestro," said Stanton, "you've just walked into the middle of one of the most hotly debated political issues on the planet."

"And this discussion is getting altogether too serious for a party," Eleanor said. "Maestro, can I get you anything to smoke, or to eat? Or perhaps you'd like to meet some of our guests?"

"Thank you, but if you don't mind, I'd like to spend some time in the laserium warming up—if it wouldn't offend you?"

"Not at all," Eleanor said. "Vera, why don't you escort the Maestro down?"

"Of course."

Wendell laughed. "Pardon me, Maestro, but this reminds me of a story I've heard about you—"

"Yes?"

"—that a well-known society hostess, some years ago, once asked you what your price would be to play at one of her exclusive parties. And it's said you gave her a price of five hundred auragrams. She supposedly agreed without flinching, then said to you, 'In that case, you realize, of course, that I will expect you not to mingle with my guests.' And you are supposed to have said, 'In that case, madam, I will charge you only one hundred auragrams.' "

Everyone laughed, especially Wendell, a confirmed self-panicker if ever there was one. "This story has followed me around for years," Jaeger said. "I only wish it were about me. It actually goes back to the celebrated virtuoso Fritz Kreisler."

"Really?" Wendell said. "I thought I knew all the great names of lasegraphy, but I've never heard of him."

Jaeger smiled wistfully; he knew too well that time wounded as often as it healed. "Kreisler was a virtuoso before the laser was even invented," he said. "He was a violin player."

Wendell shrugged.

42

A few minutes later, Vera took Jaeger down to the lawn dome. When they entered, Jaeger was happy to learn that the Darrises had a top-notch private laserium, one of the best home facilities he'd ever seen. It wasn't the pyradome, of course, but then again, what was? There were reclining couches here to seat over two hundred around the dome's perimeter, with a Tiger Pit in the center for the performer. Jaeger himself had been the one who'd tagged it the Tiger Pit after performing one night to a particularly hostile audience. The name had stuck. Jaeger found the day glow controls, since Vera didn't know where they were anyway, and he raised the dome lights. He began unpacking his instrument while Vera looked on attentively; Jaeger had no way of knowing the significance.

His instrument comprised two parts. Jaeger's console was merely a very light, very modern LCAA 1600 keyboard, not very much different from consoles in use a century before. The controls were seventy-two touch-sensitive finger panels and a dozen foot pedals, with a monitor screen and an electronic scroller for written scores; inside the console were mostly just some very prosaic oscillators and microprocessors.

The Merlino chromatic laser Jaeger owned was a different matter altogether. Aside from superlative eighty-two-year-old craftsmanship, there was nothing unusual about the array of scanners, mirrors, prisms, dichroic filters, holographic plates, and other opticals designed to modulate pinpoint laser beams into dimensional imagery. What distinguished the Merlino was an almost intangible warmth and subtlety of expression, possible only through its use of nine of the rarest, most expensive, and most perfectly cut fire gems in existence.

Nobody knew precisely what fire gems were—whether they were natural crystals or synthetic artifacts—but they had been found in some quantity on one of the asteroids. Opinions respecting whether they were natural or created by some previous human or alien civilization tended to shift with the latest theories regarding the probable existence of an ancient, exploded planet where the asteriod belt was now.

Touching a fire gem had been found to produce warm, tingling feelings in human beings, with analogous effects reproducible—but not explained—by experiments on laboratory animals and plantlife. More important from the technologist's standpoint was the fire gems' very odd behavior when subjected to various bands of electromagnetic radiation. Most important from the lasegrapher's viewpoint were the gems' ability to lase easily and continuously, with a very high efficiency of power input to output, and the gems' remarkably variable range of spectral lines in lasing, with no intermodulation to disrupt the laser's spatial coherence.

For Jaeger, this meant a laser instrument that could operate on little power, without cooling, and throughout a fully tunable spectral range.

Vera and Jaeger talked while he set up his instrument—a little about life in the habitats; a little about Vera's service experience, a subject Jaeger found particularly interesting since the habitats had never instituted any kind of service. "The worst part is the utter loss of privacy," Vera explained, "the feeling of being ordered around all the time, of being just another anonymous corporal. But there's also a feeling of doing something really important, of relieving the social pressures that might lead to another war, so you learn to forget your own personal problems and just do your job."

Finally, Jaeger plugged his instrument into a power outlet and touched it on.

Nothing happened.

Jaeger looked at an indicator on his console. "No juice," he said.

Vera looked disgusted. "My mother told me repairmen were in here all day getting the dome ready for you. They were supposed to have the problem fixed."

" 'Supposed to' is not one of my favorite expressions," Jaeger said.

"Can you run off internal?"

Jaeger checked another indicator, then shook his head. "I did a concert on Harlem Lake last night and haven't had a chance to recharge."

"Couldn't you stretch time by running the laser at quarter-power?"

Jaeger looked at Vera oddly.

"I used to play," she said.

Jaeger shook his head again. "Quarter-power is what I was counting on when I checked the power pack."

"Maybe I can find somebody up at the party who can figure out what's wrong."

"A sensible approach," Jaeger said. "Meanwhile I'll take a look around here and see if I can find the problem." He hesitated a moment. "You said you 'used to' play?"

Vera nodded.

"Why did you give it up?"

Vera paused in the dome's entranceway, moonlight framing her face. "I found myself becoming deathly afraid of the laser," she said.

"Afraid of it how?" he asked. "Afraid it would burn you?"

She shook her head. "Afraid that it *wouldn't* have burned me. That it would've gone right through me like I was a ghost. Like it was real and I wasn't." She paused a moment, shaking her head, before leaving. "I was only fifteen. Crazy the sorts of things teenagers are afraid of."

Jaeger stood watching after her as she walked back to the house. Then he began opening up cabinets and panels in the Tiger Pit.

A few minutes of rummaging around didn't produce any solution to the power problem, but Jaeger did find some lasegraphic scores that fascinated him. He was looking them over—one in particular—when Eleanor walked in. She strode to the far side of the dome, opened a blue panel on the wall, and pressed in a clear-plastic module. "Try it now," she said.

Jaeger touched his console again. "Success," he reported.

"The repairmen left the circuit breaker out."

"I thought so, but I didn't know where it was."

"If it's all right," Eleanor said, "we'll start seating at ten to eleven."

"Fine."

"I've got to run back to the party. Can I bring you anything?"

"No," Jaeger said, "thank you. One thing, though, which I'd better check with you about. While I was looking for the power problem, I came across some scores of yours. There's one in particular I'd like to play. Would you have any objection?"

"No, of course not, Maestro," said Eleanor, "whatever you like."

Eleanor returned to the party and Jaeger began his warming-up exercises.

He started by playing a composition he had written early in his career, but he ran his fingers over the keyboard without turning on his laser. The spectral scales and lissajou patterns he keyed, had they appeared in the dome, would have told him nothing he didn't already know, and would have meant nothing to a casual observer. Jaeger's *Blind Exercises* had been composed only for the fingers, not for anyone's eyes. After a few minutes, however, he judged the circulation in his fingers sufficient for some real work. He inserted the score he had found into his console and began sight-reading it. When he cycled the laser up to half-power—all that was needed in this size dome—and lowered the day glow lighting, a blue figure-8 began a dance in the sky.

It was a happy little dance. The blue figure-8 warbled and squiggled its way across the dome and around the edge. It turned somersaults and cartwheels. It metamorphosed into different shapes and sprang back again. It shrank down to a pinpoint, then rebounded into a giant. When it had finished, a red figure-8 repeated the dance the blue one had done, while the blue now weaved in and around the red figure's dance like a dog running around and between its master's feet.

When the red figure had finished its exposition, a green figure-8 began the dance still again, while the red began its own embellishments. The pattern continued with a violet figure doing the dance, then embellishing; then a yellow, then an indigo, then an orange, then the blue once again, while each of the other figures now weaved into, out of, and around the blue in a sprightly, contrapuntal moving design.

When Jaeger had finished playing the piece, he found he had an audience of one. He turned up the dome's day glow lighting a bit. "Shouldn't you be in bed?" he asked.

"I couldn't sleep. The dancing lights woke me up."

Jaeger was surprised. "I'm sorry," he said.

"I dreamed them in my head."

"You dreamed about the dancing lights?"

"Uh-huh."

"I dream about them too," Jaeger said to Joan. "Come on down here and keep me company."

Dragging a small orange blanket behind her, Joan padded over to the Tiger Pit and climbed down the three steps into it. Jaeger gestured to a spot next to him on his reclining bench, and she climbed on alongside. "Were you with my mommy this morning?" Joan asked.

"I don't know. What's your mommy's name?"

"Eleanor D'laney Darris. My name is Joan Seymour Darris."

"Yes, I was."

"Then I'm allowed to talk to you," Joan said. "I'm not allowed to talk to people we don't know."

"That's very wise," Jaeger said. "And I imagine I'm allowed to talk to you too, then."

Joan nodded.

"But I'm forgetting my manners, Joan. My name is Wolfgang Jaeger, and my friends call me 'Wolf.' You can call me 'Wolf,' if you'd like."

"Do your friends call you 'Wolf' because you bite them?"

Jaeger smiled. "Not anymore," he said. "I haven't bitten any of my friends for many years."

"Wouldja promise not to bite me?"

"I promise."

"Okay," Joan said seriously. "Are you a lasegrapher?"

"Yes, I am. And you said that very well."

"My daddy says that my sister used to be one too."

"Your sister told me." There were a few seconds of silence; Joan didn't seem to have anything else she wanted to say. "Would you like to see me make a butterfly?" Jaeger asked. Joan nodded. "Well, let me turn down the lights so we can see it better."

Jaeger dimmed the day glowing again, watching Joan to make sure she didn't mind the dark; then he began running his fingers over the key panels again. He built up the stylized image of a butterfly, line by colored line, in the center of the dome, then fixed the image and began concentrating on movement. Joan watched as a small butterfly began flapping its wings slowly, flying around the dome in larger and larger loops.

"How about two butterflies?" Jaeger asked. Instantly, a second butterfly appeared in the dome and began flying parallel to the first, and whatever the first butterfly did the second one did a split second later.

Joan watched them for a few moments. "Don't they like each other?" she asked.

Jaeger glanced down at Joan intently for a second, then back up at the butterflies in the dome. "Why do you say they don't like each other?"

"Well, *that* butterfly is always doing the same thing as *this* one."

"And that means they don't like each other?"

"Uh-huh."

Jaeger touched a panel and the second butterfly veered off in the opposite direction from the first, beginning to fly in counterpoint to the other one. "Do they like each other any better now?" he asked.

Joan thought about it for a second, then shook her head. "Now *that* butterfly is always going the other way jus' so it isn't being a copycat."

"I see," Jaeger said, "How will I know when they start liking each other?"

"Well . . . they'll start *help*ing each other 'stead of fighting all the time."

Jaeger considered this, then touched a panel which put each butterfly under discrete control; they began a complex series of complementary aerial maneuvers in which each one finished a motion started by the other.

"*Now* they like each other," Joan said emphatically.

The two butterflies looped around several more times, slowed to a halt, dipped their wings to each other in a bow, then disappeared.

Jaeger raised the glowing and turned back to Joan. "Do you know that you're a very bright young lady?" he asked her.

"Uh-huh."

His eyes twinkled. "How do you know that?"

"I saw it in the mirror," she said.

Jaeger did a double take, regarding Joan more seriously.

"There she is!" Stanton called out from the entranceway.

Stanton headed toward the Tiger Pit; very shortly, Eleanor, Vera, and Wendell followed him, Eleanor telling her wristphone, "In the lawn dome, Mac. You can stop worrying."

There was the standard back-and-forth as Eleanor and Stanton brought their daughter up on charges of Being out of Bed. Joan pleaded "guilty-with-an-explanation" and was given a suspended sentence. As soon as Mr. McIntosh arrived, she said good night to everyone, waved to Jaeger, and was carried off to bed again.

Of course, Eleanor then felt compelled to spend some time apologizing to Jaeger for Joan's interruption, and he spent some time telling her that he didn't mind at all, which naturally she didn't believe since she thought he was just being polite. In fact, Jaeger *was* being polite; the absolute truth, which he refrained from telling Eleanor, was that he considered the child who had just been dragged off to bed far more interesting company than she was.

What he did say was "Your little girl has a very fine sense of symbolic relationships. Most refreshing."

"Well, she is very precocious," Eleanor said, "and I must tell you she was completely enchanted by your performance this morning—her first concert. In fact, I caught Joan doing some drawings later, from memory, of your vistata. She got the color scale right, too."

"Most interesting."

"I put one up in the kitchen. Would you care to see it?"

"Mother, we *should* start seating," Vera said.

"I would like to see it," Jaeger said. "Perhaps afterward?"

"I was thinking, earlier today," said Eleanor, "that Joan is just the right age to start on the console."

"The perfect age," Vera said. "And in eleven years she'll be the perfect age to be floated out of a Tiger Pit on a stretcher."

"My dear," said Jaeger, "it was not by accident that I named this

48

enclosure the 'Tiger Pit.' Every lasegrapher—indeed, every artist—is a gladiator, a matador, a Christian thrown to the wild animals. Each artist must confront the ultimates many times—the Truth, the Self, Death itself—with the Lady there to reward the winners and the Tiger for the losers. Such myths are admirably accurate. It is learning to survive one's encounters with the Tiger that distinguishes the living artists from the ghosts."

Vera shuddered.

Wendell said quietly, "I wish there had been somebody to say that ten years ago."

They started seating. Soon family and guests had filled the two hundred couches, with family circle in the outermost row. When Jaeger announced the composition and lowered the day glowing once more, a rainbow appeared in the dome.

At each stage in the development of an art form, there is an individual who defines its possibilities and discovers its limits. Aristotle's *Poetics* formalized drama. Leonardo da Vinci's studies of light and of human anatomy made possible more accurate representation in painting. Niccolò Paganini's *Twenty-four Caprices for Violin* defined the limits of that instrument. Wolfgang Jaeger's *Rainbow Vistata (Vistata No. 11 in Seventh)* set the practical limits of lasegraphy.

Lasegraphy, like other performing arts, derives its power from the sexual principle. Like drama, music, and dance, lasegraphy teases. The lasegrapher seeks to communicate with others by creating a visual tension in them corresponding to their own experience of life, the release of such tension being pleasurable. The means by which tension is created, then released, defines the lasegraphic periods.

Also like other performing arts, lasegraphy gives its audience the "athletic" tension that the performer may royally screw up.

In its infancy, lasegraphy was the offspring of music and dance, relying on its two parents for its forms and patterns. Indeed, the imagery was not properly lasegraphy but choreography designed to accompany music, a practice later found only in roga. Tension and release was fleeting at best. Except for some fundamental uses of "exciting" colors versus "soothing" ones, hues usually served no function other than differentiating one image from the next or, in the case of gossamerlike interference lumia, providing a pleasant but boring interlude of swirling colors.

Over the form's first quarter-century, in its Nascent period, lasegraphers had begun experimenting with creating tension by the juxtaposition of two-dimensional shapes with three-dimensional forms. Now the first uses of color-created tension were found, which involved advancing cool-colored imagery, which the eye naturally expected to recede, and retreating warm-colored imagery, which the eye expected to advance.

In the Chaldean period, lasegraphers learned that when motion was formalized in paths the audience could expect—most characteristically, clockwise orbits around the dome's perimeter, with completion of the circle then blocked by contrary movements—tension could be raised further. In the Symbolist period which followed, lasegraphers produced tension by the dramatic conflict of putting mythopoetic images into "battles" against each other. Combined with rhythms borrowed from music and patterns common in dance, the art now had enough of its own identity to be performed without the crutch of accompanying music.

But it was in a revolt against the excesses of Symbolism that Impressionism arose. The Impressionists declared that the art form that had more control of its use of pure color than any previous form had yet to make full use of color itself to create an emotional bond between a lasegrapher and the audience.

This above all was what Jaeger did in *The Rainbow Vistata*.

Rainbows and spectral sequences, even spectral keys, were common in earlier compositions, though without much regard for the direction—violet to red or red to violet—in which the sequence departed from its key. But to compose the seven movements in descending keys of *The Rainbow Vistata*, Jaeger had to acknowledge the ancient truth that a spectral sequence and a musical scale were, in fact, both of a kind—that comparisons were not just metaphorical. In researching human color response, Jaeger learned that subconscious tension was greater at the red than at the violet, which told him what end of the scale was *up*. Furthermore, though music was capable of using multi-octave harmonics, while the spectrum of visible light takes up just about one octave, Jaeger realized that tension was created by delay in the completion of a spectral sequence—violet, indigo, blue, green, yellow, orange, red . . . *violet*—in the same way that tension in music was created by climbing the scale from *do* to *ti* then withholding the final *do*. Lasegraphy did not require a higher octave, as music did, to find unity: the color circle provided unity enough.

With the long-sought relationship between musical notes and colors finally established, much of musical form—tonic, dominant, subdominant—could now be adapted to lasegraphy; and most important, it was now possible for lasegraphy to compose the equivalent of melody—*coloratura*—with predictable results.

In variation after variation, *The Rainbow Vistata* made use of these discoveries.

The Rainbow Vistata was the composition which established as standard that scales should ascend from violet to red—the *extropic* scales, Jaeger called them—rather than from red to violet—those Jaeger tagged the entropic. It was the first composition to rely more on coloratura for its effect than merely on pattern and rhythm. It was the first composition written entirely to *lasegraphical* form.

Seventy-three years after Jaeger had composed it, performers still regarded *The Rainbow Vistata* as the most difficult virtuoso piece the art form had ever known. In fact, they competed widely to compose ever-more-difficult cadenzas for the final movement. It was this composition, therefore, with which Wolfgang Jaeger warmed up every morning. He knew that the day he could no longer play it would be the day he would end his concert career. His one hope was that he would see the coronation of his artistic heir— someone who could compose and perform a cadenza that he couldn't perform himself—before that day arrived. As yet, however, Jaeger had found no one who showed such ability.

So, as he had done countless times before, he performed *The Rainbow Vistata*.

The rainbow lighted up the dome, displaying the seven colors of the extropic scale in sequence, then spun off into discrete lines which began pulsating in the red-tonic, primal birth pains of the first movement, in Seventh. Second movement, in Sixth: the charging orange spheres bringing a rousing message of hope and good cheer. Third movement: the dazzling counterpoints in yellow lightning, brilliant and logical. The fourth "Jolly Green Giant" movement, jovial, sweeping, and grand. The spiritual, awe-inspiring waltz in the key of blue, the fifth movement segueing directly into the sorrowful, lilting indigo movement. Finally, the gentle lumias of the sensual violet movement, the impossibly fast rainbow cadenza, leading inevitably to the rebirth of the extropic rainbow, a coloratura that drew all who watched it into its compelling vortex.

The dome was pitch-black again. Wolfgang Jaeger, bathed in sweat, raised the glowing to take his bow.

He accepted the applause, then announced an encore. "For the Lady who confronts the Tiger," he said. "Delaney's *Fugue in Blue*."

There was a rumble of confusion—with several gasps in the back row—as the glowing went down again.

A blue figure-8 began a dance in the sky.

It was a happy little dance. The blue figure-8 warbled and squiggled its way across the dome and around the edge. It turned somersaults and cartwheels. It metamorphosed into different shapes and sprang back again. It shrank down to a pinpoint—

And Vera Collier Delaney screamed in the dark.

There is one lesson that lasegraphers have burned into their souls before their teachers will allow them anywhere near an audience: if you hear a scream, get the lights on *fast*. This rates in the lasegraphic catechism even higher that the theatrical doctrine "The show must go on." It may be a fire; it may be only that someone has seen a mouse. It may be an assassination; it may be that a woman has felt an unexpected hand on her knee. The most common cause is simply that someone has panicked from the darkness. But the performer is not to consider this probability, not to evaluate the content of any scream. Whatever its cause—real or imagined—it can spread into a deadly stampede to the exits in seconds.

Wolfgang Jaeger had the day glowing up to general visibility, without blinding glare, in split seconds. Yet he was not so fast that there was not time for Vera, who was in the couch nearest the exit, to be halfway outside when the lighting came up.

Jaeger took command immediately. "There is no danger. Everyone please remain seated for the moment. Mrs. Darris?"

Flanked by Stanton and Wendell, Eleanor went forward to the Tiger Pit, accompanied also by an uneasy rumble among her guests. "It's Vera," Eleanor told him softly. "I'd better go after her."

"Perhaps it would be best to continue the concert," Stanton suggested.

"If you would, Maestro," Eleanor said, "but for Goddess' sake, play something else!"

Jaeger looked deeply troubled. "I don't understand. I thought she would be pleased by my interpretation—"

"Maestro," Wendell said, *sotto voce*, "there's an old expression among us andromen: never surprise anybody by sticking your finger up his ass."

"Surprise?" Jaeger asked. "But there was no surprise. I asked Vera for permission to play one of her scores before the concert. She told me to play whatever I liked."

"Oh, no!" Eleanor turned as white as her uniform when she realized what she had done. "Maestro—" She barely got the words out. "You asked *me*."

Eleanor left the dome to find Vera while Stanton and Wendell

52

returned to their couches. "By special request, another encore," Jaeger announced as he lowered the glowing again. "Kaelin's *Gossamer Albatross.*"

Vera was not too difficult to track down at all; Eleanor found her in the kitchen leaning against the irradiation sealer. She had obviously been crying, but seemed to be past the worst of it, which Eleanor took as a good sign. "Are you all right?" she asked her daughter, putting an arm around her shoulder.

Vera shook her head.

"Will you be all right soon?"

Vera shrugged.

They didn't say anything for a little while; then Vera said suddenly, "It was *mine*. He had no right!"

"He thought you had given him permission."

"How could he think that?"

Eleanor stroked Vera's hair. "Because he asked me by mistake."

Vera slipped out from under her mother's arm. "You gave him permission to play *Fugue in Blue*?"

"He said something ambiguous about playing 'some scores of yours,' " Eleanor said. "The way he said it, I thought he just meant some pieces we had lying around in the Tiger Pit. I had no idea he meant—"

"You had no idea, you had no *idea*," Vera started. "Do you have any idea what you've done to me?"

"Vera, I'm so sorry—"

"Three *years*, Mother. Three years in a service dicteriat as a daily sacrifice to the gods of war. Three years of 'I'm gonna ram it in you now' and 'Suck me faster' and of having every square inch of my body groped eight times a day by any male past puberty who had his taxes paid up. But I knew that even though I'd never have the courage to compose another one, there was one part of me—the only *real* part of me—that no one could touch. Just so long as nobody had ever seen it—"

"Vera, I didn't mean for this—"

"Oh, yes, you did," Vera said. "You've never allowed me to have *anything* that was all my own."

Eleanor started. "That's not true," she said slowly. "I have *always* encouraged you to develop your own interests—"

"—and become a dilettante just like you. You've never succeeded at *any*thing you've started, and I'm exactly like you. How could I?"

"You are *not* exactly like me. You are a separate person with your own identity, your own soul—"

53

"Mother, if you were so cloneraping set on your daughter being different from you, then why did you *have* me in a way that made sure that when I looked in a mirror I'd see *your* face?"

"It wasn't what I expected," Eleanor said softly.

"What? I could barely hear you."

"I thought then when *I* looked in a mirror, I'd see the face of my daughter, who had reached things I could only dream about. But what I expected isn't important. The point is that I'm not living inside your body, making all the moves. You are."

Eleanor kissed Vera on the cheek, then turned to leave. "Will you come out to say good night to your guests? And Jaeger?"

Vera looked daggers at her mother. "Why don't you say it all for me? Nobody will be able to tell the difference anyway."

Eleanor paused a moment to reply, then thought better of it and went out to the lawn dome alone.

Vera remained in the kitchen a short while longer before deciding to go up to bed. On her way, she came around the other side of the irradiation sealer and saw a little girl's drawing, in the shape of a spiral rainbow, fastened to the wall.

Vera ripped the drawing down and threw it into the scintillator.

II.

λ4200Å to 4500Å

STONED OR SOBER, guests eventually go home, and good or bad, parties eventually end.

Several family-circle members did stay through brunch the next day, which gave Kate Seymour a chance to teach Joan that little song about going to St. Clive. His Gaylordship Wendell Darris declined his brother's invitation, pleading business in the Federation capital; he left the party that night, no more stoned than usual, and caught the red-eye shuttle from Newer York to Charlotte Amalie.

François Duroux left the party stoned out of his mind, and while his skymobile fetched him back to his mother's house in Montreal that night, he didn't quite make it to Legos, Ltd., the next morning.

Wolfgang Jaeger, who wasn't properly a guest—even though he *had* been invited to mingle—departed Earth for Ad Astra the next afternoon, sober as a judge.

And when they had all left, there was still Vera, who was staying on at Helix Vista, in an extended rest & relaxation, through that fall, when she would begin law school.

Another party was held at Helix Vista a week later, on April 15, though—befitting its honoree's size—this was a considerably smaller affair. Stanton Darris had assured his daughter that parties for five-year-olds were lots more fun than parties for grown-ups. Whether or not this was true as a general rule, Joan had no basis of comparison to disagree with him. If she noticed at all that of those in attendance at her fifth-birthday party, the only children were her brothers, she did not find anything extraordinary about this. And if the two recent parties needed to be compared at all, it would be only to note that Joan had a considerably lighter-hearted time at her party than Vera had had a week earlier at hers.

Of course, there were cake and ice cream and party favors. Naturally, there were presents. Kate Seymour returned to give her granddaughter a Shetland pony, which Joan—at Stanton's suggestion—named Lazy Gopher. She hugged and kissed it more than she did her grandmother, and was led around on the pony long enough for Stanton to take some holos. Then Joan allowed her brothers to take their turns, and Nick promptly lost his slightly used cake and ice cream.

Vera gave her sister a storydisc called *The Littlest Corporal.* It told the saga of a performing poodle named Tricksy, jointly owned by a little girl and her older sister, that leaves the little girl to accompany her sister when she goes off to the service. The story told the rather odd adventures the poodle had performing tricks for the women in the dicteriat, and it made a lasting impression on Joan, who didn't quite understand why Tricksy had had to leave the little girl in the first place.

Mr. McIntosh gave Joan a Snow White Talking Mirror. Mark gave her a Slinky. The twins gave her two giant turtles. And the sort of presents that two-year-old Zack was giving these days would have pleased no one but an orthodox Freudian.

Most prodigiously, Eleanor and Stanton gave their daughter an LCAA Mark 800B chromatic laser with quarter-size console. Wendell Darris (who was obviously in cahoots) had sent over a holoscreen compatible with that console so that Joan could practice, unsupervised, without using the laser.

Once it was made clear to Joan that this complicated equipment was of the same sort as that which she had seen her friend Wolf use in the lawn dome, and that she would begin lessons shortly to become a lasegrapher, she was endlessly delighted. She solemnly promised that she wouldn't treat the equipment like a toy, and that she would practice all her lessons faithfully.

Vera was not endlessly delighted with her sister's lasegraphic gifts, but limited herself to a brief remark to their mother, out of anyone else's hearing, telling Eleanor how foolish it was to begin the entire cycle once more.

The pony was beyond reach, in the stable, after dark. The story-disc lasted only half an hour, and Joan didn't feel like playing it more than once. Joan quickly bored of arguing with the mirror whether she was in fact more beautiful than Snow White, whose story Mr. McIntosh had told her, but who was a person of no particular importance to her. The twins were monopolizing the turtles. And she didn't yet know how to operate the laser, besides having promised not to play with it like a toy.

So Joan spent most of the evening of her fifth birthday playing with the Slinky.

The morning after her fifth birthday, Joan was taken to downtown Newer York by Mr. McIntosh to be fitted with an identity transponder and to be brainprinted.

The World Federation's Bureau of Immunity occupied a stately office concourse on Liberty Street, right above vaults—built deep underground on the bedrock of Manhattan Island—that had once belonged to the Federal Reserve Bank of the United States of America. That institution had ceased to exist before the new millennium had rolled around, not to mention the new Concord; its vaults—which were used primarily for storing the wealth of other nations—had survived even the devastation of the Colonial War, a century later. Nowadays these vaults housed the primary records of the Federation; the identity records of all persons known to be alive, dead, or frozen in cryonic suspension on Earth since records were consolidated half a century ago; and all Suicide Immediately After Reading military secrets of the Federation Space Corps.

This included, among other things, the brainprint of every person five years and older who had set foot on Earth in the past fifty years. But a crazed terrorist (or a committed patriot) who had managed the impossible feat of exploding a thermonuclear device inside the vaults would have been sorely disappointed: copies of the entire brainprint file were available at every police Monitor station on Earth. It was not a particularly large collection of data . . . for any pocket computer. But as provided for in the Ninth Amendment to the Articles of Federation, such Monitor copies could not even include the name of the person to whom each brainprint belonged. They stated only that the brainprint in question belonged to a person who was legally in good standing so far as the Federation was concerned, or a fugitive wanted by the authorities, or a Touchable.

In absolute fact, no one was required to wear the tiny radio transponder that converted each person's unique "primary neural modulation" into a weak broadcast signal unchanged from birth to death. But anyone not wearing the transponder was a complete nonperson, legally even less protected than Touchables, who at least still had status in the courts. Thus, while—at least, by the letter of the law—wantonly killing a Touchable was still murder, killing a nonperson was not. At worst it was cruelty to animals. Or littering.

In a society where fingers could be transplanted, larynxes could be switched, retinas could be changed, brains could be transferred into the body of a clone, the brainprint was the only reliable form of identification.

Only the mountain hermit might have missed getting fitted for a transponder. Probably even the hermit got one after being negatively "frisked" the first time . . . if the hermit survived the first time.

The Federation sold its "immunity" cheap . . . to its favored customers. Mr. McIntosh escorted one of those customers to the children's section on the forty-third floor, waited in line with her for most of an hour, then presented the information-and-consent affidavit provided by her parents. He swore an oath that Joan was the person named in the affidavit, paid the one-auragram fee, then took her to a waiting room where, among crying five-year-olds and accompanying grown-ups (except for some robot governors that, presumably, didn't grow), they sat watching holovision for another half-hour.

A robot nurse escorted them to an operating room—more like a dentist's office—and placed Joan in an operating chair, securing her head in a vise. The nurse then tied back Joan's hair and shaved the back of her head. Joan was brave about it. A human physician came in dressed in surgical greens, made some "this won't hurt a bit" sounds, and applied a local anesthetic to the back of Joan's neck.

In fact, it didn't hurt a bit. The implantation procedure, accomplished by the surgeon with a laser scalpel, was over in five minutes. The surgeon put in the transponder at the base of Joan's skull, not very far from the spot where the spinal cord meets the brain. Actual contact with the central nervous system was not needed, as the transponder was smart enough to induce the neural modulation.

After the surgeon tested the signal, she released Joan's head, untied her hair, and removed her own surgical mask. She told Joan what a good girl she was and gave her a lollipop.

The robot nurse took the actual brainprint from Joan in an ad-

58

joining office while Mr. McIntosh tried to pick up the surgeon—with no success; she was used to fending off enterprising governors.

Mr. McIntosh and his charge left the offices a few minutes later. As soon as they were down in the main concourse again, Joan threw away the unopened lollipop. It may have been her first political act.

The family's dinner was early that evening, since Vera, Stanton, and Eleanor were going out. François Duroux had discovered at Vera's ball that Stanton Darris was a fellow Marnie and had promised him an invitation to his next nightstalk. The invitation came sooner than expected when a Touchable, brought to Legos on various misdemeanors—working in a profession, working at a fixed location, property ownership, not wearing a red cloak while in public—had struck a plea bargain by revealing the whereabouts of a secret Touchable ghetto in Rochester.

The plans called for the three of them to rendezvous with Duroux's hunting party in Rochester just before sundown, in the cannabistro of the New Eastman Hotel. Duroux had promised that the party would be kept small—no more than three each of commen, andromen, and women. From the hotel the Marnies would don flying belts, and their guests would follow as closely as possible in a limousine. Vera and Eleanor would be in the limousine, since neither was a licensed Marnie—Eleanor through lack of inclination, Vera because it was only since becoming a veteran that she had become eligible. "With a little Lady Luck," Duroux had told them, "this will be a large enough hideaway that none of us will have to settle for sloppy seconds."

It was an easygoing and somewhat chaotic scene around the dinner table, since Eleanor and Stanton disliked formality as a steady diet. Vera, Stanton, and Eleanor were eating fried chicken prepared by the estate's robots according to Grandma Collier's Kentucky recipe; Mark, the twins, Joan, and Mr. McIntosh ate quiches that Mr. McIntosh had picked up from the nearest Quiche Me Quick on his way back from the city. Zack ate a toddler's porridge. Mr. McIntosh ate what the children ate, when he could, since he felt it improved his rapport; on this occasion he had the added reason for avoiding the chicken that he was a strict vegetarian.

But even quiches weren't a strong enough hold to keep the older children's attention solely on dinner. "Mom," Mark asked, "can I eat later and watch *Red Hunt*?"

"Me too!" the twins shouted. "Me too!"

Joan quietly continued eating her quiche.

Eleanor looked down the table to Mr. McIntosh. "They did all their schoolwork," he said.

"You may watch it after you finish eating," Eleanor told them.

"But the *Holy Guide* says it's on the satellite *now*."

"The holy won't forget the show, so you can just finish your quiche."

"I don't see why you let them eat such junk food," Vera said to Eleanor.

"When you have your own children," Eleanor told her, "you'll find out that you feed them whatever scat they'll eat."

"I don't want to eat scat," Vic said.

"You don't have to, dear," said Eleanor. "Just eat your quiche."

The children ate their dinners rather more quickly than usual. Afterward they were allowed to take their desserts—pieces from yesterday's birthday cake—into the den to catch the holovision show they wanted to see. Zack remained with the adults.

"As I started saying before . . ." Stanton reached for another chicken breast. "Burgess Carlisle renewed his invitation to visit him in Cair Paravel. I think he's trying to sell me a partial interest in his ferrofoam factory, now that St. Clive's restrictions on stock owner-ship by Federation citizens have been lifted."

"It *would* be a lovely vacation," Eleanor said, "before we start making Stan Junior this fall. And it would be nice seeing my grand-parents again."

"Especially if your grandmother still makes the original recipe of this chicken."

"It wouldn't be fair to Mac, though—would it, Mac?"

Mr. McIntosh shrugged. "I admit, the children are a handful at times."

"Mac doesn't have to go it alone." Vera was speaking. "I'll be here for the summer."

Mr. McIntosh began paying close attention.

Eleanor looked delighted. "I thought you wanted to do some traveling yourself."

Vera shrugged. "You know me—I've never been much for sight-seeing. Oh, maybe I'll spend a few weeks sunbathing on the Riviera, but I'll be back before you're ready to leave. When would it be, June?"

"Certainly not till after Midsummer," Stanton said. "No sense bucking the holiday crowds."

Eleanor pushed her plate away and lit a joynette. "Vera, are you sure? You really want to do this?"

"Very much, Mother. It will give me a chance to find out what it's like to have a family of my own."

Eleanor frowned slightly. Stanton said quickly, "This *is* your family, Vera."

A robot hurried over to begin removing plates.

"I mean a family with me as the mommy," Vera said. "So I'll have some experience knowing what scat to feed them."

"A mommy implies a daddy," Mr. McIntosh suggested hopefully.

Vera regarded him coolly. "Not in my experience," she said.

While the family's adults were getting ready to leave—they had to be in Rochester by six-thirty—the children and Mr. McIntosh watched *Red Hunt*—"A Mark Quimm Production, based on actual cases released by the Federation Bureau of Immunity." This week's episode was more banal than usual . . . even by holy standards.

Two Federation Monitors, Wong and McCoy, are on sky patrol in the Miami area when a report comes into their cruiser that a Marnie hunting party—bird-dogging various people by scanning random transponders and linking with Monitor computers for a status check—has alerted the computers that something fishy is going on. The computer says that a brainprint they've just read—though listed as a citizen in good standing—was picked up less than an hour ago in Budapest . . . too far away in too short a time for even a shuttle flight. The computer has answered the Marnies: "Wanted by the authorities," and the Marnies have placed the suspect under citizen's arrest, holding him until the Monitors arrive.

When the suspect is examined, it turns out that instead of a transponder, he is wearing a tiny transmitter giving out a recording of another person's brainprint.

End of Act One. Eleanor came into the den to say good night; then she, Stanton, and Vera left for Rochester.

Act Two. When the suspect's brainprint is taken at Monitor headquarters, he turns out to be a Touchable after all, using the false brainprint to masquerade as a citizen in good standing.

Act Three. The Touchable confesses to being part of a ring of renegade Touchables. With a little "persuasion," he tells how renegades kidnap people without family connections—lonely old commen, lesbians, divorced andromen—record their brainprints, then icarate them, making sure the victim's brainprint isn't filed as inactive in the Liberty Street archives. Then they sell the dead person's brainprint to Touchables at exorbitant prices.

Act Four. The entire Touchable ring is tracked down, and McCoy—the young recruit who superiors thought didn't have any guts—proves his courage in hand-to-hand fighting with the Touchable ringleader, killing the Touchable by smashing his nose into his head and propelling a bone splinter up into the brain.

Epilogue. The entire Touchable ring is condemned to the microwave ovens in time for the final commercial, a public-service message in behalf of "the Blue . . . the Butch . . . the Marnies."

Joan stayed awake through the entire show, but just barely, since she found it boring. The twins loved it. Mark started pointing out plot holes, asking Mr. McIntosh why the first Touchable's brainprint had been recorded from a person who hadn't been kidnapped or icked, and where did Touchables—who could earn barely enough to feed themselves—get enough money to buy stolen brainprints at exorbitant prices?

Duroux's hunting party didn't do quite so well as Wong and McCoy. His plea-bargaining Touchable hadn't lied outright—he had been much too smart for that. But when the Marnies got to the reported Touchable hideaway, it had—from the looks of it—been abandoned for at least two days. Duroux figured that the group probably scrammed automatically whenever one of their own disappeared for more than twenty-four hours . . . the amount of time it had taken for their informer to "crack."

The party had returned to the cannabistro at the New Eastman, and the family were back at Helix Vista by midnight.

FROM THE SKY, the two of them could see only a green-copper bubble encircled by seven smaller green bubbles; from the street, Eleanor and Joan saw the green of a monastic courtyard surrounding an ivy-strangled stone building. An iron portcullis, raised during daylight hours, lent further medieval atmosphere, protecting the courtyard from its neighbors. This had not been a fashionable area even before the War; but now it was just short of being a slum, separated by only a landing strip from Vaginatown, a walled ghetto where Touchable mothers with small children were allowed to live unmolested.

Eleanor knew firsthand that this institution had been here before the Colonial War, when the neighborhood had been part of the old borough called Brooklyn. But the domes had been golden orange, and there hadn't been any ivy, the first time she'd come here, just a little younger than Joan's current age, with her own mother. Eleanor couldn't help thinking of *The Picture of Dorian Gray* whenever she visited here: it always seemed to her that the place had aged in her stead. Nonetheless, aside from oxidation and ivy, the Malcolm Institute of Lasegraphy stood, as it had always stood, on the northern perimeter of the neighborhood called, since the War, Rainborough Park. By luck or providence, the school had been built in one of the borough's few neighborhoods left completely untouched by meteors in the Rain of Terror.

Between the ages of four and nine, Eleanor had taken lessons here from Jules Malcolm, before the War had killed him and displaced her to the farm in Kentucky. The Colliers were not particularly disposed to much besides work and prayer; they had felt that taking in their orphaned granddaughter was charity enough, without wasting money on lessons in how to give people headaches with flashing lights. The result was that when Eleanor had come back to Newer York at eighteen, she had found that nine years away from the console had been cruel, and she just didn't have the heart to begin all over from scratch.

So she had brought one daughter here to study the laser, and now, each Tuesday at 6:15 P.M., she began bringing another.

Jack Malcolm was an aristocratic-looking comman in his early seventies who, as his one concession to natural aging, had allowed his wavy brown hair to turn white. His elegance resulted primarily from slenderness combined with almost two meters of height. Eleanor thought that he now looked much as she remembered Jules Malcolm looking, but when she had first known him, he had been a gangly thirteen-year-old who always seemed to be in the way at his father's academy. Eleanor had briefly had a crush on Jack when she was nine, just before the War took her away; she had consummated the crush three decades later when she began bringing Vera for lessons. He was still unmarried.

Eleanor had not wanted to delegate to Mr. McIntosh the responsibility of bringing Joan to her first lessons, since Jack, his traumatic experience with Vera seared into memory, had not seemed eager to see Joan at all. Eleanor knew it was only because of their long friendship—and the Darris Foundation's continued aid to the institute—that he had reluctantly agreed to see Joan at the end of April—two days before Beltane—for the first time. Even so, he seemed prepared to brush them off until Joan scored so remarkably well on the Piaget tests. But he would not come to Helix Vista for her lessons, and he would not teach her by remote hookup. Jack Malcolm was a lasemeister in his father's mold: it was face-to-face lessons on the dual console in one of the lesser domes, each Tuesday from six-fifteen to seven-fifteen without fail, or it was nothing.

And Lady help the pupil who didn't practice in between.

Joan needed little of the Lady's intercession.

It would be untruthful to suggest that there weren't days when Joan didn't feel like practicing, that there weren't afternoons she would rather have spent with her pony, or even drawing with her old thermocrayons. The chromatic laser is not a rewarding instrument for a beginner: it is horridly complex and apt to discourage anyone with the sensitivity to compare one's first clumsy efforts with the soaring graces seen in a master and imagined for oneself. But Joan was too young to worry about such discrepancies—few with the sensibilities needed for virtuosity began playing over six— and she learned the instrument neither so slowly that she found the challenges overwhelming nor so quickly that endless repetitions between lessons—necessary to develop control—bored her to tears.

Some things came to her more easily than others. She familiarized herself with the thirty-six-color scale almost immediately, and was found to have the ability to identify each shade not only relative to the five hues in each of the seven color keys (not counting, of course, the thirty-sixth, invisible ultraviolet used for phosphorescence), but also discretely, absolutely. Nonetheless, it took weeks of daily practice before she was able to run her fingers, with any accuracy or fluidity, over the console's thirty-six touch-sensitive color panels. She took to the thirty-six scanning panels easily, learning to form an image's shape by FM and its size by AM. Neither did it take her long to master the step-changes controlled by foot pedals—how to bring up an interference lumia or a diffraction pattern. But to learn the basic raw-scan lissajous—the cycloids and the spirals—the mandalas, the auroras, the lightnings—took time and patience.

From her first lessons with Malcolm, Joan began learning to read

64

and write Scholastic notation, the basic scoring for lasegraphy. Malcolm, unlike many of his contemporaries, believed that early lasegraphic training had to involve the conscious mind as well as the unconscious reflexes. Joan learned how each circle on the lasegraphic staff was a complete description of a moment's frame up in the dome—the duration of each frame marked under each circle—with markings inside for type of image, its color, shape, amplitude, location, speed, direction, and dozens of other variables.

Joan did not learn this all at once, but she learned to read and write symbols for what she was learning to do as she learned to do it. This was the first written language she learned, since none of those in her household made regular use of the written form of the English they spoke, and nobody around her saw any pressing reason that she should learn to read or write in it.

Throughout Joan's first lessons, Eleanor sat off to one side in the Tiger Pit, observing. Malcolm never minded when a parent wished to observe, but this was something Vera had never permitted her; she had always complained that her mother's presence during lessons inhibited and distracted her. It was a problem Joan did not share. In fact, she barely noticed that her mother was there. But Eleanor's presence at the sessions allowed Joan to be helped with any problems arising during her practicing at home in the lawn dome, in effect giving her a second teacher.

From Eleanor's standpoint, it was almost as if she herself were getting a second chance at learning the laser, since in effect she was progressing at the same rate Joan was. She even had Vera's old console taken out of storage and set it up alongside Joan's quarter-size in the lawn dome—ostensibly so she could better help Joan with her studies, but also because she was enjoying the lessons more than anything else she had done in years.

This happy state of affairs did not last long, though. One evening in early June, when Eleanor remained in the lawn dome practicing an hour longer than Joan had, Vera suggested that if Eleanor was set on a concert career for herself, she should tell Malcolm who it was he was *really* teaching. "All you have to do," Vera said, "is forget about your trip to St. Clive . . . and weren't you planning another son for next year? I suppose you'll have to forget about him too."

After that evening, Joan practiced alone with the holoscreen Wendell had given her, or supervised in the lawn dome by Mr. McIntosh if her lesson required the laser, and Mr. McIntosh took over chauffeuring Joan to her weekly lessons.

By her eighth week, the Tuesday before Midsummer solstice, it was evident to Malcom that Joan was an exceptionally adept student. At a stage when most other students were still trying to get the left hand to speak to the right hand, Joan was playing basic repertoire—Jittlov's *Animato in Second*. It was not a terribly difficult piece, but he had assigned it to her only the week before, and she came into this lesson able to play it. She couldn't play it *well*, of course, but being able to play it at all after so short a time was impressive.

He recorded a short letter to Eleanor, suggesting that Joan's lessons be increased to twice weekly, and gave it to her to be hand-delivered to her mother. Thereafter, Joan took her lessons not only Tuesdays at six-fifteen, but also Fridays at two.

Eleanor and Stanton had several family-circle members over that Saturday, June 21, for a combination Midsummer feast and bon-voyage party for themselves. Surprisingly, two days before an election, Wendell Darris decided to attend; Stanton decided that the personal pressures of this campaign had completely fagged out his brother. But His Gaylordship's attendance prompted Joan's first performance that evening in the lawn dome. She played *Animato in Second*—the only piece she knew—to a standing ovation. The ovation was from her Uncle Wendell, who was the only person at her performance, and he had been standing near the outer wall for the entire time she played for him.

Nevertheless, it was not an unsuccessful premiere, as these things go.

Election night that Monday, June 23, brought mixed news to Helix Vista. The bad news was that the Libertarians had lost ground to the Chauvinist Party in both the Upper and Lower Manor; in particular, the Hudson Parish seat in the House of Commen, which the Libertarian Party had held since the Federation was declared, had been lost. But the Darrises were celebrating that evening, since Wendell had won a fourth six-year term as the North American Concord's gaylord in the House of Gentry.

Tuesday morning, the 24th, Stanton and Eleanor kissed their children goodbye at Soleri Skyport, gaining assurances from Vera and Mr. McIntosh that everything would hold together for the next eight weeks . . . and further promises from the twins that they would be good. Then they boarded the shuttle that would take them to Virginia Station, in fixed orbit 35,880 kilometers over Newer York. From there they would transfer to the thermonuclear torchship

Jupiter Moon for their nine-day journey, out past the orbit of Mars in the asteroid belt, to St. Clive.

Routines at Helix Vista stayed unchanged. The estate's domestic computer, aided by the robot staff, ran almost everything by itself, and what supervisory duties Eleanor had performed, Vera took over. Except for mealtimes—when Vera was constantly warning them that they'd better eat properly or they'd grow up to be Touchables—Mr. McIntosh kept charge of the children. And while their mother was missing, they certainly had the next-best-thing—in a genetic sense—for a replacement. Zack naturally assumed that Vera was his mother, and even the older children, in their turn, mistakenly addressed Vera as "Mommy."

The first one to call her that, at dinner a few days after their parents' departure, was Joan. For a moment, both their faces flushed bright red—Vera's in anger, Joan's in embarrassment—and Joan was so mortified that she ran out of the room. Almost immediately, though, Vera got control over herself. She followed Joan out to the patio and made it quite clear to her, with appropriate affection, that she didn't blame her at all for the mistake. Later, when the other children did it, Vera seemed almost pleased.

Perhaps it was inevitable that there would come a night, after the children were asleep, when Vera and Mr. McIntosh would find their eyes meeting across an empty room. It happened the first Thursday in July, shortly after 11 P.M., GMT-plus-five. The robot butler informed Mr. McIntosh, who was in the kitchen practicing the guitar, that a picturegram had just been received from St. Clive, and asked whether he wanted it played now. Mr. McIntosh asked the butler where Vera was. The butler relayed the question to the domestic computer. The computer found masses radiating a temperature near 37°C in five other rooms, but determined that only one of the masses breathed as an adult human would. It relayed this information to the butler, which told Mr. McIntosh, instants after he asked, that Vera was in the blue lounge. He next asked if Vera might be asleep; after checking again, the butler told him that her respiration was much too rapid for sleep. That should have alerted him, but didn't. Mr. McIntosh told the butler that the two of them would take the picturegram on the blue lounge's holoscreen; then he took the lift up to the fifth level.

But the blue lounge's holoscreen was already in use when Mr. McIntosh walked in. A disc was on playing *Fugue in Blue*. The blue figure-8 warbled and squiggled its way around the screen, shrinking and rebounding, then the red, then the green. As for Vera, she lay on a recliner watching, with her dress hitched above her waist, masturbating.

She felt the beginning of sensations she had not felt in well over three years. A warm excitement grew, centering in her breasts and between her legs, but gently spreading throughout her entire body. She closed her eyes, sensing the gathering-together whose delicious ripples were just approaching high tide, and searched for an image that would bring them in. She opened her eyes to help her focus better, and saw Mr. McIntosh standing in the doorway, watching her.

Their eyes met across the empty room. She didn't quite scream. "Scat, *Scat*, SCAT!"

Mr. McIntosh's pulse quickened, his eyelids were half closed, and his throat was a desert. His voice, living its own life, said, "I can make you finish."

She noticed the erection under his pants and was furious. "If the last six thousand men who fucked me didn't make me come, what makes you think you can?"

"I won't fuck you. I'll lick you out."

She was terribly frustrated, and she didn't see anything to lose. "Very well," she said. "But hurry."

Vera watched Mr. McIntosh stride across the room to her the way a master lasegrapher would approach the Tiger Pit, and she slid herself down in the recliner to allow him access. He took just a moment to position himself comfortably between her legs, blew gently across her blond pubic hair while finding her clitoris, then lowered his tongue to it, beginning to stroke rhythmically.

"Harder," she said.

He began licking harder, faster, and she began feeling the beginnings of the sensations again, that fire-gem–like warmth. After a little while, he began caressing her more tenderly again, then he would surprise her with a lightning-hard stroke; she gasped and ran her fingers through his light brown hair, pulling his head in closer. He responded by moving his hands up to tease her breasts. She noticed, somewhere near the edge of her consciousness, that *Fugue in Blue* had ended, that the disc was over. But it didn't matter anymore, she could see it by herself. He jolted her by missing a beat, then made two hard strokes together, and she would have begun spiraling down out of control when she saw Eleanor and Stanton staring at her on the holoscreen.

Every nerve ending in Vera's body stood on edge, and this time she did scream. It was not a scream of pleasure.

But Mr. McIntosh didn't realize this and he continued licking.

Vera grabbed him by the hair and yanked his head away from her, almost giving Mr. McIntosh a whiplash as he tumbled onto the floor.

"Hello, back home," Eleanor said. "We thought we'd just surprise you—"

"I can't talk now," Vera yelled at the screen, "Phone off!"

"—and not wait to let you know we arrived in Cair Paravel safely—"

Vera pulled down her dress, trying to cover herself while wondering why the phone's camera eye wasn't lit red; she supposed it was broken. "I'll have to call you back" she told the screen, more calmly. "Computer, turn the phone *off*."

"Null program," the computer said.

Mr. McIntosh tried getting his wind back to talk, but couldn't yet.

"—very nice cruise," Stanton continued, "although the free fall during turnover didn't agree with me—"

"Computer—"

"Relax," Mr. McIntosh finally managed to get out. "Crone Almighty, it's not the *phone*."

"Then how the rape—"

"It's a *picture*gram," he said. "That's what I was coming in here about. I told the computer to pipe it up here."

"What?"

"You think they'd phone from St. Clive?" He took a breath. "With twenty-six minutes between *answers*?"

"—so we'd better sign off before this gets expensive," Eleanor said. "Bye-bye."

The holoscreen cleared.

Vera felt utterly raw. She felt as raw as she had just before her collapse at the pyradome, warming up three hours before her premiere. "You stupid penis," she started in on Mr. McIntosh with her service vocabulary. She was almost crying now. "You utterly dumbjohn *scat*head."

Mr. McIntosh didn't say anything. He had seen Joan come into the lounge in her pajamas, rubbing her eyes; her bedroom was just down the hall. "I got woken up," Joan said. "I heard Mommy screaming."

"It was just a dream," Vera said wearily. "Go back to bed."

Mr. McIntosh looked at Vera with disgust, but it was too late.

"It *wasn't* a dream," Joan said. "I heard her."

"You just thought you did, honey," said Mr. McIntosh. "All you really heard was Vera and me, playing a game."

"It really wasn't Mommy?"

"No, sweetheart," he said. "Come on, I'll take you back to bed."

Mr. McIntosh took Joan's hand, but paused a moment in the doorway. "Vera, I'm really sorry," he said. "I truly am."

"Go ick yourself," Vera said childishly.

He left the lounge to return Joan to her bedroom.

Vera sat in the recliner for another few minutes, hugging her knees and shaking badly. "Cloneraper," she said.

Helix Vista was different after that night. Vera began missing meals with the family, refusing to speak to Mr. McIntosh at all. She would leave a room if he was in it, pass him in the hallways as if one or the other of them were a specter. Then, for three days, she flew off by herself to the English countryside, not bothering to tell Mr. McIntosh where she was going or how long she would be gone. When she returned, as unheralded as she'd left, she gave him no apology, though her absence had caused him to miss his day off. But Vera's time alone had calmed her down enough that she was able to resume more-or-less civil relations with him, though she still would not speak to him unless she thought it was unavoidable.

It was unavoidable on Tuesday, July 15—the day of Joan's sixteenth lesson.

VERA WATCHED from the dark. She watched the lights. She watched her little sister make them dance.

The whiny, rainy sort of day that often came to Upper Hudson in the summer was too wet, too chill, too dim even for children like the Darrises, who otherwise liked to play in the rain. It was, in fact, exactly the sort of day that had always kept such children indoors whether they liked it or not—to prevent them from getting colds had been the old reason, but since nobody got colds anymore, grown-ups found other excuses to prevent little feet from tracking in mud.

Still, even a thunderstorm wasn't usually enough to order the Darris children inside. Helix Vista was equipped with an outdoor climate-control system—to make a sunny day with anti-precipitation fields and radiant units—which was just fine unless the domestic computer said the grounds needed watering anyway.

This particular afternoon in July, the grounds needed watering. Nevertheless, a red sky at night—for Mark and the twins, delight— for Joan was the warning sailors took from red sky in the morning. A moderate deluge was made to order for a five-year-old celestial navigator to whom darkness was safety and sunlight the siren song luring her onto the rocks of her teacher's displeasure. But Joan was not yet old enough to sail the laser alone.

Much of Joan's practice could be done alone in her room, with her console plugged not into a laser but into the holoscreen her Uncle Wendell had given her. The holoscreen could simulate lase-graphic patterns as a laser would project them in the dome in all respects but two: in absolute amplitude of imagery, and in intensity of hue. The composition that Joan was preparing for that evening's lesson—Plainer's *Fantasia in Seventh*—required developing a sensitivity to both.

When it came time that afternoon for Joan to practice—preparation that properly required the laser—she had found that her usual steward was preoccupied in an activity that might most accurately be termed preventing her brothers from dismantling the house. Mr. McIntosh had disentangled himself from the boys long enough to ask Vera, who was doing some advanced reading of law discs, whether she might substitute for him in the lawn dome. Reluctantly, Vera had agreed.

Vera sat near the lawn dome's outer edge, watching Joan intently. In the Tiger Pit, Joan sat at a quarter-size console almost identical to the one Vera had owned at her age, and played the patterns across the darkened sky as if she'd been born to it. Vera could already see the beginning of technique, of Joan's personal style. The breathing of the laser matched Joan's breathing. Its spirit was her spirit, illuminating her unburdened joy. Joan made the lights her own lights. The longer Vera watched, the more uneasy the former lasegrapher became.

At first Vera did not have any idea what was bothering her. She wondered if perhaps it was her old, teenage fear of the laser, but had a sense that this feeling related to something that had started much earlier. She thought, then, that the feeling was sympathetic in nature, a reflection from Joan to herself of her own bad experience with the art, a desire to spare her sister the pain she had gone through. Since this was what she expected herself to feel, thinking herself a benevolent person, she was halfway to believing it. But almost at once, in the beat it took the laser to slash across the dome, she saw through it all.

She saw a little blond-haired girl seated at a quarter-size console not here, but in one of the domes at the Malcolm Institute. In two audience couches were a man she recognized as a still-brown-haired Jack Malcolm and a grown-up blond woman who looked exactly as she herself now looked. In the semi-dissolved way that a holovision program sometimes showed a scene from two vantage points simultaneously, Vera saw herself both as the young performer and as the grown observer. In a detached sense, though, she knew that she was the little girl, and the woman was her mother.

This particular day, near the end of a lesson after three years of such lessons, seven-year-old Vera was showing her mother and teacher that she had mastered a short virtuoso piece from the late Nascent period called *Apollo and Dionysus*. A study in contrasts—orderly, then chaotic; somber, then frenetic; majestic, then silly—it was one of those warhorses that every young lasegrapher studied for technique, and in which every audience delighted.

Her mother and teacher were no exception. When she had raised the glowing, Eleanor had applauded enthusiastically, soon joined by Malcolm, and Vera had stood up on the bench in the Tiger Pit and had taken her bow. "Excellent," Malcolm had said to her, "excellent."

"Just marvelous, darling," Eleanor had told her.

"I'm very proud at how much work you've put into this piece," Malcolm had said. "Your personality really shines through."

Vera remembered that she had taken the compliment in stride; it merely confirmed a fact she'd already known. "Thanks," she'd said. "Is that it for today?"

"You can wrap it up."

Vera had unplugged her console and begun packing while Eleanor and Malcolm chatted. Vera had paid close attention. "You know, Eleanor," Malcolm had said, "I had the strangest feeling of *déjà vu* watching Vera play this piece."

"Really? How so?"

72

"Years ago, before the War, I used to sneak into your lessons with my father, and watch you."

"I wish you'd told me," Eleanor had said. "I rather thought you didn't know I was alive."

"I was shy," Malcolm had said, and Vera had tried to imagine her confident and stern teacher as shy. "Regardless," he'd continued, "watching Vera play *Apollo and Dionysus*, I could have sworn that I was back thirty years or so, watching you play the piece. Not only does she look exactly as you did, she *plays* exactly as you did. The technique—the style—is identical."

Vera had stopped packing up her console for a moment and begun listening more closely. They hadn't noticed.

"It's a pity you couldn't keep up with your studies," Malcolm had said.

Vera had watched her mother shrug wistfully. "It doesn't matter now. Vera will be playing for both of us. I'll be happy if after one of her concerts, someone congratulates me by mistake."

Malcolm had laughed. "People *will* have trouble telling you apart, won't they? Remarkable, just remarkable. But that similarity of performing technique, I can't get over it. It's quite enough to have me start believing in genetic determinism."

Vera clearly remembered feeling decidedly odd while that long-ago conversation had gone on, and she hadn't felt any better about it when she'd asked the library computer, later that same evening, to explain "genetic determinism" to her.

Possibly, Vera now thought, as she watched Joan play in the lawn dome, this had been the beginning of her doubts. Perhaps that had been the very first time she'd had the feeling that whatever she accomplished with her life would be claimed by her mother. But more than this, if in her most personal expression it was her mother's personality that was being expressed, then how could she have any existence of her own at all?

Here, watching Joan in the lawn dome, Vera considered for the first time that it was this feeling of having no identity apart from her mother—no independent existence of her own—that had panicked her before her premiere at the pyradome. She thought back to that evening, when she was fifteen. Malcolm's prediction had come true: she *had* grown up to look so much like her mother that people were constantly mistaking one for the other, and it had struck her—backstage, brushing her hair before going into the Tiger Pit to warm up—that her mother's old wish might very well come true that

73

night. Someone *might* congratulate her mother for having composed *Fugue in Blue*; in fact, she was sure someone *would*, if not that night, then some other night. It was with this thought that she had gone into the Tiger Pit to warm up.

Thinking of herself objectively, for once, Vera considered the thought that to the adolescent girl she had been, caught in the middle of an adolescent's normal identity crisis compounded by her twinship to her mother, the formidable and pure laser light would seem to be real, and she merely spectral. Her sense of identitylessness had provided the cause for her panic, and the laser had provided the perfect embodiment of an object for her panic.

There is a moment when light first illuminates a self-revelation of this kind. In this moment, either one can accept it— and use it as the basis for examining the basic patterns of one's life—or one can reject it, and invent for oneself an even deeper strategy for hiding such knowledge. Vera rejected it. To accept it would have entailed realizing for what a pale fear she had sacrificed the only self she had ever known, and to reclaim it, how much ground she would have to cover once again.

The thought of working up throught the laser repertoire for years, recapturing lost agility, to find herself back where she had been at fifteen, wearied her beyond her conception of endurance. She rejected this path, and with it—gratuitously—the self-knowledge that had pressed it on her.

She watched from the dark. She watched her little sister do seemingly effortlessly and so naturally what she knew she would never do again. But even as she watched, she fought back the realization that her discomfort had nothing to do with any compassion for Joan. She knew that there wasn't the slightest chance that Joan would fail at the laser for lack of self, but would not admit that this logically precluded sympathy.

She had already seen Joan's singular personality shine through the laser into the dome. Joan had her own genetic pattern, a unique face, her own soul. She would never be confused with anybody else. She would never lose sight of herself.

But she refused to identify the emotion this aroused in her. Even now, if Vera had allowed herself to know that what she felt for Joan was not compassion but jealousy, she might have laughed at herself for the very absurdity of her envy. If she had admitted the feeling so she could think about it, she might have averted the very destiny that she so much wished to disbelieve. But without this conscious

74

thought, the inevitable logic of her unexamined choices would steer her course later that evening, when the consequences of her choices would long endure. Her fundamental choices now were to bring about—for herself and those she affected, but particularly Joan—just those sorts of destiny which only the possibility of free choice allowed.

The sky had rid itself of rain clouds by five-thirty, when Mr. McIntosh left Vera in charge of Helix Vista while he flew Joan and the twins into the city. Two-year-old Zack was ready for bed, Mark had stayed home to play satellite chess with a boy in New Zealand, and Vera wanted to spend that night with her law discs.

Mr. McIntosh found traffic through the inbound Hudson Corridor light that summer evening, and they made good time. Just before six, the Darrises' blue Astarte landed on the strip that divided the Vaginatown ghetto from Rainborough Park, and the twins remained locked in the limousine while Mr. McIntosh walked Joan to the Malcolm Institute for her lesson. When he returned five minutes later, after seeing Joan safely through the institute's courtyard into its lobby, Mr. McIntosh instructed the skymobile to fly the remaining three of them to a nearby fast-food emporium called Krock's AdventureWorld.

AdventureWorld had become the regular Tuesday-night stopover for Mr. McIntosh and the boys while Joan took her lesson. There was just the kind of junk food the twins loved—tonight they each ordered a Big Krock and a Krock o' Fries—and there was an amusement arcade where the twins could compete against each other to their hearts' content . . . and best of all, no girls were allowed. Krock's AdventureWorld was just about the twins' idea of heaven.

AdventureWorld had its attractions for Mr. McIntosh as well. The arcade had its own staff patrons to keep watch over the boys, leaving Mr. McIntosh free, along with other tired parents and governors, to spend a quiet hour in the cannabistro. The maître d' asked Mr. McIntosh whether he would be eating, and when he replied in the affirmative, he was seated in the nonsmoking section and offered a menu. Smoking was, of course, permitted in both the smoking and nonsmoking sections, but in the smoking section you *had* to smoke. Mr. McIntosh ordered a salad and soyaburger, and when his food arrived, he fell to.

Twenty minutes later, Mr. McIntosh was sick. At first he did not know that what he was feeling was sick. It took a while to realize since, in his recollection, he had never been sick before. But he had seen a friend of his be sick once—a rare, fatal illness—and these odd and growingly unpleasant feelings seemed to match what his friend had described to him. Moreover, like his dying friend, he was sweating profusely. He was sick, all right.

It is difficult to appreciate how this realization hit him. Physical pain he had known, injury he could deal with, but a feeling of sickness spontaneously coming out of nowhere—out of his sight or control—was something completely new to him. It was overwhelming. It frightened him. There were so few illnesses left—so many had been eliminated—that he thought this must be an incurable rarity like the one that had killed his friend. He was going to die, he was sure of it. What had begun as mere nausea was now amplified by panic; he lurched forward, knocking over his table, and he doubled over, throwing up onto the floor.

When he had finished, other customers were standing around him, staring openly in astonishment. Mr. McIntosh was as astonished as they were, and the knowledge that it was he who had done this awful thing made his panic even worse. He heard somebody ask if there was a doctor in the restaurant. Mr. McIntosh began gasping for breath. The sour taste of vomit mixed with the sweet smell of cannabis smoke, and he felt suffocated. As his panic drove him to take one deep breath, then uncontrollably another, then another, then another, all feeling drained out of his arms and legs.

He staggered a few feet and looked into a man's horrified face; then—thinking that this was his death—Mr. McIntosh passed out.

It was, naturally, nothing of the sort. When he came to, a short while later, he was stretched out on the back seat of a skymobile, and a beautiful brunette woman was holding his wrist and looking at her watch. As he came fully awake, he noticed from vibration and movement that they were in flight.

"Feeling better?" the woman asked.

"A little," Mr. McIntosh said. "I think I'd feel even better if I sat up. Lying down in a moving skymobile makes me feel dizzy."

She helped Mr. McIntosh sit up, then handed him a cup with some brown liquid in it. "Drink this," she said.

He sipped it, and it turned out to be a cola drink. But it cleared out the sour taste from his mouth, and seemed to settle his stomach. He handed the empty cup back to her. "Thank you," he said. "Where are we going?"

"Golden-Sky General Hospital. Unless—now that you're awake—you'd prefer another hospital. The restaurant manager said their insurance would cover the bill, wherever I took you."

"And you are—?"

"Dr. Natalie Shaw," she said. "I was having dinner in the canna-bistro when you fainted."

"Do you specialize in rare diseases, Doctor?" he asked "Am I very sick?"

She laughed. "As a matter of fact, I'm a specialist in andrecology. And from what I can tell—having seen hundreds of cases like this when I interned at Golden-Sky—the only thing wrong with you was an upset stomach compounded by panic. You fainted from hyper-ventilation."

"Then why take me to a hospital?"

"For your protection, and the restaurant's. It's a complicated matter involving restaurant liabilities, insurance regulations, and—for that matter—medical ethics. I'd advise you to go, even though you don't have to if you'd rather not. If it was something in the food that upset you, I rather think you wouldn't have much of a legal case without some lab tests."

"But you think I'll be okay anyway? Without the hospital?"

"I'd say so. Though I should tell you that the Good Samaritan law relieves me of liability if my diagnosis is wrong. Though it isn't."

"Then I'd better get back to AdventureWorld. I'm the governor for two boys I left in the arcade . . . Joanie!" The color drained from his face, and Dr. Shaw thought he might faint again. Mr. McIntosh checked his watch; it was already ten past seven.

"Are you quite sure you're all right? Perhaps we'd better proceed to the hospital after all."

"No, no, no," he said. "I've got to get back to Rainborough Park by seven-fifteen, before it gets dark!"

"I'm afraid we'll never make it," she said, "even if we return using my medical emergency priority—which is technically illegal. It will take five minutes before we reach the next safe turnaround in this corridor, then another twenty-five minutes back."

"Please," Mr. McIntosh said, "we've *got* to get back. And I've got to make some fast phone calls."

"Please feel free to use my video," she said.

Dr. Shaw ordered her limousine to reverse their course as soon as possible, and gained Mr. McIntosh's eternal gratitude by informing traffic control that she was still on emergency priority. Meanwhile, Mr. McIntosh got the phone code of the Malcolm Institute from Central Listings, and called it.

He was told by the institute's computer that its offices were closed for the day, but that he could leave a message.

The message he left was less than polite. Still, if Malcolm checked with the computer before he left . . .

Immediately after, Mr. McIntosh phoned Helix Vista. The domestic computer answered and was reluctant to connect him to Vera until he said it was an emergency. A seemingly endless minute passed while he waited for Vera to come on; Dr. Shaw offered him more cola, which he accepted. Finally, Vera appeared on the limousine's phone. "Yes, Mac, what is it?"

Vera looked annoyed with him even before he told her what was wrong. But when he explained, her face turned absolutely rigid.

"I'll go after Joan," she told him. "You pick up the twins and get back here at once. I'll leave Mark in charge of Zack until your return."

"You don't think she's in any real danger, do you?" Mr. McIntosh asked Vera anxiously.

"For both your sakes, she'd better not be," Vera said, then switched off. But Mr. McIntosh wondered why Vera had seemed to wear a satisfied expression as she'd said it.

"DEASIL, WIDDERSHINS, deasil, widdershins," Jack Malcolm said to Joan.

Clockwise, counterclockwise, clockwise, counterclockwise, Joan played the swirling ring-a-rosies around the dome.

Jack Malcolm sat opposite her on the dual console in the beginner's dome, waving his hand back and forth. "Deasil, widdershins, deasil, widdershins," he repeated, increasing the pace slightly. "Building, always *building*—very good—now get ready to crescendo . . ."

Joan dropped her eyes momentarily to the score—symbols

scrolling past on her monitor—and again up to the dome. Mimicking the physics by which an ice skater builds up circular momentum with arms out, then raises them overhead, she collapsed the ring inward, spinning the red lissajous faster and faster and faster down to the rosy point that ended *Fantasia in Seventh*.

Malcolm raised the glowing from his console. "Good, quite good."

Joan asked, "Do you want to see the ring-around-the-rosy part again?"

He shook his head. "But your segue between eenie-meenie-minie-moe and ink-a-bink-a-bottle-a-ink could use some smoothing out."

"That's the *hard* part," she said.

"If it's hard, it only means you have to work on it some more. I'll want to see it all smoothed out by Friday."

"Okay."

Malcolm glanced at a digital clock on his console; it read 7:21. "That's all for tonight," he said. He stood up in the Tiger Pit; from Joan's standpoint, he looked like a giant. "You'd better get going. We ran a bit late and Mr. McIntosh will be waiting for you."

Joan ejected several silver-dollar-sized discs from her console—the scores she was working on—and slipped them into a pocket on the reddish-orange pinafore she was wearing. "G'night!" she told Malcolm.

"Good night." He remained behind to power down the laser, while Joan skipped out to the central lobby.

But for the first time, Mr. McIntosh was not waiting for her in the lobby. She thought that he must have decided, for once, to wait for her in the courtyard, and went out almost at once. It was for this reason that Jack Malcolm did not see Joan when he came out of the dome and, assuming she had left with her governor, walked past the lobby into his office. He did not even glance at his message indicator as he urgently proceeded into his private bathroom.

The sun was just on the horizon when Joan left the Institute's lobby at seven twenty-two. It was the last of the day, but it was not yet night: official sunset this July 15 was seven twenty-five, GMT-plus-Five Standard Time. Joan noticed that the air was comfortably cool as she stepped into the courtyard, just before she concluded that Mr. McIntosh was not waiting for her out here either.

To say that his not being where he was supposed to be was unprecedented would have been, from Joan's viewpoint, a vast understatement on the order of telling an astronomer that Halley's comet's not showing up this time around was unprecedented. Trying to suggest to her the possibility that Mr. McIntosh might only have been delayed would have fallen on her ears in about the same way as suggesting to the astronomer that Halley's comet might *only* have been delayed.

She decided to sit down on the grass to contemplate the phenomenon, but got up immediately, finding that the grass was still wet following the afternoon's rain. But the wetness of the grass stimulated a new thought: for some incomprehensible reason, could Mr. McIntosh be waiting for her outside the courtyard on the street? When she was faced with the impossible in the first place, almost anything in the second place seemed possible. She decided to step beyond the raised portcullis and have a look.

Lights were coming on in the apartment houses across the street, but the street itself was deserted. Joan looked as far as she could in both directions, but particularly toward the landing strip. Mr. McIntosh was nowhere to be seen.

Joan would have taken this opportunity to swear, if she'd known how. Instead, as she had seen her mother do in such outrageous situations as this, she put her hands on her hips and thrust her lower lip outward. She was wondering what to do next, and had just about decided to head back into the Institute, when the last rays of direct sunlight were blocked off by the apartment house across the street, and the portcullis to the Institute's courtyard lowered to the ground.

Joan knew nothing of photoelectric gates. For that matter, aside from her expertise on the lasegraphic console, she was completely innocent of technology. She viewed machinery, as children often do, animistically, but with experience to back up mythology: when she spoke to things, as often as not they talked back.

So Joan thought merely that the gate had chosen a decidedly inconvenient time to drop, just when she wanted to go in again. "Gate, open up," she told the portcullis, sensibly; but it was an old piece of machinery, from long before the War, and it was not voice-actuated.

"Gate, please open up. I want to go *in*," she told it, but for the first time in her life, she was talking to a gate that did not hear her. For the second time that evening, she was completely perplexed. The universe just wasn't acting the way it was *supposed* to. Mr. McIntosh was supposed to be waiting for her at the end of her lesson, and gates were supposed to open up when you asked them—she had even said *please*.

So it was that Joan found herself alone, for the first time, trapped outside her world of safety, in a strange place at night.

She was not alone for long.

The woman in the red cloak was a Touchable, of course—Joan knew that. In fact, Joan knew all about Touchables. She knew that her mother always steered her and her brothers away from the Touchables who sold hoop dogs on bagels in the streets. She also knew that at the end of holovision programs, Touchables were often sent to the microwave ovens.

Joan interpreted this, from her limited experience with microwave ovens, to mean that Touchables were being sent to a kitchen somewhere and were being forced to bake bagels and reheat hoop dogs. It was these stale goods that her mother didn't want to buy from the Touchables on the street.

Thus Joan was fully expecting the woman to try to sell her a stale hoop dog when she approached. If she'd had any money, she would have bought it, too; she hadn't had dinner yet.

"You look like a nice little girl," the Touchable said to Joan. "Aren't you, now?"

Joan felt very shy, but she managed to nod. Now that she was very close to the Touchable—closer than she'd ever been to one before—Joan could see that the woman was pretty, with blond hair peeking out from under the hood, and large, deep-set eyes. Joan could also sense that the woman was very frightened.

"I *knew* you were nice, I knew it," the Touchable said. "And I'm sure a nice little girl like you wouldn't want to see anything bad happen to someone, would you?"

"Not if they didn't do something bad *first*," Joan said. Then she immediately covered her mouth with her hand because she had remembered that she wasn't allowed to talk with strangers.

But the Touchable was ready for this. "You don't have to be afraid to talk to me. I have a daughter just like you at home. In fact, it's because of her that I need your help."

This was absolutely true; the Touchable was one of the resident mothers in Vaginatown, just across the landing strip; and she was frightened because she had failed to make it back to the ghetto before sundown.

Nonetheless, her remark was well planned, having just the effect on Joan's curiosity that she expected. For the simple fact was that like most other little girls of the upper class, Joan had met very few girls of her own age.

"What are *you* afraid of?" Joan asked suddenly.

The Touchable decided to give Joan the same explanation she had given to her own daughter. "Do you know the story of Little Red Riding Hood?" she asked.

Joan nodded; she had the storydisc at home.

"Well," the Touchable said, "I'm just like Red Riding Hood. That's why I have to wear a red cloak. And I'm afraid that if I don't get right home, the Wolf will get me."

"Oh," said Joan, when she made a thoroughly logical connection. "Then you don't have to be afraid. Wolf told me that he doesn't bite people anymore."

This was a decidedly odd turn of conversation, the Touchable thought. It might have remained totally incomprehensible to her if they had not been standing right in front of an institute of lasegraphy. The Touchable knew nothing about lasegraphy, but for her generation there was a name as thoroughly associated with that art as Stokowski's had been to symphonic music, or Einstein's to physics, for previous generations. Could it be possible? Tentatively she asked, "Do you mean *Wolfgang* Jaeger?"

Joan nodded. "Do you know him too?"

This was an opportunity the woman had not expected. It was getting very dark now, and each moment she was out of the ghetto increased the danger. She knew that a Touchable crossing the landing strip into Vaginatown after sunset was a clear target for the Marnies who hunted in the area. But if she could persuade the child to accompany her across, there was a chance that she would be unmolested. While any Touchable was a legal game target after dark, she had found that most packs of Marnies had at least one member—a woman or androman—who was loath to involve a child, even a Touchable's.

All this crossed her mind in the split second it took her to decide to lie. "Yes, I do," she answered Joan, then took her lie one step further than she needed to. "Wolfgang Jaeger is a very good friend of mine."

Joan's face lit up. Concatenative friendship is the oldest and most obvious principle of human association, whether to a tribal warrior, or to a bank's loan manager, or to a five-year-old girl told not to speak to strangers. "It's okay for me to talk to you, then," Joan said. "But why are you afraid of Wolf? He said that he doesn't bite his friends."

I'll need the reflexes of a hunted animal to explain this, the Touchable woman thought. Then suddenly, by this very reflex, her mind made a connection and she remembered a newscast on the holy three months before. A news commentator was finishing up her report on Wolfgang Jaeger's visit to Earth for his centennial. "Wolfgang Jaeger," the commenter had closed. "His name translates roughly from German as 'Hunter of the Wolf Pack,' but it will be in the Tiger Pit that the master lasegrapher will be hunting tomorrow at the pyradome."

"Oh, you're getting confused," the Touchable told Joan lightly. "Wolfgang Jaeger is the *hunter* who saved Red Riding Hood from the Wolf. That's why 'wolf' is part of his name. I'm not afraid of Wolfgang, but of the Wolf himself."

"Oh," Joan said. This wasn't crystal-clear, but it seemed to make a sort of sense. "I thought *that* Wolf was just make-believe."

The Touchable decided to follow up on this before the point was lost. She couldn't be sure, but she thought she heard the distant whine of a flying belt. "No," she said, and gave a little shiver, "the Wolf isn't make-believe. But he isn't an animal, like it shows him in the storydiscs, but a very cruel man. And that's why I need your help. You see," the Touchable went on, "I have to walk home to my little girl—we live right across the runway—only the Wolf will be looking for me. But he's a very big coward, and if he sees the two of us together, he'll run right away. So will you walk home with me?"

"What about Mr. McIntosh?" Joan asked.

"Who's Mr. McIntosh?" the Touchable said quickly. She thought the flying belt might be closer.

"My governor," Joan said. "He's supposed to take me home after my lesson."

"I'll phone him as soon as we get to my home."

"Can't you phone him from here?"

The whine was *definitely* nearer. "I'm not wearing a phone, dear. Come on, we'd better hurry."

"Okay."

The Touchable took Joan's hand, and they began walking toward the landing strip.

They walked down the street slowly. The woman knew how futile it was to try to evade pursuit from a sky-belter, if they were spotted, and any attempt at running would be interpreted as resistance. The first thing one learned as a Touchable was that open resistance tended to be fatal.

Beyond the last apartment building, the street was unlighted. Since the runway itself was without lights—landing guidance relied on other parts of the spectrum—it was becoming darker with each step. In spite of herself, the Touchable began pulling Joan along more quickly. Joan started to say something, but the woman shushed her. She strained her ears, trying to hear the flying belt, but it seemed to be gone. She relaxed slightly.

They finally came to the landing strip and started across. The white plastic below their feet was slightly phosphorescent and still rain-slicked; what faint light there was from distant sources reflected up a ghostly aura. Then, suddenly, the Touchable felt it and gasped. She stopped, grasping Joan's hand tightly. One wasn't supposed to be able to tell, but after a while one always knew. Her transponder had been scanned, "We must be brave now," she told Joan, and they resumed walking across.

The light hit them at the halfway point.

The light was not the landing beacon of a skymobile in flight, but a warning flare tossed onto the ground. They halted. The flare blinded them, reflecting across the white plastic as if it were a sheet of ice, and cast ghoulish long shadows behind them.

"Out past curfew, aren't you, little mother?" the man's voice said. He was ahead of them, beyond the flare. The red-cloaked woman and Joan stood absolutely still. From the roughness of the voice, Joan was sure it was the Wolf.

"I asked you a question," the voice said.

"I can't see your medallion," the Touchable said.

"Oh, you want to see me, do you? Well, let's see how much."

A second flare was struck, and after being tossed in an arc over their heads, it landed behind them, so they could see who was there.

There was only the one man. He was wearing a flying belt and standard Marnie hunting apparel—black leather jacket and pants, high leather boots—but he was not wearing a Marnie's helmet with its official hunting medallion. The man was short by current standards, only about five feet eleven inches. His face was long, unshaved, and rattish, with sharp nose and pale-but-mottled skin. His black hair was greasy and unkempt.

"Now, answer me," he said.

The Touchable delayed long enough to allow the whine of a skymobile passing close overhead to die away.

"My little girl and I are on our way back into the ghetto," she said. "We are, as you said, a few minutes past curfew. But surely a gentleman such as you won't keep my little girl out past her bedtime?"

"I'm not any rapin' gentleman," the man said, and he grinned wildly.

"Are you the Wolf?" Joan asked him.

84

He laughed. It was not a pleasant sound. "Well, little girl, in a way. I'm Touchable, same as your mother."

If the woman had been frightened to this point, she became terrified now. While a Marnie would sexually abuse a Touchable in almost any imaginable way, it was a rule of the hunt always to leave the Touchable unharmed, available to later hunters, so long as there was no resistance. But a Touchable out hunting other Touchables was a frustrated sex criminal who might do anything. The woman grabbed Joan's hand and pulled her forward.

The man let them get a few feet away, then gave a short blast of his flying belt and jumped ahead of them again.

"If you're Touchable, you can't possibly have any real interest in me," she told him. "Let us pass."

"Wrong again," the man said. "I'm one of the lucky ones. Found a real nice doctor who, for a price, grew me another manhood and sewed it back on, good as new."

"I'm not interested in your medical history," the Touchable woman said. "And you're just wasting time. You'd better hide somewhere yourself before the Marnies get you. It's the ovens for you this time, if they catch you uncloaked with a belt and a you-know-what."

He grinned again, more ferally than before. "Suppose you let me worry about the rapin' Marnies. You want to leave? Go right ahead, little mother, anytime you like."

The woman and Joan started forward again. Once more the man blocked them.

"All I want is the pretty little girl."

Vera watched from the dark.

She had seen the groundflares on her Phaethon's initial approach, passed over them, then set down at the far end of the runway and taxied to the parking zone. When she'd passed close by the flares again on her walk back to the Malcolm Institute, she had approached to see Joan, and to hear the two adults talking, but she was far enough away not to be seen herself.

"All I want is the pretty little girl."

She had not arrived in time to hear the earlier exchange between the leather-jacketed man and the red-cloaked woman, so she assumed that the man was a Marnie out to have his way with a Touchable's child. Touchable children, as Vera knew from her beginning law studies, had an odd, mixed-up status under Federation law. Theoretically, they were full citizens, not having to be cloaked and legally immune to sexual assault. But so long as they were under the guardianship of a Touchable parent, their brainprint registrations identified them as Touchables. And from the law discs she had begun studying, Vera knew that, *de facto*, no Marnie had ever been successfully prosecuted for molesting a Touchable's child.

So Vera knew that all she needed to do to rescue Joan from the man she thought to be a Marnie was to step a few meters forward into the light and tell the man to read Joan's transponder. Once he was satisfied that the little girl did not belong to the Touchable, Vera could escort Joan away, leaving him to have his fun with the Touchable.

But she did not make a move to do it. Instead, as she thought about moving forward to get Joan, she became more and more terrified.

The human mind is, at its best, complicated; at its worst, it is inexhaustibly devious. No one has ever claimed that one can truly know, outside of God's Final Judgement, what the absolute base of a human being's motivations is, even one's own. So it may well be that even though Vera knew that no man even *half*-sane would risk the ovens to touch a veteran like herself—especially with a Touchable available—the wild look of this man was enough to make her afraid. Alternatively, it may be that her sensation of terror was merely a cover her brain was offering her, to prevent her from realizing that she *wanted* Joan to be hurt—punished—for being everything that she could not be. Perhaps both causes were simultaneous and never discrete.

In any case, at the moment when Vera thought that she could not wait any longer to walk forward into the light—at the moment she would watch the man knock Joan to the pavement—she felt the sensation of heat in her panties and down the insides of her thighs, and she became aware that she was wetting herself. The realization startled her, but she made no effort to stop. Instead, she rebelled against her terror, against her lost individuality, against her sister, against her mother, and in the stroke of an instant defected to the winning side. With the full genius of her subconscious mind, Vera slid her hand under the skirt into the golden stream draining out of her panties and masturbated herself, furiously, until she came.

"All I want is the pretty little girl."

"No!" the Touchable woman said.

"Who's gonna stop me," the man asked, "you? Hand her over, before I get rough."

"You lay a hand on her and the Monitors will hunt you forever."

"A Touchable's daughter? Don't make me laugh."

"I lied about her being my daughter," the woman said. "She's a student at the laser school over there."

The man looked down at Joan and snarled. "Is that true?"

Joan huddled closer in to the woman, but not wanting to cooperate with the "Wolf" said, "I'm not allowed to *talk* to you."

"You'd better read her transponder, if you don't believe me," the woman said.

The man uncovered his wrist scanner and took a reading from Joan's transponder. Several seconds later, the Monitor computers had answered him via satellite relay. "Cloneraping *scat*!"

He stood there a moment, fuming, then said, "I have half a mind to take her anyway. They can't kill you more than once."

The Touchable let go of Joan's hand and gently pushed her behind herself. Then she lowered her hood, revealing her face and hair. She stepped forward, provocatively, resting one hand on her hip. "What's the matter?" she said. "Can't you handle a *real* woman?"

She had done it deliberately, and now watched the man's rage, seeing his raw lust mixed in with it. He stepped forward, held himself back long enough to emphasize that *it* was deliberate, then backhanded her hard across her face. The force of the blow knocked her to the ground.

"Let her *alone*!" Joan shouted, and she launched herself at the man. She started raining blows ineffectually on his leather jacket. But he was no longer interested in Joan. He put up with her for a few seconds, then simply knocked her to the pavement.

Joan sat on the runway, one knee and elbow skinned, and began to cry.

The man walked past her to the Touchable. "Get up," he told the woman.

The Touchable woman stood, unsteadily. In one swift motion, the man pulled the red cloak over her head and threw it on the ground next to Joan. Except for a small gold cross on a thin chain around her neck, she was naked.

Joan stopped crying a little, grabbing on to the discarded cloak for a bit of comfort, and looked at the Touchable closely. Joan had never seen a naked adult woman before.

The man was also looking hard, his breathing becoming rapid and irregular. He reached down to his leather pants and released his erect penis.

Joan looked at this closely also; she had never seen anything like this either. So she was watching when the man lifted up the woman and tried to shove his penis into her, but it wouldn't go in right away. He reached up to his hair, removed some grease, and slicked it onto his organ. He lifted her up again, and this time, when he shoved, his penis went in. If Joan had been curious until now, she found this absolutely astonishing.

The man laughed. The Touchable woman knew what was going to happen now. She closed her eyes and her lips began moving silently.

With a single thrust, the man revved his flying belt, grabbed the woman tightly, and took off into the sky, almost vertically.

Joan watched as they went higher, and higher, and higher into the dark sky. She couldn't see them anymore. Then, about half a minute later, a woman's body plummeted to the runway only fifteen meters or so away from where Joan was still sitting, and exploded into a mangled heap of blood, hair, and bones.

Joan started screaming, and this time she didn't stop.

When Vera carried a hysterical Joan, wrapped in the Touchable's cloak, into Helix Vista, Mr. McIntosh tried to ask what had happened, but Vera ignored him and carried Joan up to bed. She dissolved a sedative in a cup of water and made Joan drink it. Then she sprayed Joan's scrapes with disinfectant plastice and dressed her for bed. She remained until her sister fell asleep. After telling the domestic computer to have Mr. McIntosh wait for her in the library, she returned to her own room, where she showered and dressed herself in a robe.

Mr. McIntosh was waiting for Vera anxiously when she finally entered the library. Vera regarded him coldly. "I'll expect you to be packed and out of here by tomorrow at noon," she said.

Mr. McIntosh closed his eyes, and a single tear leaked onto his cheek. He could only nod.

To Joan Seymour Darris the next five weeks were the Tiger Pit, and she was fighting for her life against the Tiger.

Its claws—leaving the Tiger's own stripes where nobody could see them—were her discovery that the world was far more brutal, and far more hideous, than she had ever imagined. Its teeth—shearing into her mind—were guilt for bringing about the attack on the Touchable, and helplessness in defending her from a man too monstrous to comprehend. Its whiskers were her longings for Mr. McIntosh; its eyes were the looks from her brothers, accusing her of causing him to be sent away. Its tongue—licking her wounds as a Tigress licks her cubs, therefore never letting her forget them—was Vera.

Vera got her licks in over and over, but in ways so subtle that perhaps at first even she did not realize what she was doing. In the next five weeks her mealtime warnings to the children to "Eat or you'll grow up to be a Touchable" took on new meaning. They expanded to almost every possible subject until, from Joan's standpoint, even the most trivial act of disobedience was potentially a capital crime.

Vera drove the point home to Joan, once and for all, in a conversation a week after the incident. Vera sat Joan down on her lap and, between Joan's tearful protests that she didn't want to talk about it, doggedly assured Joan that she shouldn't worry that what had happened to the Touchable was her fault, because only selfish people became Touchables in the first place, and what had happened was the woman's own fault for not doing what she was supposed to do.

Thereafter, Joan did everything she could to pretend that nothing at all had happened, and Vera, realizing that the only others who knew what had happened wouldn't be talking about it, found herself able to believe that she had arrived too late to do anything.

When Eleanor and Stanton returned from St. Clive, it looked to them that Vera had everything at Helix Vista running smoothly.

Their children seemed healthy and happy after five weeks under Vera's sole care. They showed proper delight at their parents' return, and even greater delight at the many presents from their parents and great-grandparents. They were delighted even with Stanton's amateur holos showing Grandma and Grandpa Collier performing zero-gravity acrobatics, and Joan was particularly thrilled with the official holos showing her parents being presented at the Court of King Elwin and Queen Lucy.

Vera's picturegram five weeks before, telling them that she'd fired Mr. McIntosh, had explained that the governor had made himself sick at a cannabistro while in charge of the children, and he had consequently missed picking up Joan after her evening lesson. "By the time I was able to fly to the Institute," Vera had transmitted, "Joan had wandered into the street and was so terrified at being abandoned in the dark that she wet herself. I feel that after dereliction of duty such as Mac's, firing him was the only thing I could do."

Vera had gone on to say that she'd given Mr. McIntosh two months' severance pay, with a letter of recommendation stating that his job performance was excellent and they were letting him go only because of a change in the family's domestic needs. Since all the Darris children would be attending school in the fall, this was almost true.

It was a dead issue by the time they returned home, but at the time of Vera's picturegram, Eleanor had wanted to reverse Vera's decision. Stanton had argued, however, that they couldn't very well second-guess Vera's judgment from hundreds of millions of kilometers away—especially since otherwise Vera's handling of the matter was perfectly sound. Their initial observations on their homecoming seemed to confirm Stanton's earlier opinion.

Nonetheless if, during their first week home, Eleanor and Stanton had any inkling that not everything was perfectly well with Joan, they could get no distinct idea what it was. She had always been quiet, but now she seemed positively withdrawn, spending almost every free minute at her console. Moreover, twice that week Eleanor and Stanton awoke to find that Joan had crawled into their bed during the night—something she had not done for more than two years.

But it wasn't until a week later, the last Tuesday in August, that Eleanor and Stanton knew that something about Joan was clearly off. Vera was busy studying more law discs she needed to cover before school started, and Stanton had decided to drop into his office for a few hours. So, for the first time, she resumed her old practice of taking Joan to her laser lessons, and it was there she got her first indications.

Joan's Tuesday lessons were now at 1 P.M. Vera had told her that the time had been changed to avoid having Joan left alone in the dark again. But Eleanor wondered why, even in full daylight, Joan grasped her hand tightly while they walked between the skymobile and the Institute, and why Joan showed no dislike of darkness as such—specifically the darkness necessary in the dome.

As Eleanor watched Joan's lesson, she saw that her little girl had made vast progress since the last time she had observed her, three months before. Not only was Joan beginning to show some real dexterity on the console, but she was playing with an intensity—a *fire*—that seemed remarkable for a student who had been studying only eighteen weeks. But along with this new intensity there seemed to be new problems, as Jack Malcolm explained to Eleanor after Joan's lesson. He took Eleanor into his office while Joan waited in the lobby with a comic disc.

"Her color sense has, to say the least, become rather extreme," Malcolm told Eleanor. "Her primaries have become overwhelming at times, especially when a composition involves heavy use of reds."

"Doesn't that indicate some sort of retrogression?" Eleanor asked.

"Normally, with a child her age, I would say so. But an incident during one of her lessons, six weeks ago, makes me think that certain colors have taken on an absolute value for her. We were working on *Fantasia in Seventh*—a red tonic playing off against a blue dominant—and everything had been going along fine for several lessons. Then Joan came in on a Friday and didn't want to play it for me. This usually means that a student hasn't been practicing, so I insisted—and do you know what she did? She played it for me, perfectly, but transposed down a third. All the reds changed into yellows, all the blues changed to violets."

Eleanor was silent a long moment. "Six weeks ago. That was the Friday after she was left outside here in the dark?" Malcolm nodded. "Did you see any other sign that something was bothering her?"

"Nothing at all," Malcolm said. "It was quite a relief after my conversation with Vera that Wednesday when I got Mr. McIntosh's phone message."

"What message?"

"The one telling me to hold on to Joan after her lesson, because he couldn't make it back here by dark. I called Helix Vista immediately, because there was a squad of Monitors scouring the neighborhood that morning, and I was terrified they might be searching for Joan."

"What was it?"

"Nothing unusual," Malcolm said. "Some Touchable got herself icked. It's always something, around here. The ghetto, you know. Anyway, when I spoke to Vera, she blamed me as much as Mr. McIntosh for letting Joan get outside, and she was all set to stop Joan's lessons entirely. But I wasn't about to have her ruin Joan's career the way she ruined her own. I'm afraid I had to threaten her with calling His Gaylordship before she agreed that all that was really necessary was an earlier lesson."

"You don't think Joan could have gotten involved with that icked Touchable, do you?"

Malcolm shook his head. "I can't imagine a hunting party icarating a Touchable anywhere near a little girl. They'd lose their medallions—might even pull a stiff fine. Besides, Vera would have to have seen something, wouldn't she?"

"Yes, of course," Eleanor said. "I wasn't thinking."

Still, she couldn't help thinking about it, back at Helix Vista later that afternoon. Stanton had flown home with his belt and had decided to show off for his children, who were playing touch squatball on their course. But when he approached them, Joan ran frantically toward the house, screaming; went inside and grabbed on to Eleanor; then wouldn't let go.

Whatever doubts Eleanor had about what might have happened to Joan during the summer were pushed out of her mind simply by the onslaught of fall. Eleanor became pregnant with her fifth son. She packed Vera off to Espiritu Santo, New Hebrides—the campus of Federation University Law School. Mark and the twins returned to their Astoria School, while Zack was started mornings at a piagetic nursery school. Lastly, Joan was enrolled for the first time at the Erika Blair Girls' Academy in Manhattan.

With her mornings free, Eleanor decided that she could wait awhile before breaking in a replacement for the sorely missed Mr. McIntosh. She felt she could do without gubernatorial help at least until spring, since the baby wasn't due until next June.

She also decided that now that she was back from vacation, and Vera was no longer around to taunt her about it, there was nothing preventing her from using those free mornings to take up the laser again. During the same conversation with Jack Malcolm in which she arranged for Joan's lessons to be shifted to after-school hours,

Eleanor fitted herself into Jack's schedule for weekly lessons Thursday mornings. She swore Jack to secrecy about the lessons—particularly from Vera and Wendell, though for opposite reasons—but she also told Stanton about it. She swore him to secrecy also.

Joan did not take to school the way a comman takes to the dicteria.

Her teacher at the Blair Academy, Mrs. Martingale, was a bored young widow, who, when Mr. Martingale had drowned while scuba diving, had found herself with a considerable fortune, plenty of time, and an education degree. She gave Joan a representative sample of what she could expect on the very first day, when she sat her down at a computer terminal and told her to recite, if she could, all the numbers between one and one hundred.

Joan, who had already been taught some math by Mr. McIntosh, said, "Uh-huh, that's easy."

"Just *do* it!" Mrs. Martingale said, scaring Joan halfway off her chair.

Things went downhill from there. Several weeks later, during a lesson in light penmanship, Joan complained to her teacher that she couldn't write because her hands were sweating, and the light pen kept on slipping out of her grasp. Mrs. Martingale just ordered her to go back to writing. When Joan persisted that she couldn't write because of her sweaty hands, Mrs. Martingale took it as a sign of open rebellion, told her that she was a bad little girl who—if she wasn't careful—would grow up to be a Touchable, and sent her down to the principal's office for punishment.

Dr. Blair, a slightly built Englishwoman in her nineties, asked Joan why she had disobeyed her teacher's order to write. Joan simply repeated, "My hands keep on sweating and the light pen keeps on *slipping*. And I won't grow up to be a Touchable, I won't!"

"I see," Dr. Blair said. She recorded a quick note on her desktop terminal, transmitted it up to Mrs. Martingale's classroom, and told Joan to return to class.

Afterward, during light penmanship lessons, Joan was given a piece of towel to dry off her hands as needed.

The dozen other girls in her class interested Joan only until she discovered that they knew nothing of lasegraphy, and didn't seem to be able to talk about anything even half as interesting. Moreover, aside from Visual Language and Numerical Manipulation—what previous generations had called the Three R's—Joan found the lessons to be nothing but the memorization of unrelated facts, the imposition of rules for their own sake, and learning to be able to respond satisfactorily to a question on a subject to which she hadn't been paying any attention.

She also quickly learned how to invent games and draw pictures on her terminal, but always have them erased from memory by the time Mrs. Martingale punched to monitor her desk on the teacher's master display.

Perhaps it was a useful education after all.

In mid-December, a week before the Yule Solstice vacation, the class was given an introductory lesson in lasegraphy. There was, of course, nothing in this lesson that Joan didn't already know. But in the course of it, Joan discovered—to her absolute delight—that the school computer was programmed in Scholastic laser notation.

Thereafter, her secret games took a more specific direction. She began noodling around with rearranging sequences from various compositions she had been studying with Malcolm, and without realizing it, she began composing original sequences of her own. Since she didn't dare leave them in the computer, where her teacher could find them, Joan simply memorized the parts she wanted to keep.

Of course, there came a day, in early February, when Joan got so deeply involved with one of her compositions that she failed to notice, during a history lesson, that Mrs. Martingale was monitoring her. Naturally, the teacher again sent Joan down to the principal's office to be punished for failing to pay proper attention in class. She also transmitted a note down to the principal stating that if she expected her to maintain discipline with the other girls, her punishment of the Darris girl had to be backed up this time.

There was another discussion between Joan and Dr. Blair, a phone conversation between Dr. Blair and Eleanor—while Joan waited in an empty classroom next to the principal's office—then a second phone call from Dr. Blair to Jack Malcolm. Afterward, Dr. Blair spent a good twenty minutes trying to figure out what to do. She decided while looking in on Joan.

From then on, whenever Mrs. Martingale sent Joan to the principal's office to be punished "for not paying attention," Dr. Blair assigned Joan the punishment of being made to sit all by herself, for one hour, in that empty classroom. From Mrs. Martingale's viewpoint, this was a perfectly acceptable punishment—one that was an effective deterrent for the other girls in her class. In fact, Mrs. Martingale would have intensely disliked such a sentence herself.

Perhaps, then, it was just as well that Mrs. Martingale didn't know that Dr. Blair was leaving Joan alone with an active computer terminal in that classroom—with access to private, permanent memory—and that Joan was using those solitary hours to compose to her heart's content.

III.

λ4600Å to 4900Å

In the April of Joan's twelfth birthday, the Lasegraphy Company of Ad Astra—better known as LCAA—sponsored a weeklong festival at the McDanald Media Temple—better known as the pyradome. It was to be a lasegraphical extravaganza the like of which had never before been seen on Earth—so the publicity said, and the publicists did not have to exaggerate much. Not only were LCAA Records' top classical and roga artists appearing—including its classical superstar, Wolfgang Jaeger—but the festival would be a showcase for aspiring composers and performers. Prizes to be won included, in the senior competitions, recording contracts and financial backing for concert tours, with scholarships and instruments to be awarded in the junior competitions.

Jack Malcolm considered that he was a winner even before the festival started: five of his institute's students were performing at the festival. One was an alumnus of the Malcolm Institute now on the roster of LCAA's featured recording artists. Three current pupils—including Eleanor Darris—were performing in student showcases. Lastly, and most exciting of all to Malcolm, Joan Darris would premiere her own *Vistata No. 1 in Sixth* at the festival, and on the basis of a transcription of its first movement submitted with Joan's application, the festival's judges had unilaterally switched Joan from the junior to the senior competition—the youngest composer to be so honored. Inasmuch as Joan had no pressing need for either scholarship money or a free instrument, Malcolm suggested to Joan that she had nothing to lose by the move.

At the moment, however, Joan was next to Malcolm on a couch in the Institute's box at the pyradome—with Stanton, Vera, Wendell, Kate Seymour, and five of the seven Darris boys in their family box right behind them—and in a few minutes it was Eleanor who would be making her debut in the Tiger Pit.

Eleanor's avocation had been a well-kept secret for more than six years: only the previous November, when the festival's acceptances were sent out, had family or friends other than Malcolm, Stanton, and Joan learned that Eleanor had taken up the console again. Eleanor had restricted her time with the laser to hours when her older sons were at school and her younger sons were off with their governor, Seth Whitehead, an elderly gentleman who nonetheless belied his name with a thick crop of brown hair, and who mooted the point by insisting the entire family call him "Gramps." Still, if Eleanor had been expecting extreme though opposite reactions from Vera and Wendell when they found out, only His Gaylordship's was true to form: he had dipped into his lasegraphic collection to give Eleanor a virtual relic of the art: an original cinematic print, almost two centuries old, of Ivan Dryer's *Laser Image*—the earliest recorded lasegraphic performance. When Eleanor had met Vera in downtown Newer York to tell Vera of her new career, over lunch in the Legos courthouse's exclusive Marsupial Club, Vera had merely said, "How marvelous for you," and had gone on eating her fruit salad. Eleanor was not sure that she wouldn't have preferred outright hostility.

Such hostility as Vera felt for Eleanor before the performance was stored somewhere Vera didn't have to look at it. But Wendell, on the couch to Vera's right, had long ago learned that in his profession reading people was more important than reading proposed laws, and he observed that Vera's program leaflet was already reduced to shreds of twisted foil. Wendell turned his head to Vera and told her, "Cheer up. It's only a concert, not an execution."

Vera turned to him, startled, then allowed herself a slight smile. "At least when I'm on the bench," she said dryly, "I'm the one handing out the executions."

Wendell harumphed, and turned his head back up toward the

dome. Vera turned her head leftward, to Stanton, and searched out his hand with her own. "My Goddess," Stanton whispered when she'd found it, "your hand's a *puddle*."

In the box ahead of them, Joan turned to Malcolm. "That tunnel is so *ghastly*," she whispered. "At least when I was in there, you were waiting with me."

"That was so I could get the quiche," Malcolm said, and they both smiled.

Four years before, in the Malcolm Institute's annual student recital the year she was eight, Joan had made her debut at the pyradome. At the lesson before the recital, Malcolm had offhandedly told Joan that he was hungry, and somewhat abruptly had turned the discussion from pedal technique to favorite foods, discovering in the process what Joan's favorite was. It had seemed an uncharacteristic and somewhat forced familiarity for the usually nononsense lasemeister, but Joan had not thought about it until after she had made her debut, playing Jaeger's formidable *Vistata No. 18 in Fourth*. Amid thunderous applause, Malcolm had marched down the pyradome's center aisle to the Tiger Pit, where he had presented Joan with an enormous quiche Lorraine. She had, however, been much too excited to swallow more than a mouthful.

The day glowing flickered twice, and on the couch behind His Gaylordship, Kate Seymour turned to her only redheaded grandson, five-year-old Stan, Jr., and told him, "Hush up, now. Your mother's about to play."

Also with thoughts more suited to a death house than a laserium, Eleanor Delaney Darris stood at the mouth of the tunnel leading into the pyradome's Tiger Pit from backstage, waiting for the signal light to change from yellow to green, as it had changed from red to yellow seconds before. Her palms were as wet as her throat was dry, and she was wondering at the moment how the Christ she'd ever got herself into this situation.

Some wise and kind soul had foreseen her discomfort, for right next to the entrance were a tissue dispenser and a water cooler. Eleanor mopped her palms and took a short drink, then noticed that there was a bucket as well. She preferred to think that it was only for disposing of the tissues, though she suspected otherwise.

She smoothed her floor-length black gown unnecessarily, then smiled as she remembered what Malcolm had said at her last lesson. "When you stand in that tunnel," he'd told her, "watching your life pass before your eyes, remember that someday you'll look back on the terror of this hour as the high point of your life." He'd then leaned back in his couch, grinned, and said, "Life really scats, doesn't it?"

The light changed from yellow to green. Eleanor took a breath and walked into the Tiger Pit.

She could hear the applause, but with the spotlight on her, she couldn't see the audience at all. Thank the Lady for that, at least, she thought; she knew that if she'd caught even a glimpse of Wolfgang Jaeger or Geoffrey Moulton sitting in the jury box, that would have been it for her, right then and there.

Eleanor bowed at four, eight, and twelve o'clock to the audience surrounding her. Then she seated herself, adjusted the couch, wiped imaginary dust off the console, lowered the glowing to pitch blackness, and began to play.

She started with the first of three pieces she would play in her hour-long showcase, Partyka's *Ad Astra Suite*. Written on Earth before the space habitat by that name had even been planned, it was a somewhat programmatic series of five themes-and-variations describing—as the composer had written on the score—"Human Aspirations That Will Take Us to the Stars." The themes were titled, in sequence, "Observing the Eagle Soar," "The Hot Air Balloon," "Amelia Crossing the Atlantic," "The X-15," and "The Eagle Has Landed."

Eleanor flew beautifully through the first three sections, poured on everything she had for the devastatingly fast "supersonic" variations, then reintroduced, in a brighter key, the transformed statement of the original "Eagle" theme for the alternately graceful then rocky final touchdown.

The audience was warmly receptive as Eleanor raised the glowing for her first bows, as they were again when she'd completed her second piece, Pfirsichbaum's *Apollo and Dionysus*. She lowered the glowing again as the applause died down.

It was the time for the premiere of *Nocturne in First* by Eleanor Delaney Darris.

While the pale-violet shadow of the day bowed three times to him, a deep-red sunset yawned, fading into the distance. Slowly, ponderously, the blue moon stretched, shook herself, and began to awaken from her sleep. She began lumbering around—back and forth—marching a call for her sons and daughters to awaken with her.

In a cool, clear blue voice, she summoned forth the planets and the stars—the great galaxies and clusters of galaxies—to arise with her for the Night's Great Dance.

She asked all assembled what the night's dance should be, and all sorts of suggestions were made.

There were calls for reels and rigadoons, one-steps and two-steps, fox-trots and turkey trots. There were factions for jigs, horas, and kazatskis; jitterbuggers, bunnyhoppers, and cakewalkers argued; now there were demands for gavottes and pavanes, minuets and mazurkas, sarabands, tangos, and fandangos . . .

Enough! danced the moon; I will decide.

It will be a waltz. Follow me:

> *Rising*:   Violet, Indigo, Blue ♭;
> *Falling*:   Yellow, Green, Indigo.
> *Rising*:   Violet, Indigo, Blue ♭;
> *Falling*:   Red ♭, Orange ♭, Indigo.

Reluctantly at first, they began to waltz in the established coloratura—rising and falling, rising and falling—isolated, seconded, and answered. At first only a few began, timidly, but soon with greater confidence. Then all were waltzing—faster and more innovatively—swirling and entangling, showing off and taking grand risks . . .

A burst of red, then to orange, then to gold: the planets and the stars—the great galaxies and clusters of galaxies—paused, then slowly began breaking up into smaller groups to head home.

The moon bowed three times to the risen sun, yawned, then—with a final flash of white—retreated into darkness for her rest.

Eleanor Darris raised the glowing to an ovation of applause and shouted *bravas* and *bravissimas*.

Eleanor was the final contender in her category. The jury, though exhausted from watching lasegraphers since ten that morning and the day before also, deliberated only an hour—though it seemed forever to Eleanor and fourteen other hopefuls as they paced the greenroom, smoking joynettes. For some of the younger ones, away from their parents and governors, it was a rare chance to toke with the grown-ups.

Just before midnight, Geoffrey Moulton—as president of the jury—called five finalists back to the Tiger Pit. Eleanor was among them. When it came her turn, he placed around her neck a fire gem set into a palladium medallion, then kissed her wetly on both cheeks.

Eleanor had tied with a fourteen-year-old Oriental boy from Antarctic Province for a year's study with Moulton at the LASER Institute in Van Nuys, Pacifica—the academy founded by Ivan Dryer himself a century and a half earlier. On the second day of the LCAA festival, Thursday, April 22, Eleanor had tied for second place in the classical Junior Competition.

It was too late to hold a celebration that night, but there was some debate between Eleanor and Wendell regarding the proper night for throwing a party—above all, an excuse to play host to the top names of lasegraphy at Helix Vista for an evening. Wendell thought it should be the next night, Friday— a night the festival was devoting to roga—while Eleanor thought it might be better to wait for Tuesday the twenty-seventh, the night following the senior competition, in which Joan was playing, and the last day of the festival.

It was not only a question of Eleanor's wishing to share her laurels with any Joan might win, but a matter of protocol. With one exception, the celebrities they most wished to invite were not only on Eleanor's jury but on Joan's. Inasmuch as many of them were already acquainted with Eleanor and Wendell through grants from the Darris Foundation, there was the possibility that another candidate would charge that having them to Helix Vista before Joan competed was prejudicial.

Wendell discussed the problem with the "exception," Wolfgang Jaeger, right after Eleanor's award and just before Jaeger left for his hotel. Jaeger laughed when he heard of their quandary, assuring His Gaylordship that the lasegraphic community was so incestuous already that such an affair would be a teardrop in a cloud factory—such "influences" were so common as to cancel out. Moreover, since some of the most prized guests would be leaving Newer York Monday night immediately following the Senior competition, the only chance of getting most of them was this Friday—already today.

The celebration was scheduled for the following night.

"Do you have anything to say before sentence is passed?"

It was a drama that had been played out in courtrooms throughout history. The prisoner in this case, a frightened-looking teenaged Touchable girl with raven hair hanging out from her red-hooded cloak, stood in the dock. Her attorney—a portly androman looking somewhat like a manicured Rasputin in his lavender capote—stood next to her. The prosecutrix, in her pink cloak, sat at the prosecution table at the left of the chamber. The jury of six women and six andromen were in a box on the right side with a court recorder, a robot, just in front of them. The court clerk in his blue cloak—the only comman in this courtroom as an officer—sat at a desk just below the judge's bench, watching an array of video monitors and wearing a headset that permitted the judge to speak to him privately.

The visitors' gallery was large and filled, as usual, with witnesses, spectators, and holovision technicians; several cameras were suspended at discreet—but strategic—points around the courtroom. Two burly-looking bailiffs, both in lavender, stood in opposite aisles of the visitors' gallery, each with his legs planted apart and his arms folded across his chest, looking like genies awaiting their next command.

Her Honor Vera Collier Delaney sat at her bench, raised higher than anyone else in this chamber, the Legos, Ltd., corporate logo with its motto "LEX SCRIPTA, LEX TERRAE" prominently displayed on the seal in front of her. She wore a black cloak. An enormous holovision monitor above her showed, at the moment, a close-up of the Touchable.

The image on the holoscreen cut to Vera, trying to look patient waiting for the prisoner's reply to her question, then back to the Touchable once again.

The Touchable looked at the jury, looked at the prosecutrix, looked up at the huge monitor—now showing an encompassing view of the gallery—then lowered her eyes to meet Vera's. Softly, but amplified by a pickup, she said, "Forgive them, Father, for they know not what they do."

Vera kept the Touchable's glance and smiled slightly. "How melodramatic," she said. "How . . . *touching*. Is that all?"

The girl in red nodded.

"Very well," Vera said. "You grant us mercy, we grant you justice." She pressed a panel on her bench. "Court clerk will read the sentence."

The text appeared on the clerk's monitor board. He pressed a panel on his desk, swiveling it around to face the gallery, then in a professional-sounding baritone began reading from his monitor. "Thank you, Your Honor. Touchable Number 264-7RT-399 will be taken for a last shuttle ride on TransMeridian Skylines to the Federation Execution Facility at Detroit, Ontario. There she'll be given a sumptuous last meal courtesy of Chez Bernie's Restaurants. Then, at midnight Sunday the twenty-fifth of April, she'll be taken into the fabulous Radarmatic Microwave Oven for her personal execution."

The Touchable gasped deeply, and had to be held up by her lawyer.

The clerk allowed himself a pause, as the huge holoscreen showed a recorded insert of a Touchable being led into the oven, then went on cheerfully. The holoscreen accompanied him with appropriate visual displays: "Some of the witnesses during this trial have received consideration from, and promotional fees have been paid by, Newer York's beautiful downtown Nova Cancy Hotel—'At Nova Cancy, there's always room for one more!'—by TransMeridian Skylines—'On TransMeridian, we'll fly you from morning to night!'—by Chez Bernie's Restaurants dateline to dateline—'For the finest French cuisine you'll eat, *allez vite* to Bernie's suite!'—and by Radarmatic, Inc. Back to you, Your Honor."

Both bailiffs turned to face the gallery, uncrossed their arms, and began applauding wildly, leading the spectators—with intermittent frantic waving—to applaud likewise.

When the clapping died down, the holy zoomed in on Vera, who said. "So Mote It Be!"

She banged her gavel. The spectators began applauding again.

The bailiffs escorted the Touchable out of court in the brief recess—during which Vera phoned Stanton at his office for a lift to Helix Vista for Eleanor's celebration that night—and when the proceedings had come back from promo, Vera turned to her court clerk and asked, "Who do we have next, Johnny?"

At a little past six, Stanton's company limousine called for Vera in front of her green foam house on Earth Street. The skymobile waited for her while she took her time slipping into a black evening formal, allowing her blond hair to fall loosely over bare shoulders; then she told her domestic computer where she could be reached, grabbed her overnight case, and climbed into the limousine. Vera watched a recorded summary of her day in court on the vehicle's holoscreen while the skymobile taxied up Manhattan Boulevard to the Darris Tower. She greeted Stanton warmly when he got in. Shortly, they were cleared for takeoff, and five minutes later they were climbing to 3,000 meters for their flight north, via the Hudson Corridor, to Helix Vista.

They talked casually about work for a few minutes, then proceeded to a recapitulation of the last hunt they had gone on together and talked of the next hunt to which they looked forward. Over the past few years, Stanton and Vera had teamed for Marnie hunting parties quite a few times. Eleanor and Vera had both become Marnies, but Vera had substituted for Eleanor while she was pregnant with Collier and later Delaney, while (unbeknownst to Vera) Eleanor practiced—and largely owing to Eleanor's growing dislike of hunting. It had all been very innocent, though, and while Vera and Stanton had frequently helped the other to have sex with a Touchable, they had never committed the indiscretion of being alone together for long.

Conversation about hunting bogged down momentarily, and there were several heartbeats of silence. A word from either of them could have broken the moment easily. Instead, neither said anything. It was long enough for Stanton to notice how much Vera was like Eleanor before she had got so preoccupied with that raping laser of hers, and it was long enough for Vera to remember how envious she had been of the Touchable she had pinned down for Stanton on their last hunt together.

The silence lasted just a little while longer. Then Vera smiled, took Stanton's hand, and lifted it to her lips. His mouth opened, astonished. They were at 1,000 meters. She rested his hand on her knee, and moved it slowly up the inside of her thigh. They were at 1,500 meters. She ran one hand through his red hair while with her other she guided his hand to her hollows. She gasped. He hesitated only an instant longer, then grabbed her with all the frantic urgency of a fifteen-year-old satiating his starvation for the first time. They were at 2,000 meters.

Her tongue tried to swallow his as his hands explored the textured curves of her body. They were at 2,500 meters. As they pulled clothes out of the way, their eyes stared into the other's, then shut tightly. They were at 3,000 meters.

"I'll have you," she said, her voice like molten lead.

"You do," he answered.

Two bodies tried to crush themselves into one. When he thrust into her, it was an act of time-travel and of conquest—not conquest of her, but of a wife who no longer seemed to need him to complete herself, and of his long-dead father, who during his lifetime had measured his son's manliness by the number of women he took to bed. When she encompassed him, it was an act of theft so complete that she didn't even mind when in his moment of near-unconsciousness he called her Eleanor. His moment triggered hers—the first time since she'd entered the service nine years before that she'd been brought to release other than by her own hand.

It was only after they were descending into Helix Vista, as they assembled clothing and heavily breathed in each other's musk, that

105

they realized the inevitability of their moment. Each of them knew that their act had been a statement of the same kind, born out of the same void. But each saw the future filled differently.

THE LCAA MARK 800B chromatic laser, the model given to Joan Darris on her fifth birthday, is generally regarded as the best commercially produced instrument of its time. It was also the most expensive. Unlike the free-electron lasers used in cheaper instruments, and like the handmade instruments of the Impressionist period—such as Wolfgang Jaeger's classic Merlino—the Mark 800B was an injection laser making use of between nine and twenty individually cut fire gems, different for each instrument LCAA made. Cutting the gems to tune them for the color wavelengths needed in lasegraphy is a delicate and expensive proposition—more than an art, less than a science. Thirty-five spectral lines—from 3,800 Ångströms in dark violet to 7,600 Ångströms in dark red, plus the thirty-sixth ultraviolet line at 2,970 Ångströms—must be located at mathematically precise wavelengths, so if there are a few extra lines at odd points in the spectrum, they can be ignored or filtered out.

Joan's instrument had several such extra lines among its twelve gems, including a wolf at 10,600 Ångströms in the infrared, an unavoidable but invisible line in her laser's darkest red gem.

But this was not the only Wolf attending Joan in the lawn dome at Helix Vista, as she practiced to the last possible moment before her mother's celebration.

In a front-row couch of the lawn dome, Wolfgang Jaeger watched Joan practice. There was no conflict of interest in seeing Joan play before judging her competition performance, since he was not serving on Joan's jury. Jaeger had told LCAA that he would serve only on the jury of the Junior Competition, saying that with five of his students in the Senior Competition, it would be impossible for him to remain objective. That was what he said. His actual reason had more to do with not wanting to expend energy arguing with another committee when even standing up in this abominable gravity well was an effort.

Thus, having arrived early for the party, he reclined in the dark, blissfully watching Joan run through her Vistata.

First movement. A leitmotif in orange dances against a green field surrounded by a violet perimeter; outside the perimeter is a slowly dimming red glow. The orange leitmotif dances from one edge of the green to the other, as if searching for something, then notices a gap in the perimeter. The leitmotif dances through the gap from green to red, loops around several times, and is about to dance back into the green when the gap closes up.

Second movement. The orange leitmotif makes several more attempts to get back to the green, unsuccessfully, while the red glowing shifts increasingly to dark violet. When the shift is complete, a red leitmotif joins the orange on the now violet backdrop, and the two leitmotives carefully engage each other in conversation. When the dance is completed, they begin a cakewalk in larger and larger circles.

Third movement. The red and orange leitmotives start dancing slowly across a phosphorescent white field, even as their own patterns take on a ghostly aura (provided by the thirty-sixth hue in ultraviolet). The leitmotives stop, the red circles cautiously around the orange several times, then the two leitmotives resume their journey across the phosphorescent white.

Fourth movement. Halfway across the dome, a bright flaring in yellow stops the two leitmotives, casting violet shadows behind them. A second flare from the opposite side doubles the shadows, signaling the ominous appearance of a leitmotif in dark blue. As the orange leitmotif backs away, the blue leitmotif engages the red in an apache dance; but the red disengages and, rejoining the orange leitmotif, continues across the phosphorescence.

Fifth movement. The blue leitmotif dances in rage, time and time again blocking the red and orange leitmotives, encircling them, trapping them.

Sixth movement. The red leitmotif dances between the orange and blue leitmotives, and begins circling the blue enticingly. The blue responds to the red by attacking, and the red falls. The orange leitmotif counterattacks the blue, but with no effect. With one swift shove, the blue sends the orange spiraling across the field.

Seventh movement. The blue circles the red, slowly, and as it circles, the red leitmotif changes into a leitmotif in bright gold. The blue leitmotif begins circling the golden leitmotif, drawing it higher and higher and higher toward the center of the dome, until their patterns are so small that they look like one green leitmotif . . . then the gold leitmotif spins to the dome's edge as a shockwave, turns red again, and expands toward the center until the entire dome is bathed in a dying red glow, broken only by a small, pulsating remnant of the orange leitmotif.

The dome went black. Wolfgang Jaeger applauded as his "Bravissima!" echoed through the empty dome. Joan raised the glowing.

When he had stopped applauding, Joan said, "How about an encore?"

Jaeger chuckled. "You're prepared to outdo yourself?"

Joan twisted a lock of red hair around her finger. "No, you."

"Not another rainbow cadenza, I hope?"

"Next year," Joan said.

She dimmed the glowing again, began running her fingers across the console, then built up a stylized image, line by colored line, in the center of the dome. She fixed the image and began concentrating on movement. Then Joan touched a foot pedal to bring up a diffraction, and fingered a key to place each image under discrete control.

"*Three* butterflies," she said, as they began looping around one another in three-way counterpoint.

Jaeger laughed resonantly. "My God, you remembered that?"

"I remember almost everything, Wolf," Joan said.

"Thank the stars, I don't," said Jaeger.

"Composer?" said Geoffrey Moulton to Jack Malcolm. "The man is *color-blind*. That blue jay couldn't compose a competent Yulegram, much less a vistata. If you judge by the duration of his 'pieces,' he probably suffers from premature ejaculation."

Eleanor had given up an hour before trying to keep the discussions from getting serious. When lasegraphers got together, they argued lasegraphy; similar discussions were in progress all over the terrace, interrupted only by a robot with canapés, or a trip to the cannabistro, or a shift in factional loyalty. Near the cannabistro, one small crowd was gathered around the white-haired Jack Malcolm and his contemporary, Geoffrey Moulton, who alternated between coming across as a petulant young man and as the holder of keys to eternity.

"Nevertheless," Malcolm answered Moulton, "Roland Church sold approximately five times as many recordings last year as the total sales of everyone at this party."

"With choreography set to *music*," Moulton said.

"That is the convention of the medium," Malcolm replied, snagging a pimento crust as it went by.

"Pandering to the lowest impulses of the public."

"I've seen him perform," Malcolm said. "He has some lovely coloraturas."

Moulton threw his lavender cloak backward and snorted. "I suppose the next thing you'll be telling me is that you intend to allow *music* in your practice domes."

"No," Malcolm said. "With a few exceptions, my students are too lazy to allow that. They'd begin composing by ear, rather than by eye, and never learn how to draw out the implications of a theme."

"But Good Goddess, Malcolm, that's what I've been getting at all *along*. This roga doesn't have any form of its own, any logic. You can do anything so long as it follows the beat of the music."

"It isn't quite that lawless. Its dialectical phrases—"

"All right. A few simple progressions. A key change to the dominant. Any first-year student could do as much."

"Perhaps. But could you?"

"Why the caldron would I want to?"

Malcolm turned to the cannabistro for a moment, then returned with a joynette. "Perhaps," he said, "because we get so wrapped up in form and technique that we tend to forget ours is a medium relying on mythic archetypes. And what better place to look for archetypes than in the collective unconscious that buys so many Roland Church recordings?"

Moulton rapped on his chest, the sound muffled against the heavy fabric. "In here, that's where. I don't need to look at sales figures to know what's an archetype."

"How odd," Malcolm said. "That's almost word-for-word what Roland Church said to me when he started taking formal training with me last fall."

Moulton's jaw dropped, and Jack Malcolm lit a joynette. "And he isn't color-blind. I tested him. As for being premature, my friend," Malcolm said, laying his hand on Geoffrey Moulton's shoulder, "you'll have to test that for yourself."

The group around them broke up, laughing, as the two lasemeisters headed over to the court around Jaeger, which included the hostess, her red-haired daugher, His Gaylordship, and most of the other lasegraphers.

"So you see, Maestro," said Graham Ingrams, a spindly but short comman in his thirties, "neither the coloratura nor the graphics in my *Color-blind Vistata* rely on traditional forms. The sequences, in fact, were arrived at by spinning a roulette wheel and transcribing the numbers to achieve a new, achromatic logic."

"I'm beginning to see," said Jaeger, tugging at his cloak. "Tell me. What has the audience response been to these achromatic compositions of yours?"

"As is to be expected with new forms," Ingrams said, hurt rising up in his voice: "anger, distrust, and maintenance of disbelief. But I'm sure in time this will change. Weren't your own pathbreaking works accepted only after initial resistance?"

"Of course," said Jaeger, pulling at his shoulder again. "Damn these cloaks. I'll never get used to them. Still," he went on, "in my search for new paths I always heeded the Tao that it's better to follow the river than dig oneself into a trench."

Ingrams turned chilly. "If one doesn't like where the river is going, isn't one free to dig a canal?"

"Just don't follow the alimentary canal, or you'll reach a bad end."

"The Maestro has gotten too obscure for me," Ingrams said.

"And for me also," said Wendell.

"Very well," said Jaeger. "Has anyone here ever been to the concert of a symphony orchestra?"

"My class at school went last year," Joan said. "The Tokyo Repertory Orchestra was at the Television Museum."

"Would you evaluate the concert?" Jaeger asked her.

Joan shrugged. "They didn't play nearly as well as the old recordings we heard in class before the field trip."

"Thank you. I rest my case."

"Maestro," Ingrams began, "I'm afraid I still don't see—"

"Then *look*," said Jaeger. "Ingrams, when I was just about your age, I attended one of the last concerts of the Boston Symphony Orchestra, the last major orchestra there was. It was pitiful. At the peak of symphonic music, there were orchestras in every major city, and most minor cities had at least community orchestras. Yet by the mid–twenty-first century, symphonic music was dead. At the concert I attended, the orchestra was down to three-quarters strength and the audience was two-thirds empty. The performance was a disgrace compared with recordings they'd made half a century earlier. Their audience could get a better performance staying at home listening to their audios than going to a live performance, so the orchestras lost out. Today a few repertory orchestras are all that's left of a once major artistic industry."

110

"I don't see how that addresses my vistata," Ingrams said. "It seems more an attack on the recording industry."

Jaeger shook his head. "What killed the symphony orchestra was not competing with their own recordings," he replied, "but not having any new symphonic compositions to compete with. And this was due to a sort of Gresham's law—counterfeit music driving out real music—that you would unleash upon lasegraphy."

Ingrams drew back. "Why, I'd never—"

"Listen, Ingrams," said Jaeger. "What you do with your career is your affair. I just want to see things sold with the proper label. You want to use an achromatic form, it's not a new idea. In music they called it 'atonality': compositions made up of sounds without harmonic tonality, without melody or chords—chaos without letup, tension without release. But music is defined by its harmonic tonality—just as lasegraphy is defined by its concordant chromatics—and music without harmony was, in effect, music without music, just as lasegraphy without chromatics is lasegraphy without lasegraphy. And when two generations of symphonic composers, performers, and critics labeled musical tonality as a relic of the past, force-feeding their ever-dwindling audiences on noise sold as 'modern' music—while simultaneously definitive performances of past tonal masterpieces accumulated on recordings—the audiences withdrew from the concert hall to their living rooms, and a great art form was dead. Every composer, performer, and critic who backed this counterfeit music with his or her reputation was a party to the murder of classical music—no, scratch that—to its *genocide*."

Before Ingrams could reply, Stanton Darris caught Eleanor's eye and nodded. "The supper is served," Eleanor announced. She took Stanton's arm and added to him under her breath, "Thank the Lady."

Vera was alone on the terrace, refilling a hash pipe with Mixture No. 23, Assassin's Blend, when the woman came up again to get her handbag. "Oh, there you are, my dear," she said to Vera. "I've been looking to get you alone all evening. But shouldn't you be down at the supper?"

"I'm going down in a moment," Vera said. "But why were you looking for me?"

"Oh, of course. I'm Martha Silberstein from the *Gazette-Holograph*. I was on your jury."

Perhaps it was the hash, Vera thought, but she had no recollection of the woman from any recent case. She tried to place a bony, olive-skinned woman with a hairdo like a layer cake, and came up short. This was embarrassing; she decided not to show it. "Of course," she said, unconsciously mimicking the woman. "How are you this evening?"

"Quite well, thank you. You know, my dear," she said, "I've served on many juries, but I've never been so impressed as I was watching you at work."

"Thank you," said Vera. "Perhaps I shouldn't press my luck by asking, but what impressed you so much?"

"Oh, don't be so modest, my dear," Silberstein went on. "It doesn't take a reporter's eye to see that you have a great career in store for you. I expect to see you go all the way to the top."

As a matter of fact, Vera did have long-term plans, involving His Gaylordship, to gain a seat for herself in the Upper Manor. "How nice of you to say," she said.

"Have you made any plans for next year?"

"Why, no."

"Do you plan to move to Pacifica, or just commute?"

"Pacifica?" Vera asked.

"Why, yes. Pacifica. I know we're supposed to be provincial, but I'm sure you've heard of it. On the Pacific Ocean, you know."

"I'm not planning to go to Pacifica," Vera said, missing the humor.

"Oh, but my dear, you must. This is a priceless opportunity."

This was *definitely* strong hash, Vera thought; she no longer had any idea what this conversation was about. But she was in too deep to walk out now. "I'm afraid I don't see it that way," she bluffed. She frowned. "Have you at least discussed it with Geoffrey?"

"Geoffrey?"

"Maestro Moulton, of course," Silberstein said.

Came the dawn, and Vera felt so relieved to discover that her mind wasn't gone that she hadn't yet noticed that something worse than her worst fears had come true. "I beg your pardon," Vera said. "You have me confused with my mother, Eleanor Darris. I'm Vera Delaney."

"Oh, my dear, I'm so embarrassed. But you must play, yourself?"

"Why must I?"

"If you don't, what jury could you have been thinking of?"

"That's the amusing part," Vera said. "I'm a justice for Legos, Ltd."

112

"Oh, that *is* amusing," she said, lighting a joynette. "But I do seem to associate a Vera Delaney with lasegraphy. Are you sure you've never been in the Tiger Pit?"

"Well," Vera admitted, "not for many years."

"Of course," Silberstein said. "Sixteen years, isn't it? You were supposed to premiere at the pyradome but fell ill. I was assigned to cover your debut."

"You have a remarkable memory," Vera said tightly.

"My dear, in my business you must."

"Mine also," Vera said. "I must admit I found it quite embarrassing not being able to remember what jury you were supposed to have been on."

"How darling," she said. "But I wouldn't worry about the mistake happening again. You'll never find me on a jury of that sort. My mind doesn't operate in that sphere at all. I don't know anything of law, never did, and no doubt never will. Do you think we should be getting down to the supper?"

"Go right ahead," Vera said, relieved at the end of this conversation. "I want to enjoy the night air awhile longer."

Martha Silberstein headed to the lift, then turned back for a moment. "You don't play anymore?"

Vera shook her head.

"A pity," she said. "You were supposed to be quite a prodigy." The lift arrived and took her down.

Vera stood at the cannabistro a moment longer, just looking at the stars twinkling through the anti-precipitation field; then she turned and filled her hash pipe for a third time with Mixture No. 23, Assassin's Blend.

It was well past 1 A.M. Saturday morning when the last guests flew out of Helix Vista. Joan's LCAA Mark 800B chromatic laser, with its full-size Model 1600 console, was still set up in the Tiger Pit of the lawn dome, as she had left it when she went up to the party hours before with Wolfgang Jaeger. Vera was thoroughly stoned when she glided into the lawn dome, powered up the laser to 860 milliwatts, and sat down at a lasegraphic console for the first time in sixteen years.

She didn't bother with *Blind Exercises*; she wanted to see results immediately. Slowly—excruciatingly slowly—she began her old warm-up routine, a series of progressive lissajous. So far, so good. She played through spirals, double helixes, and opposing mandalas;

and as long as she didn't try to go too quickly, there were no difficulties beyond a few minor fluffs.

It was time to try it again.

It was a happy little dance. The blue figure-8 warbled and squiggled its way across the dome and around the edge. It turned somersaults and cartwheels. It metamorphosed into different shapes and sprang back again. It shrank down to a pinpoint, then rebounded into a giant. When it had finished, a red figure-8 began repeating the dance the blue one had done . . . and Vera found she no longer had the facility to handle even a simple counterpoint. Her hands and feet just couldn't synchronize. *Fugue in Blue* tumbled to a halt.

She tried it again, slower, but it still wouldn't work. She tried it a third time and a fourth, slower each time, with no better results.

She keyed the laser into standby mode, rested her arms on the console, and lowered her head onto her arms.

A few minutes, dark and silent, passed like this. But soon, Vera turned off the laser, disconnected it from its console, plugged it directly into the power outlet—bypassing the console's circuit breaker—and aimed the instrument not straight up at the dome's center, but almost horizontally at the wall. It was not the first time she had gone through this procedure. The first time was the day she'd returned home from the hospital after her aborted premiere.

When Vera released the power dampers and turned the laser on again, it focused its full spectrum in a tight beam with a power output of 86 watts, burning a hole one third of a centimeter in diameter into the wall. Even a meter away from the beam, off axis, she could feel its heat. She was wearing black, she thought dimly; good: black would absorb the entire spectrum.

She was contemplating the puzzle of whether the beam would continue straight through the black or refract through the skin under it when Eleanor walked into the dome.

She was also still in her black evening formal.

Eleanor saw the laser beam burning into the wall, and knew what it meant. She took a breath, and said calmly, "If I was able to begin again on the laser after fifty-five years, then you can after sixteen, if you want to."

"So I can follow in your footsteps again?" Vera asked.

"I followed in your footsteps," Eleanor said, "when I reasoned that if you had the innate ability to compose *Fugue in Blue*, I had the same innate ability to attempt *Nocturne in First*."

Vera laughed bitterly, and moved in closer to the beam. "I'm surprised you never went to law school."

Eleanor walked a few steps closer to the Tiger Pit and stopped again. "Then we are different," she said. "I never wanted to."

"Neither did I," Vera said.

"If you need to find yourself through art," Eleanor went on, moving another step closer, "there are media other than lasegraphy, in which you wouldn't have to compete with me."

"I watched you, Mother," Vera said. "You tried them all. Dance, music, painting, sculpture, your Little Holy group. If you couldn't find yourself that way, neither can I. Besides, I'm not looking to find myself. I know what I'd find. You." She moved closer to the beam.

Eleanor walked slowly to the edge of the Tiger Pit. "This is no answer, Vera," she said.

" 'I never would be missed,' " Vera paraphrased. "Except by Stanton, maybe. Oh, didn't I tell you? We fucked on the way to your party."

"He told me," Eleanor said.

"What?"

"He told me." Eleanor stepped down into the Tiger Pit. Just half a meter more . . . "We've been drifting apart for years. We've both known it. Perhaps the only thing that's kept us together this long has been the children. Or the tax shelter seven sons provide," she added with bitterness of her own. "We've made plans to separate when I move out to study with Moulton in Pacifica."

An expression of terror appeared on Vera's face as she realized the full implication. "My Goddess," she shrieked, "I can't even steal your husband, except as his spare part!"

Eleanor took another step.

"Don't come any closer," Vera said.

"Vera, you mustn't do this to yourself," Eleanor pleaded.

"What are you worried about, Mother? It's more real than I am. I'm just a ghost, remember? It'll go right through me as if I'm not even here."

Vera moved closer to the laser and Eleanor made her move, trying to push Vera away from the instrument.

Eleanor fell in front of the beam's path, and the beam burned into her from her shoulder to her waist. She fell to the floor of the Tiger Pit, unconscious.

Vera screamed. And she never knew whether, in that last instant, her mother had slipped in front of the laser, or whether her mother had lost her balance as Vera had tried to step out of her mother's way.

13

VERA'S SCREAMS brought Stanton to the lawn dome quickly. For a brief moment he thought it was Vera on the floor and Eleanor screaming. Then he saw the fire-gem medallion around Eleanor's neck. His expression in that instant, as he realized how much she meant to him, was truly desolate. His first impulse was to sweep the lifeless-looking body of his wife into his arms. But he knew enough of first aid not to assume her dead—or to move an accident victim—so he left her as she was, on her back. Eleanor was not bleeding; the laser had sealed the blood vessels it cut.

"Quiet!" Stanton ordered Vera, to stop her from screaming; she took a sharp intake of breath and fell silent.

Fifteen-year-old Mark showed up at the lawn dome seconds after his father. "Don't come in," Stanton told him. "Your mother's been hurt. Get Gramps up and tell him to keep everyone else out of here."

"Do you need anything?" Mark asked.

"The robots will get anything. Move it!"

Mark left as Stanton punched his wristphone for the domestic computer and began barking orders in staccato bursts. "Stanton Darris, emergency priority. Begin sequence. One. Family limousine is to taxi to the lawn dome, soonest. Two. Phone emergency room of Kingston General Hospital and notify them of an injury accident involving a laser at high power. Interrupt sequence—Vera, turn that raping laser off—sequence resume, three. Place me in phone contact with hospital on-duty medic, soonest. Four. Domestic robots are to bring one videophone with medical sensor kit and one emergency medical kit to the lawn dome, immediately. Interrupt sequence." Was there anything else? "Resume sequence, uh, four—correction, five. Place Darris company limousine on standby. End sequence."

"Readback emergency priority sequence," the domestic computer began. "One, family limousine—"

"Waive readback. Uh, record in permanent. Stand by. Don't touch her," Stanton told Vera, who had shut off the laser and was now kneeling next to her mother.

"I wasn't going to," Vera said.

The family's blue Astarte parked in front of the lawn dome just as Mark ran in, carrying the videophone, medical sensors, and emergency kit. "I thought I told you to stay out of here," Stanton said.

"The robots were taking too much time," Mark said as he brought the equipment to Stanton.

"All right, good work," Stanton said. "Now get out."

"But—"

"*Now!*"

Mark got out. Stanton placed an oxygenator on Eleanor's nose, then attached sensors to her forehead, chest, and right earlobe.

With no further action possible for a few seconds, he looked dully at Vera. "What happened?"

"It . . . it was an accident."

"A lasegraphic instrument can't burn like this by accident."

"I'd . . . set it up that way. I was trying to—"

Stanton shushed her as his wristphone buzzed. It was the emergency-room physician, a black woman who spoke with an Afrikaans accent. She looked at Eleanor's injuries through the videophone, read her EEG, temperature, heartbeat, respiration, and blood color, then turned back to Stanton. "It's bad," she said. "I'm dispatching an ambulance with paramedic team. We'll know more when we get a look inside. Do you have her medical history available?"

"Our computer has it. I'll transfer it."

Stanton gave orders to the domestic computer, and a few seconds later the doctor was reading Eleanor's chart.

The doctor said, "This says that your wife is taking mannitol supplements as part of her antigeric regimen. Did she take it today?"

"If she's supposed to take it, she took it. Eleanor's a fanatic about such things."

"Her fanaticism may pay off. Next. Whose laser did this? We'll need exact technical specifications."

"It's my daughter's," said Stanton.

"I want her to accompany your wife to the hospital."

"She's only twelve years old," he said. "This is her *mother*."

"Can she handle emotional shock?"

Stanton did not answer immediately.

Vera said, "Yes, she can."

Stanton looked at Vera questioningly.

117

"Then you'd better get her," the doctor said.

"I'll do it," said Vera, and she left for the house.

By the time Joan was roused and dressed, the ambulance had come, picked up Eleanor, and returned to the hospital. Stanton, Joan and Vera followed in the Astarte a few minutes later. They paced, worried, and drank hot cups of coca mocha in the emergency room's waiting area for most of an hour before Dr. DeVries, the medic who'd examined Eleanor over the phone, invited them into her office, reassuringly.

She motioned to them to sit, then lit a joynette and seated herself at her desk, ordering her computer to transcribe the conversation. She spoke to Vera first, asking questions about the accident, but only such questions as were medically pertinent; she had no desire to file an official report with the Monitors. Vera told Dr. DeVries that Eleanor had fallen in front of the beam of a lasegraphic instrument putting out its full spectrum at absolute power.

"That's eighty-six watts!" Joan exclaimed, bewildered.

Dr. DeVries just nodded, taking another toke. "There was extensive damage," she said, "involving the cardiovascular system, major organs, and bones. Luckily, there has been no damage to the brain, even though it was deprived of oxygen for about twenty minutes." She turned to Stanton. "Your wife was clinically dead when the ambulance got to her. You can thank the mannitol she was taking that we were able to save her. It prevented the oxygen-starved brain cells from swelling against the braincase, which would have crushed the brain to death. But there are some things about this accident I still don't understand. I was under the impression that a lasegraphic instrument puts out energy only in the visible wavelengths and ultraviolet. That sort of damage I can account for—'sunburn' lines from the ultraviolet, coagulation of blood from lines in the greenish-blue. But what I don't understand are burns that look as if they were produced by a surgical laser."

"How is a surgical laser different from my daughter's?"

"Aside from more power output—except, it seems, in this instance—surgical lasers operate in the infrared."

Joan bit her lip. "My instrument has an extra line in the infrared—it's called a wolf—at 10,600 Ångströms."

Dr. DeVries nodded again. "That would explain it. That's right in the range used by many laser scalpels. If your laser had been putting out lines only in the visible spectrum and ultraviolet, we might have been able to do more. As it was, young woman, I'm afraid the worst injuries inflicted on your mother were caused by this wolf."

Joan froze, and even Vera had no idea why.

Dr. DeVries went on. "I'm afraid conventional treatment is ruled out. But we reintroduced oxygen flow to the brain in time, and Mrs. Darris is now most of the way into controlled hypothermia. That's all we can do."

"I see," said Stanton. "Then how long must my wife stay here?"

"I suppose you can take her out anytime."

"You mean damage was light enough to heal by itself? Eleanor can come home? Is she awake yet?"

"Why, no," Dr. DeVries said. "She is comatose, with irreparable damage to much of her body."

"I thought you said you'd saved her!"

"We did. Oh, I'm sorry. I see you didn't understand. Mr. Darris, we've placed your wife into controlled hypothermia. We're supplying her brain with a cryoprotective artificial blood while reducing her body temperature to four degrees Celsius, where there won't be any further deterioration. Mrs. Darris can remain here like this until you can make arrangements to place her into cryonic suspension, have a surrogate body grown for her, and have your wife's brain transplanted into it. I'd say the prognosis for her complete recovery is excellent."

"But . . ." Stanton almost couldn't ask the next questions. "How long until the transplant can be performed? Is it possible to obtain an already-grown surrogate body so they could operate immediately?"

Dr. DeVries shook her head. "For a brain transplant to avoid tissue rejection, the surrogate must have your wife's own genetic pattern, grown from one of her own cells. Since her ova are intact, they will probably grow the surrogate by a parthenogenic process, rather than cloning. The body will, of course, have its brain—except for parts needed for autonomic functions—inhibited in its embryonic stage to prevent personality formation. But a compatible host mother will have to carry the fetus until induced parturition at the sixth month, when a radical lobotomy is performed; then the surrogate is placed in a vivarium until puberty, when the brain is transplanted."

" 'Compatible host mother,' " Stanton said. "Ideally, that's a close relative, isn't it?"

Dr. DeVries nodded. Stanton looked over to Vera. When she realized that he was seriously thinking of her as a host mother for

Eleanor's new body, she shuddered visibly. "I'm opposed to cerebral abortion on principle," she lied.

"As for how long," Dr. DeVries went on, "I'm not a specialist, so I can only estimate. It depends on Mrs. Darris's genetically predetermined growth rate—age of first menstruation and so on."

"Can't they speed things up?" Joan asked.

"I'm afraid not. Accelerating the growth of a surrogate body beyond the natural rate causes progeria—premature senescence and death."

"Then . . ." Joan could hardly speak. "How long until I get my mother back?"

"Give or take a year or two," Dr. DeVries said, taking another toke, "I'd estimate about sixteen years."

The Darrises' blue limousine left the hospital, minus Eleanor, just after four that morning. The flight back to Helix Vista was just as blue, with the necessity of explaining the accident weighing heavily on Vera, but neither Stanton nor Joan wanting to ask in such confined surroundings. They hardly spoke a word.

Mark was in the living room, the only one waiting up for them, when they came in. Stanton gave his oldest son the news, then offered both Mark and Joan the sedatives Dr. DeVries had supplied for the family. Mark took his and went right up to bed.

Joan stayed. She turned to Vera as soon as Mark was in the lift and out of earshot. "I want to know what happened to Mom with my laser," she demanded.

Vera looked at Joan wearily. "This is no time for an interrogation. Go up to bed."

"Maybe other people can't tell the difference," Joan said, "but you're not my mother and can't tell me when I go to bed. I'll go when you answer me. Did Mom release the power dampers? Or did you?"

"I'll tell you in the morning. If your father says I should."

Joan looked over to her father. "Vera hasn't even told me yet," Stanton said. "We'll see tomorrow."

"One way or another, *I* will," Joan declared, then followed her brother up the lift.

When Joan was also out of earshot, Stanton looked to Vera. "Tell me now," he said.

Vera took a breath and blinked back tears. "I tried to kill myself. Mother tried to stop me. I guess she was too raping successful."

120

Stanton shook his head. "She wasn't successful enough. She left it for me to finish the job."

Vera looked frightened. "Of killing me?"

"Of saving you," Stanton said. "Or should I say, saving each other?"

"Oh, Stan," Vera said, and she fell into his arms, whimpering.

A few minutes later they took the lift up to what last night had been Eleanor and Stanton's bed, and was now theirs. Neither of them took a sedative.

It was a short night with little sleep for Stanton, Vera, and Joan, who were awakened by Mark Saturday morning before nine to tell the rest of his brothers the news about their mother. Mark had already briefed Gramps with what he knew. The twins, fourteen, took the news hard but managed not to cry in front of the others. Nine-year-old Zack and six-year-old Stan, Jr., did cry. Collier, four, and Delaney, two, were both too young to worry about their mother's having gone away for a while; "a while," for them, meant anything from a few hours to whenever. They spent the morning, as usual, watching serials on the holy with Gramps.

Stanton spent the morning on the phone—with his mother, with Wendell, and with his lawyers. He recorded picturegrams to the Colliers and Eleanor's three brothers, and made arrangements for Eleanor to be frozen into cryonic suspension at the Forest Hills Vivarium in Queens.

After lunch, Vera took Joan aside in the yellow lounge and told her that she'd been very depressed at the party last night, mostly from having had to sentence a young Touchable girl to the ovens earlier in the day, and this combined with smoking too much hash had caused her to try taking her own life in the lawn dome. Their mother, Vera explained, had tried to stop her and had fallen in front of the laser while trying. Vera asked Joan to forgive her.

Joan hesitated for a few moments, then said, "I'll forgive you when Mom tells me to."

"Do you really hate me that much?" Vera asked.

"Did you hate the Touchable you sent to the ovens?" Joan answered.

"No. I was just doing what I had to do."

"So am I."

"Even that Touchable girl forgave me," said Vera.

"It was her choice," said Joan.

121

Vera turned red. "It's not wise," she said, "to carry around hatred for so many years. You should forgive me now for your own peace of mind."

"If it makes you feel any better," Joan said, "how I feel about you doesn't have anything to do with either my peace of mind or the reason I can't forgive you."

"You're too raping logical for twelve," Vera said, "but you're going to find out soon there are things logic can't protect you from."

Joan got up to leave.

"Where are you going?" Vera asked sharply.

"To practice."

"Crone Almighty," Vera said, "haven't you had enough of lasers after what happened to Mother? How can you go anywhere near the lawn dome after last night?"

Joan paused in the doorway. "It's funny," she said. "That's what I was thinking of asking you about Mom's bedroom." She waited another moment, then left. But Joan left for the practice console and the holoscreen in her own room, rather than for the lawn dome and her laser.

Monday evening at six, Jack Malcolm dropped Joan off at the pyradome to set up her instrument in the Tiger Pit for the competition. As per lots drawn, Joan was scheduled to compete at seven-thirty—considered a prime spot, since she would be the first performer the jury would see after their final dinner break. But there was a surprise waiting for Joan in the Tiger Pit when she arrived: an arrangement of roses, set into an ascending color scale, with a hand-written note from Wendell that said simply, "I'll see you Over the Rainbow."

After she had set up and tested her laser in the huge dome, Joan went back to the greenroom, where half a dozen of her competitors—all in their late teens and early twenties—were engaged in animated discussion. By remaining on the fringes of their conversation—but watching their reactions to her—Joan concluded that the news about her mother had not yet got out. No one ventured a "Tough luck, kid," or—worse—suggested that the jury might rule in favor of Joan out of sympathy. Joan hoped the jury hadn't yet heard; she didn't want to go through the rest of her life wondering if her first "break" had been due more to sympathy than to talent. Assuming she would win, that was.

Joan had her mind set at rest on that point just past seven, when

Wolfgang Jaeger came back to wish several of his students "Over the Rainbow," then pulled Joan into the corridor to wish her the same out of their earshot. Jaeger told Joan that Jack Malcolm had told him earlier in the day about her mother's deanimation, but that her jury did not know; Jaeger could state this for certain since he had just come back from dinner with them, during which Eleanor's name had come up with no reference to her accident. Jaeger told Joan that someday Eleanor would be very proud of her, and after being assured by Joan that she would be all right, he returned to the greenroom to lend moral support to his students.

Joan waited at the mouth of the tunnel, next to the water cooler, tissue dispenser, and bucket, waiting for the red light to turn. Jack Malcolm had offered to wait with her again, but Joan had turned him down, saying that this time she had to be alone. Jack had tried to talk her out of it, but Joan had insisted. At seven twenty-five, the light turned from red to yellow, and precisely at seven-thirty, it turned to green.

To the sound of thunder and the sensation of blinding light, Joan entered the Tiger Pit. She bowed blindly at four, eight, and twelve o'clock to the audience around her; then—in the Tiger Pit of the pyradome—Joan sat down to play her laser for the first time since it had struck down her mother.

She lowered the glowing to pitch blackness, then began to play the only composition she had elected to compete with, her own *Vistata No. 1 in Sixth*.

First movement. Joan is in the grass courtyard of the Malcolm Institute, looking for Mr. McIntosh; outside the courtyard, the last rays of day shine onto the street. Joan skips through the gate, still searching for Mr. McIntosh, and is about to head back in when the gate drops.

Second movement. Joan makes several more attempts to get back inside the courtyard, unsuccessfully, while day shifts increasingly to night. When the shift is complete, the Touchable arrives, and the two of them talk for a few minutes. When they have finished, they begin the walk to the Touchable's home.

Third movement. They come to the phosphorescent white landing strip and start slowly across; what faint light there is takes on a ghostly aura around them. The Touchable stops Joan, tells her they must now be very brave, and they start across again.

Fourth movement. Halfway across the landing strip, the light from the flare hits them, casting ghoulish shadows behind them. But it is not until the second flare is tossed behind them that Joan first sees the man the Touchable has warned her against, the man who admits to Joan that he is the Wolf.

The Wolf. The Wolf that had killed the Touchable who asked Joan to be her daughter.

The Wolf. The Wolf that the doctor said had inflicted the worst injuries on her mother.

Suddenly, Joan was no longer in the pyradome, playing a composition, but for a split second actually back on the landing strip with the Wolf.

Then another beat, and Joan was again in the pyradome, but fully aware that her hands were stroking the laser, which, both in substance and in composition, unleashed the Wolf that had attacked her mother.

She was back on the landing strip again, her hands guiding the Wolf's attack on the Touchable. A scream welled up in Joan's throat; but she was back in the Tiger Pit, where her compulsive training never to start a panic denied her even this release.

She forgot where she was in the piece and froze. For one beat. For two beats. For three beats. No, *No, NO!* she thought; not like Vera—*not like Vera*— and with her final reserve, she jumped in at the only place that would come to her, the end of the last movement. It was a fatal mistake. She saw the Wolf taking the naked Touchable higher and higher and higher . . . and when she fell, Joan fell with her.

When Joan came to, she was lying on a couch in the greenroom with Wendell, Malcolm, and Jaeger standing around her looking concerned and talking animatedly. She was disoriented a moment; then she remembered and sat up in a panic. "I've got to go out and finish!"

"Shhh," Wendell said, "you don't have to go anywhere. Just rest here for a few minutes; then I'll take you home."

"I have to go back or I'll be disqualified!"

"You already have been, honey," said Malcolm. "It doesn't matter."

"Doesn't matter?" Joan cried. "Do you think I want to end up like Vera?"

"You'll never be like Vera," Wendell said. "You couldn't be if you live twice as long as Maestro Jaeger."

"It was too much for you, too soon," Malcolm said. "I never

should have let you compete tonight . . . not so soon after the accident."

Joan shuddered. "I never want to play that laser again. Never."

"I don't blame you," Jaeger said. "It would be like trying to do sculpture with Lady Macbeth's dagger."

"Not *Macbeth*, Maestro," said His Gaylordship. "*Hamlet.*" Wendell turned to Malcolm. "Are you familiar with the play, Jack?"

"What?" Malcolm said. "Yes, of course."

"Hamlet would have saved everybody a lot of trouble if he'd simply left Denmark."

"I see your point," Malcolm said. "But do you two think you can pull it off?"

"Leave my brother to me," Wendell said.

"What are you all taking about?" Joan asked.

"My dear young lady," Jaeger said, turning to Joan. "How would you like to come back with me to study in Ad Astra?"

THE FIRST THOUGHT that Joan Seymour Darris had about Ad Astra, even before she ceased marveling about how light she felt standing on the surface of this new inside-out world of hers, was that there were so many women all around—even girls her own age or younger. The second thought she had was that so many of the Astrans were wearing less clothing out in public than she wore to bed back on Earth. And the third thought was that so many of these people were walking around in mixed couples—couples of any sort, for that matter—and they looked so, well, *carefree* together.

Her fourth thought was that she'd better find a rest room at the docking station immediately; though the space liner had been boosting under gravity for all but half an hour, she hadn't wanted to tangle for a second time with the ship's free-fall toilet—obviously designed by a male—which another woman had referred to as "the velvet maiden." She'd barely managed to conceal the evidence of her first try at it.

All told, the trip out from Earth had taken her and Wolfgang most of a day, beginning with her tearful goodbye at Soleri Skyport to her father, her brothers, Gramps, and Jack Malcolm. Joan had even given Vera a kiss on the cheek, accepting one from her sister in return. There were, of course, all sorts of useless going-away presents, and one very useful one from Wendell: *The Diplomat's Guide to the Habitats*. It was a fact-filled, etiquette-crammed, opinionated, and anecdotal pocket library compiled by one of the Federation's most successful ambassadors, His Excellency Burke Filcher, who early in his career had negotiated the Rainbow Compact that formally ended the Colonial War and restored trade between Earth and its space relations. Burke Filcher had since gone on to a powerful seat in the House of Commen, and his manual had since been issued to all Federation officials traveling abroad.

The shuttle ride up to Virginia Station took just over an hour. Then there was a two-hour layover that Joan and Jaeger spent down in the Wheel shopping, at lunch in the Tokomak Lounge, and gawking at Earth through coin-operated telescopes. Finally, they boarded the *Yuri Gagarin* for their five-hour trip to Ad Astra.

For Joan, the worst part of both the shuttle ride and the cruise in the *Gagarin* were the periods of free fall. She had taken anti-nausea pills, so she didn't experience any spacesickness, but the sensation of weightlessness was exactly like endless *falling*. She spent the free-fall periods of docking maneuvers and the mid-flight turnover of the *Gagarin* strapped tightly into her acceleration couch, watching a holy program that she could barely apprehend.

The Diplomat's Guide to the Habitats (latest edition) described Ad Astra and its oldest city, Nova Paulus, where Joan was moving, as follows:

The firstborn of the North American Concord's former colonies, Ad Astra is a cluster of manufactured habitats situated in the LaGrange Two orbit one-sixth of the way out again past our moon, about 450,000 kilometers from Earth. This cluster consists of ten pairs of habitat cylinders—each cylinder being 35 kilometers along its major axis and 7 kilometers in diameter—with each pair of cylinders rotating along parallel axes pointed toward the sun, but rotating counter to its twin cylinder for gyroscopic balance linked together by an 80-kilometer-long bridge.

The people live inside these cylinders.

The current combined population of Ad Astra is about 50 million, divided roughly equally between male and female, and distributed more-or-less among the twenty cylinders. Four more cylinders are under construction.

In the Ad Astra cluster are also pairs of several hundred smaller cylinders used for agriculture, heavy industry, research, and anything dangerous to inhabited areas.

As an introduction to comprehensive treatment, this abstract will examine the Nova Paulus habitat, a city of 2,327,000. Except for being in the opposite season, its twin cylinder, Minneanova, is structurally identical.

Three land valleys the cylinder's length, and a bit over 3 kilometers wide, are alternated by similar-shaped dichroic window arrays with segmented planar mirrors orbiting overhead, creating a natural-looking sky above each valley. The mirrors change angle gradually to simulate a natural movement of the sun across the sky, day into night. For the last thirty years, the Astrans, as they like to be called, have settled upon a sixteen-hour day and a nine-hour night as metabolically optimum; however, natural sunlight is on tap—through a system of mirrors and optic fibers—twenty-five hours a day to any residence desiring it.

Nova Paulus's three valleys are Valle de Sol, Sunny Glen, and Sundale. I surmise the name-givers were from Encino.

In Nova Paulus's endcaps, mountains rise 3,500 meters (one climbs *inside* the mountains), while finger lakes line the mountains' base. In the Eastern endcap is Mt. El Capitán, a tourist center owing to its low-gravity attractions; in the Western endcap, Mt. Capistrano provides communities to senior citizens for similar advantages.

Each valley has a land area of about 10,900 hectares, with the endcaps adding usable mountain land of about 4,400 hectares, resulting in a usable land area in Nova Paulus of about 371 square kilometers. Population density is about 6,270 people per square kilometer, roughly equal to Newer York today, six decades after the War.

Rotation along Nova Paulus's major axis (a three-minute period) provides simulated gravity, approximately two-thirds Earth normal at the lowest point in the valleys. Higher into the mountains, gravity reduces considerably, reaching free fall at the cylinder's axis.

Nova Paulus's axis is the home of its most popular attractions: its free-fall sports arena, its aviaries—where anyone may take wing and fly like a bird—its honeymoon hotels . . . and its red-light district. As hard as it is to believe in this day and age, prostitution is legal here. But then, so is virtually everything else.

The arrangement of homes, recreation, and shopping reflects a pleasant diversity of the best aspects of polyurban living today, with no disruption from the intermingling of residential and industrial areas.

Weather is controlled to public comfort, transportation is cheap and convenient, and street crime is virtually unknown—a wonder of wonders, since the wearing of personal weapons is quite common.

The people are easygoing and well mannered—even toward tourists, whom they regard much as a rancher views cattle. Their soft-spoken, but sometimes quite animated, way of talking seems to be the only universal trait in this pluralistic culture.

Since secession, the Astrans have relied exclusively on the Ad Astran Union's General Lease for their social contract. All residents must be signatories to the Lease or local merchants will not house, feed, or in any way do business with them. An exception is made for children, the retarded, and tourists, whose presences are vouchsafed by a sponsor—a signatory to the Lease who agrees to take on their liabilities. Such liabilities may be insured, and are routinely taken on by tourist bureaus eager for business.

The Lease has no positive obligations—no taxes, duties, or compulsory service—and specifically forbids the Union from imposing a cost on anyone without prior consent. The cost of all common goods and services—foreign defense, maintenance of thoroughfares, even the manufacture of air—seems to have been absorbed into the prices of salable products. I suspect they've figured out a way to make the tourists pay for them. There does not seem to be a single instance of what economists on Earth refer to as the "public goods" problem of externalities.

The concept of criminal justice is completely dormant here; even murder is treated as a tort. Dispute settlement is private, ranging from arbitration based on mercantile concepts of common law . . . to dueling.

The only remnant of democratic processes, since the War, is the yearly elections to decide on time and climate. This seems to be a local sport as much as anything else, and campaigns can be quite heated. Literally so: a recent climate campaign slogan was "Fry the bastards!" I believe they fried them.

The most frustrating thing about Ad Astra is that, having no government to speak of, it has no use for an old political hack such as me. There being only honest work here, I would quickly starve to death, should I ever be foolish enough to emigrate to this space island paradise.

—BURKE FILCHER, M.H.C.

As soon as Joan had returned from the rest room, and Jaeger had arranged for their baggage to be sent on ahead, there was the matter of Joan's legal status—child, tourist, or resident? Joan and Wolfgang discussed the matter with the Leasing Agent in the docking station's shipping office. The agent, a dark-haired girl only a few years older than Joan, pointed to a copy of the Lease mounted on the wall, and asked Joan to read it to her aloud. "When in the course of human events—" Joan began, but the girl interrupted her. "You can read," she said.

"Haven't I seen that opening paragraph somewhere before?" Joan asked.

"Plagiarism is our second-largest industry," Jaeger told her.

"What's the first?" Joan asked.

"You are," the agent said, "unless you claim resident status."

"What's involved?" Joan said.

"Signing the Lease," Jaeger said. "In essence, the Lease demands only one thing—that in exchange for the right to do business with people here, you agree to accept responsiblity for any costs you incur at the expense of someone else. You agree that if you buy something on credit, you'll pay for it. You damage somebody's property, you reimburse them. You agree to do a job and don't deliver, you absorb the cost of having failed to do it."

"What's the most I can get stuck for?" Joan asked.

"If you murder someone, except in defense, you can become the property of their heirs."

"What if I don't sign?"

"Then," the agent said, "you buy a ticket out of here right now—the Merchant Association will risk lending you the ticket if you can't afford it—or you find a sponsor to guarantee your debts."

"That would be I," Jaeger said. "But if I sign for you, I am your legal guardian and you have to obey any decision I make for you."

"Can they make me accept a guardian?" Joan asked.

"No one," the agent said, "can be prevented from signing the Lease on her own behalf, so long as she is legally competent—which you proved by reading the Lease—or unless she has an outstanding debt against her name which she refuses to honor."

"It doesn't matter how long I stay?"

The agent shook her head.

"I can sign and be treated like an adult?"

The agent nodded.

"I can see why we Astrans don't think much of tourists," Joan said, as she reached for a light pen to sign the Lease.

15

THE DRYER SCHOOL OF LASEGRAPHY had its campus on Lakeview Boulevard at the eastern end of Valle de Sol, just west of Auberon Avenue, where Wolgang Jaeger had his condominium. From the campus it was just a ten-minute walk to 14010 Captain's Row, a Garrison Colonial house owned by Michael and Rita Rubinstein.

Both were native Astrans in their early fifties, married to each other for twenty-six years; they'd met and married while at graduate school in Kibbutz. Dr. Michael Rubinstein headed the Department of Chairistic Heuronomy at the University of Ad Astra at Nova Paulus; Dr. Rita Rubinstein was principal of the Günter Grass Kindergarten.

The Rubinsteins had three children, all girls—Shoshana, Astrid, and Debbie. Shoshana was twenty, married, and studying in Tsiolkovskiigrad, Lenin, to be an ecological engineer; Astrid was thirteen, already *bat mitzvah*-ed, and a student at Dryer; Debbie was nine and a budding free-fall Olympic champion.

Astrid had moved into Shoshana's old room two years before, Debbie had moved up to Astrid's room, so Joan moved into what used to be Debbie's room. It was a third the size of the room she'd had at Helix Vista, but somehow—maybe it was the lower gravity—it seemed almost as large.

Astrid and Joan hit it off right away, and remained friends even when Astrid learned that Joan, though a year younger, was leap years ahead of her in lasegraphic accomplishment—and treated so by Jaeger. It didn't matter. Living at Helix Vista had isolated Joan from her fellow students at the Malcolm Institute, her singular interest had isolated her from the other girls at the Blair Academy, so she was delighted to have, for the first time, a girlfriend who shared her primary interest—even if Joan did have to talk more than listen on the topic. It balanced out: Astrid was more sophisticated than Joan in other areas—in what holovision performer was the current explosion (they called it HV here, not the holy); in what design of shorty-short jumpsuit "just everyone" was wearing this spring; and in what boys at Dryer Astrid thought were really boosty.

After setting Joan up with a practice dome on campus, and with a new instrument—one without any infrared wolves lurking about—Jaeger simply told Joan to keep her fingers nimble, then gave her six weeks to acclimate to her new home. The Rubinsteins—aware that the quiet spells to which Joan were subject reflected longings for her mother—drew her into their family life as much as possible. The first Sunday they took Joan with them on a cruise through the Finger Lakes, the next on a picnic halfway up El Capitán, one Saturday night they went on a Family Pub Crawl, and on Friday nights she went with them to synagogue.

The only place Joan didn't go with them was to an exhibition of free-fall acrobatics that Debbie was performing in. Joan hung back that Tuesday evening, even though she knew it was only a matter of weeks before she would have to go.

130

In the habitats, lasegraphic performances took place in free fall.

Joan found the religious aspect of the Rubinsteins' family life confusing, inasmuch as the Blair Academy had been Orthodox Wiccen and not at all inclined to give equal time to other faiths. The Friday night after the service for a particularly high holiday, Joan pulled Astrid aside and conducted a mini-seminar on comparative religion. "Let me see if I've got this right," Joan said. "You say that the Jewish religion doesn't say whether God is male or female, right?"

"That's right."

"Then how come Jesus Christ is always referred to as male?"

Astrid shook her head. "You're getting it all confused with Christianity. Jews don't believe Jesus is God."

"Then how come whenever your father wants to swear, he always says 'Jesus Christ!' or 'Christ Almighty!'?"

Astrid suppressed a smile. "I guess it's easier to swear with a name you don't really believe in."

"But you said your family doesn't really believe in God?"

"Well, not literally."

"Then what difference does it make whom he swears by?"

"I guess it's an emotional difference."

"Well, then, why is it important to refer to God as 'Him' or 'the Lord,' and why did the rabbi correct me when I referred to God as 'Her' and 'the Lady'?"

"It's a way of keeping our people separate from other religions, because we've been persecuted so much. It isn't any different with witches, is it?"

"We don't have a holiday celebrating Salem every year," Joan said. "Which leads to my real question. You said that just before I arrived you celebrated Passover, which is in memory of God's not killing the firstborn sons of Israel while He went after the firstborn of Egypt."

"Right so far."

"Then why, tonight, did you also celebrate Never Again, which seems to call God to account for standing by and not doing anything while the Nazis killed millions more Jews than He saved from Pharaoh?"

"You ask harder questions than the *Mah Nishtanah*." Astrid considered her answer for a few moments. "I think," she said, finally, "that it doesn't really matter whether what we remember is good or bad, just so long as Jews don't forget we're the Chosen People."

131

"Chosen for what?" Joan asked.

"Don't ask," Astrid said. "We haven't figured that out in six thousand years, and by now, a lot of us are afraid to find out."

Joan's trouble with free fall came to a head, as it had to, within the week she started lessons with Jaeger. "I think it's time we let you try out the Cathedral," he said.

Joan stood absolutely still and didn't say anything.

"You don't seem particularly thrilled by the prospect," Jaeger said.

"I'm scared to death, Wolfgang."

"I know," he said gently. "But there are drugs to take care of that."

"I can't drug myself for the rest of my life."

"You wouldn't have to," Jaeger said. "The drugs merely suppress your 'fight-or-flight' syndrome long enough for your body to accustom itself to whatever you're phobic about. When your body has learned the desired response, you don't need the drugs anymore."

"Can the drugs tell the difference between something you're supposed to be afraid of and something you're not?"

"No," Jaeger said, "but you can."

"Then I shouldn't need a drug to do it," Joan replied. "Let's get this the rape over with."

The tram climbed the monorail up El Capitán slowly, with Joan clutching Jaeger's arm so tightly she was leaving red marks in his flesh. By the time the tram reached the axis, Joan was sweating profusely into her orange jumpsuit. "I think I'm gonna be sick," she said.

"Take a deep breath," Jaeger said, "and think about something else. Try running a vistata through your mind—mmm, make it my *Eighteenth*."

Joan closed her eyes, took a deep breath, and swallowed hard. But it was too late. Jaeger barely got the sick bag to her in time to catch her vomit.

When Joan had finished, Jaeger handed her a peppermint and told her to suck on it. "You won't throw out twice," he said. "Now just hold on tightly to my belt—or the guideline—and follow me. The Cathedral is right nearby."

Joan held on to both belt and guideline, which slowed them down considerably. They passed through a minor tube into the La Paz Artery, where people floated quickly past in both directions—past

132

several brothels, past a storefront bubble with a salesman demonstrating zero-G cookware, past the Ricardo Aviary—and an endless ten minutes later, Joan followed Jaeger through the irised entranceway to Garmire Cathedral. It was pitch-black until Jaeger raised the glowing.

When he raised it, Joan was inside a perfect globe, about half the size of the pyradome but accommodating as many viewers. The lasegrapher performed not from a Tiger Pit but in the Avocado Pit at the globe's geometric core, with the audience facing both "upper" and "lower" hemispheres. By a system of image-splitting, whatever the lasegrapher projected onto the dome above was repeated exactly onto the demimonde below.

After Jaeger pulled Joan along the guideline to the Avocado Pit, he showed her how to belt herself into the performer's frame so she could use her feet to oppose the console's pedals.

Finally, he cycled the laser up and dimmed the glowing. "Play something happy," he said.

"I think I'm gonna throw out again!"

"No, you won't! Tell me, what are you afraid of?"

"Falling, I'm falling!"

"What frightens you about falling?"

"I don't know!" Joan wailed.

"Yes, you do!"

Tears began forming at the corners of Joan's eyes, and began breaking away and floating off as globules. "Have you ever seen anyone icked?"

"What?" he said.

"I did, when I was five."

Jaeger started, and had to pull himself back to the Avocado Pit with the guideline.

"Listen, Joan," Jaeger began. "Nobody in Ad Astra has ever—" Suddenly, Jaeger made the connection. "Is that what your vistata was about?"

Joan shut her eyes tightly and could only nod.

"My God," Jaeger said, "my God. Listen closely, now. No one has ever been icarated in Ad Astra. We're civilized here; we don't do that to people."

"Tell that to my stomach," Joan said shakily.

"Listen to me. Two-thirds of the audiences you'll ever play for will be in free-fall cathedrals such as this one, and the worst thing you'll have to worry about is a bad review—which, I admit, is bad enough. Now, on the count of three, I want you to open your eyes and begin playing my *Eighteenth Vistata*. I guarantee in five minutes you'll forget all about your nausea."

But Joan already had. Jaeger watched an arc of yellow liquid jetting out of Joan's shorts and continuing past the frame.

"I'm wetting myself!" Joan said, nearly hysterically.

"Never mind that, now," Jaeger said. "Play, damn it!"

And a few seconds later, Joan opened her eyes and began playing Jaeger's *Vistata No. 18 in Fourth*.

Two days later, to celebrate Joan's baptism in the cathedral—simultaneously of fire, air, and water, he realized—Jaeger took Joan and Astrid out to a holodrama imported from Earth.

The Guest Host was a second-rate thriller about an Earthwoman who wants to bear a clone of herself, but is medically unable. Therefore, she and her husband hire a Touchable woman to be host-mother of the cloned daughter. In the early stages of her pregnancy, the Touchable woman becomes the mistress of the genetic mother's husband—who has a fetish for pregnant women—and when the genetic mother finds out what the Touchable and her husband are up to, she threatens to throw them out.

The Touchable and the husband murder the wife—the genetic mother of the child the Touchable is carrying.

After the murder, the Touchable, with the husband's help, moves to another city and takes over the murdered wife's identity by wearing her brainprint in a fake transponder, and has the murdered mother's daughter as her *own* child.

The clone-daughter grows up with a dislike for the woman she thinks is her own mother, but actually is only her host mother and the murderer of her genetic mother.

When the daughter grows up, she learns about the murder by stumbling across the fact that her own brainprint is identical to the one her supposed mother is giving out, and since they don't look at all alike, she can't be her clone or parthenogenic daughter, and therefore, her real mother's brainprint must have been stolen . . . as it was, from her genetic mother.

The daughter turns the Touchable in to the authorities, and the murderess and the husband are brought to justice.

Normally, an insipid plot such as this would have made no impression on Joan, who informed Astrid and Wolfgang that the scenarists had cheated: a clone wouldn't have his or her parent's brainprint. Joan knew because Vera had Eleanor's genetic pattern but still had a brainprint of her own, and it worked the same with a clone. But, as it happened, Joan would remember *The Guest Host* for the rest of her life.

When she returned home with Astrid after the show, a picturegram from Joan's father was waiting for her.

Stanton hemmed and hawed his way through the message—using such phrases as "We've thought this over very carefully" and "Neither Vera nor I can stomach the thought of cerebral abortion"—but what the picturegram added up to was that Stanton and Vera had decided not to grow a new body for Eleanor. Eleanor was to remain, indefinitely, in cryonic suspension at the Forest Hills Vivarium.

The message chopped off.

For the second time in her life, Joan Seymour Darris made a promise to herself. This time, she vowed that someday she would return to Earth, win custody of her mother, and impregnate herself with Eleanor's new body, giving her mother life once again.

IV.

λ5000Å to 5500Å

AT THE SUMMIT of Mt. Capistrano, a woman floated, naked and relaxed, gazing into the brilliant celestial night that no one had ever seen from Earth. She often came to this sanctum when she needed to think. This afternoon, she needed to make a decision.

Even at repose, she was a woman of striking presence, tall and slender, with the lithe power that poets always attributed to the lioness but that was more properly human. Enhancing her physical aura, encircling her face like a corona around one of the stars she was watching, she wore a reddish mane that could have crowned a male lion.

Judging by nonessentials, astrologers made the same mistake about her that poets made when comparing humans and lions. By their rules she was not a lion but a ram. But she had no desire to live among sheep—even as their ruler—and had broken from the herd while a lamb.

In the age of two-dimensional photography, she might have been a model. She was large-eyed, sharp-featured, and small-breasted enough to be. In the age of three-dimensional holography, she never would have found a day's work in front of cameras that would have searched in vain for soft cushioning and found only unyielding angles.

It didn't matter. She never would have enshrined her outward appearance any more than she would have enshrined her internal arrangement. Just so long as both did what they were called on to do, she gave them required maintenance and otherwise left them to fend for themselves.

An alarm sounded, signifying that the time she had paid for in the sanctum was up. But she had already reached her decision. Taking a deep breath, she stretched, let out her breath with an exuberant squeal, then performed a somersault to align herself with the corridor to the changing room.

A few minutes later, once again possessing minimal weight, she climbed into her jumpsuit and ran a comb through her hair. Then she realized she'd better get home if she wanted time to get ready before her celebration. Today, April 15, was her birthday. Joan Darris was seventeen today.

She caught the first tube express back to El Capitán, took the tram back down the mountain on that end, and twenty minutes later was walking through campus, bypassing Auberon, Booth, and Clementine Avenues. Just past campus she turned onto Davis Avenue, and two blocks farther on entered the fifty-story building where she now lived.

It was a small, one-bedroom apartment with a clear view of Lake Goddard; a number of Dryer students lived here, along with students from the nearby Business annex of UAANP. Joan had lived in this apartment a little over a year and a half, and though compared with Helix Vista it was still puny, it was positively expansive after one small room at the Rubinsteins'. Besides, after three and a half years of kosher food, she was happy to be able to heat up a simple quiche Lorraine, without checking the package to make sure its cheese had originated in a soybean and its bacon had come from a pig genetically engineered to chew cud as well as walk with a cloven hoof. Life was complicated enough without having to worry about the nature of pigs' digestions. Still, since her birthday dinner was at the Rubinsteins', she didn't mind putting up with their foreign customs once again.

Since early in January, when she had completed the quadrivium at Dryer and been awarded her Bachelor of Fine Arts degree, Joan had been taking postgraduate master classes with Jaeger and supplementing her allowance from her father by playing roga on weekends at The Sure Thing, a mocha house up El Capitán. She remembered her first lesson with Jaeger after another of his students had told him she was playing there, two months ago. "Don't go back there," Jaeger had ordered her.

"I fully intend to," she'd answered. "It teaches me a style I can't learn from you."

"I don't intend to waste my time on a student who'll throw away her talent playing garbage."

"Then I suppose there's no lesson today?"

"If you're going back to that dive next weekend, no."

Joan had got up to leave.

Jaeger had called to her. "Do you really think you can reach your true potential without me?"

"Do you really think I can reach my true potential by letting anybody—even you—decide for me what I can and can't play?"

"If you know so much, why have you bothered studying with me at all?"

"If my artistic impulses are so unreliable, why have you bothered teaching me for close to five years?"

"You always get right to the point, don't you?"

Joan rarely scored off her teacher, and had smiled slightly. "Just like a laser, Wolfgang."

Jaeger had just groaned.

"We're wasting time," he'd said, then had started her lesson.

Neither of them brought up the subject again.

In fact, Joan's time at The Sure Thing was an attempt to work through an artistic problem that had plagued her since she'd begun lessons with Jaeger.

It was not that she wasn't learning a tremendous amount studying with the Maestro. But there was an unforeseen cost to her artistic development. Jaeger had a powerful voice—both literally, in his criticisms of her compositions, and figuratively, in his own—and all Joan's compositions had been dominated by his influence.

At first, everything she'd tried to compose was "no good." Then, everything she'd composed had come out looking like Jaeger. An attempt to eradicate his vision and find her own again had resulted in almost two years of not being able to compose at all. Finally, she had begun composing again, but everything she'd turned out was either so lightweight as to be little more than a lasegraphic pun—such short pieces as *Contract Bridge*—or so repressively formal as to be Chaldean, such as *Syncopations in Fifth*. It was only playing roga, allowing music to set the dances, that Joan felt free of Jaeger's overpowering genius and was able to breathe her own images again.

But it wasn't her night to play roga. After blowing out the candles on the birthday cake Mrs. Rubinstein had baked for her, it was her night to watch it. Astrid Rubinstein had managed to get two pairs of impossible-to-get passes to see Roland Church record a holovision program at Garmire Cathedral.

More accurately, Astrid's boyfriend, Moshe McCoy, had got them. He was a graduate student at Dryer, born and raised in St. Clive, who explained at dinner that he'd gotten the studio passes from Church's bass fortissimo player, Hill Bromley, a friend of McCoy's father.

Joan's date, another Dryer student named Édouard Casals, was more interested in McCoy's oxymoronic name, and hesitantly inquired about it on their way up El Capitán. "Don't worry about it," McCoy said. "Everybody asks, sooner or later. But there's no great mystery. My mother is Jewish and my father is Mere Christian."

"Where does that leave you?" Casals asked.

"Hard to say. I've been both baptized and *bar mitzvah*-ed. I qualify as both Christian and Jewish, depending on whose rule book you subscribe to."

"My mother says that you're Jewish," Astrid said, "because your mother is. That makes you kosher to date, as far as she's concerned."

"And since my father's family practices infant baptism, I qualify there also. See?"

"But isn't there a conflict of interest?" Joan asked.

"No more than there was for Jesus," McCoy said. "He was both *bar mitzvah*-ed and baptized too."

"I think you've just proved my point," Joan said.

"Did I? The conflict wasn't in the way He viewed Himself, but in the way other people viewed Him. Besides, the conflict between my parents is nothing compared with the differences between my paternal great-great grandparents before the Church unified. My great-great grandfather was green and my great-great grandmother was orange."

"What?" Casals asked.

"Irish Catholic and Irish Protestant."

"You've still lost me," said Casals.

"There was a civil war going on in Belfast at that time," McCoy explained. "When my great-great grandparents got married, it was a lot like *West Sidereal Story*."

"But if the inhabitants didn't get along together," Casals asked, "then why didn't half of them build another cylinder?"

McCoy looked disgusted. "This was back on Earth, before they emigrated."

"Oh." Casals looked sheepish.

"Wake up and smell the mocha," Astrid said. "Everyone knows that Irishland is back on Earth."

Joan exchanged glances with Moshe, but neither felt it necessary to correct her.

They arrived at Garmire an hour before the scheduled rolling time of twenty o'clock, and after being piloted to their pallets in the studio audience by a production-company seraph—who made sure they strapped in before flying off—they watched several dozen technicians setting up the Avocado Pit in aerial maneuvers that looked, more than anything else, like a Brushfire War dogfight.

When some of them cleared away, McCoy pointed to a large, muscular man with hair as red as Joan's, dressed only in black trunks and vest, who was running his hands along a cylindrical pipe about the length and diameter of a fence post. As his hands ran up and down the pipe, so ran the musical scales he was warming up with, at a pitch not much above that of a shuttle blasting off from Earth, and at a volume—comparing the amount of air involved— not much quieter. Joan felt a low rumble in the pit of her stomach as he played. "That's the bass fortissimist who gave us the passes," McCoy told them. "That's Hill Bromley."

Church's other backup musicians began warming up—his antithesist, percussionist, keyboarder, and two tenor fortissimists. At ten after twenty, they began rolling and Roland Church jetted in.

By some accounts, roga was the oldest form of lasegraphy, harking back to the days of planetarium shows and krypton-gas lasers, in the very infancy of the medium. But during the long rise to ascendency of classical lasegraphy performed in silence, music was an unwelcome guest in the laserium, looked upon much as an ecdysiast would be at a wedding. She would not be shown the door because she wasn't inherently entertaining; it was just that people would tend to lose track of the bride.

Along about the time Wolfgang Jaeger was finishing up *The Rainbow Vistata*, a young man named Thomas Sofer smuggled music back into the laserium through a side door when he premiered his lasegraphical accompaniment to Alexander Scriabin's 1911 symphonic composition *Prometheus*, which Scriabin had originally written to be performed with a color organ. Unlike the 1911 premiere, this one was a critical and popular success. Scriabin's music and Sofer's lasegraphy became the background to several holodramas . . . and several dozen HV commercials.

Over the next few decades, lasegraphers found there was extra money to be picked up composing lasegraphical accompaniments to other musical works, and the generation after the Colonial War found a home among the *bohs* at mocha houses, and at private parties, to perform the improvisational lasegraphy that had come to be called "roga."

Nobody was quite certain where the name came from. But it was thought that the term derived from "rogue" lasegraphy, combined with characteristic phrases that were loosely based on the ragas of Hindu music.

Roland Church, a thirty-two-year-old native Bantu from Uhuru with an unpronounceable Swahilian cognomen, had emigrated with his family to St. Clive while he was still a small child. He had adopted his *nom-de-lasegraphie* at fifteen, when he'd begun performing roga. His first backup musicians were three of his five brothers, who began playing with him when he was ten; he had later added his oldest sister and a blond girlfriend, Estelle, who became his first wife. By the time Roland Church was twenty, he had a second wife—consecutively, not additively—a new backup band (which retained only Estelle, his keyboarder), a long-term recording contract with LCAA, and two palladium albums. His career had not faltered in the twelve years since.

Joan, of course, had seen Church perform on holovision and—without telling Jaeger—had been buying his albums for years. But she knew there was a big difference between a live performance and one that could be stopped, redubbed, overdubbed, and edited. She even knew a case Jaeger had told her about in which some difficult passages in another lasegrapher's recording of one of Jaeger's vistatas had been cut in from Jaeger's own recording.

So Joan was doubly impressed when the hour-long program, from the moment Church jetted in, was recorded straight through, with no retakes, and that Church's performance was fully up to those found on his albums.

He was, she had to admit, quite good. While roga did not have the complexity, logic, subtlety, or pastoral beauty of classical lasegraphy, roga surpassed classical in sheer speed and energy—not unrelated, Joan suspected, to the "coca" in the mocha houses where roga grew up. Neither was there any of the standoffishness in the audience that characterized so many classical performances; the audience clapped in rhythm to the imagery, whistled their approval of a dialectical display of pyrotechnics, and brought the performance to a complete halt at the end of one of Church's silent riffs.

She knew the exhilaration a performer felt at such moments. She'd felt it herself during recitals she'd given while at Dryer ... and on weekends at The Sure Thing.

At the end of the program, McCoy led them back to the greenroom to thank their host.

They swam downstage with little problem—McCoy's name was on the guest list—but the list was long, the corridors were chaotic, and it required some care to make sure that one's foot did not end up in someone else's eye, or vice versa. Once inside the jam-packed greenroom, McCoy spotted his father's friend and introduced Bromley to his friends from Dryer. Then McCoy accidentally on purpose mentioned to Bromley that it was Joan's birthday.

"A birthday girl, eh?" Bromley said. The bass fortissimist reached up and grabbed a booted foot, pulling Roland Church down to eye level. He gestured at Joan. "A birthday girl," he told his boss.

"Hey, everybody!" Church shouted. "A birthday girl!"

"My God," Joan said, "I'm not the first one!"

"Hey, Estelle," Church said, "It's your turn. Lead off!"

And Church's keyboarder, his former wife, began singing *Happy Birthday*, soon joined by everybody in the greenroom and on out to the corridor.

When they got to, "How old are you now?" Church took pity on Joan and told them all to knock it off; everyone laughed and applauded, and the chaos resumed.

"And what can I get for the birthday girl?" Roland Church asked Joan.

"You wouldn't happen to have a hole for me to crawl into, would you?" she asked.

"Your wish is my command," Roland Church said.

The "hole" that Church commandeered for Joan was a canna-bistro a little down El Capitán called The Last Ditch. The entourage was kept down to Church and his current wife—and antithesist—Claire; Hill Bromley and Estelle—but they weren't really "with" each other, Estelle explained—the Birthday Girl; and her three friends from Dryer.

After they ordered—Church insisting on ordering the evening's second birthday cake for Joan—Estelle explained that her boss and

143

former husband had never had a birthday party until she'd given him one when they were married, and since then Church never let a birthday go by uncelebrated.

"He does this sort of thing to everybody," Claire Church went on. "On my last birthday, he got the entire audience singing to me in the middle of a performance."

After a plate of breaded mushrooms was set down, interrupting the birthday talk for a few seconds, Joan managed to get a word in to Church. "I think we have a teacher in common," she said. "Jack Malcolm."

"In common indeed—my comman, Jack," Church said. "Jack Malcolm is one massive friar, a *mass*ive friar. But if you're one of Jack's students, what are you doing so far from home?"

"I'm at Dryer now," Joan said, "studying with Jaeger."

"Now, there's a *real*ly massive friar," Church said, "the Wolf Hunter. For him to be teaching you, you must be pretty *mass*ive yourself."

"Well, someday."

"Don't let her fool you," Astrid said. "There isn't anybody at Dryer who can even come close to her."

"Astrid," Joan objected.

"Well, it's true! Isn't it, Moshe?"

"She plays rings around me," Moshe admitted.

"Hey, no glow, that's just *fine*," Church said.

"I'm just starting to study roga," Joan said. "Seriously, I mean; I've been buying your albums for years. I've been playing weekends over at The Sure Thing."

"My old alma mater," Church said. "I played there years ago, when I was just getting tight. Maybe sometime when I'm back here I can catch your set."

"Jesus," Casals said.

"Oh, I couldn't, not yet," Joan said. "I haven't been doing roga long enough to be really tight. Besides," she continued, "I'm going back to Earth in a few weeks."

"What?" Astrid said. "You didn't tell me—"

"I just decided this afternoon," said Joan.

"Well, look, princess," Church said. "My friar Hill, here, owns a mocha house back in Los Angeles, where I work out new material before we take it on the road. If you're ever out that way, give us a call there, and maybe come in and play for us."

"That's very generous," Joan said. "Thank you."

144

"Consider it as a favor I owe to our friar in Rainborough," Church said. "He told me to pass it on."

On the tram back down El Capitán, after splitting off from the others, Astrid started grilling Joan. "Have you told the Maestro yet that you're going back?"

"Tomorrow," Joan said.

"He's not going to like it. He wants you in the St. Clive Competition next April."

"It'll have to hold for a year. I've got business on Earth I can't put off. Besides, I don't have anything ready to enter."

"What about your first vistata?"

Joan shook her head. "Too many bad memories associated with it to use it in competition."

"Well, what about *Contract Bridge*?"

"Come on, Astrid. It's a joke, not a composition."

"It's precious," said Astrid. "I like it."

"Thanks, but you don't get the King of St. Clive to hand you a medal by being precious."

"What about *Clockwork*?"

"Too stiff," Joan said. "Let's face it, I'm a Molly Monochrome. I had one good idea for a vistata and that was it. I might as well stick to other people's compositions—or to roga."

"Seventeen," Astrid said, "and already flamed out."

"I don't know," Joan said. "But I don't think my teacher has to worry about my coming up with a new rainbow cadenza before he retires."

17

"I'VE BEEN WAITING for the other shoe to drop since you started roga," Wolfgang Jaeger said to Joan. "Well, don't stand there looking like a criminal. Sit down."

Jaeger's condominium, like one of his vistatas, was an exercise in unity. His architect and decorator, after long discussions with their client, had decided that since the Maestro would be using their creation to compose color sequences of his own, their thoughts should not impinge on the Maestro's in his own home. The entire penthouse—walls, carpets, furniture, and all but one *objet d'art*—was done completely in black-and-white. The exceptional *objet d'art* was the sculpture of Iris, the Rainbow Goddess, who watched over the entranceway.

The apartment's one structural oddity was a half-size Tiger Pit in the center of the living room with a dome raised into the ceiling. On the other side of the Tiger Pit from the entranceway were two cat-ercornered chairs. Jaeger gestured to Joan to take the white. He sat in the black.

"It doesn't have anything to do with roga," Joan said.

"I know," said Jaeger. "But roga is a symptom of why you're leaving."

Joan shook her head. "I've talked to lawyers back on Earth about my mother," she said. "While I can't try to win custody of her body until my next birthday—when I'd be drafted into the Federation Peace Corps—the Federation's Copyright Law—the next-of-kin clause—grants me the right to impregnate myself with one of my mother's cells. I'll deposit the surrogate with the vivarium, and au-thorize a cerebral abortion, in the sixth month. I'm hoping that by presenting my father and Vera with a *fait accompli*, without leaving them the excuse that they're responsible for a cerebral abortion, they'll have to give authorization for the transplant of my mother's brain into the already-brainless surrogate, once it's fully grown."

"Have you talked it over with them?"

"No. Vera especially might try to stop me if she knew. Since back on Earth I'm a minor, she might succeed."

"But why do this now, at the very beginning of your career?"

"I can't do it later," Joan said. "I have no intention of waiting al-most twenty years until I'm past the draft age before returning to Earth—my mother might be declared legally dead by then and her brain destroyed—or resisting the draft openly and being declared Touchable. Aside from the horror of it, as a Touchable I wouldn't have the right to sue for custody of my mother. But I don't intend to be drafted, either. *No*body *any*where has any claim on three years of my life, and I'd willingly press the button on a microwave oven to cook anyone who says they do. My only chance of saving my mother without sacrificing my career is to deposit my mother's sur-rogate before I'm eighteen, and to resume my residency out here so

I can legally inform the Federation that I've declared for extra-terrestriality before they can issue a draft notice."

"Do you intend to continue lasegraphy while you're pregnant?"

"Are you joking?" Joan said. "Just because I have to try saving my mother's life doesn't mean I'm giving up my own."

"You're taking a great risk," Jaeger said. "You know there are only two more years in which you'll be eligible to compete for the St. Clive Medal before you'll be past the age limit."

"I'm not risking all that much, right now," Joan said. "You know I haven't been able to compose anything up to competition level."

"That's what I meant when I said that roga is a symptom."

Joan nodded, suddenly alert. "Do you mind if I smoke?"

"I didn't know you did."

"I didn't want you to know." She pulled out a joynette.

Jaeger lifted a lighter out of his chair and lit it for her.

Joan took a toke and exhaled. "Wolf, I need the time away from you. I've been trying so hard to have my compositions avoid looking like imitation Jaeger that I haven't had any energy left to have them come out looking like original *me*."

"That's not your problem," Jaeger said.

"If it's not my problem, then whose is it?"

Jaeger laughed. "You didn't understand me. What I meant was that you solved the problem of imitating me years ago. All my students go through that phase. The bad ones never get out of it, and I send them packing. If imitation were all you were capable of, you wouldn't be here now. You've learned what it is I do in my compositions—the logic and the discipline—but you've used me, as I intended, as a point of departure. I know my characteristic phrasings. I see them all the time in the work of other lasegraphers; not only my students, mind you—I'm talking of lasegraphers who have been around almost as long as I have been. But my personality is not to be found in the work of Joan Darris. The trouble is, neither is *yours*. Do you know why?"

Joan took another toke, nervously, and shook her head.

"Well, I do."

He remained silent for so long that Joan was not certain that he hadn't fallen asleep with his eyes open.

"Aren't you going to tell me why?" Joan asked.

"I've been waiting for you to ask me that for two years," Jaeger said. "But now that I think about it, I realize that it's something in which I have no right to supersede your own introspection with my

147

speculations. But however long it takes you to figure out, I assure you that your natural gifts will enable you to deal with it."

Jaeger stood up, signaling an end to the conversation.

Joan stood also.

"I know that this is not the form of your beliefs about the way this universe works," Jaeger said, "but may God always be with you in your trials."

They hugged and kissed each other. Jaeger kissed Joan on both cheeks.

Joan snuffed out her joynette, then paused in the entranceway before the sculpture of Iris, and had the awful feeling that she might never see her teacher again. She tried to cover up her sudden emotion. "I didn't know that you believed in God," she said.

Jaeger smiled understandingly. "I didn't want you to know."

The weeks before a move are always hectic, as the following two were for Joan. She had to sublet her apartment through August, when her lease expired; this she accomplished with the help of a trimester student at the Business annex of UAANP. Then almost all her clothing was inappropriate back on Earth, so the more expensive items were divided up among Astrid, Debbie and another girl from Dryer, while the more ephemeral items were just thrown out. The task of replacing the lightweight and comfortable habitat styles with the more rigidly stylish, but far less comfortable, apparel now being worn in Newer York was a task Joan did not really enjoy.

Finally, there was the night before her departure, which she spent over at the Rubinsteins', avoiding saying goodbye to a family toward which she felt far more warmth than toward her own.

When Joan Darris, wearing a tightly cut grey business suit with matching beret, handbag, and high-heeled pumps, arrived back at Soleri Skyport on May Eve, the night before Beltane, she had two desires. The first was, so far as she knew, unquenchable: she wished Ad Astra had diplomats so she might have known one who could have given her *The Diplomat's Guide to Earth*—a work that so far as she knew didn't exist, and a glaring omission in the accumulated knowledge of humankind, so far as she was concerned. Her second desire was more practical and immediate: she wanted to get off her feet and into a hot bath. After five years in Valle de Sol's two-thirds-gee spin, her tolerance of Earth's unrelenting, now half-again-as-heavy gravity had worn off, though she felt that Newer York's thicker air seemed to help a little.

So when the Federation customs inspector asked her "Do you

have anything to declare?" Joan was too tired to say anything more devious than "Everything I've got with me, I suppose."

Naturally, she ended up in the Customs Supervisor's office for the next hour. She phoned Helix Vista, found everyone out but the domestic computer, and was told that the family's new pink Artemis limousine was on the way to the skyport to meet her. She spent the rest of the hour sitting on a bench and massaging her calves.

By the time it was straightened out, an additional half-hour after she finally got to speak to the supervisor, that except for new clothing everything she had with her—including her LCAA instrument—had been purchased more than a year before and was therefore exempt from import duties, Joan had already been holographed, brainprinted, inspected for three viral infections more common in the habitats than on Earth, and inoculated against two diseases she'd had immunity against since birth.

As she rode the slidewalk to the skymobile loading zone, a robot baggage cart rolling along on the ramp beside her, Joan was worn out, sore, and contemplating how many asteroid mines the Earth could provide if blown up properly.

When Joan reached the loading zone, she received a shock. It was only a Touchable woman, selling flowers to arriving passengers. At first Joan wondered how a Touchable could be out after dark, until it came to her that it was May Eve and Touchables were granted temporary immunity. Then Joan realized how quickly her mind had asked the appropriate question, and it brought home more profoundly than clothing, gravity, or red tape what returning to the planet meant.

Joan bought a box of mixed flowers from the Touchable, paying her an auragram and receiving a blessing for telling her to keep the change; then Joan's wristphone homed her in on the limousine, where she received a second shock. An athletic-looking blond boy was sitting in the bubble top, waiting for her. "My God," Joan said when she saw her oldest brother. "Mark, how long have you been waiting out here?"

Mark laughed. "My Goddess," he said. "You really have been in the colonies a long time!"

Joan got in, they kissed, and after the robot had loaded Joan's belongings, the Artemis departed on automatic for Helix Vista.

"I spoke to the domestic computer," Joan said. "Where is everyone?"

"They're all at the Astoria School tonight, Joanie," Mark said. "The second grade is putting on a production of *The Boys in the*

Band, and our littlest brother is playing Emory. You should see Delaney camp it up. He's hilarious. I left after the first act so I could pick you up."

"That was sweet," Joan said.

"The rest of the family circle is coming back home afterward to celebrate Beltane. I'll give you three guesses what 'maiden from the stars' is guest of honor."

"Lovely," Joan said. "But I hope my feet hold up. This gravity is killing me."

"In a week, it'll be as if you've never left."

Joan tended to doubt it, but held back her reservations. "So," she said. "How do you like Yale?"

"I'll survive," said Mark. "Another year, then law school. Vera says that if I keep up my grades, then right after I pass the bar I can go to work as her law clerk."

"Isn't she worried about being accused of nepotism?"

"Accusations from whom? She's Chief Justice now."

"I know, but doesn't that just make it worse?"

"Why should it? How else does anyone get anywhere?"

"I see your point," Joan said. "You wouldn't happen to have a joynette, would you? I ran out on the trip."

Mark gave her one, took one himself, and lit both.

"You know the twins just went andro," he said.

Joan toked and nodded. "Daddy told me in his last phone call."

Mark grinned. "They're calling themselves 'Nicque' and 'Vicque' now." He spelled out the names for her.

"Charming," Joan said dryly. "What about you? Still in blue, I see."

Mark nodded. "I tried going andro a few times in Sex Ed, but it didn't take. I just don't like it enough to give up women for good." He took a toke. "I wish to Goddess I did. It'll take forever to get a bench of my own as a comman."

Joan nodded. "Any interesting women friends?"

He shook his head. "Just in the dicteriat, along with everybody and his brother. Hey, you'll be going in around a year from now, won't you?"

"Well, I'll be eighteen next year," Joan said carefully.

"That's what I meant," said Mark. "You've really grown up since the last time I saw you, Joanie. You know, you've really filled out in all the right places."

"Thanks," Joan said. "You look like you've grown a head taller and have been lifting weights."

"A little," Mark said. "But it's mostly been playing squatball. I think I'll make first string next year."

Joan took another toke and nodded.

"It would be really funny if you and I ended up in the same dicteriat sometime, wouldn't it?"

Joan spent the next few seconds trying not to choke.

"What made you think of that?" she said sharply.

"Well, there's a guy on the first string who told me in the locker room that the computers made a mistake, one time, and he ended up getting assigned to his own sister."

Joan looked at Mark carefully. "What did he do?"

"What do you think?" Mark said. "He wasn't going to risk getting sent to the end of the line for another month. So he fucked her."

"Oh," Joan said. She looked at her brother more closely, pitying him for the kind of pressure he must be under, then added quietly but firmly, "I wouldn't believe everything you hear in the locker room. Your friend was probably just telling a story to keep up his reputation."

"I suppose," Mark said quietly.

They didn't talk much for the rest of the flight.

As it happened, the delay at customs had wasted so much time that the rest of the family circle had made it back to Helix Vista before the Artemis arrived with Joan and Mark. The next forty-five minutes were spent kissing; being kissed; assuring her younger brothers that no, you really couldn't fall from one edge of the cylinder to the opposite edge; and observing that her father and her brothers treated Vera exactly as they had once treated Eleanor—as if Eleanor Darris had never left Helix Vista at all.

Joan found it spooky watching Vera act as guest host for their mother; and worse, she had the eerie feeling that living in Eleanor Darris's house, with Eleanor Darris's husband, raising Eleanor Darris's other children, Vera Delaney had in some sense *become* Eleanor Darris, and as long as she was, she was no longer susceptible to the insecurity and lack of identity that had driven her to near-suicide.

Joan wondered if perhaps Vera's suicide attempt had been more successful than she had realized; whether in the lawn dome that night it was not Vera who had died, while the spirit of Eleanor Darris lived on in a body emptied of its soul.

Worst of all, Vera reacted toward Joan exactly as Eleanor once had—greeted her just as Eleanor would have, questioned her about her studies with Jaeger just as Eleanor would have, told her how good it was to have her back home just as Eleanor would have. The only indications that this was Vera Delaney and not Eleanor Darris were the occasional references to her work at Legos, Ltd., and the lack of references to work in a laserium. Joan was grateful for these indications: it prevented her from drifting into the comfortable delusion that had captured the rest of her family that Eleanor Darris was still with them, and relieved them of any need to rescue her from her icy sleep.

The only person Joan was certain would not have been taken in could not be there tonight: His Gaylordship Wendell Darris was in the home stretch of the most difficult electoral race he had ever run, and was too busy campaigning for a sixth term in the House of Gentry to be with his family for the holidays.

Just before midnight, Vera donned her green High Priestess robes and brought the family circle together for the Beltane Sabbat, a celebration of the Maiden Goddess' coming of age. Aside from Wendell, and in addition to her own father, seven brothers, and Gramps, the rest of the Darris clan was here: Joan's Grandmother Kate, Aunt Melentha and Uncle Rudy, their daughter Elizabeth—two years younger than Joan—and Joan's male cousins, of whom the only one she found at all personable was twelve-year-old Jeremy. At the appropriate time, Joan was called to deliver the "I who am the beauty of the Green Earth," and she had the odd feeling while reciting the words of the Wiccen ritual that the meaning was exactly the same as the *bat mitzvah* she had seen Debbie Rubinstein recite back in Nova Paulus. She wondered why there were always religious wars. Retiring at last to her old bedroom, she found it seemingly unchanged since she'd left it, five years before.

Beltane was on a Friday this year, so the three-day weekend began earlier rather than ended later. The family ran around their Maypole, and watched the ceremonies on the holy around the much-larger Maypole in Moscow. After the feasting, Joan stayed on the sidelines—still tired from fighting the gravity—while her family spent the evening playing touch squatball. Eventually Joan became bored with this and retired into the house to watch *I Love Lucifer* on the holy.

Saturday, May 2, Joan borrowed her father's company limousine and spent the day with Jack Malcolm in Rainborough. She demonstrated to him what she had learned, told him anecdotes about her studies at Dryer and with Jaeger in particular, and brought him up to date on her recent meeting with Roland Church.

Sunday, May 3, Joan decided it was time to start getting some exercise to speed up her acclimation; she took out a black stallion named Hierophant from the family stables and spent several hours on the Darrises' bridle paths alone. When she returned, a bit sore in her thigh muscles but definitely invigorated, she took a little time to visit with Lazy Gopher, who was on his last legs, as ponies go.

The rest of Sunday Joan spent in the lawn dome, practicing.

On Monday, May 4, Joan flew to Manhattan in the morning with her father, telling him she wanted to shop, and as soon as she left him at the Darris Tower, she grabbed a skycab to Forest Hills. She spent several hours at the vivarium filling out legal forms, and another hour undergoing medical examinations before the staff physician and insurance underwriters would assent to the procedure. Then, while she was waiting until she was needed, Joan visited her mother's capsule in the Hall of Preservation.

The attendant told her that it was exactly like being asleep, except there weren't any dreams. All these horror stories on the holy about the soul endlessly trying to escape its frozen body were just nonsense. When the sleeper waked, it would be as if no time had passed at all.

When Joan left the Forest Hills Vivarium that afternoon, after a necessary hour in Manhattan making unnecessary purchases, she was just on time to meet her father at the Darris Tower to return home with him. But what Stanton did not know was that since that morning Joan had become most assuredly pregnant with an ovum that, properly handled, would someday be her mother.

18

JOAN HAD TAKEN very thorough precautions to make certain that no one from her family would discover either the fact of her pregnancy or the specific nature of it before she wanted them to know.

To begin with, Joan had invoked a little-used clause in the Federation Copyright Law—which she'd discovered while still in Ad Astra in discussions with a lawyer from Earth—that forbade the Forest Hills Vivarium from disclosing to anyone, under threat of losing its operating license, that a surrogate was being grown. The clause had been added to the law some years before during a period when murder prosecutions were relying on gangsters' not discovering that witnesses whom they thought dead were being brought back from the grave to testify against them.

Secondly, Joan had shown the vivarium's assistant director—as proof of kinship to its charge—a birth-record printout that was authentically her own in all respects but one: it showed her birth date as one year earlier, to bypass the need for parental consent. Joan had also "casually let it slip" that she was looking forward to entering the service in two years, when her student deferment was up.

Third of all, to make certain that no one from the vivarium would try to reach her at Helix Vista, Joan had listed her permanent address as 14010 Captain's Row, Valle de Sol, Ad Astra—the Rubinsteins' house—and she had previously instructed Astrid to call her person-to-person collect if anything important-sounding was sent to her there.

Finally, Joan intended staying at Helix Vista only for the first seven or so weeks of her pregnancy, before she would show, and had already sent a deposit for a five-month retreat at the LASER Institute's Hermitage on Mt. Shasta beginning at Midsummer solstice.

What Joan had failed to take into account, nor could the lawyers advising her—of necessity unfamiliar with her family—have foreseen, was that the Chief Justice of Legos, Ltd., was not bound by the same legal restrictions as an ordinary citizen—or even Federation Monitors. Within seventy-two hours of Joan's impregnation at the Forest Hills Vivarium, its insurance underwriters—as required by law—had registered the operation in Federation computers. Once it was there, a standing request for any listings under the surnames "Collier," "Darris," "Delaney," "Duroux," "Seymour," and several others forwarded the registration to Her Honor Vera Collier Delaney at her courthouse offices in Newer York.

She found a listing for the registration report among her mail on Friday morning. She punched it onto her terminal.

Vera looked at the report and turned ashen. "So that's why she came back," she said softly to herself.

"I'm sorry, Your Honor?" Vera's clerk said.

154

"Hmm? Oh, nothing, Ted. Why don't you take a mocha break? I need some time alone."

"You're due in conference with Justice Duroux at ten."

"Call me at a quarter to."

The boy left and Vera sat reading the report carefully, growing angrier by the second. Rape it, it wasn't fair! Joan had everything she wanted in life: her career on the laser. Now this *half*-sister of hers—a half-truth, since Joan was Vera's half-sister while Vera was Joan's full sister—was going to bring their mother back and take away the only happiness Vera had ever known. Just when she'd finally got her life in some semblance of order, the whole cloneraping battle would begin all over again. Joan hadn't even the decency to discuss the issue with her.

Oh, she'd loved her mother as much as Joan, Vera told herself; but let the dead past bury its dead! Who knew what her mother might do, even sixteen years hence, when she found out that she and Stanton had decided against reviving her?

But this thought came perilously close to causing Vera more guilt than she allowed herself these days, and she shut it off quickly.

Her sister had played it very shrewdly, Vera thought, trying to finesse her into a situation where she couldn't object in front of the family. But Joan would soon find out she was a poor amateur at this sort of game—no, strike that: she wouldn't even know what hit her.

Vera studied the registration carefully. She looked at the date of birth listed for Joan—was that right? No, it couldn't be; she had to have made herself a year older to bypass her father's consent. Was this sufficient? But Vera soon realized that it would be far too easy for Joan to provide proof of her actual age and put off her fate another year—far longer than was needed. She would have to find another way.

Vera found it two lines farther down.

14010 Captain's Row, Valle del Sol, Ad Astra.

The fool had listed herself in a legal document on file with the Federation as a "permanent resident" of the habitats. This would do nicely.

Vera instructed her terminal to reprint the registration report on the left side of the terminal and to list the address of the Upper Hudson Parish office of the Ministry of Universal Service on the right side. This done, she ordered the address stored, the right side cleared again, and began dictating a short letter:

155

The enclosed document has come to my attention. As an officer of the Upper Manor, it is my duty to inform you that the said Joan Darris, a native of Earth, has falsified her age on this document—seemingly in your favor—but with the actual intent of carrying a pregnancy through to term and returning to her "permanent" address outside your jurisdiction before the usual draft age. Under Paragraph Five, Section Two of the Federation Universal Service Act—which states that a female citizen of the Federation is liable for universal service at the convenience of the Federation from any time between menarche and menopause—I suggest immediate induction as a precautionary and disciplinary measure. Address notice to Joan Seymour Darris at HELVISTA, Hudson.

As per Federation Statute No. 39,557, correspondence regarding a potential inductee between a judicial officer and M.U.S. may not be reproduced, released, or used in evidence.

VERA COLLIER DELANEY
Chief Justice, Legos, Ltd.
"LEX SCRIPTA, LEX TERRAE"

Vera hesitated only a second, just long enough to feel sufficiently guilty to qualify in her own mind as a human, then ordered, "Transmit both sides to stored address with my verification code."

"POSTED," her terminal printed out; and "Posted," it said aloud.

Vera's intercom sounded; she brought up the image of her clerk. "It's a quarter to, Your Honor."

"Yes, Ted?"

"Your ten-o'clock conference with Justice—"

"On my way," Vera said.

Vera checked her hair and makeup, slipped on her jacket, and thought that she must be forgetting something. Just before she stepped out the door, her terminal said, "Correspondence received, M.U.S. Upper Hudson."

Ted ran after Vera before she'd reached the lift and tossed her the briefcase Her Honor had forgotten. Vera slipped it into her jacket pocket. By the time she reached the ground, Vera was convinced that she'd only been doing her civic duty.

Joan lay on her bed in her old room at Helix Vista, playing with her Slinky. She'd found the toy while rummaging through her clothes closet to make room for new wardrobe.

Joan played the Slinky back and forth between her hands, feeling the weight build up first in one hand, then in the other, and wondered why such a simple, silly little toy was so much fun. It was like a roga phrase in miniature, she thought. A coiled spring built up tension on one side, then released it and built up tension on the other, always searching for a center of gravity. Back and forth it went, with the rhythmic certainty of a heartbeat, or a Chaldean metronome.

She wondered why it was only in roga that she could let her feelings run free. Jaeger was right. She hadn't managed to get any of her feelings into her compositions since her first vistata. Could it be that she was avoiding dealing with her feelings—bringing them into her view, into her work—because of the shock she'd experienced with the composition at its premiere? Was roga a safe retreat—a sanctum—for her, since it was incapable of representing abstract ideas the way classical lasegraphy did? Was this what Jaeger had seen in her—that she was afraid to represent anything meaningful to her because it might cause her pain? Had Jaeger seen her true color—and it was yellow? Was this the judgment her teacher had refused to render?

She played the Slinky back and forth between her hands. It was a spiral, such as Jaeger had used at the finale of his *Resurrection Vistata*. What had he said the spiral meant? A novelist-philosopher from the last century of the old millennium had written that the line was the best geometric symbol of the pursuits of Man because it was an abstraction rarely found in nature, which relied more on the always-repeating cycles represented by the circle. But Jaeger said that this philosopher had seen only part of the truth, looking at the symbolism in terms of two-dimensional shapes, rather than three-dimensional forms.

If you looked at a circle flat-side on, Jaeger said, you saw a closed, continuous loop; but if you shifted around ninety degrees, the circle could just as easily be an ascending spiral. And since every cycle in nature was always a little different from the previous one—each orbit of a planet around its sun at a different space in its galaxy, each cycle of a galaxy at a different place in its cluster, each spring season in the year different from the resurrection of the previous year—Jaeger had thought that the spiral—a synthesis between the circle and the straight line—was the most appropriate symbol of all.

Joan thought about it. The line arguing against the circle, forming into the spiral. It had the proper dialectic of a roga phrase. Line, circle, spiral. Thesis, antithesis, synthesis. Jaeger, of course, disliking roga as much as he did, had never seen it in these terms. The sequence was completely missing from *The Resurrection Vistata*.

It was so obvious to her. She began making lists in her mind of various spirals: spiral nebulae, the double helix of the DNA molecule, spiral staircases, the spiral path the soul was supposed to take on its way to heaven, the path of an object caught in a vortex or whirlpool, the spiral that appeared when one divided a rectangle into squares and continuously drew the resulting radii—Jaeger had used this last in the finale of *The Rainbow Vistata*. Why, the very house she was in right now was a representation of that principle, combining the ancient Chaldeans'—the real ones'—rainbow ziggurats—the Tower of Babel that the Rubinsteins had told her about—with a spiral. Even Helix Vista . . .

Joan laughed. Then she left the Slinky behind on the bed, walked over to her practice console, and switched it on. Helix Vista, of course. Had she gone away for five years just so she could see with some perspective—some distance—what had been staring her in the face since she was born?

It couldn't be called anything else but *The Helix Vistata*.

She switched the console into record mode and began making some initial sketches.

Let's see. The first movement would have to state the dialectical roga phrase. Start with the thesis—the circle? No, the *line*. Classical development of its implications. What color sequence? A standard progression would do for a start. Okay, then come back with the antithesis—the circle; now develop it, reverse the coloratura; now something dramatic—perhaps a roga segue—to introduce the rotating synthesis of the two into—

"Joan?"

She didn't even look up. "Not right now, Vicque."

"It's Nicque," her brother said. "And it can't wait. There's a Monitor here to see you."

Joan finally looked up. "Come on, Nicque. I don't have time for jokes right now."

"I'm not joking."

"Well, what does he want me for?"

"How should I know? But he's pretty good-looking. Maybe he wants to take you out."

"Well, if he does, he's come at the wrong time." Joan flipped her console from record mode to standby and followed Nicque down the lift.

"Can I have him when you're through with him?" Nicque asked.

"You'll have to ask him out yourself," Joan said as she went to the foyer.

The Monitor, a young, dark-haired man with striking blue eyes that matched his uniform, was as good-looking as her brother had indicated. "Yes?" Joan said.

"Joan Seymour Darris?"

"That's me."

The Monitor handed Joan a foil envelope. "I'm serving you with this officially," he said.

"What is it?" Joan asked.

"Open it."

Joan ran her thumb along the foil and the envelope opened. She took out a piece of official stationery, which began, as these things had always begun, "Greetings from the First Lady of Earth. You are hereby ordered to report for a physical examination to determine your fitness to serve . . ."

The Monitor didn't quite have to catch her.

"Next."

A dark-haired girl got up from the bench and went down a long corridor into the examination cubicle with its light flashing. There was one more girl ahead of Joan, who was dressed as if she'd come here for a wedding. Looked at in the right way, perhaps she had.

Customs must have given them some sort of warning, Joan thought miserably as she sat on the bench in the Poughkeepsie office of Universal Service, waiting for her physical. It was about the two-hundredth time that she'd considered the thought in the two weeks since she'd received her notice. She suspected it would not be the last.

Joan looked around the waiting room. Drab civilian clerks sat at rows of computer terminals. One wall displayed the flags—in descending order—of the World Federation, the North American Concord, and Hudson Parish. On the opposite wall was emblazoned the Federation Peace Corps official motto. Joan had learned the motto's origin from a history professor at Dryer. It seemed to her a poor joke on the world. The motto was "MAKE LOVE, NOT WAR."

"Next."

The bridesmaid on the bench next to Joan—or was she now the bride?—got up and walked down the aisle to the cubicle with the flashing light. I'm next, Joan thought, even while she was still wondering whose sick sense of humor was responsible for a pregnant virgin's catching the bouquet.

Joan's ability to thwart the draft had dead-ended immediately. After consulting with her lawyers—*in corpore,* this time—Joan had learned that she had, in fact, been liable for the draft since her first menstruation at thirteen, and that the draft age was merely the *de facto* earliest age a girl would be drafted. The only reason Joan had received her notice prematurely was the Ministry of Universal Service's administrative judgment that as a long-term resident of the colonies Joan was a particularly high risk for evasion; as a simple precaution it had issued a jeopardy summons.

Normally, such an early summons might be fought with a plea for a student deferment. Such deferments were routinely granted up to age twenty-five. But Joan could not qualify. She had already received her bachelor's degree, she was not currently engaged in postgraduate work regarded as essential, and her idea that she might claim to be engaged in detached postgraduate study at the Dryer School not only would fall on deaf ears, but more than likely would confirm their view that she was leaning toward extraterrestriality.

Neither, with a jeopardy assessment on file, was there any possibility that she would be granted a deferment to carry her pregnancy to term.

This left only the possibility of claiming conscientious-objector status, which also turned out to be a *cul-de-sac.* Such exemptions were granted only to religious orders of Lesbian Wiccens—a small, but politically powerful sect; Joan had no provable link to any such sect, nor could she establish one in time, even if she'd wanted to. As for Christian orders, those left on Earth had either accepted the secular view propagated by the Peace Corps that their service was a charitable duty performed to prevent war, or accepted the life of a Touchable as witness to their faith. Those Christians whose beliefs were irreconcilable with the Federation's policies had long ago emigrated to the colonies, the largest single exodus building up the St. Clive habitats to a population of a quarter-billion over the past half-century.

Joan had learned immediately that her father, brothers, grandmother, and other relatives had never considered the possibility that Joan wouldn't serve. Vera cannily pointed out to Joan that even their mother had served. Ever since the Colonial War, when there had been suspicion that family sympathies lay with their financial interests in the colonies, the Darrises had always bent over backward to establish their patriotism to Earth—hence Eleanor's volunteer work for the U.S.O. after her marriage to Stanton.

The one relative Joan thought might have both the sympathies and the means to help her was Wendell; but Vera had anticipated this direction and informed Joan that anything in which she might try to involve His Gaylordship would be at her uncle's expense. Did Joan really wish to involve Wendell in the political scandal of obtaining special privileges for a relative while he was engaged in the fight to save his career? Vera even obliquely suggested that since Wendell had always pushed his party toward a free-trade policy with the habitats, Joan's premature notice might have been the result of action by His Gaylordship's protectionist enemies in Federation customs, trying to trap him through his favorite niece into just such a false move.

Vera's suggestion worked. Joan had refrained from seeking out Wendell—not for the sake of politics, or her belief in Vera's conspiracy theory, but for the sake of the only animate relative who shared her love of the laserium.

But this might not have prevented Joan from attempting escape to Ad Astra, where she could have carried the surrogate until she could have placed it in a vivarium, had she not learned in her consultations one more odd fact. Joan Darris, on Earth at seventeen, was a minor and legally unable to sue on her own behalf to obtain custody of her mother's deanimate body. Joan Darris, draft evader living in Ad Astra, would be a permanent fugitive from Earth—declared Touchable *in absentia*—and being unable to sue for custody of her mother's body, would have to rely on her father's and Vera's goodwill for her mother's reanimation—goodwill that had been glaringly absent so far.

But Corporal Joan Darris would reach legal majority on Earth immediately upon induction, and would be free to institute legal proceedings for custody at once.

"Next."

Joan got up from the bench and walked down the corridor to the cubicle third from the end on the left, with its light flashing.

Inside the cubicle, a robot nurse instructed Joan to strip completely and get up on the examining table. The next hour was spent under the robot's direction in all sorts of routine measuring, testing, holography, sonography, radiography, probing, scanning, and scrutinizing that the medics could trust to be done routinely, without the application of human intelligence. Joan also provided blood, urine, fecal, and tissue samples, as well as smears from several parts of her anatomy. A human physician never came in at all; Joan was simply told to get dressed and report to Room 101.

"Room 101" had a talking door that said, to anyone who came within a meter, "Dr. Chertok's office. Please go into the waiting room and sit down." Joan went into the waiting room and sat down along with a half-dozen other women her age. A roga set with all the juice squeezed out of it was being played on a holoscreen; Joan always found LAZAK depressing—even though she knew the commercial lasegraphers who recorded it made a small fortune from it—and did her best not to watch.

Twenty-five minutes later, another robot nurse instructed Joan to go into Dr. Chertok's office. It was merely a parlor with a desk, comfortably furnished with plush chairs, a couch, and a mocha machine. Dr. Chertok, a homey-looking woman whom Joan assigned a rough age of eighty, sat behind a desk looking at her terminal. "Please sit down," she said without looking up from her display, "Ms. Darris, isn't it?"

"Yes." Joan took the chair opposite the desk. "Do you mind if I smoke?"

The doctor looked up. "It's a bad habit, particularly unwise in the first trimester of pregnancy."

Joan started slightly. "Are you suggesting that I'll be allowed to carry my pregnancy to a point where it matters?"

"No. Your current pregnancy will, of course, be terminated. The advice is simply for a time, three years from now, when you'll be free to have as many babies as you wish."

"I see," Joan said.

"I don't," Dr. Chertok said. "You're an unusual case, Ms. Darris. I don't get very many women sitting in that chair who are simultaneously pregnant and the possessor of an unruptured hymen."

"May I smoke, now?" Joan asked.

"Hmm? Oh, go right ahead." The doctor reached over and speeded up the ventilation a bit.

Joan lit up and didn't say anything.

"Ms. Darris?"

"Yes?"

"Aren't you going to tell me?"

"I didn't know you were asking," Joan said.

"Couldn't you have assumed my question?"

"I'm not here by choice, Dr. Chertok. I'm not assuming anything anymore."

Dr. Chertok scribbled a note on a pad in front of her. Joan, who had found it useful in zero gravity to be able to read upside down, read to herself, "Passive-aggressive tendencies."

"Are you a psychiatrist, Dr. Chertok?"

Dr. Chertok smiled. "You're an extremely bright woman, Ms. Darris."

Joan inclined her head slightly.

"Why do you resent the service, Ms. Darris?"

"I don't resent it," Joan said. "I abhor it."

"Is that why you've chosen artificial impregnation? Because you're opposed to sex?"

"I have no idea whether I'm opposed to sex or not," Joan said. "I have no experience to judge from, as you just got through pointing out."

"Pardon me for a moment," Dr. Chertok said. She turned back to her terminal and typed in a question; an answer came back in seconds, "I'm sorry," she said. "I can see that you're upset because the service will require you to postpone the recovery of your mother."

Joan looked startled for the second time in a few minutes. "You have access to *that?*"

"Why, yes," Dr. Chertok said. "Is there some reason I shouldn't?"

"I demanded full confidentiality," Joan said.

"Such procedures are always on file with the government," Dr. Chertok said, "though it is rare for us to be allowed access."

Joan took another toke. "I see," she said tightly. A suspicion arose in her mind. "How could you have obtained access, then?"

"That's a question to address to the Ministry's Counsel General," Dr. Chertok said, "but at some point a court order must have been issued. Such files are kept sealed unless unlocked by a judge."

A notion that Joan had filed away as "impossible" was suddenly refiled under "likely." But it didn't change her opinion of Vera in the least.

"You're a great boon to the service, Ms. Darris," said Dr. Chertok. "With a young woman otherwise in good health, as you are, we sometimes have to spend thousands of auragrams—and use up to six months of service time—to perform reconstructive surgery on a face, or improve a figure, or straighten a set of teeth. We won't have to do anything of that sort with you."

"Does the Ministry pay a kickback to my ancestors?" Joan asked.

Dr. Chertok laughed. "If you maintain your sense of humor for the next three years, you'll do just fine. Thank you, Ms. Darris, that's all. You can pick up your induction orders at the main desk up front."

That evening after the family's dinner, Joan cornered her sister alone, reading in the discotheque. "I want a straight answer," Joan said. "Did you arrange to have me drafted?"

Vera shut off her reader. "What ever gave you such an idea?"

"Did you think I wouldn't find out? With the vivarium's registration report on my pregnancy in my draft file?"

"A pregnancy registration? What in the world are you talking about? Are you saying you're pregnant?"

Joan looked Vera straight in the eye; Vera met her gaze straight on. "You know very well I am," Joan said, "and in what manner and for what purpose. The registration report on my impregnation was on file with the Federation where only a judge would have had legal access to it."

"So you jump to the hasty conclusion that I must be that judge?" Vera said haughtily. "Do you think that Wendell's political enemies wouldn't have judges of their own they could use?"

"If you knew I was pregnant with Mom's surrogate, it would have been a natural move for you to stop me any way you could."

"And on this circumstantial evidence, and amateur psychology, you build a case against me?"

"I see that you're not surprised when I mention that I'm pregnant with Mom's surrogate."

"It was a logical conclusion when you mentioned 'pregnancy' and 'the vivarium,'" Vera said. "Honestly, Joan, you'd never make a lawyer. You try to badger me into admitting that I'm involved somehow in getting you drafted, just because some report is on file in the wrong place, without even bothering to research the simple fact that no evidence pointing to the source of the file would be allowed to be entered—" Vera stopped suddenly.

Joan smiled.

Vera took a breath and smiled back. "I withdraw that last opinion," she said. "You'd make an excellent lawyer. I've never seen a more skillful cross-examination."

"Shall we cut out the compliments and get down to business?" Joan said.

"We have no business to discuss," Vera replied. "You know as well as I do that you were planning to escape back to the colonies before your draft notice. I was merely doing my duty as an officer of the Upper Manor—regardless of any family sentimentality."

"That wasn't your motivation and you know it."

"I know no such thing, so how can you?"

"Why don't we tell Wendell and let him decide?"

"Go right ahead, if you wish to make more of a fool out of yourself than you're already doing. Do you think that even His Gaylordship won't recognize that I was merely saving him from political scandal? Scandal which still could lose him the election, if you talk?"

"I won't argue the point," Joan said, "since both of us know that Wendell is the only other person walking around on this planet, aside from me, who sees right through your self-deceptions. I'll offer you a straight trade. You withdraw your objection to transplanting Mom's brain into a surrogate body that I'll supply as soon as I get out of the service, and I'll not only go through the Peace Corps without a peep like a good little girl, but I'll never mention to anyone, including Dad, who was responsible for turning me in to Universal Service."

"You can go right to the caldron," Vera said.

"I'll fight you, Vera," Joan said. "I'll make a big stink about it in court. You'll find yourself with my father on one side and me on the other, crushed between a meteor and the moon."

"Go ahead," Vera said. "Your father is just as aware as I of why it's better that our mother not be revived so long as he and I are living together. As for court, you'll find out that this is one squatball course where I own the squatball, the nets, and the lariats."

Vera turned on her reader again, but held down the pause control. "Enjoy the service, dear," she said. "I think it will do you some good to think of something other than your selfish desires for a change. And I definitely think it's about time you had to give up your childish obsession of playing with colored lights, for once, and learned what it means to be a woman." Vera released the pause control and began reading the disc again.

Joan took the lift up to her bedroom and prostrated herself on her bed. She wished Vera hadn't sounded so cloneraping much like her mother.

ONE MORE ACT was left that Joan Darris felt she had to perform before her induction in two weeks, and she went about it—as she did everything else—wholeheartedly and systematically. In some respects it was an archaic and futile gesture, of the sort she had seen in countless period holodramas, with no meaning anyone on Earth could take seriously these days. But Joan lived her life by injecting her own meaning into empty symbols, and there was one more symbolic act that she decided she owed herself.

The Federation Peace Corps might very well be impressing her into working its fields for the next three years, but she was not going to hand over *droit du seigneur* as well. Her mind, her spirit, and her soul were her own, and by the time the lord came to claim his harvest, Joan would make sure that the best he could hope for was damaged goods.

The only question was whom she liked well enough to gift-wrap her virginity for as a present.

It was not an easy problem. Living at Helix Vista in virtual purdah, she just did not know that many single commen. If Moshe McCoy had been on Earth, she would probably have asked Astrid if she could borrow him for the night. She considered Jack Malcolm, age difference and all, but decided that no matter how much she liked and respected him, to try shifting him from the role of teacher to that of lover not only would place a strain on their friendship, but would imply promises she was not willing to make. Incest was out for similar reasons: Mark might just as well go back to the squatball course. Finally, she was not about to attempt a blind pickup, for reasons involving both taste and prudence. Not only did she have no experience in making a line decision on that field, but it would be too much like granting the world's premise without a fight.

She thought about it for a few days, then decided on a course of action. There were built-in problems, and it was not sure that she would reach her intended outcome, but there were secondary and tertiary aspects that appealed to her, so she proceeded full speed.

On Saturday night, June 6—approximately thirty-six hours before her scheduled induction—Joan made her move.

Getting away from Helix Vista turned out not to be any problem. Her father and Vera were going hunting that night, and were taking

Stanton's company limousine; the family's pink Artemis was left at home. Since the skymobile was not preprogrammed to accept voice instructions from her, Joan simply told the Helix Vista domestic computer—which was—to relay orders to the Artemis that she would be taking it out that evening. Inasmuch as neither Helix Vista nor the Artemis had been instructed to disobey such an order, she got use of the family limousine without a hitch. And since Mark was away at Yale, the twins had their own wings, and Zack was sitting for his younger brothers that night so Gramps could take the evening off, there was no competition.

Joan didn't think her father would particularly mind if his daughter flew out for a fling before leaving to the service; but if he did, what would he possibly do before she left on Monday? Ground her till she left?

She found the comman she was looking for sitting in the canna-bistro of a roga cabaret called The Dichroic Scale in the avant-garde section of the Bronx. She was sure it was he even though he had grown a mustache since the holograms she had used to find him had been taken; still, she recognized him. It had not been hard to track him down once she found his home address: he had left a message on his apartment's computer telling any callers where he would be for the evening. Joan guessed he didn't consider himself a target for burglary.

The Dichroic Scale had both cover charge and minimum; Joan also had to show her false birth-record printout before she could get in. The roga wasn't scheduled to start for another hour, so it was not yet crowded. Joan found a small table facing her target and sat down. When he caught her glance, she smiled.

"Do you come here often?" he asked, then laughed. "Goddess, that's a stupid cliché. Shall I try again?"

"Why not?" Joan said. "In squatball there's five down before you're out. You've asked two questions, so you're down two."

"Let's see. 'A lot of weather we're having lately'?"

Joan shook her head. "The amount of weather is a constant; it just changes forms."

"Ah, a Linguistic Analyst," the comman said. "I can see I'll have to upgrade my approach. How about 'What would you say are the metaphysical implications of the early-Renaissance philosopher Carson's statement that "If you buy the premise, you buy the bit"? ' "

"I would say—and do—that if you're going to start calling early-Renaissance television comics philosophers, you might start by asking whether McMahon was Carson's Boswell. You have one more down," Joan said.

The comman looked at her thoughtfully. "How about 'May I buy you a toke?' "

"You see?" Joan said. "That wasn't so hard, was it? My table or yours?"

"Yours," he said, moving over and signaling to the cannabist.

"I'm Joan," she said.

"Andrew."

"Do your friends call you 'Andy' or 'Drew'?"

"The commen call me Andy, the andros call me Drew."

"What do women call you?"

"Mostly, they don't."

"Self-pity?" Joan asked.

"Self-honesty," he answered.

"Well, Andrew," Joan said. "If you'll allow me to ask you some questions without asking any in return, your luck will have changed."

His eyebrows raised.

"Just one question," he said.

"All right, one."

"You're not working for the Monitors—or anyone else—as a police siren, are you?"

"No, I'm not," Joan said. "And you don't get to ask why you're so lucky tonight. Just leave it that I think you're acute. Deal?"

"Deal."

The cannabist arrived and took their orders.

"What do you do for a living, Andrew?" Joan asked.

"I teach guitar," he said.

"Do you like it?"

"It keeps the rent paid."

"I gather you'd rather be doing something else."

"You gather correctly."

"Then why do it?"

"Because the only strings attached are on the guitar."

"Seven points," Joan said.

The cannabist arrived with their tokes. Andrew paid him.

"You remind me of someone," he said.

"Someone you liked?" she asked.

He nodded. "Someone I could never have."

"Someone whom you would have allowed strings," Joan said.

"Someone who wouldn't have pulled them," he said.

168

He and Joan toked simultaneously.

"You've been bitter for a long time, Andrew," Joan said.

He nodded again. "Twelve years."

"What happened twelve years ago?"

"I was fired from the only career I'd ever wanted."

"Did you deserve to be?"

"Yes," he said. "I failed in a trust that had been placed in me, and let my employer down very badly."

"Why did you do this?"

"I fell ill," he said. "I've never wanted any responsibilities since."

"My skymobile is outside," Joan said.

"My flat is two blocks from here,'" Andrew said. "I live alone."

His apartment was a studio, medium-sized, comfortable, but not very modern. A pair of music stands in the corner, and a guitar hanging on the wall, attested to his current livelihood.

After they got inside, and the door was closed, he turned to look at Joan. "Sing a song for me, Andrew," she said.

"All right." He went to the corner and took the guitar off the wall, spending some seconds tuning it. "What would you like to hear?"

"Do you know *Going to St. Clive*?"

"Is the President andro?" he asked.

He began singing,

> "As I was going to St. Clive
> I met a man one-hundred-five
> Who's with his ma, one-hundred-thirty,
> Who's with her pa, one-hundred-sixty.
> Sixty, thirty, hundred-five—
> I hear they're living in St. Clive,
> But how long can they stay alive?"

He sang it in a clear Irish tenor, with perfect intonation, and had no trouble at all with the words, singing them faster and faster and faster until finally, out of breath, he hit a final chord on "alive" and stopped.

He took a moment to catch his breath, then said, "Any other requests?"

"Show me your bed, Andrew."

"Bed," he ordered, and a section of the floor opened up to show a bed sunken into the carpet.

"Anything else?"

Joan smiled. "If you don't mind, I think I'll let you take the initiative from here."

"Have you had your shots?" he asked.

"I'm already pregnant," she said.

"This is going to be interesting," he said, rehanging his guitar.

They spent the next twenty minutes caressing each other and undressing, raising each other's passion, until there came a moment when both were naked, and as ready as they were going to be.

At his first attempt to enter her, he found his way blocked, and Joan gasped.

"But you said—"

"No questions," Joan said, "Again!"

"But—"

"You're the only comman I'll trust, Andrew."

"You don't even know me," he said.

"You told me your entire life tonight," she said. "Please?"

"I think I could love you," he said.

"Tonight will be your only chance to," she said.

When he thrust again, she screamed and dug her nails into his back, then gradually relaxed and fell into his rhythm. It was warm, and tender, and marvelous, and went on for almost an hour, but every time she neared release, she pulled back out of his reach. Finally, he reached his own climax and fell asleep with his head on one of her breasts.

She managed to disentangle herself from him and got dressed again without waking him. Just before she left, she ran her fingers through his light-brown hair one more time and kissed him tenderly on the cheek.

She paused in his doorway and thought that she had lied to him: she still couldn't trust him enough, even though she now knew it hadn't been his fault. But she had no time to grant third chances, knowing that his strength did not match hers and she could never carry him to the stars. "Good night, Mac," she whispered as she left. "And thank you." But he was asleep and never heard her.

V.

λ5600Å to 5900Å

"RAISE YOUR RIGHT HAND, place your left hand above your ovaries—like this—and repeat after me . . ."

In the assembly hall of the Poughkeepsie branch of Universal Service, forty-six young women between ages seventeen and twenty-five—varying in face, figure, dress, ethnic background, but **not in their universal trepidation**—stood in five uneven ranks, nine women per row except for ten in the first. In front of them stood an imposing brunette woman in the pink uniform of the Federation Peace Corps, with a silver ankh on each collar, who a few moments earlier had introduced herself as Mistress Selene Cooper. Behind Mistress Cooper stood the Flag of the World Federation—the old United Nations Flag with its stylized white world map circled by olive branches, backed by a light-blue field—but the Federation had colored the olive branches pink and lavender.

In the front rank of draftees, owing to a surname beginning with the letter "D," Joan Darris raised her right hand along with the other young women, and placed her left hand across her lower back.

Mistress Cooper said, "I—state your name—"

"I, Joan Seymour Darris—"

"—do solemnly swear—"

"—do solemnly swear—" Joan and the other forty-five repeated in unison.

"—faithfully to execute the duties required of me as an Officer of the World Federation Peace Corps—

"—to obey the lawful orders of the Federation First Lady and all Superior Officers—

"—to perform the feminine biological functions required of a Corporal to maintain a free and peaceful world of men—

"—to love, honor, and cherish all commen—

"—without stint, measure, or reservation: to this end I pledge my troth—

"—so help me, Goddess," Mistress Cooper finished.

"—so help me, Goddess," they repeated.

"Congratulations," Mistress Cooper said. "You are now Cadette Corporals in the Federation Peace Corps. From now on, you will address me as 'Mistress Cooper,' 'Mistress,' or 'Ma'am.' "

She began walking back and forth across the first rank as she talked. "For the next six weeks, you will be known collectively as 'Taurus Twenty-five Sorority.' You are being sent to the Federation Peace Corps training facility at Camp Buffum, Long Beach, Pacifica, leaving here at oh nine hundred hours—that's nine A.M.—which is thirty minutes from now. After you are given the order to fall out, you may use those thirty minutes to retrieve your belongings, say any goodbyes, and learn how to gynuflect, inasmuch as you will be expected to know how to deliver at least a passable gynuflection to your Drill Instructor when you arrive at Buffum. You will regroup in front of this building, where your bus will be waiting. You will *know* it is your bus because it will say 'Taurus Twenty-five' on the front. From the time you are ordered to fall out to the time you arrive at Camp Buffum, you will be subject to the orders of your Temporary Harem Leaders—whom I will appoint—and to the orders above all of your Temporary Drill Instructor, whom I will also appoint." Mistress Cooper handed out five harem rosters to the inductee at the farthest left of each rank. "You five are the Temporary Harem Leaders. You will be responsible for making sure that each member of your Harem—the women in your row—is on that bus on time. You will be subject to the orders of your Temporary Drill Instructor until you report to your permanent D.I. at Camp Buffum."

Mistress Cooper returned front and faced the women again. "Cadette Corporal Joan Darris—one step forward."

Startled, and a little confused, Joan hesitantly stepped up. Mistress Cooper handed Joan a small library and a complete sorority roster. "You are Temporary Sorority Drill Instructor," she told Joan. "It is your responsibility to see that everyone on this roster arrives at Camp Buffum as ordered, and that every cadette knows the ranks, insignia, basic organization, decorations, and gynuflection of the Peace Corps by the time your bus arrives at Camp Buffum. You don't have anyone to say goodbye to, do you?"

"No, Ma'am," Joan said. She had said her goodbyes back at Helix Vista, taken the family limousine to Poughkeepsie, and sent it back.

"Very well," Cooper said. "Order the sorority to fall out."

Joan turned around to face the other inductees. "Sorority," she shouted, "*fall out!*"

The other women began scattering. Mistress Cooper told Joan, "You're in complete charge until the bus arrives at Camp Buffum, where your permanent Drill Instructor, First Corporal Georgia McDonough, will meet you—what's so funny, Cadette?"

"Nothing, Ma'am, except I seem to know a lot of the Irish."

"Very well. I suggest you delegate the memorization drilling to your harem leaders—it will spread the resentment out a little bit. Understand me?"

"Yes, Ma'am."

"Good. Your bus has an autopilot and knows the way; simply tell it to go as soon as everyone's aboard. Call the roster again onboard. I won't hold it against you if stragglers hold you up, but I will if anyone is left behind. If someone from a harem is missing, send that harem leader out to get her and wait. If there are any further problems, come and get me in my office down the hall or phone from the bus."

"Ma'am," Joan asked softly, "why me?"

Mistress Cooper smiled slightly. "Because Dr. Chertok tells me you're a potential troublemaker—which translates onto my roster as leadership potential. Keep it all under control and you'll find things going easier for you—all right?"

"Yes, Ma'am."

"Good. Make sure you know the drills better than anyone else on the bus by the time you arrive at Camp Buffum."

"What about lunch, Ma'am?"

"Good Goddess, I'd forgotten. There's a galley at the rear of the bus. Have your harem leaders each pick out a cadette from her harem to serve, and stagger the meals between about noon and one o'clock—that's twelve to thirteen hundred in dicterial parlance. There are also snacks you can hand out around fifteen hundred, and airsickness pills for anyone who wants one. Still with me?"

"Yes, Mistress."

"When you arrive at Long Beach, line up the sorority in formation in front of the bus, and order them to gynuflect Corporal McDonough when she arrives."

"How will I know her, Ma'am?"

"She will be the only First Corporal—the insignia on her collars will be silver yonis—who approaches your sorority, and you will not be rebuked for that assumption if someone else approaches in her place. Uh, you do know how to gynuflect, don't you?"

"Like this, Ma'am?" Joan put her left foot forward and bent her right knee, causing her hips to swivel as she lowered.

"Not so deep," Cooper said, "or you'll wear yourself out. Give me another one—wait for me to return it, since I'm standing—when I dismiss you."

"Do we gynuflect any superior officer we see, Ma'am?"

"No. Gynes are given just in dress formation, when reporting to or leaving the presence of a superior officer, and when acknowledging an order. Ready, Cadette Darris? Dismissed."

Joan gynuflected Mistress Cooper, received a gyne in return, and left.

The eight-hour bus flight to the other coast was completely uneventful, if one didn't consider it an event, an hour into the flight, when Cadette Sommers threw up onto Cadette Fairman. Certainly Cadette Fairman wasn't inclined to consider it an event. More out of a sense of responsibility than out of a sense of compassion, Joan cleaned up both cadettes and the seat herself, and found that her treatment by all the other cadettes was considerably warmer afterward. Joan was happy that she'd taken an airsick pill herself, though, inasmuch as she'd been inclined to queasiness since her visit to the vivarium.

By the time the bus descended onto the landing strip in Camp Buffum at 1415 hours, GMT-plus-Eight, it was a close decision as to which harem would be up front.

First Corporal Georgia Gaffer McDonough, a broad-shouldered

and stocky woman with a roundish race to which she had to devote eternal vigilance so that it wouldn't look pixyish, waited until the women were in formation in the parking area before she approached the bus. When she was almost in front, Joan shouted, "*Sorority* . . . ten-*hutt!*' Dress right . . . *dress!* Taurus Twenty-five, gynu-*flect!*"

Corporal McDonough looked surprised, but returned the gyne.

Joan turned to McDonough, gynuflected again, and said, "*Ma'am,* Taurus Twenty-five Sorority reporting to Corporal McDonough as ordered, Ma'am."

McDonough gyned again in return. "Your name, Cadette?"

"Cadette Corporal Joan Darris, Temporary Drill Instructor, Ma'am."

"At ease, Cadette. We don't expect pink-and-polish on the first day."

"Yes, Ma'am." Joan went into "at ease" stance.

"Though it seems a shame to waste it. Cadette Darris, in ascending order, tell me the Peace Corps's ranks with their insignia."

"Ma'am," Joan said, "the ranks of the Peace Corps with their insignia are: Cadette Corporal, Virgo; Second Corporal, gold yoni; First Corporal, silver yoni; Mistress, silver ankh; Lieutenant Matron, palladium dove; Full Matron, 'N.D.' circle of peace; Matriarchs, Venus crosses, *Ma'am.*"

McDonough approached a woman in the first rank—Alpha Harem. "What is the insigne of the First Lady, Cadette?"

"Ma'am, as a civilian, the First Lady doesn't have one, Ma'am."

The dark-haired D.I. went to the next cadette. "What are the organizational levels in descending order, of the Corps—and what rank commands each level?"

"Ma'am," the cadette said, "the organizational levels of the Peace Corps with their commanding ranks are: The Corps, commanded in descending order by the First Lady, the Ministry of Peace, and the Supreme Matriarch; the Conglomerates, commanded by a Three-Cross Matriarch; the Corporations, commanded by a Two-Cross Matriarch; the Divisions, commanded by a One-Cross Matriarch; the Cleavages, commanded by a Full Matron; the Dicteria, commanded by a Lieutenant Matron; the Troops, commanded by a Mistress; the Sororities, commanded by a First Corporal; and the Harems, commanded by a Second Corporal, *Ma'am.*"

McDonough went to a cadette in the second rank. "Cadette, what are the Peace Corps decorations in ascending order?"

"Ma'am, the Peace Corps decorations in ascending order are: the Copper Pentacle, the Gold Pentacle, the Cross of Earth, and the Federation Medal of Honor. Ma'am," she added a split second late.

"Describe the Medal of Honor."

"Ma'am, the Medal of Honor consists of a Venus Cross with a Pentagram in its circle, Ma'am."

"Do you expect to win the Medal of Honor in the next three years?"

"Ma'am, I hope not, since it's only awarded posthumously, Ma'am."

No one laughed.

Corporal McDonough returned to face Joan. "Order the sorority to stand at ease."

"Sorority," Joan commanded, *"at ease."*

The women relaxed their posture, moved legs apart, and clasped their hands behind their backs.

"Well done," McDonough said. "I have never before seen a sorority arrive so well prepared. Keep this up for the next six weeks and you'll find there are special privileges to be won. In the meantime, I am making permanent the temporary appointments of Harem Leaders, and the Temporary Drill Instructor will now be my *Assistant* Drill Instructor." She turned to Joan "Do you object, Cadette?"

Joan thought back to the advice Mistress Cooper had given her. "Uh, no, Ma'am."

"Good. The Harem Leaders and Assistant Drill Instructor will be breveted to Second Corporal for the duration of training—unless you or they do something to cause me to bust them back—and as such will wear both the Virgo and the gold yoni. I trust I will not have to remove the latter insigne. If I do, you all will be sorry.

"The schedule for the rest of today and tomorrow is as follows: stow your belongings in your assigned dorm rooms by eighteen-fifteen, supper in the mess hall from eighteen-fifteen to nineteen hundred, orientation lecture in the dorm assembly hall at nineteen-fifteen, and time to get your dorm rooms in regulation order from twenty-one hundred to lights out at twenty-two thirty. Reveille tomorrow morning is oh six-thirty, breakfast from oh seven hundred to oh seven forty-five, and medical examinations from oh eight hundred to whenever the doctors say you're through. When you are through, depending on the time, you will report directly either to the quartermistress for uniforms, or to the mess hall and *then* to the quartermistress. Tomorrow evening will be spent in a second orientation lecture followed by a personal and dorm-room inspection.

"You will be living in Steinem Hall for the next six weeks. There will be three cadettes to a dorm room, except for the Assistant Drill Instructor, who will share a room with me. When you are given the order to fall out, report to your dorm, decide who will bunk with whom, and leave me out of it. If there are any disputes, consult your harem leaders and assistant D.I., in that order." Corporal McDonough turned to Joan. "The tram will be here momentarily," she said softly. "The departure code is 'Steinem,' and the dormitory computer will tell you what rooms your sorority will have. I'll expect you to get them all to the mess hall by eighteen-fifteen for roll call. Got that?"

"Yes, Ma'am."

"Take charge of your sorority, Corporal."

"Yes, Ma'am." Joan gyned, received a gyne, and turned to the formation. "Sorority, by harems, fall out and retrieve your belongings!"

"Alpha Harem," their leader shouted, *"fall out!"*

Beta through Epsilon harems fell out in sequence. "Amazing," McDonough said to Joan. "How did you do all this in eight hours?"

"Ma'am," Joan said, "I had the harems compete against each other in learning the drills, with snacks as prizes, then assigned their ranks and letters by score, with the top harem up front."

Corporal McDonough laughed.

The medical examination, Tuesday morning after breakfast, was virtually a repeat of the one Joan had been given in Poughkeepsie two weeks earlier, with the exception that this time everything was done by a live doctor, Lieutenant Matron Torres. Joan found it considerably less comfortable than with the robot. This time, though, Lieutenant Matron Torres told Joan, "You might as well get uniformed and have lunch with your sorority. I'm scheduling you for an abortion at fourteen hundred. In the meantime"—she took a bottle of dark liquid from a shelf—"drink this."

"What is it, Ma'am?"

"It's just a dye. Go on, drink it. It's not bad-tasting, and it won't do much of anything to you."

Joan hesitated a moment, then unsealed it and drank it down. It had a wintergreen flavor.

"Get dressed," the doctor said, "and report back here at fourteen hundred."

After dressing once more in her civvies, Joan took a tram across the camp to the quartermistress, was ordered to strip naked, fed her civilian clothes to a machine which cleaned, folded and boxed them for her, then stepped into a tailor's closet, the same sort one might find at any Manhattan Boulevard couturier's. A low-powered laser measured her from tip to toe and fed her measurements into the tailoring mechanism, which in five minutes provided her with a white dress uniform, five pink jumpsuits, five pairs of pink tights, two pink nighties, and matching shoes and accessories for each outfit. She didn't have to bother trying them all on to know that they would fit her perfectly. She just put on one of the jumpsuits, which was regulation for all-around wear while on duty.

The quartermistress personally handed her the Virgo and gold yoni insignia, which she pinned onto her collar.

Properly attired, Joan dropped the other clothing down a delivery chute with orders to send it to her room, and caught a tram outside back to the mess hall. She didn't, however, have much of an appetite for lunch.

At 1400, Joan reported back to the medical building, and found that Cadette Sommers—the one who had thrown up in the bus—was scheduled for an abortion just ahead of her.

Sommers was crying. "They have no right!" she kept telling Joan over and over again. "It's my body and they have no right to make me have an abortion!"

Joan really didn't know what to say to her. She had already had the same thought many times, ever since she had received her draft notice. All Joan could think of was the phrase "submit to the inevitable," but she also thought that the old maxim was wrong, and should have been "Inevitability is the last refuge of the scoundrel." She ended up not telling Sommers, and herself, anything more than "This too shall pass."

Sommers went in first. She was inside only five minutes before she came out. She was still crying.

"Did they postpone you?" Joan asked.

"No," Sommers said. "It's over already."

"Corporal Joan Darris," Lieutenant Matron Torres said.

Joan got up and went into the operating room.

"Get undressed," the doctor said, "then lie down on the table."

Joan stripped naked, for the third time that day, and climbed up onto the operating table. "Don't I get an anesthetic?" she asked the doctor.

"You won't need one," she answered. "You won't feel anything, really, anyway. Now, just lie down on the table and hold still."

When Joan lay down on the operating table, able to look straight up, she could see that rising into the ceiling above her was an apparatus she recognized as a surgical laser. Of course, she thought dimly; it couldn't have been anything else. If the rainbow was supposed to be God's promise never to destroy the human race again, then the laser had to be His sword, made from the same coherent light that spirits must be.

The laser projected a spot of light onto Joan's lower abdomen, but she knew that this was only a rangefinder, searching for the embryo; if it had had any power behind it, it wouldn't have been moving around so much.

The doctor's voice, coming from behind a shield, said, "On the count of three, I want you to take a deep breath and hold it until I tell you to let go. One."

The Sword of God, Joan thought.

"Two."

It had given her everything of importance in her life, but it also took everything of importance away.

"Three."

Joan took a deep breath and held it; a few seconds passed while the optical laser found its definitive target; then there was an instant-long pulse, and Joan felt something within her die.

The doctor came out from behind the shield. "That's it," Torres said. "You can get dressed now."

Joan got off the table and began to put on her uniform again. She hadn't felt the laser, which was tuned to a wavelength that treated her as if she were transparent and had acted only on the dye-soaked embryo, which would be expelled with her next period. The laser had left no mark on her skin.

Joan didn't say anything. But she was thinking of words she had heard in a synagogue in Ad Astra, and thought that for her they should have been: The Laser giveth and the Laser taketh away.

Blessed be the Name of the Laser.

CORPORAL GEORGIA GAFFER McDONOUGH's second-night orientation lecture always began the same way. "You cadettes are here to learn to do a job. It's a necessary job to prevent men from blowing their tops and leading us into another war—one that might incinerate the surface of this planet next time. Some people may still think it's a dirty job. Well, maybe it is. It still has to be done. You may not like it at first, but it's necessary, and you're going to learn it or I'll know the reason *why*. If you do as you're told, after a while you may even find yourselves beginning to like it."

Thus began in earnest the basic training of Taurus 25 Sorority. Minus three women who had been pulled out of the sorority by doctors who decided they needed more recovery time from plastic surgery, they spent their first week at Camp Buffum in orientation lectures with various specialty personnel, having their physical prowess and stamina tested, performing calisthenics before breakfast and aerobic dancing before taps, and being told a lot that "I don't care how you learned to do it back in Poughkeepsie, Cadette—from now on you do it the Corps's way!"

The first week's training was an odd mixture of disciplines from various different sources. There were hygiene classes, sensuality training, anatomy lectures that taught where pleasure centers were to be found and where pain centers were to be avoided. There was a lecture on the sexual theories of Wilhelm Reich—and his treatment of "body armoring" as a cause of violence—as well as demonstrations of orgonomic massage, theoretical explanations of oral erotic technique, posture drills, formation and marching drills, makeup, hairstyling, sexual ethics, and History of the Corps.

One lecture in particular piqued Joan's interest. "Orgasms," Corporal McDonough began. "They are both the Corps's greatest prize for you women and our greatest curse. Properly handled, your orgasm can be your best friend, giving you the fuel to make it through your three-year term. Improperly handled, it can be your worst enemy. If you aren't achieving enough orgasms, you can become too bored to perform efficiently. If you are achieving too many orgasms, you can exhaust yourself so you don't have the strength to complete your duties."

Somehow, Joan thought that she would not be worrying too much about the latter problem.

Joan, having decided to enter the Corps at all, decided to learn these lessons better than anyone else. For once in her life, she was the complete conformist. Once in a while, she couldn't help wondering if the Touchable she'd seen icked could possibly have been one of Corporal McDonough's washouts.

It was not impossible. McDonough was inclined to dorm-room chats with her brevet assistant for hours past lights-out—no major problem, since neither of them needed more than six hours' sleep a night—and Joan learned that the sixty-year-old D.I. had been at her job for half her life, turning down promotions so she could stay "with the girls." "Six times a year," McDonough told Joan, offering her a joynette and lighting one herself, "five thousand scared young women are dumped onto this base. For most of them, the way they will feel toward sex, marriage, men, children, and life in general will depend on the lessons they learn here. In many of the sororities, you'll hear the D.I. call cadettes pussies if they show any emotion, and drill into them that the commen who come into the dicteria are nothing but stupid penises—Mister Dumbjohns." She took a toke and lit the other joynette for Joan. "I don't permit that. My women will have to live with and love both themselves and their commen when they leave the Corps, and if I can send them off to the dicteria with the right attitudes, I'll feel I'll have given them a good start toward that goal."

Joan's already-high opinion of McDonough rose even further when a cadette from Delta Harem did wash out. The maternal D.I. ruled a phobia discharge with no criminal or civil penalty attached. Joan thought that if she hadn't begun to like McDonough so much, she could have tried for a Paragraph 23 herself—though at this point there was no great hurry to be anywhere else until she could win custody of her mother.

The only other person Joan became close to at Camp Buffum was Cadette Adele Sommers, though the relationship was clearly demarked with Joan as Big Sister to the pale, slight blonde, albeit Sommers was a year older. Even though she explained that her pregnancy had been unplanned—she'd neglected to get her shots—Adele was still upset about her abortion and turned to Joan as a co-survivor of a common tragedy, drawing Joan into speaking *ex cathedra* on weighty moral issues.

Sommers began tagging after Joan to meals and wherever else

Joan would let her, but sensed when Joan wished to be alone and didn't press beyond that point. Joan knew Adele's interest wasn't purely sisterly, though. She was inclined to physical affection— even kissing Joan on the lips— and Joan realized clearly she could have expanded their relationship as much as she wanted; there were unused dorm rooms to which the assistant D.I. had easy access. Joan, however, did her best to keep any sexual conversations between them purely official.

On Friday at 1900 hours, Taurus 25 Sorority was in Steinem Assembly Hall for Corporal McDonough's final orientation lecture. After a discussion of technical matters, the D.I. changed to a different subject. "On your first day here," she told the sorority, "I said that if you kept up the diligence with which you impressed me on your arrival, there would be special privileges to be won. Well," she said, almost allowing her pixies to win, "here's the first. After this lecture, you are all granted a three-day pass."

Even dicterial discipline couldn't restrain the cadettes from cheering.

Corporal McDonough ignored the disciplinary breach, waited for the noise to die down of its own accord, then raised her hand for complete silence again. "You are all due back in this assembly hall at twenty-one hundred hours, Monday, fifteen June. On Tuesday morning, we will dispense with theory for a while and each of you will be assigned an androman as a sexual tutor."

McDonough waited a few minutes to let her words sink in. "Medical examinations show that at least seventeen of you girls are probably still virgins—I say probably because I've heard about elastic hymens, though I've never encountered one. Well, it doesn't matter who the virgins are—the Corps doesn't really care. But by Tuesday evening, every one of you will have experienced penile penetration.

"So if any of you are still virgins, my advice to you for this pass is 'Go get fucked!' If you fuck someone you care a little bit about, it won't be so shocking the first time—and won't waste the time of your tutors, who I assure you don't find this enjoyable work, are all Doctors of Sexology, and cost the Corps a bloody fortune to keep on our civilian staff. The Peace Corps has no need of your cherry, so give it to someone you like.

"One last thing. Federation elections are coming up shortly, and some of you women are eligible to vote for the first time. If you are interested in voting, register at the terminal on the first floor. The program code is 'Vox populi.' Corporal Darris, dismiss the sorority."

Joan stood and said, "Sorority, ten-*hutt!*" The other women stood. "Gynu-*flect!*"

Corporal McDonough gyned the sorority in return, then left the assembly hall.

"Taurus Twenty-five," Joan said, "dis-*missed!*"

There was cheering again, and war whoops that ranged in pitch from soprano to contralto, as the women ran to the lifts to begin packing in their rooms.

Joan took her time. She wasn't at all sorry that she had jumped the gun, so to speak, in dispensing with her virginity. Mac had been nice, even if this did take the edge off her gesture of rebellion.

Besides, Corporal McDonough's last words had given her an idea of where and with whom she wanted to spend her first pass—if His Gaylordship could find the time just before elections to invite her to the Federation capital. And considering what she had seen on her two previous visits to the capital, they probably didn't allow any real ones in the Virgin Islands anyway.

Wendell could and did find the time to invite his favorite niece for a visit, but he could not be there immediately, as he was making campaign appearances that night and Saturday across the South. His Gaylordship offered Joan several choices.

The first was for Joan to take a shuttle immediately that night to Mexico City, campaign with him on Saturday, then fly back to Isle of Persephone with him in time for dinner at his home with a close political ally from the Lower Manor.

Or Joan could enjoy herself around Southern Pacifica that night and Saturday morning, catch a Saturday-afternoon shuttle to the Virgin Islands, and be there in time for dinner.

Finally, she could catch a shuttle to Wiccensted Skyport that night; tour the islands; lounge around Wendell's almost-empty estate, Villa Olga; spend all day Saturday practicing at his full-size lasegraphic console—or sunbathing on his private beach—and join His Gaylordship and his guest when the two arrived at dinnertime.

Joan opted for the final choice.

After phoning PanCord for reservations, she packed—including extra pinks, dress whites, and civilian clothing in her valise—then made it via tube to Queen of the Angels Skyport by eight-thirty, where she caught the nine-twelve shuttle to Alamo City Skyport. The shuttle she caught out of Alamo flew her the rest of the way to Wiccensted, and by 3 A.M., local time, she was in a taxi from Wiccensted, Isle of Artemis, to Charlotte Amalie, Isle of Persephone.

Joan spent most of her time in transit fending off advances from wolves who took her pink uniform as an open invitation, and she considered that it might be worth the extra bother on her return to travel in civvies and change back into uniform in a skyport rest room just before returning to base.

Charlotte Amalie at night was a colorful and magnificent city, Joan had to admit, with its stately hilltop palaces, towers, museums, monuments, and open beaches just a few kilometers away from the narrow, bustling streets and orgiastic nightlife in Cha-cha Town.

Villa Olga was within a kilometer of Cha-cha Town, overlooking the Caribbean, and except for some necessary modernizations and additions, it was essentially the same almost-three-century-old villa that had been the Russian Embassy under Tsar Nicholas II and later a popular resort for the literary world. It was said that many famous authors had written their best-known works here.

The sight-seeing was not what had attracted Joan this time. She had seen the buildings of state, the museums, and the monuments on her two previous visits before she'd left for Ad Astra. Her first visit, when she was ten, had been a field trip with her class from the Blair Academy. The second time, a few months before her departure with Jaeger, had been when her parents, brothers, and the rest of the family circle had gone to the capital to see Wendell sworn in as Vice President Pro Tem, right after Vice President Ramundi's assassination.

So this visit, Joan settled into Wendell's home immediately with the aid of his robot staff, took a pre-dawn skinnydip in the blood-warm Caribbean Sea, had the butler prepare her a piña colada—an alcoholic delicacy she'd never tried but had heard about—and spent an hour before she went to bed at the console. A week without practicing had seemed forever.

Her last thought before she fell asleep that night was how good it felt to lie in an intelligent bed.

Joan didn't leave Villa Olga at all the next day. She spent the morning swimming and sunbathing (again in the nude; when Wendell had said the beach was private he'd meant it) and after lunch played through five of Jaeger's vistatas before she felt her fingers could forgive her.

She thought about working a little bit on *The Helix Vistata*, but she just didn't have the will to try. She hated the idea that she might get a fresh idea on the composition only to be forced to let it grow stale by the time she could get back to it. It was better to let the whole thing alone until she could give it the attention it deserved.

At four-thirty, Joan took one more dip in the ocean, went from there to a shower, fixed her hair, then decided that she would amuse her uncle by wearing her dress uniform to dinner. Besides, she felt the white gown was more appropriate in this climate than anything else she'd packed.

At five-thirty His Gaylordship and a very handsome guest arrived. Joan and Wendell hugged and kissed each other—their first greeting in more than five years; then His Gaylordship introduced Joan to their tall, well-built, and roguish-looking dinner companion, His Excellency Burke Filcher, Majority Leader of the Libertarians in the House of Commen. "Oh!" Joan said when she heard his name. "The author of *The Diplomat's Guide to the Habitats*."

His Excellency grinned, and one could have lit up a laserium by his teeth. "You've read my *Guide*?" he asked.

"Watch it, Joan," Wendell said. "Compliments can be tricky."

Joan shrugged. "To be honest, I practically memorized it. My uncle gave it to me when I left for school in Ad Astra. It was indispensable."

"Now you've done it," Wendell said.

"Wendell," Filcher said, "I believe I'm madly in love with your niece."

Wendell shook his head and sighed. "I tried to warn you, dear. But you'll have to learn that when you compliment an author on his work, you're creating a loyalty more binding than the one between a pair of Siamese twins."

"Then I don't have to worry," Joan said. "It wouldn't be binding at all in this city, if the twins disagreed on a crucial issue—am I right, Your Excellency?"

Filcher laughed. "It wouldn't be any problem in the House. I'd simply arrange to pair their votes."

Wendell groaned. "One more like that, Burke, and you can eat in the kitchen."

"I won't mind," His Excellency said puckishly, "if your charming and intelligent niece would care to join me in the cabinet."

Joan discovered over dinner that Burke Filcher's predilection for pretty young women who liked his writing was exceeded only by his predilection for bad jokes. This aside, he was an excellent dinner companion, as urbane, traveled, and witty as his *Guide* suggested. Wendell informed Joan that Filcher was well known around Charlotte Amalie for being able to talk glibly on any subject for at least half an hour, whether he knew anything at all about it or not.

He impressed Joan with his wide-ranging knowledge, his succinctly stated and often-caustic appraisals of capital politics and social life, and his good-humored cynicism about his profession. Joan was sure this attitude, shared by her uncle, was the main nonpartisan bond between the men.

Joan was also quite certain that beyond his personality, Filcher's still-boyish good looks—jet-black hair, baby-blue eyes that he used like an expert, and the body of a squatball champion—made him a model for the commen who voted for him: the Confirmed Bachelor Women Couldn't Resist. He even had a sarcastic comment about his looks, mentioning to Joan that he had worked his way through college, sixty years before, as a model for coca mocha advertisements.

After dinner, on the veranda, with the ocean rhythmically rolling in to the beach, the three of them broke out the cannabis and allowed the discussion to turn serious.

"How do you like the Corps so far?" Filcher asked Joan.

She smiled slightly. "You wouldn't want an honest answer."

"I admit," he said, "one doesn't get one very often around here, but it's always welcome."

"Wouldn't I be violating some sort of unwritten law by speaking against the Corps while in uniform?"

"Why, no," Filcher said. "I believe we've *written* a law on that very subject. But I won't turn you in. Will you, Wendell?"

"Speak your piece, Joan," Wendell said. "You may never get another chance."

Joan shrugged. "I think that if there were a button here," she said, "and by pushing it I could blow up this planet to avoid subjecting myself to the next three years, I wouldn't delay pushing it for a second."

"Well said!" Filcher declared. "Now can you formalize the charges beyond an emotional desire?"

Joan laughed. "I wasn't propagandized in Earth schools long enough, Your Excellency—"

"Burke," he said.

"Burke. Do you expect me to be unaware, after five years in Ad Astra—a place you know as well as I—not only that the Corps is essentially three years of continuous rape—beginning with legalized kidnapping and maintained as legitimized slavery—but that it's completely unnecessary for a society to have any such institution?"

"Any further charges, before I present a defense?"

"Rape, kidnapping, and slavery isn't enough? You want more?"

"Please."

"All right. I'm a lasegrapher. The draft takes me away from my profession for three years—years that are crucial to my artistic development."

"You can't know that," Filcher said.

"How can anyone know for certain what might have been? How many lasegraphers, musicians, painters, inventors, medical researchers, and architects are being interrupted by the draft—and what has this planet lost by stealing part of their lives?"

"The argument from the unseen—and elitism. Is that it?"

"You may proceed, Counselor," Joan said, taking a toke.

"I've never faced a prettier prosecutrix," Burke said.

"Out of order," Wendell ruled.

Filcher inclined his head slightly. "As you wish, Your Honor." He lit a pipe and took a few tokes before turning back to Joan.

"A while back," His Excellency began, "a Libertarian named Randolph Bourne coined the proverb 'War is the health of the State.' It was true enough. It was only during wartime that even supposedly democratic republics could commandeer the lives and property of their citizenry in any fashion the rulers saw fit. But by the mid–twentieth century—when weapons of universal destruction first became available—war was much too dangerous to be used to keep political societies healthy. All-out war was genocidal, the Brushfire War proved that limited wars had irreparable consequences to the economic well-being of a country, and the Colonial War proved that in any conflict between Earth and space, space had the clear upper hand—pun intended, my dear."

"Forgiven," Joan said.

"Moreover, with the habitats producing at an outrageous pace—space has clear advantages in a number of ways—national wars on Earth placed our planet at an intolerable disadvantage—one we couldn't bear for long without becoming the economic colony of our offspring."

Filcher took another toke. "But the Lady smiled her luck on us. The very sexual imbalance that the Brushfire War had inflamed also provided the solution to our political problems—if we handled them intelligently. We simply changed the equation from 'War is the health of the State' to 'Rape is the health of the State.'"

"You admit it's rape?" Joan said.

"Does it pay for a statesman to deny obvious truths? Not that you'll ever hear me speak this way in public. The theories are too technically involved to be understood except by a doctor of political philosophy—and not all of *them*."

"Then why explain it to *me*?" Joan asked. "Or is this more flattery?"

"You *might* have been able to understand this if you hadn't lived in the habitats, but I would say that's your main advantage here. Very well. I will concede not only your charge of rape, but also kidnapping and slavery. I intend to justify all three to you before I'm done."

"That I'd like to see," Joan said.

"Let's start with a comparison," Filcher said. "Isn't the Corps and its draft a small price to pay compared with wars and the military drafts that left men, women and children crippled, dismembered, and dead?"

"I object to both equally," Joan said. "But I will point out that you are completely free from this 'price' that you claim saves us from war—completely free from what you admit is rape, kidnapping, and slavery. Is that fair?"

"Life is rarely 'fair,' my dear—especially when the needs of a world are involved. For centuries, governments imposed military conscription exclusively on men, with women, if you will, getting the benefits without paying the price. Was that any fairer? Do you think if wars were possible today without destroying the planet—if we men could fight it out as we used to, with swords and shields on fields of honor—that we wouldn't gladly pick up our swords and shields to spare our women this burden? We do not have that choice. Again I concede, ours is an ignoble age. But when it comes right down to it, is the service so bad?"

"I wouldn't know yet. I expect it to be intolerably boring."

"Millions of women have 'tolerated' it—and some of them didn't even have the variety the service offers: they had to tolerate their husbands. But even if it is boredom, look at the bargain. For three years of boredom, you women provide the world with virtually unlimited freedom, peace, and prosperity—more than this sorry planet ever saw before. Moreover, immediately after the service, you are one of the prime beneficiaries of that peace and prosperity—one of the privileged ruling class. Is that such a bad deal?"

"I have no interest in being part of any such ruling class."

"You were born into it," Filcher said, "and have already received the benefits. Let's not fall into the fallacies of hypocrisy, Joan. Weren't you born into a family wealthy enough to allow you a luxury handed few generations—the possibility of pursuing your artistic talents virtually unfettered? Were you required, as previous generations were, to spend your hours cooking, cleaning, tending your younger brothers, and performing the other drudgeries women were subject to?"

"I don't suppose you attribute the robotics revolution to the draft also?" Joan said.

"I don't have to," Filcher said. "All I suggest is that there would have been no guarantee that Joan Darris would be born into such a condition if society weren't free from war, and if our planet's current policies didn't make certain that only the wealthy and successful produce offspring."

"The habitats get along just fine without rape, kidnapping, and slavery," Joan said. "Remember, I've lived there."

"That is their nature," Filcher said, "one we cannot share. I believe you're used to thinking septimally, aren't you? Seven colors of the dichroic scale, seven movements to a vistata, and so forth?"

Joan nodded.

"Very well. You can divide things up almost any way you please, but for your convenience, let me say that there are seven principal interests of humankind: war, adventure, money, sensuality, religion, creative work, and children."

"What about love?" Joan said.

" 'Love ain't nothing but sex misspelled,' " he quoted. "War—as we have seen—is no longer a safe pursuit; so we substitute sex and adventure. But the habitats are populated by those who have rejected this pattern for other *specific* alternatives. In spectra, we might say Ad Astra thrives on money to creative work, primarily. Kibbutz from religion to creative work to money. Lenin almost entirely on religion."

"A Leninite would disagree with that," Wendell said.

"Not a self-honest Leninite," Filcher said.

"That's a contradiction in terms," Wendell said.

"As you wish. St. Clive thrives on religion to creative work and children; Daedalus primarily on adventure—need I go on? Without exception, each habitat has chosen primary interests other than the ones that make peaceful life with our gender ratio possible. Their patterns work beautifully—for them. But not for us. By the Lady, Earth had fallen into a gender imbalance which put sex at a premium—an artificial scarcity inflamed by stupidity and intervention during the Brushfire War—and this left our planet with a way to move from organization around war—chauvinism, racism, protectionism—to a World Federation organized around sex. Instead of drafting young men to go to war and be maimed and killed, wasn't it better to draft young women for a three-year term of comparatively harmless rape?"

"Rape is an act of violence, not an act of sex," Joan objected.

"Then how can you claim the Corps fosters rape when there is no violence permitted? You contradict yourself. No, Joan, you corporals are raped because the essence of rape isn't violence, but *trespass*. But we satisfy the taste for violent rape also, through licensing Touchable hunting—institutionalizing satisfaction of the two main reasons for war: the hunt and its thrill of conquest; and the foot soldier's main spoils throughout history—rape of enemy women. But more than this, it gives us a controllable society without the inefficiencies of prisons. Outright criminals are declared Touchable and subject to public abuse; lesser problems can be dealt with either through the draft—for young women—or by threatening to cut off dicterial and hunting privileges—for young men. Those immune from these controls—older women, lesbians, married men, andromen—naturally become our ruling class—though we're above all a gerontocracy."

"I hadn't thought of it that way," Joan said.

"Then I'm not wasting my time," Filcher said. "I'll wrap this up, then. The most important thing about the Corps—and a world order based on sex—is that it spurs competition as never before, which is good for both our economy and our evolution as a species. Men know that only the top seventh of them will ever be able to interest a woman in marriage and get out of the dicterial rat race, so you women act as the spurs to men's greatest efforts, which is proved by the fact that in economic terms the Federation has begun gaining on the habitats in innovation and economic production. Moreover, only the top seventh or so of the male population reproduce—I'm including those andromen rich enough to hire a hostmother so they can clone themselves. Only the richest, best-looking, best-educated, most-charming—whatever the rape you women look for in a man—reproduce. The next generation—no matter how much more affluent their parents' production has made the world—will be faced with just as much competition. Economics is no longer a prime motivation, since it can be wiped out by closer and closer approaches to economic post-scarcity. Each child born on this planet is born with a silver spoon in his or her mouth. We *have* no starving children. And each son must compete against his brothers for the one daughter from another family, so he can marry and reproduce. The only device that lets us use this economic and evolutionary tool is the draft. The only tools at our disposal are rape, kidnapping, and slavery. I don't think we are unjustified in using them. If you could convince me that we could achieve the same benefits, economically and evolutionarily, without coercion, I might change my mind. But I have seen little evidence of it. Our planet is prosperous, peaceful, and competitive with the habitats at a grave economic handicap—our atmosphere and gravity well. I attribute our success to the sexual pattern we've adopted that makes competition so tough for us. Moreover, I suspect that in a few hundred years the evolution will show its first effects, and you will see the 'wolves' from this planet rise up and eat up the 'sheep' in the habitats."

Wendell dumped his dottle into an ashtray. "You know, Burke," he said, "as soon as you do away with the concept that the individual has a right to be free of any burdens, any costs, that he or she hasn't voluntarily agreed to—no matter what the supposed benefits—you justify any and every system that fits your whimsy and justify it in the name of the good of the race, or the good of the nation, or the public good, or other sophistries of villains."

"Now you're over the rainbow!" Joan said.

"As you know, my dear fellow," Filcher said, "the *a priori* assumption of individual self-ownership—which is necessary to such a proposition—is one I have never seen a reason to make."

Joan looked Filcher straight in the eye. "It's an assumption," she said, "that anyone is blind to at his own risk—and possibly over his own dead body."

His Excellency smiled at Joan. "My dear, in your case I do believe it would be worth the risk."

JOAN SPENT SUNDAY alone at the villa with Wendell. There were several things she wanted to accomplish before she reported back to Camp Buffum, and His Gaylordship was free until a holovision speech he was to record that evening.

Joan's first objective was accomplished at breakfast—discussing her planned lawsuit to gain her mother's custody. Wendell was sympathetic. He told Joan that he had tried the very Saturday of Eleanor's accident, when Stanton had phoned him, to convince his brother that he must make arrangements to revive his wife. Their mother—Joan's grandmother, Kate—had made a similar plea, with just as little success. They had both been one night too late: Vera had convinced Stanton in pillow talk that there was no point in complicating their lives by reviving Eleanor—from whom Stanton would have separated anyway—as long as the two of them were living together. "I knew this when I arranged your schooling with Jaeger," Wendell said. "It was primarily to save you from Vera's influence—and knocking your head against a ferrofoam wall—that I thought it would be best to get you off the planet."

Joan breathed in deeply; much of this was news to her. She'd had no idea that her parents had been planning to separate anyway. "They waited six weeks to tell me," she told Wendell; "then they said it was because they objected to cerebral abortion."

"The morality of cerebral abortion is a tricky proposition, I must admit," Wendell said, sipping a cup of mocha, "but I assure you it was not a paramount concern in their decision. Vera's motivation you know as well as I. But your father's is somewhat more complex. In essence, what comman has the opportunity to marry his wife twice, and the second time get a newer model with none of the boring familiarity of the first? Plus, when it came right down to it, your mother was not as good for your father's ego as Vera is. They hunt together, and your father—who has always had a dreadful inferiority complex to *our* father—feels he's proving his masculinity with every Touchable he catches. And instead of staying at home accusingly, as your mother began doing, Vera goes right along with him and even helps."

"Vera told me as much when I confronted her about it."

"Vera can be amazingly honest for someone who lies to herself and others so often. But what I find even more amazing," Wendell said, "is the courage *you* showed in coming back here at all, to try saving your mother. I wish you could have known my father. You and he are really two of a kind."

Joan blushed. "Thank you," she said softly. "That's the nicest thing anyone has ever said to me."

"It won't be an easy court fight," Wendell said. "Expect to have access to your father's money cut off as soon as he learns of the suit."

"I've already thought of that," Joan said. "But what I'm more

192

worried about is that my father might use this as an opportunity to try getting my mother declared legally dead."

Wendell smiled. "Don't worry your head about *that* possibility," he said. "They won't make any move on that, because as soon as your mother is legally dead, you inherit a quarter-share of the estate."

"What?"

"You mean you haven't seen your mother's will? Very frankly, when you first told me you were going to sue your father, I thought you meant to declare your mother legally dead yourself, so you could inherit your share of the Darris millions."

"I almost feel like slapping you for that," Joan said. "How could you think so little of me?"

Wendell grinned. "I try never to see the better side of people. That's why I've gotten as far as I have in politics. But before you sidetrack me—have you thought of what you'll use to pay your lawyer?"

"I intend to use the Corps's Legal Aid Office," Joan said.

Wendell buttered a brioche. "You'll use my attorney, right here in Charlotte Amalie. I'll foot the bill. I would have filed suit myself, five years ago, if I'd had a chance in the caldron to win."

"Wendell, you're going to make me cry for the first time in years," Joan said. She leaned across the table and kissed him on his cheek.

Wendell busied himself behind his brioche. "Now, don't go sentimental on me," he said. "You wanted to slap me just a few seconds ago, remember? Drink your mocha and we'll see my lawyer first thing Monday morning."

Joan's second objective was accomplished later that afternoon, with the aid of a powder Dr. Torres had given her before she left the operating room. She had told Joan that if she didn't get her period by itself within four days, she should ingest the powder and it would bring on her period within hours. Joan took it at breakfast and went swimming nude in the ocean again that afternoon, and when her period came while she was swimming, she gave her surrogate embryo a burial at sea.

She reminded herself that as soon as she returned to base she had to visit the doctor again, to get the first of a series of shots that would in essence make her a freemartin—with no days lost to menstruation—for the time she was in the Corps.

Wendell took Joan that evening to an expensive dinner at The

Pirate's Cove in Cha-cha Town, after which they went to the holo-vision studio on The Hill where Wendell recorded a half-hour speech for broadcast election eve.

Monday morning at ten o'clock, Wendell and Joan visited Wendell's attorney, Linda Klausner of Deyo, Abrams & Greenberg, and Joan signed the electronic documents necessary to begin court proceedings.

She flew back Monday afternoon to Pacifica—in civilian clothing, this time—made a purchase at the skyport outlet of a disc-store chain called *Civilization and Its DisContents*, then changed back into pinks and was back on base by supper. She found a note from Corporal McDonough on their dorm-room terminal saying that the D.I. wouldn't be back on base until just before roll call at 2100.

Joan saw Lieutenant Matron Torres just after she ate, got her anti-ovulation shot, and spent the time until McDonough returned reading the disc she'd bought at the skyport. It was called *The Physiology of Orgasm in the Woman*, and getting this disc, or its equivalent, had been Joan's third objective while on leave. She memorized and rehearsed the parts she needed and disposed of the disc down the nearest scintillator just before Corporal McDonough came back.

Cadette Sommers was missing at roll call, but late that night she arrived back on base, and was present at morning formation. Corporal McDonough gigged her, with a punishment of confinement to base for the sorority's next pass, which she told Joan privately would probably be in two weeks.

After breakfast, Taurus 25 Sorority were assigned their tutors. Joan's was a muscles-on-his-muscles androman named Boyce Blaine, Ph.D., who she was certain had to be andro by choice, since his looks could have gotten him as many women as he wanted. Aside from his build, he was tall, blond, and blue-eyed, with a dimpled, jutting chin that could have been used to bust knuckles. Joan thought he was as close to physical perfection as any man she had ever seen, and she was completely repelled by him.

She had the distinct impression that the feeling was mutual.

Joan and her tutor were assigned Training Boudoir 46, where Blaine ordered her to strip. Joan turned around and unfastened her jumpsuit. When she stepped out of it, naked, and turned around, her tutor was already stripped bare. He did not have an erection.

"We'll start with basic fellatio," he said, walking over to the bed. "It's very important to remember at all times that the most sensitive parts of the penis are—what are you waiting for?"

194

"I can't do this," Joan said. "I thought I could, but I *can't*."

"Listen, there's nothing to it. Half an hour from now you'll be an old hand at this sort of thing. And don't worry about my coming in your mouth. I take forever, and I'll give you plenty of warning."

"It's not that," Joan said. "I'm sure you're a very good tutor, but I can't go through with this."

Dr. Blaine looked tired. "Why do they give me all the virgins?" he asked rhetorically.

"I'm not a virgin," Joan said.

"You might as well be, as far as I'm concerned. Listen, Cadette Darris—"

"*Corporal* Darris," Joan said.

"Not if you keep up this nonsense another thirty seconds," he said. "I have tutored approximately nine hundred seventy-five cadettes over the past ten years, and just about half of them were sure going in that they 'couldn't go through with it.' I thought that since you were the assistant D.I. I could save some time and bypass my usual bedside manner. I see I miscalculated, and for that I apologize. All right, we'll ease into this. Lie down on the bed."

"But—"

"You won't have to touch me, I promise. All you have to do is lie there and allow me to lick you to orgasm at least three times in the next hour. Believe me, after the Blaine Treatment you won't have any reservations left about doing the same for me. I know about this; trust me."

He took a step closer to Joan. "The alternative facing you," he went on, "is that we get dressed right now and tell your D.I. that her assistant has washed out. I think she likes you; she'll probably decline to sit on your court-venereal. Now, which is it, Corporal?"

Joan hesitated a second. "Let's go back to circle one," she said. "Basic fellatio."

Her tutor shrugged. "Four years of college, five of graduate school, and ten years in this business, and I *still* can't figure women out. All right, let's get going."

Dr. Blaine lay down supine on the bed and Joan positioned herself kneeling between his legs. He told her to grasp his penis. She did.

"We'll begin with an operation known as 'fluffing,'" he said, "since we do not yet have an erection. About twenty-five percent of the commen you encounter in the dicteriat will need to be fluffed. As I started saying before, it is crucial to remember that the most responsive parts of the penis are the glans and the underside of the

195

shaft. Begin by withdrawing your teeth behind your lips and take the tip of the penis in your mouth, gently massaging it with your lips."

Joan did as she was ordered, orally massaging the head of his penis until Blaine had reached erection.

"Very good," he said, propping himself up on his elbows. "Now, there's a standard order to proceed from erection, and we have a mnemonic called the Three T's—Tongue, Teeth, Testicles. Repeat that."

Joan began to repeat it, but he interrupted her.

Dr. Blaine giggled. "Didn't your mother ever teach you never to talk with your mouth full?"

"And, with one-sixteenth of one percent of the votes from North America in," said satellite-anchor Bruce Farmer, "our panel of U.H.I. computers has declared the winner in the hotly contested race for the Concord's two seats in the House of Gentry."

Joan and a dozen of her dorm-mates were gathered around a communal holoscreen on election night, Tuesday, June 23, watching the live worldwide coverage.

Joan watched with a mild interest in her uncle's fate. She had been eligible to vote for the first time, but had not registered. "I don't believe in playing rigged games," she had told Adele, when she'd asked. "The power is always at the center, regardless of what the election outcome is."

"You won't even vote for your own uncle?" Adele had asked, astonished.

"Especially my uncle," Joan had said. "I like him too much to help him even symbolically—by casting a statistically meaningless vote—to continue playing piano in a bawdy house."

"What in the world does that mean?" Adele had asked.

"Never mind," Joan had answered. "I've just read too many history discs. Maybe the only way I can explain is to say that the old statesman Edmund Burke was wrong. The only thing necessary for the triumph of evil is for good men to go into politics."

"If you don't vote," Adele had said, "you have no right to complain about the outcome."

"You'll believe every piece of scat they fed you in school, won't you? Do you think I consider the course of my life subject to the whim of any plurality?"

"Well, if you don't believe in voting, how do you think people can change anything?"

"Things would change just fine by themselves," Joan had said, "if everybody would just mind their own raping business."

"And the winner of the Upper Manor's pink seat," Farmer said on the holy, "is Chauvinist Party challenger Anita Morgan, defeating two-term Libertarian Lady Frances Clark, who chaired last year's controversial hearings on alleged heterosexual behavior by andromen in the Upper Manor. Defeated along with Clark is five-term veteran Libertarian Gaylord Wendell Darris, chairman of Gentry's powerful Ways and Means Committee. This stunning upset is the first time that the Chauvinists have held North America's seats in the Upper Manor since the Federation was declared, and our computers show that the margin of victory will have been tight, coming in at a little over one-half percentage point in each parish."

"You see?" Adele told Joan. "*Your* vote might have made a difference."

"Thanks," Joan said. She smiled. "I'm not used to thinking of myself as omnipotent."

"Don't you even feel bad about your uncle?"

"I empathize with him. I don't sympathize with him."

"Honestly, Joan, sometimes I really don't know what you're talking about."

"—go now to Clark-Darris Election headquarters in Washington, Potomac, where correspondent Ravi Panikkar is with Gaylord Darris."

"Shh," Joan said to Adele, "I want to hear this."

The holy cut to Wendell and the dark-skinned, lavender-Nehru-jacketed correspondent. "Your Gaylordship," Panikkar said, "just a few minutes ago you heard U.H.I. declare Vidal Vidal the winner of the lavender seat in the Upper Manor that you have held for thirty years. What are your thoughts at this moment?"

Wendell grinned, and Joan had the feeling that her uncle was in the dorm with her, grinning at her personally, though intellectually she knew perfectly well that everyone watching holovision around the world had exactly the same impression.

"Well, Ravi," Wendell said, "first of all, I'm always amazed at how you news people would have me throw in the wet towel when out of twenty-five million votes you project a winner on the basis of the first fifteen thousand six hundred counted."

"Your Gaylordship," Panikkar said, "I'm sure you know that out of thousands of electoral-race projections, U.H.I. has been wrong only once."

Wendell shrugged. "Call me old-fashioned, but I *still* prefer computers that look backward rather than forward. But I'm evading your question."

"Uh, I *was* trying to avoid saying that, Your Gaylordship."

"Well, you can just relax about all this 'Your Gaylordship' formality, Ravi—didn't you just say I've been voted out?"

"Uh, you don't seem upset about it," Panikkar said.

"Oh, I feel bad for all my campaign workers, who have worked their tails off during the campaign, but three decades in the Upper Manor can be a long stretch, Ravi, and very frankly, I feel the way I did as a young boy, this time of year, when I'd leave school on the last day of term for summer vacation."

"The difference this time, Your—uh—"

"Wendell."

"—Wendell, is that you won't be returning in the fall."

"Oh, I wouldn't write me out of the game so fast, Ravi. It's only the third down, and our team is ahead. I'm sure my party will find some useful work for an old snareman like me."

"Do you have any advice for your successor in the seat?"

Wendell grinned wickedly. "I'd advise him to keep the eyes in the back of his head wide open, because this election was pretty close, and after a term with the Chauvinists administering the Concord you're just likely to see this old snareman pull out his lariat and rope the netman one more time. Aside from that, Vidal Vidal is a fine androman and I wish him all the luck the Lady can smile on him. He'll need it, if my colleagues still in Gentry have anything to say about it."

"Thank you, Your Gaylordship. Back to you, Bruce Farmer."

The anchor returned to the screen. "And thank you, Ravi. We go now to the Sixteenth Parish race in the House of Commen, where Pacifica Parish Representative Burke Filcher has just been declared reelected in our U.H.I. projection for his fourth term—"

"See?" Joan said to Adele. "Uncle Wendell doesn't seem much more bothered by this than I am."

"I don't know," Adele said. "One thing for sure, though. If I were in your position, with what you told me about your upcoming lawsuit, I'd much rather have an uncle in the House of Gentry, where he could rope the netman if he has to, rather than one who's just lost his lariat."

24

THE TRAINING of Taurus 25 continued on the parade ground and in the lecture hall, on the dance floor and in the boudoir. After her first all-day session with Dr. Blaine, Joan immediately assumed the standard routine of three sessions with him a week, two hours per session, on Mondays, Wednesdays, and Fridays. After the run-in at their first session, Joan "submitted to the inevitable" and did pretty much as she was told. But she tried to keep his physical contact with her body as limited and dispassionate as possible. Blaine observed this with a professional's eye, deciding to see if it would work itself out.

The problem came to a head abruptly in Joan's ninth session with him on Friday, July 3—the afternoon before the second weekend pass Corporal McDonough had granted all but Cadette Sommers. It was almost halfway through the session, approaching the break, with Joan spread-eagled on the bed and Dr. Blaine between her legs. He was, of course, performing cunnilingus on Joan, trying to break through her barrier of unresponsiveness.

Joan was breathing in quick, shallow breaths, her face and chest were flushed, and her nipples were hard. Suddenly, she grabbed his head, pulled it in tight to her crotch, began panting and vocalizing . . .

And Blaine pulled away from her. "*Stop it,*" he said. "Stop it!" He jumped off the bed and stood over Joan, looking as if he might strike her. Joan drew away from him, frightened.

"How *dare* you?" he said. "How dare you lie to me like that! Do you realize I could have you court-venereed for insubordination?"

"What are you—"

"Cut the scat! Do you think that after ten years of this I don't know the difference between a real orgasm and a faked one?" He stood back, catching his breath, and fuming.

Joan didn't say anything. He had caught her red-handed, red-faced, and red-breasted.

After a minute he tossed her a robe. "Put this on," he said.

"Are you going to tell Corporal McDonough?"

"That's entirely up to you," he said. "Right now, I'm going to take a joynette break and give you a few minutes to think about what *your* choices are."

"Could I have one?"

He lit two joynettes and gave Joan one.

"I'm sorry," she said. "It doesn't have anything to do with you. It's me."

"Look, Darris, my ego isn't involved here, so you don't have to massage it. Why do you think the Corps hires andros for this job?"

"Because a comman would get too excited and come too fast?"

Blaine took a toke and shook his head. "Out of thousands of applicants, they could find as many commen as needed with the required self-control. Uh-uh. They use us because we won't get *emotionally* involved. It's not an infallible system, of course—what is?—but it doesn't happen that an androman switches over to comman all that often, so it's a statistically insignificant risk. If you're thinking that you've offended me, think again, you haven't. If you're thinking that you can butter me up, bat your eyelids, and maybe even cry, you can forget that too. I'm immune. Your only choices are to come clean with me or, so help me, ten minutes from now you'll be confined to quarters awaiting trial. Clear?"

"Clear," Joan said.

"All right. You can start by telling me why you'd pull such a stupid stunt."

"You've probably figured it out already."

"Don't play games with me, Corporal. Of course *I* know. I want to see if you're self-honest enough that *you* know."

Joan shrugged. "The Corps can take my body, it can extort labor out of me, it can invade my privacy. It *can't* tell me what my most private feelings are going to be."

"No, you're right. They can't force you to feel. But since they can require you to be somewhere doing something you obviously would rather not do, my question is—why make it hard on yourself? What can you possibly gain by turning yourself into a robot for three years?"

"My self-respect," Joan said. "I don't *ever* want to forget that I'm being *forced* to do this."

Blaine took another toke and looked disgusted. "Maiden, Lady, and Crone—Corporal Joan-of-Arc, ready to march into the fire for the right to make herself miserable."

"Sometimes pain is the only reminder you can have that you're not selling out."

"Corporal, get this through your head and get it through there quickly: whether or not you *enjoy* the next three years is of no consequence to me, to your D.I., to the First Lady, to the commen who'll be fucking you—or to anyone else on this planet but *you*. The only reason the Corps prefers orgasmically responsive women is that women who don't come are a *discipline* problem—which is exactly what we're having right now. Beyond that, nobody gives a good *scat*. If you need to remind yourself that you're being forced, why don't you simply program your terminal to sing you a song about it each morning?"

Joan couldn't help laughing in spite of herself.

Blaine allowed himself a slight smile also, but went on. "Tell me, are you a Christian?"

Joan shook her head.

"Well, then, who do you think is going to send you to hell—or bar the way to heaven—if Corporal Joan Darris has an orgasm while she's in the Corps? What will happen—who will be injured—if you come while you're being forced to fuck? And who's going to decorate you if you somehow manage to make the next three years total drudgery for yourself?"

"No one," Joan admitted.

"You're cloneraping right, no one! Are you any freer from coercion if you don't come?"

Joan shook her head.

"As a matter of fact," Blaine said, "by making the question of an orgasm a personal obsession, whom are you locking up? The people who decided that Joan Darris would be forced into the Corps, or you?"

"It's just . . . I feel if I'd be enjoying it at all, I'd be committing some sort of treason."

"To whom?"

"To every woman who's being coerced this way."

"Does your not having an orgasm make things any better for them?"

Joan shook her head.

"You implied before," Dr. Blaine said, "that you didn't want to allow your feelings to be owned by the Corps. Why should your orgasms be the property of other women? If you think you *own* yourself, don't you have the right to as much pleasure as you can muster from an otherwise unpleasant, coerced service?"

"I . . . I guess I didn't see it that way."

Joan took another toke.

"I'm not sure . . . I don't think . . . I could come with someone I don't love or trust completely," she said.

"Joan." He startled her by using her first name. "Sexual responsiveness isn't conditional on what other people do or don't do. You *own* every orgasm you have—it's property no one can take away from you. What turns you on, how you fantasize to get there, isn't any of my business, and I'd never ask you about it. That's a place in you that no one can ever touch—unless *you* choose to share it. Okay?"

"Okay."

Blaine snuffed out his joynette. "Look, this has been a rough day for you. I can call it a session and we can get going again on Monday, if you'd like."

Joan thought about it a few seconds. "I think . . . if you don't mind . . ." She took off the robe again. "I'd like to try it again. For real, this time."

"All right."

Blaine sat down on the bed next to Joan, put his arms around her, and kissed her. This time, Joan opened her mouth and cooperated.

They proceeded naturally from kissing to caressing to touching each other in the pleasure centers the manual spoke about, and soon he slid down on the bed again and resumed licking her most pleasurable center.

A few minutes later she was again breathing in quick, shallow breaths, but her mind was 450,000 kilometers from Earth, and surprising herself a little, she saw herself watching Roland Church's bass fortissimist, Hill Bromley, with his muscular arms rippling against his black vest and the bulge in his black trunks when he hit the instrument's lowest notes that shook her to the core. She watched him, with his hair as red as her father's, his quick, feral smile that went through her like the vibrations from his fortissimo. Abruptly, he left his fortissimo floating in the Avocado Pit and sailed over to her pallet in the audience, only the audience was gone. He grabbed her roughly. He was running his hands over her breasts, pressing his open mouth tightly against hers, crushing her against the pallet, his red hair mingling with her own—she felt a sudden pressure between her legs . . . and she was *there*, free-falling with him, falling, falling, falling . . .

Then she was back on Earth, sobbing silently, utterly drained and defenseless. But she was also utterly free, for the first time, and she knew that this was a freedom that no one could ever steal away.

The Teapot Dome, at 9100 Sunset Boulevard in Los Angeles, served a brew that was probably closer in appearance to crude oil than to tea; but if there were any scandals—political or otherwise—

in the closet of this mocha house, no one had yet found a skeleton key.

Later that evening, after entering her charge code and conjuring up the Friday Late Edition of the *Los Angeles Times* onto her dorm-room terminal, Joan changed into a summery, rainbow dress, put on rose perfume, and caught the tube to Hollywood.

After finding a line of roga fans around the block to Doheny, waiting to get inside to see Roland Church, Joan walked back around to the stage door and spent a few minutes batting her eyelids at the security guard before he would agree to send her name in to Roland Church or Hill Bromley. Ten minutes before nine she was put onto the guest list, motioned inside, and given a ringside seat near the Tiger Pit at the owner's table.

The owner, Hill Bromley, could not join her at the table, of course, being otherwise occupied with his bass fortissimo in the Tiger Pit. But Hill did see Joan at his table while he was warming up and gave her a friendly wave.

Joan waved back to him enthusiastically. Perhaps a little *too* enthusiastically, she worried. But her concern was more than overpowered by her relief at finding out that Bromley—who Estelle had explained back at The Last Ditch was not "with" her—was wearing, according to local custom, vest and trunks not of lavender, but of blue. It would have been just a little too much to find out that the first man she really had the hots for was andro.

At a few minutes after nine, Roland Church came out—to tumultuous applause—into the Tiger Pit for his first set. He accepted his reception for a few minutes, then held up his hand for silence. "Thank you, thank you, friars and sisters," he said. "We're going to try something a little different, tonight—something very special that I've been working up for the past few years. It's not like anything I've ever done before—hell, I don't think it's like anything *anyone* has done before—and I hope you like it. I call it *Kama Roga.*"

The house glowing went down: Church shouted to his percussionist, Phoebe Norton, "One, two, three, *four!*" and his backup band began to play, soon joined by Church.

It was a fast-moving, violent expression of the prime Hindu dialectic. Perusha—matter—as thesis, symbolized by the Phallus of Shiva; Prakriti—energy—as antithesis, symbolized as the Yoni of Shakti—synthesized into Matter and Energy creating the World.

The idea was pure roga, but the complexity of development and the coloratura were pure classical, and Joan realized that the form of the composition was as dialectical as the subject matter. Roga was the thesis, classical was the antithesis—and the synthesis was, well, something too new for Joan to know what it was. She felt a thrill up and down her spine of the same sort she'd felt the first time she'd seen a performance of *The Rainbow Vistata*, a sensory equivalent of the statement: This is new and different; this is the way I want to feel about the universe.

The audience in The Teapot Dome obviously felt the same way—whistling, applauding in rhythm, stamping their feet and pounding on the tables—but this was Church's crowd anyway, and Joan hadn't expected any different. When Church turned her way, she yelled, "Bravo!" He grinned.

The rest of the first set was pretty much the same standard roga Church had always done, and included several pieces Joan had seen in the recording session in Ad Astra, two and a half months before.

During the break, Church and Bromley came over to the table and joined her; the other members of the band had decided to spend the hour across the street watching a new roga band at a showcase club called The Pink Panther.

"So," Church began, "how's my massive little sister been?"

"I was drafted," Joan said.

"Oh, scat," Bromley said, and it was the first time Joan had really seen him react to anything.

"Scat, indeed," Joan said. "I haven't had a minute on the console in almost three weeks. I can *feel* my fingers turning to clay."

"Well, we can do something about that, can't we?" Church said to Hill. Hill nodded. "How'd you like to take my next set?" he asked Joan.

"What?" Joan could barely speak. "I haven't played in weeks—no roga since April—and you want me to perform in public?"

"This isn't the pyradome," Bromley said. "If you blow a phrase or two, we can cover you with the music and who'll know?"

"But—"

"Now, I've got just the thing for you," Church said. "I've got a new arrangement I've just worked up on the practice console back in the greenroom. Why don't you go warm up, give it a try, and if you feel okay with it in an hour, I'll send you in with it—okay, princess?"

"Well, okay. But I'm not going on unless the fingers work."

"That's a lady!" Hill said, and Joan felt warm all over.

Church caught the feeling. "Hill, my friar, would you do me the honor of escorting the princess back?"

An hour later, Joan was standing in the dark at the edge of the Tiger Pit. Her palms were as wet as her throat was dry, and she was wondering at the moment how the Christ she'd ever got herself into this situation. Hill gave her a thumbs-up and grinned. Then Church came into the spotlight, took some applause before waving the audience into silence, and began working the crowd. He wasn't about to deliver up Joan to an audience of his fans—expecting *him* to play—without a proper setup.

"How you feelin' tonight?" he started.

Shouts of "Just fine," "Coked to the moke," and other genialities passed back to him.

"Do you feel fine enough to get a treat even *I'm* looking forward to?"

There was more assent.

"Do you feel fine enough to give a warm welcome to a massive little sister of mine? Friars and sisters, give a massive Teapot Dome greeting to a friend of mine from Ad Astra, Joan Darris!"

Joan took a breath, then walked into the Tiger Pit, under the spotlight next to Church. Church conducted the applause up and down for a few seconds, then cut it away completely, and the audience laughed.

"How you feelin', princess?"

"Uh, 'coked to the moke'?"

The audience laughed; it was obvious that Joan wasn't anythinged to the anything.

"Well, that's just *fine*," Church said. "Friars and sisters, this massive little princess is the Number One Ace of the Hunter of the Wolf Pack himself, Wolfgang Jaeger. Now, it merely happens that me and the band just finished working up an arrangement of one of Jaeger's *magna opera*, set to music. But to tell you the truth, I don't want to give it a shot in public before I see how my sister here plays it—I mean, she's got to have this Jaeger friar *down*. Now, I'll be back at one A.M. for my next set, but in the meantime, I'm going out to join *you* for once, and let somebody else fight the Tiger. It's all yours, princess. Over the rainbow."

The audience applauded again, Church climbed out of the Tiger Pit and took his place at the owner's table—the very seat from which Joan had watched his set—and Joan took her place at the console.

She lowered the glowing, started the console's recorder, took a breath, and said to Phoebe Norton, "One, two, three, *four*!"

The rainbow lighted up the dome, displaying the seven colors of the extropic scale in sequence, then spun off into discrete lines which began pulsating in the red-tonic, primal birth pains of the first movement of *The Rainbow Vistata*. The music pulsated along with the imagery.

Second movement: the charging orange spheres bringing a rousing message of hope and good cheer, while the music spun out a charging, wintry melody. The dazzling lightning counterpoints of the third movement were the natural element of Claire Church, whose job it was as antithesist to counterpoint all visual expressions with melody anyway. The music loped and swept with the green movement, waltzed in blue, lilted in indigo. The quiet ripples of the violet movement; then—silence.

Joan began playing a roga dialectic she had worked out from the previous thematic material—the red movement as thesis, the blue movement as antithesis; the orange movement as thesis, the indigo movement as antithesis; the yellow movement as thesis and the violet movement as antithesis. Then, parallel development—playing the theses and antitheses in simultaneous progression, accelerating through the Golden Rectangle, back and forth, from thesis to antithesis faster and faster and faster . . .

Until Joan's rainbow cadenza reached a height of tension, and she signaled the musicians to rejoin her for the rebirth of the extropic rainbow which synthetically resolved the entire cadenza, a coloratura that drew all who watched it into its compelling vortex.

When the final white flash from the laser concorded with Claire Church's final chord, the audience nearly tore the house down.

Joan played *Contract Bridge* as an encore, with Claire Church following her by eye and the other band members following Claire. Then, while Joan was taking her bows, Roland jumped into the Tiger Pit and kissed Joan on both cheeks.

It was a moment of triumph that lasted for hours—through the break before the next set, which Joan used in feeding the recording of her rainbow cadenza into Church's transcriber and immediately posting the score to Jaeger at the Dryer School; through Church's 1 A.M. set; and through the wind-down session after hours with the band.

One by one, the band members packed it in for the night, until it was down to Roland and Claire Church, Bromley, and Joan. Then Roland and Claire left also, and it was down to Joan and Hill Bromley, alone at 3 A.M. in the empty club.

Hill had Joan fill out a request for a waiver from the local of the

206

lasegraphers' union, since her only union membership was in the almost anarchic union in Ad Astra that existed solely to allow Astran lasegraphers to perform on Earth. Then, while Bromley went around closing up, they chatted. When he had locked up, they went outside to Sunset Boulevard, and they looked at each other silently for a moment. "I'd like to sleep with you tonight," Joan said.

Bromley looked as if he were in pain. "I know you would," he said. "Come on, I'll walk you back to the tube station."

They began walking toward the slidewalk. When they got on, Joan said, "Do you have a wife back in St. Clive, or something?"

Bromley shook his head, but smiled slightly. "Roland likes to play games about it," he said. "That's why he keeps throwing pretty girls—like you—my way. He doesn't approve of my sexual life-style—he thinks it's disgustingly unnatural. Aside from that, we don't usually tell this to anyone because, well, it's not a good idea to be known as one on this planet. But," he said, "you were almost right when you said I had a wife back in St. Clive."

"Almost right?" Joan asked. "You're engaged?"

"I might as well be—I took a vow to her. You see, Joan," he said gently, "I took a vow of celibacy. I'm a priest of the Mere Christian Church."

THE LAST TWO WEEKS of training went quickly and fairly uneventfully. There were no more difficulties with Dr. Blaine—with whom Joan now cooperated freely, though there was no repeat of that first climax—and her acclimation to service life proceeded smoothly.

Joan received three harsh items of correspondence in those final weeks, though. The first was from her father, offering her an immediate 50 percent of her inheritance if she'd drop her suit. Joan was so angry that she was afraid she'd curse her father incoherently if she spoke to him. She phoned Linda Klausner and told her to decline. Joan's allowance from her father stopped two days later.

The second item of correspondence was from Wendell. For him it was good news; for her, bad. Burke Filcher had passed a bill through the Lower Manor confirming Wendell as Ambassador to St. Clive. Wendell had agreed to St. Clive's condition that he honor its laws against homosexuality for his stay there, and would be leaving in mid-September. Joan tried to feel happy for him. It was impossible.

The third item of correspondence was from the Dryer School of Lasegraphy. Wolfgang Jaeger said in his picturegram, "When my eyes uncross, and I climb down off my apartment ceiling, I'll tell you what I think of your new cadenza to *Rainbow Vistata.* For what it's worth, I can't play it—but that's because I have no desire to try. I've asked myself a hundred times in the past week: am I getting so old—am I so afraid to die and let someone else go beyond me—that I can't appreciate genius when I see it? Or is this cadenza the worst obscenity ever to be perpetrated on lasegraphy? I haven't decided yet. I may *never* be able to decide. I'll probably have to live with this discord till the day I die. Can you?"

She decided that she could live with it. Joan had already decided that she could live estranged from her father, and with her only sympathetic relative a quarter-billion kilometers away.

But there were nights when she lay in her bed shaking, trying to avoid waking McDonough with her mewing. She had never felt so suffocatingly lonely before—not even at five years old on the landing strip. She began to realize that the worst attacks in life came not from outside, but from within. She began to know that the most fearsome enemy in life was not the Wolf, but the Tiger.

On Monday, July 20—the one-hundred-ninety-eighth anniversary of Armstrong and Aldrin's first steps on the moon, though Greenwich Mean Time chauvinists claimed those steps for 2:56 A.M. the 21st—Taurus 25 Sorority of the World Federation Peace Corps officially completed their basic training and were given their assignments to the dicteria.

Joan wasn't going to have to relocate very far at all. "You're getting the best dicteriat in the Corps," Corporal McDonough told Joan before breakfast, "and you can take the tube over from here. Take the express to North Hollywood; get off at the Eleven-thousand block of Burbank Boulevard. Eleanor Roosevelt Corporation, Nine Hundred Ninety-fifth Dicteriat—the 'Best Whores in the Corps'—commanded by Lieutenant Matron Gerry Perlulone: 'The Motherfucker,' to her women."

"You seem to know it," Joan said.

"It's my old outfit," McDonough said, "and I made sure you'd get it."

"Thank you," Joan said.

"Gerry went through with me; DeJarnette was commanding then. Old DeJarnette—I won't tell you what we used to call *her*."

"I hope the rest of the sorority does as well."

"Can't possibly—the computers usually make the assignments of new corporals."

"May I see the roster?"

"Why not? You'll be reading it off after breakfast." McDonough instructed the terminal to display the roster.

About a third of Taurus 25 had been distributed among Roosevelt's ten divisions—45,000 women per division, divided into ten cleavages with ten dicteria per cleavage. The others had been sent to divisions in the Concord's only other corporation, Susan B. Anthony—except for one cadette from Buenos Aires who was being sent to Evita Perón Corporation in the South American Union.

Joan checked the roster. Adele Sommers had been sent to Susan B. Anthony's 811th in Alamo City. She dropped a floor down to Sommers's room to say a preliminary goodbye.

Sommers's roommates had already gone to breakfast, leaving Joan and Adele alone for a few minutes. Joan gave Adele advance posting of her assignment, and told Adele hers.

"You always land on your feet," Adele said to Joan. "You'll be close enough to hop over to Hawaii on weekends."

"Space available on Corps transports," Joan said. "I don't have the money I used to."

"Listen, you promise to phone me occasionally, won't you? And maybe you can visit us in Fort Lauderdale for Yule."

"I'd like that," Joan said. "I'll let you know later."

Adele nodded, then hesitated as if something important were on her mind—which there was. "There's something I've been meaning to tell you for a long time," Adele began. "But you have to promise you won't repeat this to anyone. Okay?"

"I promise," Joan said.

"You remember how I was late getting back from our first pass?"

"How could I forget?" Joan said. "I was calling the roll."

"Well, I wasn't late getting back by accident. I almost deserted."

Joan nodded. "I understand."

"Not yet, you don't," Adele said. "My boyfriend—I told you about Preston—was all set. He had tickets to Disney, Ad Astra, for both of us, and he'd bribed an exit permit for me. We could have made it. We were already in Soleri's final boarding area when I changed my mind."

Joan knew what was coming—what *had* to be coming. She braced herself, as if for a beating.

"I changed my mind because of you," Adele said.

Joan took a breath.

"I know how much you dislike the Corps. I knew it from the day we had our abortions together. And I thought, If Joan could go through that and still think sticking with the Corps is so important—when she hates it as much as I do—then maybe I'm wrong? I know you're smarter than me, Joan. And you're stronger, too. I felt I'd be letting you down if I—why are you crying?"

Joan stood there bracing herself against the wall, tears leaking freely down her face. She felt sick to her stomach. "You fool," she practically whispered.

"What? Joan, how can you say that to me after—"

Joan managed to shake her head. "Not you, Adele," she said miserably. "Me."

Adele got up and put her arms around Joan. Joan cried copiously for five minutes. But she couldn't bring herself to look Adele in the eye again, and she could never bring herself to explain why she'd been crying.

In architecture, organization, and housekeeping operations, the 995th Dicteriat was not really different from a luxury apartment house.

Each corporal was assigned her own apartment with kitchenette and dining alcove—though room service and several in-house commissaries were also available to the women at no charge—with a private living room, terrace, bedroom, and bath. This private apartment was available to the corporal from a private corridor that led to the other corporals' private apartments, and in which outsiders were never allowed.

Adjoining each private apartment—available to the commen through a public corridor—was the corporal's individual Hospitality Suite, with its whirlpool bath, sunken bed, love seat, and LAZAK screen. There were also two more bathrooms—one for the corporal, one for the visiting comman.

The schedule could be varied within certain limits, but each corporal was required to receive 41 commen per week, 48 weeks a year for the three years—assuming there had been no time lost to the doctors and dentists. All other things being equal, this was 1,968 visits per year per corporal, or 5,904 visits in three years.

The schedule called for each comman to receive a fifty-minute hour of treatment, with at least ten minutes between visitors for the corporal to bathe, brush her teeth, relubricate herself, dress, apply makeup and perfume, and fix her hair. Each corporal had three serving robots to perform several of these tasks simultaneously—a process not unlike that undergone by a quick-change actor in a live holoplay—while another two robots refreshed the suite for the next comman and made sure that the previous one was robed and—if slow or recalcitrant—escorted back to the locker room by Dicteriat Security.

The corporals were not visually or aurally monitored by the Corps in either the Hospitality Suites or the private apartments. But by use of a code word—Joan's was "Dumbjohn"—or telemetry of her emotional state, if she could not speak, a pair of armed and expertly trained andromen from Security just down the hall would be there in seconds to take care of a comman causing the corporal trouble. As for the performance rating of the corporal, the Corps relied exclusively on rating surveys taken from commen on their way out.

Joan requested, and received, a schedule that left her evenings and weekends free. This meant three commen from 9 A.M. to noon, an hour for lunch—which Joan found it easier to take in her apartment—five sessions in the afternoon, and dinner in the commissary at 6. One weekday evening per week, Joan took a session between 7 P.M. and 8, to reach her weekly quota. Other than the work, a fortnightly session with her Sorority Adviser, and one evening of assembly and drill per month, her time was her own.

Immediately upon her installation in her apartment, Joan sent a shipping company to Helix Vista to fetch her laser, her console, and her holoscreen. They were delivered a week later, along with a voucher from Zack saying that the company had made its pickup at 2:14 P.M.—from which Joan inferred that her father and Vera had been out. She set up her console and holoscreen in her living room, with her LCAA Mark 1000 laser in her closet, packed and ready to go.

And occasionally, go it did—to The Teapot Dome for an evening of performing roga. It became a regular practice, on a weekend, for Joan to take one of Roland Church's sets—or the entire evening one night when Church was scheduled for a recording session that didn't require his backup band—and it gave Joan a chance to become good friends with Hill Bromley. She found that behind his silent exterior was a man with an immense love of life and immense compassion; but she also felt there were immense sorrows that he wouldn't share with anyone, and a scent of intrigue that made her wonder if he was as candid as he seemed.

Evenings, and weekends when she wasn't spending time at The Teapot Dome, Joan again began working on *The Helix Vistata*. There were many nights, however, when she was just too emotionally drained to do any more than the most perfunctory of sketches, with the rest of her evening spent reading, watching the holy, or in bull sessions with her sorority-mates on her floor. Joan was careful, though—her wretched experience with Adele Sommers still fresh in her mind—not to let any of them know what her feelings were on anything important, and she kept herself emotionally aloof from them.

The only person in the Corps with whom Joan kept up regular contact was Georgia McDonough. Occasionally, on a weeknight, they would meet for a holodrama, or for dinner at a restaurant in Marina del Rey; and one weekend Joan invited McDonough to watch her perform at the mocha house.

Some nights, Joan didn't want to do anything more than walk around alone in the warm Pacifica climate that reminded her of Ad Astra—a memory that was stimulated each time she passed the private club, several buildings down from the dicteriat, with its motto DE PROFUNDIS AD ASTRA. Joan looked up the meaning of the Latin by accessing an encyclopedic dictionary on her terminal, and found that it meant, Out of the Depths to the Stars. She decided if she were to have a personal motto, this would be it.

But the stars were for later; now she had to deal with the depths.

The commen who came into her boudoir, eight times a day, were all freshly bathed, medically certified, shaved and manicured, and in a category according to weight, height, and phallus size to make sure they would not place her under undue stress.

Aside from that, no two were alike. Joan never saw any comman more than once. But she found that after a week she couldn't tell one from the next.

Her routine usually began with offering the comman a joynette or a glass of wine, then either sitting with him and talking for a few minutes while snuggling up to him, or leading him into the whirlpool bath for a massage.

The number of orgasms a man was entitled to during his fifty minutes was not specified by the Corps, and this left some variety.

Some men wanted to talk, neck, or be massaged. Some merely wanted Joan to hold them and caress them. Some men weren't interested in the more sensual parts of the service at all, and simply wanted to get their rocks off as many times in the hour as possible. One comman surprised Joan by managing to ejaculate four times in the fifty minutes—though there wasn't all that much physical ejaculate by the fourth time.

One comman, who stood out from the others in Joan's mind, didn't want to have sex at all. He spent the fifty minutes reading Joan love poetry he had written. It was good, she thought, and she was sorry that regulations forbade giving her name to a comman, or asking him his.

Only one time in the first months at the 995th was it necessary for Joan to summon security.

It was halfway through her last session of the day, and the comman she was with had come almost immediately at the beginning of the hour. He wasn't particularly interested in talking, so Joan spent some time while he was recovering massaging him; then he asked her to lie down on her back, while he straddled her.

Joan did as he asked. But as soon as he was in place over her, with his legs astride her belly, he took a breath, exhaled deeply, and began peeing on her.

She was so frightened, at first, that she couldn't even scream. Then she realized what he was doing and did scream—but her pulse rate must have already triggered an alarm in the security office, because two andromen were in the door before she could get out the word "Dumbjohn."

Joan had never felt so humiliated in her life, and couldn't bear to look the guards in the face. But they understood, dragged the comman out quickly—kicking and screaming that his hour wasn't up—and left her alone.

She spent the next two hours in the bathtub.

On Sunday evening, August 30, Joan received a phone call from Capistrano General Hospital in Ad Astra. A receptionist informed her that the hospital had traced her after first calling Helix Vista and receiving a forwarding address from her brother Zack. The receptionist told her that Wolfgang Jaeger had suffered a massive heart attack, was in the intensive-care unit, and would probably not live out the night. The only person he'd asked to speak to was Joan Darris. Would she please hold while she transferred the call?

A dead weight began pressing on Joan's diaphragm and spreading out from there to her entire body. Then the image of Wolfgang Jaeger came on the screen. He looked a century older than the last time she had seen him, four months before, and had an oxygenator on his nose. But his eyes were alive, and he was able to speak—slowly. "Joan?"

"Yes, Wolfgang, I'm here . . . can't you hear me?"

There was a delay that seemed forever. Then he said, "Don't forget the three-second time lag. I may be slow, but I'm not dead yet."

Joan couldn't help smiling through her tears.

"I suppose they've told you I'm dying?" he asked.

"Yes, Wolf. They told me."

"Well, don't place any high wagers on it," he said. "You made me so mad with that *Vershlungener* cadenza of yours that I've decided I'm not ready to accept a deep-space orbit yet—at least, not without a fight. You still following me?"

Joan nodded, then decided to say "Yes" also.

"All right," Jaeger said. "I won't have to explain this, since you've been through it once already. I've made arrangements to be cryonically suspended the moment my metronome stops ticking, and also made arrangements to have a surrogate clone grown for me."

Joan gasped, and when the three seconds were up, she could see Jaeger trying to smile.

"Now, you're probably thinking that an old brain in a new body doesn't go very well. I've talked it over with the doctors, and they give me about a fifty-fifty chance of waking up after the transplant. After that—assuming I wake up at all—there's no guarantee that I'll live a day, or a week, or a month—or another one hundred sixty-seven years. But it will be about sixteen years before they know. Do you understand?"

"I understand, Wolf."

"Good. If I wake up, will you marry me?"

Joan's jaw dropped, but the only delay before her answer reached him was caused by the speed of light.

"Yes, Wolf. I'll marry you."

Jaeger smiled. "I don't expect you to live the life of a nun until I'm resurrected. Promise me you won't."

"I promise, Wolf."

"Good. I didn't want you waiting around only to find out that God had already put me to work designing solar systems, or some such thing. But I'm taking a chance that time isn't as important to Him as it is to us, and that a few decades more or less doesn't make any difference to Him. If God is anything, He has to be patient. Now, don't smile like that—don't you know it's not polite to smile around a dying man?"

"I love you, Wolf."

"And I love you," Jaeger said. "This had better work, or else I've spent the past one hundred sixty-seven years waiting around for nothing. *Au revoir*, Joan."

The picture faded out.

The news services Monday morning carried the story of Jaeger's death.

VI.

λ6000Å to 6300Å

26

ON THE EVENING of Friday, September 18—three days after Wendell Darris left for St. Clive—Second Corporal Joan Darris was being drilled along with the rest of the 995th Dicteriat for their participation in Monday's Samhain Day Parade. Half an hour into the drill, Joan was called out of formation by her sorority's First Corporal, April Elman. "The Motherfucker wants to see you in her apartment on the double," Elman told Joan. "You bite a comman in the wrong place, Darris?"

"Uh, not that I can remember, Ma'am."

"Well, when the Motherfucker calls for someone on the double, it means something *big*. So don't bother gyning me; move your ass."

Joan moved it. She grabbed the lift up to the penthouse and announced herself to the door; a moment later, a sharp "Come in!" answered and the door slid open.

Joan went in, waited for Lieutenant Matron Perlulone to look up from a disc she was reading, then gyned and said, "Second Corporal Joan Darris reporting to the Commanding Officer as ordered, Ma'am."

Since Perlulone was sitting, she did not have to return the gyne.

That was why Joan was absolutely astonished when the statuesque blonde rose and gyned her in return. "Congratulations, Darris," Perlulone said. "Though you won't have to gyne me on your way out. It's *Lieutenant Matron* Darris now."

Joan could barely believe her ears. *"Ma'am?"*

Perlulone shook her head. "We're the same rank now. Call me Gerry. Would you like a cup of mocha?"

"Uh, yes, please," Joan said. She still couldn't believe this was happening. "No disrespect intended, Ma—uh, Gerry, but are you *sure?"*

Perlulone smiled. "Oh, there's no mistake. Do you think I would receive orders for a triple bump in rank without checking? I can't recall ever having heard of one in this Corporation before. Do you take sugar?"

"Uh, just cream, please," Joan said. She accepted the cup and sat down in the opposite seat toward which Perlulone gestured her.

She took a gulp of the mocha, burning her tongue, then said, "But why *me?"*

"It goes with the transfer," Perlulone said. "You've received a Congressional Appointment to the House of Commen Dicteriat in Charlotte Amalie. You're on a week's leave as of now, and you report there on the twenty-eighth to Matriarch Lilith Graves."

"Uh, you wouldn't happen to know *who* appointed me, would you?" Joan asked, though she felt she already knew.

"Of course I know," Perlulone said, "it's right on the orders. His Excellency Burke Filcher, the Member of Commen from this parish. Each Member is alloted one appointment per year. Filcher has made appointments from this Cleavage before, but never from my dicteriat, and never—I believe—anyone below the rank of mistress before. Now," Perlulone went on, "I realize your appointment is probably as much as anything else a compliment to your uncle, but you've still brought a proud honor to this dicteriat, and I thank you for it."

Joan couldn't think of anything more original to say than "You're welcome, Matron Perlulone."

Perlulone put down her cup of mocha. "It's traditional when this happens to throw a party, but I'm afraid with the parade coming up Monday I couldn't manage that. But a friend came up with something perhaps even better. First, however—" Perlulone removed Joan's gold yonis and put them in a box for her. Then she said, "Come in, now."

218

First Corporal Georgia McDonough came in from the bedroom and gyned Joan. Joan started to get up, but McDonough shook her head.

Lieutenant Matron Perlulone went to a sideboard across her living room and ordered its top drawer to open. She returned with a small box, and handed the box to Corporal McDonough. "These belonged to Margaret DeJarnette," Perlulone said, "Georgia's and my commander, and the best raping officer in the Corps. She's a two-cross Matriarch now. When I took over the Nine Hundred Ninety-fifth, Margaret sent me two of her old sets of doves. I'm wearing one set now. Georgia was supposed to get the other, but she's asked me to give them to you. Corporal, would you proceed?"

Corporal McDonough pinned a palladium Dove of Peace on each side of Joan's collar, then stepped back and gynuflected Joan again.

Joan returned the gyne to her Drill Instructor.

Perlulone kissed Joan on both cheeks, stood back, and presented a gyne to Joan herself. Joan returned this gyne also.

Unaccountably, even though the Corps meant nothing to her, Joan found herself misting up—partly at how much this honor seemed to mean to the other two women, and partly at the great kindness they were showing her. "Thank you very, very much," Joan said, and she did not need to pretend any warmth. She felt it.

Then Perlulone took out a joynette, broke it into three parts, and lit one for each of them.

Corporal McDonough presented the toast. "To Lieutenant Matron Joan Darris—recently of Taurus Twenty-five Training Sorority, presently of Eleanor Roosevelt Nine Hundred Ninety-fifth Dicteriat, and soon to be of the House of Commen Dicteriat. May you always bring love into every room you enter."

McDonough and Perlulone toked simultaneously.

Then it was Joan's turn. "Uh, I don't know any of the right toasts," she said.

McDonough smiled. "Any old toast will do."

Joan thought for a moment, then raised her joynette and said, "May you always have an extra stash if you're out of money, or enough money to buy an extra stash."

This time, all three of them toked, and—according to custom—they crushed the three parts simultaneously into an ashtray.

Lieutenant Matron Perlulone turned to Joan. "How would you

like to sit with me, Monday, in the reviewing stand of the Samhain Day Parade?"

Joan smiled. "I think I'd enjoy that—especially the look on Corporal Elman's face when she sees these doves on my collar. She'll probably scat."

McDonough smiled at Joan. "If you don't mind my saying so, Ma'am, you've got a wicked streak in you a klick wide."

Lieutenant Matron Perlulone nodded her agreement. "Widen it a couple of klicks, Matron Darris, and soon they'll be calling *you* the Motherfucker."

Rank Hath Its Privileges—and with Joan's new rank came a much-higher pay grade, top priority on Peace Corps shuttles to any part of the globe—no charge, of course—and one heck of a pension plan. Joan didn't imagine she would be staying with the Corps long enough to have to worry about her retirement, though.

The other privileges did come in useful, however. Right after the Samhain Day Parade, Joan hopped a shuttle to Newer York, checked into the Nova Cancy Hotel—watching the First Lady's speech giving thanks this day, among other things, "for the valiant women of the Federation Peace Corps who have wiped the scourges of war, poverty, and rape from the face of this planet"—then phoned Jack Malcolm and talked him into the exclusive use of one of his domes for the week. He agreed—but only on the condition that he allow him to take her out for dinner and a show the next night. Joan agreed.

The next morning, Joan phoned Deyo, Abrams & Greenberg and instructed Linda Klausner to send the bills for the custody lawsuit to her directly, rather than to Wendell. Her second call that morning was to the local Corps motor pool, giving orders for a skymobile to be placed at her disposal for the week. It was waiting for her in front of the hotel by the time she finished breakfast. Then she flew to the Malcolm Institute and spent the day making final sketches for *The Helix Vistata*.

Joan completely forgot about time and about lunch. She probably would have worked all night long if Jack Malcolm hadn't come in at five-thirty to remind her of her deal. Joan changed into her dress uniform in Jack's bathroom, ordered the Corps skymobile to return to the hotel by itself, and flew with Jack in his craft back to Manhattan for supper atop the pyradome. After dinner, they went uptown to the Metropolitan Soap Opera House and saw its production of *Luke and Laura*.

They stopped for mocha and a late snack at the Rinso Café across from the Metropolitan; then Jack dropped Joan off at the Nova Cancy and returned to Rainborough.

Malcolm hardly saw Joan for the rest of that week, even though they were only a few meters away from each other. But by Sunday the 27th, Joan had a completed first draft of *The Helix Vistata*. She left a score of it with Jack for his critique, and flew off to Charlotte Amalie Sunday evening feeling more lighthearted than she'd felt in months. She slept Sunday night in the Commen Dicteriat's B.O.Q.

Monday morning, Joan reported to her new commanding officer, Matriarch Lilith Graves. Except for ceremonial occasions, gynes were not used among officers of the rank of lieutenant matron and up, so when Joan greeted Graves it was with a handshake and a smile.

The smile was not returned with much enthusiasm, but then again, Joan surmised that it probably hurt the woman's face. Graves was a large, square-faced woman in her nineties who looked as if she might have had a good figure three decades before. She kept her mousy brown hair cut in a short style that hadn't been popular for half a century, and wore far too much makeup.

"Welcome to Commen, Matron Darris," Graves said. "Have a seat. Would you care for a cup of mocha?"

"Only if you are, Ma'am," Joan said.

"Never touch the stuff anymore," the officer said. "Keeps me awake nights, and I lose enough sleep over this desk. But feel free."

"Thank you, Matriarch, but it's not necessary. If I may suggest it, Ma'am, I've found that a tryptophan, inositol, choline, and potassium compound counteracts the stimulation quite well for a night's sleep."

"Do you have medical training, Matron?"

"No, Ma'am. But I tend to be a night person, and when I had to get up for classes in the morning at school, I consulted a chemist for something to help me get to bed earlier. I should warn you, though, it tends to produce rather vivid dreams."

The matriarch made a note on her desk terminal. "Thank you, Matron. I'll have the pharmacy make some up for me."

"That's not necessary, Ma'am. It's sold commercially under the brand name Dreamspinners."

Matriarch Graves turned to her terminal again and ordered a bottle to be on her nightstand by her bedtime.

"Now, to business," Graves said. "Do you understand how the assignments work around here?"

"Only what I read in the manual, Ma'am."

"Well, then, there's not much I have to explain. You'll be providing exclusive services to His Excellency Burke Filcher, at his convenience. I'm afraid that your days of set routines and limited duties are over: R.H.I.P., but Rank Hath Its Burdens also. You'll be escorted by His Excellency to state functions, will be on call to him twenty-four hours a day, and your leaves will be arranged according to his desires and schedule. You'll also find out that there is much more variety in the sexual services the Members of Commen are entitled to—no more andromen down the hall to burst in if there are any unusual requests. Do you follow me?"

"Uh, yes, Ma'am."

"Don't look so glum. He can't require you to do anything that would cause you physical harm."

"What about emotional damage, Ma'am?"

"That's what the Corps has Advisers for, Matron. If you have any difficulties in adjusting to your new assignment, I'll see that you get time off to have regular therapy sessions. Just remember that there is very little that's new under the sun, and there really isn't any sexual behavior that hasn't been practiced routinely by some civilization, group, or tribe throughout history—and considered by them perfectly enjoyable and valid. We of the Corps—especially of the Commen Dicteriat—pride ourselves on our ability to provide just about any service physically possible—cheerfully, imaginatively, and expertly. Do you follow me?"

"Yes, Ma'am."

"Good. His Excellency has informed me that he has obtained a private residence—conveniently near his own—for you to live in. Here is the address." She handed Joan a printout.

Joan looked at the address, then did a double take. It was the address of Villa Olga—Wendell's estate.

"His Excellency will be expecting you for dinner at his home this evening at eighteen hundred hours. A ground taxi will be sent for you at seventeen forty-five. Until then, you're free to get yourself settled in at your residence and acquaint yourself with the islands, if you'd like. You'll find this a remarkably beautiful place to live, year round."

"I know, Ma'am. I've visited here before."

"Fine. It's been a pleasure meeting you, Matron. I owe you one for the sleep aids, if they work. If you need a favor in return, let me know."

Joan stood. "Thank you, Ma'am. I've enjoyed meeting you also. Good morning."

Joan could hardly believe that she had this luxurious Caribbean estate all to herself. Villa Olga was almost as large as Helix Vista, but she did not have one "room" here that was hers; she had the whole estate—with every modern luxury available on Earth and a full staff of robots at her beck and call.

Neither was she just a temporary guest in Wendell's house: she learned that the estate had been Wendell's only so long as he was in the Upper Manor; its title had reverted to the Federation, and Filcher just happened to be the sort of Member powerful enough to commandeer such a choice property for his own use—by largesse, now Joan's.

Joan spent the day on her solitary beach, swimming and tanning, the latter aided by a drug that prevented freckling, burning, or stroking. Then she prepared for her dinner with Filcher and met the taxi on schedule.

At dinner—just the two of them and a staff of robots—Filcher was just as charming as at their first meeting. His estate was not quite as large as Villa Olga—though much more modern—but possessed both indoor and outdoor swimming pools, full health-club facilities, the largest holy screen Joan had ever seen in a private home—and its own laserium dome.

After dinner, Filcher asked Joan to play for him in the dome. She played *The Rainbow Vistata* for him with her new cadenza, of which he was properly appreciative; but he wasn't interested in an encore . . . at least, not any encore she could perform with a laser.

He literally swept Joan into his arms and carried her off to the master bedroom—somewhat of a feat in itself; Joan was not a small woman. He laid her down on his bed, and they began undressing each other.

A few minutes later, Joan discovered that Filcher hadn't chosen her carelessly. He was hung—according to the Corps's classifications of penis size, borrowed from the *Kama Sutra*—like a horse. This meant a "high union"—a tight fit—since Joan's classification according to the measurements of her unstretched vagina was "mare."

Burke hovered over Joan for a second after he made sure she was ready for him. He noticed her expression when she saw his phallus size. "Why do you think they call us Members?" he asked.

223

That he did not wait for Joan to finish laughing proved it was a rhetorical question.

Joan had her days pretty much to herself, and she spent them around the islands sight-seeing and shopping, and at home swimming and practicing—but her nights were spent with Filcher. She had not yet reached a climax with him, but had the feeling that it was only a matter of time. He was an expert lover—innovative, considerate, and sensuous. On Thursday night, however, Joan had her first indication that the honeymoon, as far as she was concerned, was over. "Get yourself outfitted with a flying belt tomorrow," he told her. "I'm taking you on your first hunt tomorrow night."

"But I'm not a Marnie," Joan objected.

Filcher produced a medallion. "You are now."

The hunting party, Friday night, was made up of commen, ladies, gaylords, and their guests—sixteen in all—who hopped a private shuttle to Alamo City late Friday afternoon and were suited up an hour before dusk. The plan for the evening was for the party to break into eight pairs—tracking as many Touchables as possible to what looked to be their final destination for the night—then compare notes and see if any location came up more than once on the map. If it did, they would suit up and perform the same tracking with skybelts and "hawks"—robot belts with scanning equipment—in the "hot" sector. Immediately after dusk, they would triangulate on the area in the hopes of finding a camp.

Just exactly where Touchables went for the night was the problem that, as far as Filcher was concerned, made Touchable hunting a sport. There was no immunity from capture—even in a private home—but a home offered natural protections anyway: it could not be entered without a search warrant affirming probable cause, and the only way a Marnie could get such a warrant was to get a firm tracking on the Touchable's brainprint signal to a stable destination. Anything over five minutes of the same signal from the same location was enough to permit the Marnie to move in—after, of course, getting the legal go-ahead from Federation computers.

Hunting parties from the Manors had been notoriously bad about ignoring the legal amenities, but Filcher disapproved of that strongly. It was not particularly the law he cared for—it was the "ruining of the sport of it."

The main difficulty with getting a sufficient signal, though, was that the brainprint transponders put out a signal so weak that almost anything thicker than air would block it. It was, perhaps, possible to implant brainprint transponders with a higher efficiency of converting body heat to radio signal, but the traditionalists in the Marnies had always opposed such action. They liked the hunts just the way they were, and anything giving them too much advantage would ensure that a Touchable never stuck his or her head out at night.

As it was, just so long as a Touchable was uncloaked—illegal, but not unduly punished unless compounded by other crimes—there was a fair chance that he or she could move around at night without being caught.

The best hunting strategy of all—though it seldom worked, since Touchables were by necessity such a tight-lipped lot—was to capture one Touchable and offer immunity in exchange for providing the location of an entire ghetto. Immunity included not letting the other Touchables know who had squealed. Aside from whatever loyalties Touchables had toward one another, the main difficulty with this approach was that the Judas Goat might decide that simply being absent during a pogrom would be considered by the others evidence of his or her guilt.

But this night it worked.

It was Gaylord Hernández's ward, Denis, who actually made the capture. He received a hot reading and swooped down like a bat, confronting the Touchable in a vacant lot. He was an old drunk—red-cloaked, but obviously of no interest to anyone sexually—but he could be bought for the price of a bottle. "These old ears hear things, they do," he told Hernández. "Certainly you wouldn't begrudge an old man a quart of the good stuff—say, a bottle of real Scotch?"

"Straight liquor is illegal, old man," Hernández said. "You know that, so why bring it up?"

"An important gentleman like you, the law's no problem for you," the old man said. "That's my price to tell what I know."

"I'll give you money, old man. Enough to buy a case of wine."

The old man shook his head. "Wine I've got plenty of—I've got a lot of customers, I do."

Hernández spat on the ground, then phoned the others. It turned out that Lady Moslow had anticipated the problem, and had left a bottle back in the shuttle; she phoned the shuttle and ordered a robot aide to fetch it to Hernández.

Twenty minutes later, the old man had his Scotch and Hernández had his address—a camp inside an abandoned stadium in the northern part of the city. Hernández and his ward waited with the old man until the others signaled him that they had hot readings in the area of the stadium; then Gaylord Hernández and Denis flew to join the others.

It was a bonanza. There were thirty Touchables encamped under the bleachers—enough that no one had to have sloppy seconds. The Touchables offered no resistance as the hunting party lined them up and proceeded to make their choices. Filcher chose for both himself and Joan. He chose a young, dark-haired girl—perhaps only fourteen, and so scared she was wetting herself. "Take her," he told Joan.

"I'll pass," Joan said. "Enjoy yourself."

"That's just what I intend to do. Take her."

Joan looked disgusted. "What do you want me to do?"

Filcher smiled. "You'll figure out something."

"It's all right, sweetheart," Joan told the girl. "I won't hurt you."

Joan unstrapped herself from the flying belt, removed her leathers and helmet, and proceeded to kiss, caress, and lick the Touchable girl. Filcher stood back and watched.

A few seconds later, there was a high-pitched scream from across the stadium. Then a second and a third.

Joan stopped. "What was that?" she asked Filcher.

"I believe Lady Moslow has brought out the whips and chains," he said. "Go on with what you were doing."

Joan glared at Filcher and got her first reaction out of him that night—a bulge under his leathers. She went back to licking the girl while Filcher stood back and watched, the screams continuing in the distance.

Later that night, after they returned to Charlotte Amalie, he took Joan into his house and stopped her. "You didn't like the hunt, did you?" he asked.

"I thought it was reprehensible," she said.

"Excellent," he said. Without another word, he ripped Joan's clothes off her and took her right in the entranceway. He came as soon as he entered her. Thus did Joan get her first real notion of what motivated Burke Filcher.

"THIS HEARING is again in session."

It was in a conference room, rather than in a courtroom, that the case of *Darris* v. *Darris and Delaney* was heard. Linda Klausner had suggested—Stanton and Vera's attorney, Marv Hastings, had agreed—that the custody suit could be best handled in arbitration rather than in a public courtroom battle. By contract, however, the outcome would be just as legally binding.

The judge in the case was a short, dark-haired attorney, an androman specializing in copyright law. He had been assigned to judge the case by the North American Arbitration Association, to whom Joan's and her father's attorneys had taken the case. His name was Arthur Endicott, and Joan thought he looked very judicial.

The first part of the hearing, before lunch, consisted mainly of the attorneys' presenting the facts of the case to their judge—essentially amplifications of materials they had already presented to the association before the hearing began. Endicott had listened to both sides without any comment—though Joan noticed that their judge spent as much time watching the emotional reactions of the disputants as he did listening to the facts.

Neither side had seen any need to clutter up the issues by calling any witnesses.

The reactions of Joan to her father and Vera, of Stanton to Joan, and of Vera to Joan were restrained. They greeted each other politely when they saw each other, but did not go any further than that. There would have been no point in words—the attorneys would simply have told them to shut up.

"All right," Endicott said. "I'm ready to hear final arguments Plaintiff may proceed."

"Thank you, Mr. Endicott," Linda Klausner said. "I'll be brief The issues here are simple. My client's mother, Eleanor Darris—whom she loves very dearly—lies frozen in cryonic suspension, and her guardians—the defendants—have taken no action to revive her even though the medical procedures are well established, with no risk to the patient. Plaintiff has offered to take upon herself all pains, costs, and burdens necessary to reanimate Eleanor Darris but defendants have refused. Plaintiff contends that the defendants are in conspiracy against Eleanor Darris—Stanton Darris's wife and Vera Delaney's mother—principally because the two defendants are living together as man and wife now—though not legally recognized as such—and the reanimation of Eleanor Darris would prove inconvenient to their affair. In the meanwhile, Eleanor Darris is being deprived of her most basic right—the right to breathe. We petition for custody of Eleanor Darris's suspended body so that her reanimation may proceed at our expense, and will accept any court supervision required to that end."

"Thank you. Defense may proceed."

"Mr. Endicott," Marv Hastings said, "this is more of an emotional quarrel within a family than anything else, with strong passions and feelings on both sides. Plaintiff's notion of a conspiracy against her mother is ridiculous—the defendants in this case are Eleanor Darris's *husband* and first *daughter*. Regardless of the fact that the two defendants are living together, they have made no move to have Eleanor Darris declared legally dead, or to discontinue her suspension—for which they are paying—nor has Stanton Darris made any move to divorce his wife, though he could easily obtain a decree. Defendants have informed plaintiff that their decision not to revive Eleanor Darris is solely for the reason that such reanimation would require the surrogate for Eleanor Darris to have its brain cerebrally aborted—a procedure to which defendants have profound moral objections. The defendants can sympathize with plaintiff's desire to reunite with her mother—as they themselves would like to do if this reanimation could be accomplished by less drastic means—but they are not prepared to abandon their moral principles even out of love for the plaintiff's mother."

"I'd like to thank you both for being so concise," Endicott said. "All right. I don't see any point in going back and forth over this again—as I would if there were some possibility of mediation here. Given the case as you have presented it to me, there just doesn't seem to be any way to divide this one down the middle. It requires an all-or-nothing decision. I'll render my decision now. First, I admire the plaintiff's loyalty to her mother. It's aesthetically pleasing to me that for once I don't have a case where brothers are squabbling to make the rest of the family pay for the reanimation of a loved one. I am less moved by the defendants. It is a primary principle of law for parties to come into court with clean hands—and I'm afraid that the fact that the two defendants sleep together while Eleanor Darris lies suspended makes their hands, in my view, less than clean. Still, their defense—that they object to cerebral abortion—is one I find both legally and morally valid. I do not feel I have the right to deprive them of their right to make this moral choice. Therefore, I find against the plaintiff. Arbitration costs will be assumed by plaintiff entirely."

Endicott shut off his recorder and turned to Joan. "I hope, if I'm ever suspended, young woman, that my ward will be as loyal to me as you are to your mother. I apologize that I couldn't see my way clear to helping you."

Joan sighed. "I understand, sir."

Endicott left the conference room. Stanton said, "Marv, we'd like a few minutes with my daughter." Hastings nodded to Stanton and left. Joan nodded to Linda Klausner that it was all right; she left too.

"You're still my daughter and I'm still your father," Stanton said to Joan. "The question remains where we go from here."

Joan laughed bitterly. "Fine. I'm not due back in Charlotte Amalie until tomorrow night. Why don't you lend me a flying belt, and we'll go on a family hunt together?"

"What the rape does hunting have to do with this?"

"I started wondering what sort of men used their flying belts to hunt after I saw a Touchable use one to ick another one when I was five."

"No, it was a Marnie," Vera said. Then she bit her tongue.

"No, another Touchable—you *were* in time!" A shiver ran up Joan's spine as she realized the import of what Vera had accidentally let out. "You could have stopped him! And then you had the audacity to blame Andrew McIntosh?"

"Look," Stanton said, "I don't know anything about this—and what does a dead Touchable matter, especially after twelve years? You say you're free tonight, Joan? Why don't you stay at Helix Vista?"

Joan tried to calm herself. "To what end, Father?"

"Well, for one thing, you might want to see your brothers."

"Did Mark or the twins make any effort to see me when I needed them? Zack I can see elsewhere, where we won't be so strained. As for my younger brothers, when they are old enough to make a choice in this matter, I'll take it up with them individually."

"I'm not talking about 'this matter,' " Stanton said. "I'm talking about reuniting our family."

"You may begin by reuniting me with my mother," said Joan.

"You have no right to judge me this way!" Stanton said.

"Talk to my sister. She's the judge in this family, not me."

"I told you earlier," Vera said to Stanton, "that you'd be wasting your time with her."

"Have you no feeling left for me?" Stanton asked.

Joan looked at her father directly. "Yes, Father. But I'm too discreet to tell you of it."

Stanton fumed up. "All right—to the caldron with you! Nobody can ever say that I didn't try to make peace with you."

"Father," Joan said, "there is a debt of honesty I must settle with you. Do you remember when I was four years old, the night of Vera's coming-out party? You flew your belt onto my terrace, climbed in my window, and I asked you to sing a song for me. You sang *Going to St. Clive*. After you sang it, I told you that you sang much better than Mr. McIntosh."

Stanton nodded, hesitantly. He remembered the night well.

Joan stood up and paused at the door. "I loved you that night. And because of it, I lied about your singing," she said.

On Friday, December 18, the Yule recess of both Manors began, and Joan moved into Burke Filcher's estate for the duration of recess. In one sense she was grateful to be having to spend the holidays with him—it gave her a valid excuse to decline Adele Sommers's renewed invitation to spend Solstice with her family. Otherwise, she was not particularly thrilled to be at Filcher's beck and call twenty-four hours a day for the next three weeks.

Oddly, the week of Solstice went smoothly. Filcher left Joan to trim the Solstice Tree and otherwise practice in the laserium as much as she wanted. He gave her a bedroom of her own and did not approach her sexually all week; he slept in his own bedroom. They spent Yule Eve at a congressional Solstice party with those who had not returned to their home districts for the holidays, sang Yule carols such as *Ruby the Red-Nosed Reindeer*, and exchanged gifts Solstice morning—Joan giving Burke a set of hand-embroidered blue silk pajamas, and Burke giving Joan a copy of the new biography of Wolfgang Jaeger, a documentary called *The Wolf Who Hunted Tigers*.

The only thing that Joan found particularly strange during the week was that Filcher had decided that the two of them would eat nothing but fruits and vegetables—a "cleansing routine," he called it—and while by the end of the week Joan wanted a steak so badly she told Filcher of visiting the Television Museum in Newer York and watching episodes of *The Twilight Zone* starring Rod Sirloin, she had never been so regular in her life.

The point of all this became clear to her the morning of Saturday, December 26, when Filcher instructed her to join him—in her dress white uniform—for breakfast in his bedroom. He wore the new silk pajamas Joan had given him for the first time.

Breakfast was in bed, consisting of omelettes, croissants with butter and jam, fruit juice, and mocha. Joan ate enthusiastically; while there was no meat, it was a better meal than she'd had in a week. After her third cup of mocha, she got the urge to relieve herself—as she did every morning after drinking mocha—but Filcher kept on delaying her, chatting away merrily on meaningless subjects.

Finally, the situation was desperate. "Burke, I've *got* to *go*."

"Eh? All right. What are you waiting for?"

"I was waiting for you to finish talking. Goddess, you're talkative this morning!"

Joan started to get out of bed.

"Where are you going?" Filcher said.

"Haven't you been paying attention? I have to go to the bathroom."

"No, you don't," he said.

"Come on, Burke, this isn't funny anymore. You said I could go to the bathroom just two seconds ago."

"I didn't say anything about the bathroom," Burke said.

"Burke, if I don't get in there in about fifteen seconds, I'm going to mess my pants!"

"Now you've got the idea," Filcher said.

"You're crazy!" Joan said, and she started for the bathroom.

Filcher was faster, though; he hopped out of bed and blocked her way.

Joan was practically crying, now. "Burke, let me through! I'm holding back so hard it's *awful*."

Filcher didn't move. He just stood blocking the way and smiled.

Joan started for a bathroom in another room, but she got only a few steps before Filcher grabbed her and started fondling her. She struggled, but he was much stronger than she was.

She struggled against him, and against herself, for almost a minute more, until there came a spasm of pain so great that she was helpless against it. She stood there, tears coming freely out of her eyes, urine pouring down her legs, and scat being pushed out to form a massive paddy in her panties.

The smell of scat drifted upward . . . and without even touching himself, Burke Filcher ejaculated into his silk pajamas.

He let Joan go. She managed to make it into the bathroom before she started throwing up.

An hour later, Joan had finally managed to clean herself up and bathe. Filcher brought her a pink jumpsuit, and she put it on.

When she came out, she faced him off. "Don't you *ever* do anything like that to me again!"

"Don't be absurd," he said. "I haven't enjoyed you so much since you threatened my life at our first meeting."

"Either you promise to knock off this humiliation routine of yours or I'll be in Matriarch Graves's office first thing Monday morning requesting a transfer back to the regular dicteria—cut in rank and all. She owes me a favor. She'll do it."

"She does, and she'll find herself busted back to second corporal," Filcher said. "Don't underestimate me, Joan. I have you; I have the power to keep you."

"I'll tell my uncle," she said.

Filcher laughed. "What makes you think your uncle can do anything from St. Clive? Even if he were here, he's no longer in Gentry."

"Maybe not, but I'll bet he has friends who still are."

"There's no one in either Manor closer to your uncle than I am. You see, Joan, he and I were lovers for ten years."

Joan took a breath. "You're lying—you couldn't have been!"

Filcher dropped himself down onto his bed, put his arms behind his neck, and smiled. "Regulations forbid only heterosexual practices by gaylords. Any other alliances are perfectly legal—and quite popular. You've heard the expression 'Politics makes strange bedfellows'? Joint-Manor conferences can become quite interesting."

"I still don't believe you," Joan said.

"It doesn't matter what you believe," Filcher said. "As a point of fact, it doesn't matter if you believe me that it was Wendell himself who introduced me to the practice of the Brown Handkerchief. Now, I don't want to argue about this any longer." He sat up in bed. "I'll tell you what. I'll take you into Cha-cha Town tonight for a five-centimeter-thick steak. Peace?"

Joan thought for a moment. "I'll have to return home first. I put my dress uniform into the scintillator. My only spare is at my house."

"All right," Filcher said. "Why don't you spend the day on your beach? I have some legislation I can look over this afternoon, anyway. I'll come by for you at seven."

"As you wish," Joan said.

"That's my girl!" Filcher got up and kissed Joan on the cheek, then went down to his study.

Even though she'd just taken a bath, Joan immediately returned to the bathroom and washed her face thoroughly before she left.

Now she knew why they called them Members.

SHE DIDN'T THINK anybody had been watching her.

A skymobile from the Corps motor pool arrived at her estate at 1400 hours—though she might as well begin thinking of it as two o'clock in the afternoon, she considered. She took only one, civilian-issue ferrofoam suitcase, another case with her LCAA laser and console, and a third case with the practice holoscreen Wendell had given her what seemed like a millennium ago. As a final thought, she took the biography of Jaeger. A disc was a disc, regardless of the source.

She made a stop at her bank and withdrew virtually her entire accumulated service pay—a substantial sum—from her account. She'd spent hardly a centigram since she'd entered the Corps. She had not received a bill from her attorney, nor would she. Linda Klausner had told her that the Ambassador had already sent her a sum quite sufficient to cover all costs, and Wendell had refused to accept a refund. Joan was grateful for the reserve in her account, and decided that she would settle her legal bill with Wendell when she saw him.

Going to St. Clive, especially in time for the Competition, was not all that simple, though. The first ship leaving for any of the habitats was the *Michael Collins*, departing Virginia Station on January 12th for Daedalus, in the asteroid belt. The first ship to Ad Astra was the *Joan Baez* on the 16th—she thought she might like to take that one for personal reasons. The first ship directly to St. Clive was the *Robert A. Heinlein* on the 28th. It wouldn't be possible for a deserter from the Federation Peace Corps to get through security—either in a skyport or in Virginia Station, which was legally part of Earth—by any of those dates without considerable preparations.

The sort of preparations she needed were going to require help. And Joan knew only one place on Earth where there were people with the inclination and the contacts to supply it.

Joan had read somewhere that there were two main phases in any escape. The first was breaking contact with the pursuer; the second was putting as much cold trail between the escapee and the pursuer as quickly as possible. Joan did not know for certain that she was being pursued, but assuming that she was and trying to lose whoever might be following her seemed the prudent policy. She proceeded methodically.

The first step was getting to a place where she could change to a more anonymous mode of travel, such as a bus or shuttle, and lose the Corps skymobile—which, if it didn't have a tracer on it when it was sent for her, would surely have one within a few hours. Joan flew the skymobile from Charlotte Amalie to Canaveral Skyport, smashed the vehicle's flight recorder, then told it to return to the motor pool back in the Virgin Islands. With any luck, it would run out of power and splash somewhere in the Atlantic.

It was now 3:30 P.M. back in Charlotte Amalie. If Filcher had called the estate to check up on her, there might be Monitors looking for her already. She could have left an automatic satellite relay from her domestic computer to her wristphone—telling Filcher, if he called, that she was talking to him from the beach—but Joan had felt safer turning off her wristphone and leaving instructions with Villa Olga's domestic computer to tell any caller that she was taking a siesta.

She had to decide whether it was safer to alter her appearance now—which might delay her another hour—or whether she should risk getting on a shuttle before it was likely that her brainprint would be read as "Wanted by the Authorities."

She compromised, buying a hat at the skyport gift shop that would conceal her most noticeable feature, her red hair; then hopped the three-fifteen shuttle from Canaveral to Queen of the Angels Skyport. She breathed an extra sigh of relief when she was finally out of the automatic brainprint readers of skyport security. So far, at least, there was no general alarm out for her. It was 1 P.M., GMT-plus-Eight, Standard Time, Saturday afternoon.

She was the last appointment of the day in the Ziegfeld Follicles Hair Salon in Beverly Hills. She would have preferred to have this done at a more crowded hour, but decided perhaps it was better to be slightly more memorable to one hairstylist than to be seen by a shopful of customers. She asked, and received, only a haircut. "Are you sure you want to cut off all that beautiful hair, honey?" the stylist said to her with hesitation in his voice. "It seems such a shame."

"I'm up for a part in a holodrama at Zōētrope," Joan said, "and I want to *look* the part at the audition."

"Maybe you shouldn't cut it until you've got the part for sure," the comman said.

Joan shook her head. "It's a period piece, and I just can't get into the part *emotionally* unless I look right. But I do want to ask a favor. Could you be extra-careful to save *all* my cut hair, so I can have a wig made from it?"

"That's a splendid idea," he said.

Joan had him cut her hair as short as his own. He boxed the hair he had cut off and gave it to her. Joan wasn't at all sure that she would get around to doing anything with it before she left Earth—it seemed unlikely—but she had wanted to make sure that there weren't any samples of her hair anywhere it could be analyzed.

She took the tube to Monica that evening, had dinner at a steak house, registered at a hotel of the sort not requiring I.D., then spent the night in her room, bleaching the hair still on her head albino white.

Sunday morning, Joan went to the Lavender Department of Phil & Roebuck and purchased several sets of android clothing—belated Yule presents, she told the salesman. Then she returned to her hotel room.

Binding her breasts with self-stick elastic was uncomfortable, but no great problem. Joan had always regretted how small her breasts were . . . until now. It took an extra layer of fabric to conceal her nipples, which just made it look as if she had a male's well-developed chest muscles. Finally, she put on one outfit and looked at herself in the mirror.

"Not bad," she said aloud to her mirror. "A choice little chicken if I say so myself."

She was checked out of her hotel room by noon, tubed her luggage on ahead to the checkroom at Sunset Station, then went into a lavender cannabistro to see how she fared.

She had two offers within five minutes. But she declined, saying that she had just come in for a quick toke before meeting a friend.

She spent the afternoon in a holodrama double feature, then tubed herself to Hollywood by six.

The Teapot Dome was not yet open for business when Joan arrived, but the stage door was open, so Joan let herself in. No one was in the greenroom, or inside the club itself, so Joan took the spiral staircase up to Bromley's office. He was in, working on what looked to be accounts. Joan rapped softly on the door.

Hill looked up. "How did you get in?"

"The door was open, friar," Joan said, "so I just let myself in."

"We're not open yet," Hill said. "Why don't you come back in a couple of hours?"

"I didn't come looking for action, friar," Joan said. "I'm looking for a gig. I play roga."

"Sorry, I'm not hiring. Try The Pink Panther."

"I'm real good, friar," Joan said. "What's more, I'm a personal friend of Roland Church."

Hill sat back in his chair and smiled. "Are you, now? Well, what's your name?"

"I'm calling myself J. D. Harrison," Joan said.

"Well, I'll tell you, Friar Harrison," Hill said. "I know just about everybody Roland Church has laid eyes on in the past ten years, and he's never mentioned you."

"That's 'cause he *knows* me by another name, friar."

"So? What name is that?"

"Joan Darris," she said, and smiled.

She had to help him up off the floor. He had fallen backward laughing.

Hill Bromley listened to Joan's story, then said, "I'll help in any way I can. And I know just the man you'll need to see."

That was that.

"J. D. Harrison" made his premiere at The Teapot Dome that evening—three unscheduled sets backed by recorded music, since the Roland Church group was off that night—and after picking up her luggage, she accompanied Hill back to his apartment in a high-rise complex on North Van Ness.

Bromley had a visitor's bed sunken into the living-room floor, which he made up for Joan himself—there being no robots on the premises; then Joan went into his bathroom, slipping out of her binding. It was the first time she could breathe comfortably all day. Bromley lent her a pair of his pajamas, since she had nothing suitable, by his standards, with her; then they toked a joynette together and went to their separate beds. Joan was amused when she saw the lock on his bedroom door flash into activation.

She found herself exhausted and fell asleep almost immediately. She didn't even need to take a Dreamspinner.

Monday the 28th, before breakfast, Hill phoned an acquaintance of his and made an appointment at his own apartment for noon. Joan spent the morning practicing with console and holoscreen, and Hill spent the morning reading.

The acquaintance arrived at noon with a ferrofoam suitcase. He was a medium-height, medium-build comman with the sort of face one had a hard time remembering five minutes after he'd left the room—and even his voice was the sort it was difficult to listen to for more than a few minutes without feeling drowsy. "Meet the Invisible Man," Hill told Joan when they were introduced. "He's been in a Monitor lineup three times, and all three times someone else was identified; twice, it was a Monitor planted in the lineup."

"Father Bromley," the man said in simple acknowledgement, "I am your humble servant. How may I help you this time?"

"Free to the Church, as usual?" Bromley asked.

"Do you need to ask, Father?"

"You weren't at Midnight Mass on Christmas," Bromley said. "I was beginning to wonder."

The Invisible Man smiled weakly. "I was detained," he said.

"Business, no doubt," Bromley said. "I've never known you to be drawn to sins of the flesh."

"Now, Father," the man protested. "You don't want to look a gift horse in the mouth, do you?"

"Always," Bromley said. "If the Trojans had, they could have saved themselves a lot of trouble. You'll be there next Sunday?"

"I'll try, Father."

"Hmmph!" Bromley inclined his head toward Joan. "A complete outfitting, good enough to get by security at both skyport and Virginia Station."

"How long until departure?" the Invisible Man asked.

"Between two and four weeks," Bromley said.

"You won't need a deader, then," the man said. "The chances of a double reading in a month are negligible."

"What's a 'deader' and a 'double reading'?" Joan asked.

"A deader," the Invisible Man explained, "is a brainprint recording taken from someone recently deceased, as opposed to a 'live' or 'icicle.' A 'live' is a recording from someone still walking around, and an 'icicle' comes from someone who's in frozen suspension."

237

"How do you get a reading from someone who's dead or frozen?" Joan asked.

"You can't," the man said. "You get it *before* they're dead or frozen."

"I suppose you then 'get them out of the way'?" Joan asked.

"That's not a polite question, J.D.," Hill told her. "And do you think I'd do business with someone who did such a thing?"

"What other way is there?" Joan asked.

"The Father provides me with donor recordings," he explained. "When one of them dies or is suspended, we put it into the active file. The donors arrange things in such a way that their brainprints are never put into the Federation's 'inactive' file."

"Oh," Joan said, "I apologize for misjudging you."

"I forgive you," the Invisible Man said, then smiled pointedly at Bromley. Bromley shook his head sadly at him, but couldn't resist smiling. "As for a 'double reading,' " the man went on, "that's what happens when a 'live' reading is taken almost simultaneously from the borrowed recording and the person it's been borrowed from— too far apart for it to be the same person, as far as Federation computers are concerned. This tips the computers off that something is fishy—"

"—in our case, in the Christian sense of the term—" said Bromley.

"—and an alarm is sent out on that brainprint. But we use deaders—very rare and very expensive—only for someone who needs a safe brainprint for a long time, or permanently. We can use a live one for you with little risk, since you're leaving Earth so soon."

"There is one safe source of 'live' brainprints we didn't mention," Bromley said—"Christians back in St. Clive who visit Earth once, then donate their brainprints so they can be used by Christian Touchables on Earth. Since they never return to Earth, there's no possibility of a double reading. That's one of the reasons being known as a priest on Earth is so dangerous—it would make my work hazardous to everyone around me. But I don't think we'll be able to use this source much longer. There's a bill pending in the Upper Manor that would file the brainprint of anyone leaving Earth as 'inactive.' "

"But a new brainprint isn't all you'll need," the Invisible Man said. "You'll also need an exit permit—can't be faked; it'll be checked with the computers. And"—the man turned to Bromley—

"perhaps you'd better see about getting this young fellow's looks changed before the holos?"

"She already has," Bromley said.

The Invisible Man did a double take, then smiled.

"Should you have told him that?" Joan asked Bromley. "The less he knows, the less that can be forced out of him."

"I'm afraid our friend must know everything about you," Bromley told Joan. "He'll need the information to get the exit permit through his usual channels."

"I have money," Joan said. "I can pay my own way."

"Make a donation to the Church in my name," he said. "Since you're with the Father, your money's no good with me."

"Is that how you really feel," Bromley asked him, "or is it just because I'm your best source of brainprints?"

The man smiled sheepishly. "Only God can say, Father."

"He will, my son, He will."

The Invisible Man opened up his suitcase and they proceeded to business.

A false transponder was a different sort of device than Joan had thought; she realized that she had never seen one portrayed in a holodrama exactly right. Essentially, all false transponders did the same thing—mask one's own brainprint and put out a radio signal with another, previously recorded brainprint—but there were several types, depending on what one needed. There were false transponders that could be surgically implanted instead of a real one. There were transponders that performed the double duty of scrambling one's own transmission while simultaneously transponding the false brainprint—these could be used short-term and discarded, without the necessity of surgery. Finally, there were units of the latter type that could pickpocket the brainprint of someone in close proximity to it, then broadcast that brainprint to any scanner that read the pickpocket transponder.

Possession of any of these devices by anyone other than Federation security personnel was good for immediate sentencing to being a Touchable. Possession by a Touchable was good for a trip to the ovens.

The Invisible Man provided Joan with the temporary, nonsurgical sort, with the recorded brainprint of a woman from St. Clive who had made a trip to Earth a year before, then returned home. He told Joan that he would "assign" that brainprint to her in his files for the next two months. After that, she should assume that it would be resold whether she had made it off Earth or not. She would have to get back in touch with the Invisible Man if she needed an extension of the time.

After he had taken the holograms of "J. D. Harrison" needed for the official exit permit, the Invisible Man took down the information about her he needed, and told Joan that she would have her exit permit in her new name within a week. Once she had it, J. D. Harrison could book passage wherever was convenient with no security problems.

The Invisible Man was all set to go when Joan stopped him. "I want to buy from you—at my expense, this time, and for cash—half a dozen pickpocket transponders."

"You planning to go into business for yourself?" he asked.

"I just like to plan for all contingencies," Joan said.

"I'm not sure that using such a device is quite ethical," Bromley told Joan. "Even if you're only using it temporarily, you *are* stealing someone's identity without consent."

"I don't intend to use them for immoral purposes," Joan said. "But I've read enough old novels to know that it's always prudent to have what used to be called a 'hole gun.' "

"Just don't get caught with them," the Invisible Man told Joan. "I had a friend who was. By the time the ovens were through with him, you couldn't have told him from a used-up joynette."

JOAN HAD NO INTENTION of being caught with them—or without them.

She prepared six packages, one pickpocket transponder to each. The outermost packaging of each was marked with the return address of Sewell Lasegraphic, Ltd., with instructions: LASEGRAPHIC COMPONENTS; DO NOT SUBJECT TO EXTREME HEAT OR COLD. There actually was an assortment of lasegraphic components in each package, along with an invoice on Sewell Lasegraphic forms—some with a letter apologizing profusely for the delays caused by a change of ownership or shipping problems from a parts supplier in Ad Astra—dating an order from a time between April and November appropriate for the address to which that package was being sent. Enclosed also was an updated price list.

Sewell had formerly run his business out of his home in Van Nuys, not far from the LASER Institute, and the business now consisted solely of a postal address J. D. Harrison had leased for this one use. Sewell had gone out of business two years before, but his business license was still on file. Joan was surprised how cheaply Mr. Sewell had sold his company name, some outdated business-form and stationery software, and two cartons of obsolete laser components he'd had in his garage. She had a feeling that if she had bargained a little longer she could have induced Sewell to pay her just to get the junk out of his garage.

She addressed one package to Joan Darris c/o the Malcolm Institute; one to herself c/o Deyo, Abrams & Greenberg in Charlotte Amalie; one to herself via C.P.O.; one to herself at Villa Olga—and two to J.D. Harrison, one at General Delivery, Newer York, and one to him at a duty-free shipping address in Virginia Station. The packages addressed to the Malcolm Institute, to her attorney's office, and to J. D. Harrison were marked, DO NOT FORWARD: PLEASE HOLD FOR ADDRESSEE, and—to protect Jack Malcolm from implication in her crimes—she added the warning on the package sent to her at the Malcolm Institute: MAY BE OPENED BY ADDRESSEE ONLY.

Her insurance taken care of, Joan forgot about the packages and occupied herself with more immediate concerns.

Living in Bromley's apartment, Joan discovered just why Hill was so reticent to get into discussion with anybody he didn't know and trust. The Teapot Dome was only one business he operated, but, he said, as far as he was concerned it was actually owned by the Church. He ran several other firms, each providing him access to things and people necessary for his actual work on Earth as a Christian missionary to the Touchables.

The most important of these businesses was the Hasty-Tasty Hoop Dog Company, which employed Touchables as street vendors. It was in these offices that he had easy access to—and a legitimate cover for—his meetings with Touchables, his recruitment of Christian Touchables as field agents to bring other Touchables into the Church, and the hovercart barn that doubled as the Church itself.

Every Sunday morning an hour after dawn, and before business hours of the hoop-dog company, when the Touchables took out the hovercarts, Bromley held a secret Mass. He took confessions on

Wednesdays, and Saturday mornings he held religious classes. The only Mass he held during night hours was the extremely risky midnight Christmas Mass—the most important commitment to their faith that the Touchables could make. That was why he had been so miffed at the Invisible Man for not attending—it showed a lack of spirit.

"He's a Touchable also?" Joan asked.

Bromley nodded. "All the parishioners in my church are."

Bromley went on to explain that he was only the chief administrator of the Church operation; he had delegated ownership-of-record and as much authority as possible in the hope that if he were ever captured or killed, the mission could go on without him.

Joan expressed a desire to attend Mass with him, but Bromley told her that with the high risks involved, he would allow her to come only if she was serious about converting to Christianity and taking Communion. Since Joan wasn't, she declined. But he would allow her to attend one of his Saturday-morning classes—if she was willing to don a red cloak for that morning and wear a transponder identifying her as Touchable. "Nobody except a Touchable attends these classes," he explained, "because none of the other Touchables would show up if an outsider were allowed in. These people are very touchy—excuse the pun—about outsiders."

"Then how can they trust *you*?" Joan asked.

Hill smiled. "I was waiting for you to ask me that."

"Shouldn't I?"

"Only if you want the full story," he answered.

"Yes."

"They trust me because I also am Touchable," Bromley said.

"There are many ways one can get to be a Touchable," Bromley explained, "but the two most frequent are women who evade the draft or desert, and men who commit rape. I think you can guess which category I am in," he said.

Joan looked at him carefully. "You're a rapist?"

"I was," Bromley said.

"I wouldn't have thought that a man like you would be capable of such a thing," Joan said.

"Men—and women—are capable of just about anything," he said, "given the necessary causes."

"But—" Joan looked embarrassed. "You're not—you still have

a—It is *real*, isn't it?" She blushed. "Just professional interest, you understand."

Bromley grinned. "Since you're going to great lengths to give up that profession, I'd say it's more like morbid curiosity. But, yes. It's real. The Church required me to have a penis cloned and reattached before it would ordain me. It was ruled that I couldn't properly repent my sin unless I was subject to the temptation, so that I could strengthen my faith resisting it."

"But—" Joan hesitated. "Am I invading your privacy by asking how you could be brought to doing such a thing in the first place?"

Bromley shook his head. "It's only in talking about our own sins that we can be a witness for others to our redemption. My case isn't very complicated or unusual. When I was fifteen years old, and living under my original name with my clone-father and his ward—"

"You're a clone?" Joan interrupted.

"Yes."

"I'm sorry. Go on."

"I was living in Edmonton, Alberta, with my clone-father and his ward, and when I was fifteen, my parents were divorced. A few months later, my father came home one night stoned out of his mind, and I think you can guess what happened."

Joan shook her head.

"You've heard the expression 'cloneraper'? I was the other half of that expression—the clone who was raped."

"Goddess!" Joan said. "Oh, sorry."

"I'm not offended," Bromley said. "God's gender is not an important issue with me. But to continue: later the same night my father raped me, I passed it on one more step. I'm not sure if it was purely out of anger and humiliation, or whether I was trying to prove my masculinity to my father and myself. You see, I'd already told my father that I'd decided to be comman rather than androman, but as far as women were concerned, I was still completely innocent. I was even too young to get into a dicteriat. In any event, the first woman I saw alone on the street that night became my victim. I don't remember what she looked like—it wasn't important to me when I raped her, and I couldn't bring myself to look at her for long in court. But since she remembered very well what *I* looked like, picking me out of a lineup, I was convicted, declared Touchable, and peotomized."

"Couldn't you tell them what your father had done to you?"

"There was no way to prove it," Bromley said. "The day I was arrested—at school, two weeks after the rape—my father killed himself."

Joan couldn't manage to say anything. She just stared at him.

"I almost followed him," Bromley said. "I thought my life was over. But there was something—I didn't know what it was at the time—that wouldn't allow me to give up. I managed to get hold of a false transponder, peddled my ass until I had enough money for a ticket and a bribed exit permit, and escaped to St. Clive, where I got a job working in an asteroid mine. It was then that I was drawn into the Church—mostly thanks to a fellow miner who preached to me in the bunkhouse."

"And then you just became a priest?" Joan asked.

"Then I just became a priest," Bromley said—"eighteen years later. In the meantime, I'd started playing music. That's how I ended up with Roland—I met Estelle when they were married. She and I sang in the choir together."

"The rest of the band—they know all this about you?"

Bromley nodded. "So do all the Touchables in my parish. You see, it's my experiences that make it possible for me to talk to them and be taken seriously. They know that I've been there. If there were such a thing as destiny—which I don't believe in, since I accept the doctrine of free will—I'd say that this vocation was chosen for me. I don't know of any other way, than bringing those who are raped and those who commit rape to God, that I could repent my past."

"I think you're being too hard on yourself," Joan said. "What you did was wrong, but a jury should have found that there were mitigating circumstances."

"There is only one Judge whose opinion interests me," Hill said.

"You know I don't believe in God, Hill."

"I know that what you believe in is not called by that name. But I know you are possessed by the Divine Spirit every time you sit down at the laser console."

Joan smiled. "It sometimes feels, when I'm composing, as if I'm possessed—I mean, things come out that seem much more coherent and intelligent than I thought they could be—but I simply attribute it to the workings of my subconscious mind."

"Where else but inside you somewhere—it doesn't matter if you call it the subconscious mind, or the heart—could something from outside this universe reach you?"

"How can something be 'outside' the universe—if the universe is everything that exists?"

"If you identify 'everything that exists' with the word 'universe,' you can't," Hill said. "It would be a self-contradiction. But if you use the term 'universe' to mean all we know from the experience of our five senses to exist—the universe of space-time-gravity-mass-energy—then one leaves open the possibility of a realm organized differently."

"How could that be?"

"Talk to a physicist about subatomic probabilities—and then ask if there is any necessary mathematics that says things *have* to be the way they are. Saint Clive himself wrote on this subject over two centuries ago in his book *Miracles*."

"You can't ask if 'things could have been otherwise,' " Joan said. "That's where you *start*—with the universe as it is."

"Ah," Hill said. "The argument from Objectivism."

"The argument from what?"

"There were two main exponents of rationalism in the twentieth century," Bromley said. "One was Saint Clive Lewis, and the other was the philosopher-novelist Ayn Rand."

"Jaeger mentioned her," Joan said. "She was the one who used the symbol of the straight line as the abstraction of man's goals."

"Very good," Hill said. "Both those thinkers were virtually flaw-less practitioners of deductive logic. Each was also a master at the art of creating metaphors to explain abstract philosophy. Yet Saint Clive was the foremost apologist of Christianity of his time, and Rand was the foremost exponent of atheism. Both were logically self-consistent to their premises. But their conclusions contradicted each other. Can you tell me why?"

" 'If you buy the premise, you buy the bit,' " Joan said. "Different data produce different conclusions."

"Precisely," Hill said.

"Where did they get fundamentally different premises, though?"

"They had one essential epistemological difference, and it led to different metaphysics, which in turn led to diverging—though sometimes remarkably overlapping—moral codes. Read Rand's and Lewis's attacks on Immanuel Kant side by side and you'll see what I mean. The only major disagreement is one of style: Saint Clive was politer. The epistemological difference arose on the ques-tion of what, precisely, were to be allowed as sources of data—'tools of cognition,' Rand called them. Rand said that the only valid tools of cognition were the five senses—which presupposed an objective universe completely apprehendable by them, and discounted any feelings that might contradict logical integrations—sensations into

245

percepts into concepts—built up without contradictions from those senses. Where Saint Clive differed was that he postulated the possibility of a realm 'farther up and farther in'—a concept he adapted from Plato—that could be reached only from following a feeling of longing for that realm which he called *Sehnsucht*—a German word that simply means longing. Saint Clive said that not only were these feelings cognitively valid—or at least, he believed them to be—but they were more important than cognition from the other five senses—an idea which appalled Rand, and which she attacked endlessly."

"But," Joan said, "both of these seem to beg the question. They start with a premise of a certain metaphysics, then attempt to prove their premise by their conclusions based on what they *admit* as data. I was taught at Dryer that this is a classic methodological fallacy."

"It was for Rand. But Saint Clive made the entire question of his metaphysics a hypothesis to be validated by empirical methods, rather than a basic premise in itself. The 'experiment,' however, requires a leap of faith. Rand defined faith as acceptance of that which hasn't been—or can't be—proved true. Saint Clive defined faith more like an epistemological equivalent of loyalty—maintenance of a belief after being convinced, even in the absence of constant reminders. Here's mine: faith is the epistemological device necessary to test the internal data from this other realm—the same 'willing suspension of disbelief' applied when entering into any other creation provided by an artist. It is the only way spiritual information can be leaked to our world."

"Define 'God,' 'spirit,' and 'heaven' for me."

"Heaven: a realm where mass and energy—if my theories are correct—synthesize into a common plasma, transcendental to the entropic requirements of our universe—not governed by time, space, or gravity—which is coherent in such a way that the laser is only an energy metaphor of it. The substance can assume holographic consciousness, and becomes a Being of Spirit. This is not Church doctrine; I'm speaking off the record. God is the fountainhead of this spiritual consciousness."

"The Hindus," Joan said, "also speak of matter and energy creating the universe."

Bromley nodded. "The Tower of Babel syndrome," he said.

"What?"

"Do you know the story—Old Testament—of the Tower of Babel?"

246

"Built by the ancient Chaldean priests," Joan said.

Bromley nodded. "The story says that God destroyed the Tower of Babel—an attempt by men to get into heaven without His permission—then divided humanity into a multitude of tribes, each speaking their own language, to disorganize humanity so we couldn't try it again. Sort of a 'No Trespassing' sign—though we've been trespassing against one another ever since. What the multitude of languages accomplished more than anything else was a multitude of religions—like the parable of the blind men and the elephant— each religion teaching part of the truth, but vehemently denying parts taught by the other religions. Christianity against Judaism against Hinduism against Witchcraft against Objectivism against Scientism. If we all ever started *listening* to each other instead of squabbling all the time, we might learn something—the password Saint Peter needs to let us through the gates. Another metaphor: it doesn't have to be an actual gate. Today, we have a worldwide Federation—no more nations fighting against nations, with English fast becoming the central language spoken on this planet—yet we are divided as much as ever: men against women, the old against the young, the Witches against the Christians, and so on. One World, but no World Community. An example," Bromley went on, "and you just brought it up. Why is it that we Christians celebrate the Eucharist—also called the Mass—and the Hindus speak of Perusha, best translated as 'mass,' and scientists speak of a central, fundamental property of matter called mass—and nobody ever asked whether we're all talking about the same thing?"

"Come on, Hill. You're basing your theology on a bad pun?"

"The pun—a synthetic abstraction of two concepts into one word—is the simplest model of dialectical creativity. And it's a pun only in the most widely spoken language of our time," Hill said. "As Saint Clive might have asked: with God planning things from a vantage point outside time, can this be a coincidence? The words *derive* differently. The scientific term 'mass' derives from the Greek word *maza*—a barley cake—and the same root as the Corn King legends that preceded the arrival on Earth of Our Lord, and symbolized by his use of matzoh at the Last Supper, The Church's use of 'Mass' derives from the Lation *missa*—a message. Is it a pun that in the modern, worldwide Language of Science the two words reunite? And even if it is a pun, didn't Christ Himself show a predilection for this form of metaphorical humor when He said, 'Thou art Peter, and upon this Rock I build my church?' The Catholics took

247

Him literally—perhaps The Lord's Pun—as the justification for basing the Church out of Rome. If the Church could take a pun literally, why can't I?"

"Hill," Joan said, "my basic rejection of Christianity—as I understand it—is not only empirical but ethical. I could never accept any doctrine that demands that I sacrifice my life to others—I don't care how many others: even a worldful."

Bromley nodded again. "Again, you seem to be a natural Objectivist. Not surprising, considering your lasegraphic training and background. But again, 'If you buy the premise, you buy the bit.' The ethics involved—the very question of what is and is not a sacrifice—depends on one's primary values and what reality is. Is it a sacrifice if you sell your own life to buy the life of someone you love?"

Joan thought about it, then shook her head. "But I would first try to save both our lives."

"If you have that option, fine—but what if you can't? Look at Christ's sacrifice. He said, 'The wages of sin is death.' This starts with the story of Adam and Eve in Genesis. They began as latent immortals, poached a bad apple from one of God's trees, and were punished by being reduced from *zōē* life—a life of spirit—to mere biological life, subject to entropy and eventual death."

"They were just trying to learn the difference between good and evil," Joan said. "The legend seems to be an attack on human reason—our primary moral cognitive faculty."

Bromley sighed. "I think that's where we have a language problem again," he said. "It was the tree which bore the fruit of the 'knowledge of good and evil.' We may take 'tree' and 'fruit' to be poetic renderings, but the word 'knowledge' has changed meaning since that was translated. It means 'congress with'—as used in the old phrase 'carnal knowledge.' God wasn't punishing Adam and Eve for gaining an intellectual appreciation of what evil was. We may assume He gave them at least a basic education in morality before setting them up on their own. What God was doing was withdrawing His sanction from two hell-raisers who'd had 'knowledge of evil'—congress with it, active participation—and were no longer to be trusted with the immense powers a Being of Spirit must have. Look at our history—and how close we came to destroying ourselves with nuclear weapons—then ask yourself what if two J.D.'s with spiritual powers—each many times more powerful than a nuclear weapon—were allowed to run around free? God had already got into that problem with the revolt of His angels led by Lu-

248

cifer. I suspect creating a being somewhere between *zōē* and *bios*—having aspects of both—was His attempt to circumvent that problem again—making it possible to test us in a closed-loop system before He let us enter into a World where He could no longer destroy us.

"But you sidetracked me; I was trying to explain what Christ was up to. God—in His aspect of the Trinity as Father—had never quite got over His disappointments with human beings. So He split off a part of Himself into the entropic universe—sent that part of Himself into the closed loop, rather like the path an electron takes in a circuit—with orders to let people know there was a way to correct the error—get out of the entropic death trap—if they really wanted to. But it could be done only on a case-by-case basis—we are created to be individuals, first and foremost. Christ said that He loved all Mankind. If He did—and His death and resurrection were going to save the lives of those He loved—then what sacrifice was there? It seems a rather good bargain for both Him and the rest of us. I would venture to say that if Rand's metaphysics had been different, she would have portrayed John Galt doing the same thing. As it was, Galt is portrayed to show every propensity for risking his life to save the woman he loved—and Rand declared John Galt to be the foremost proponent of the selfish glorification of Man's life on Earth. Well, if that's all there is, Rand was right. But what if Saint Clive was right? It changes the data—doesn't it?"

"What about those who talk about sacrificing themselves for the survival of their species?"

"If biological life is all there is," Bromley said, "then either they are preaching sacrifice for its own sake—Kant's doctrine, which both Rand and Saint Clive reject—or they value sheer numbers. I see no reason, if the basis of all values is biological life, that an individual should care about anything beyond the circle of his own life and those he loves personally—an anthropomorphization of the principle of the Selfish Gene. From a personal vantage point, why are the lives of one thousand or one million or twenty billion people one doesn't know—whether they exist now or merely as a future potential—more valuable than one's own life and its enjoyment? Why give up a bird in the hand for two in a bush that will die in a few billion years anyway, more or less?"

"Your heaven may not exist," Joan said.

"That's a calculated risk, based on internal data that I cannot share with anyone else. Communication without a common referent is impossible."

"But the referents keep on changing," Joan said. "You say God, the witches say Goddess—one deity, many deities. Nobody can agree."

"The Tower of Babel again," Hill said. "The Trinity of God is three Personalities in One, and it is my personal belief—again, none of this is official doctrine—that at least one of those Personalities is female—hence the earliest concepts of God as female."

"Witches say all three aspects are female—Maiden, Lady, and Crone," Joan said.

"And the Hindus say a male and a female principle synthesize to create the world—matter as male, energy as female. If I were to take a guess—again, unofficially—I'd say from my personal feelings that the Holy Spirit of the Trinity is the female aspect—a form of plasma energy; Christ as the male aspect, incarnated in matter; and God the Father the spiritual synthesis of the two."

"The Sword of *Goddess*," Joan said.

"What?"

"Never mind. Go on."

"It makes sense mythologically and psychologically. Read the psychiatrist Carl Jung. He wrote that each of us has a latent personality of the opposite sex in us—women have their male 'animus,' and men have their female 'anima.' The search for love is the attempt to find this latent personality fully developed in another person. I would also surmise that in andromen their anima is the dominant personality, and in lesbians the animus is in charge—ambisexuals seem to have both developed about equally. This microcosm of the opposite in each of us may be a microcosm of the basic structure of God and Heaven—we *are* supposed to have been made in God's image. If you ever have trouble understanding the opposite sex, don't look outward at them. Look within yourself. Inside is where the wisdom to process all externally derived knowledge resides."

Joan looked at Hill Bromley, shook her head, then smiled. "I don't know whether to believe anything you've said, Hill, but you've succeeded in challenging every fundamental I've lived by. I think I will attend that class of yours next Saturday."

Hill smiled back at her. "You're still welcome, but it's not really necessary. We have just covered my next year of seminars at one gulp."

"DO AS YOU WOULD BE DONE BY."

There were thirty red-cloaked Touchables seated in a conference room in offices adjacent to the Hasty-Tasty hovercart barn, with a large, red-haired and red-cloaked man addressing them. Joan, also cloaked in red and sitting in the third row of chairs, thought that perhaps Hill had been overly modest in his assessment of his lecture series, and she had decided to attend this Saturday morning, January 2, anyway—at an hour so early her eyes weren't quite open.

Joan still hadn't quite recovered from the New Year's party at Roland and Claire Church's house in Malibu. She remembered the party mainly for its incessant loud music, no place to sleep where there wasn't carousing in progress, a stoned androman named Henry who kept hitting on J. D. Harrison all night, and no way to escape, since her "date" for the evening was the bass fortissimist of the band that was providing the incessant loud music. She had finally fallen asleep around 7 A.M. New Year's in Hill's skymobile, and had awakened that afternoon in her bed in his living room. She surmised without being told that Hill had carried her in.

She was not sorry she'd come this morning, though. Hill was as lively in the lecture hall as he was talking one to one, and his lecture tracing the Golden Rule from its earliest statements in almost every major culture on Earth—with applications ranging from the Law of Equal Liberty through business ethics—was interesting throughout.

More interesting to Joan, though, was the lively question-and-answer session following the talk. Joan saw that Hill's role among these Touchables was not only priest, confessor, employer, and teacher but also psychiatrist and judge. A clear example of this came up in a question posed by two Touchable men—Harry and Roger—having to do with hovercart territories. Harry claimed that he had a contract with Roger to switch territories with him, had already paid him the money promised, but that Roger now refused to honor the agreement. "Is this true?" Hill asked Roger.

"Yes, Father," he said, "but I agreed and took his money because if I didn't switch with him, he would have beaten me up."

"Is that true?" Bromley asked Harry.

"Well," Harry said, "I let him *think* I would've beaten him up if he didn't switch with me, Father, but I wouldn't actually have done it. Even so, he promised to switch with me and took the five aura-grams I offered him."

"I tried to give it back to him," Roger said, "but he won't take it."

"A deal's a deal," Harry said. "We have a contract."

Hill shook his head. "One of the oldest principles of law is that any agreement made under duress isn't binding—legally or morally. You don't have any agreement or contract, Harry. You'd better take your money back. I suggest if you want Roger's route, you offer him what he wants for it."

"Fifty auragrams," Roger said.

"That's how much extra I'd make in the next six months!" Harry said.

"That's what you said when you threatened to bean me," said Roger.

"Settle this between yourselves after class," Hill said. "Just remember, Harry, if you get a reputation for trespassing the rights of others, there will always be someone bigger and stronger around who can do the same to you. Next question."

At the end of class, Hill led them in a hymn. They sang "For He's a Jolly Good Fellow."

Joan asked him about it after the Touchables had filed out. "It wasn't exactly Handel's *Messiah*," she said.

He smiled. "For the last six millennia, people have been singing the praises of God in the most grandiose terms possible. Most people don't believe any of it. With these people, I'll be happy if they believe God is jolly good."

That night, J. D. Harrison played once more at The Teapot Dome between Roland's two sets. After the middle set, the representative of the World Confederation of Lasegraphers, Denny Ronaas of Local 47, came up to the owner's table, where Hill was sitting. Joan was in the greenroom with Church and the rest of the band. "Hill," Ronaas said, "we've got a problem with that new lasegrapher of yours. I don't have a listing in my roster."

"Denny, I filed for a waiver—" Hill cut himself off. He was about to say that he had filed for a waiver with the local which Joan—whose membership was in the Astran union—had first played The Teapot Dome back in July, but realized in time that Ronaas was talking about "J. D. Harrison." He was in a double bind, this time—damned if he filed and damned if he didn't. "Denny, I'm sorry," Hill said. "I thought I filed but just realized I raped up."

"It's okay, Hill," Ronaas said: "you're still within the two-week grace period. But have it on my desk Monday morning, will you? I'd hate to see the Dome on the Unfair List."

"This is his last night," Hill said. "Do you still want to go through all that filework?"

Ronaas thought about it. "Don't bother, Hill. But give a comman some warning next time, will you?"

"Thanks, Denny," Hill said.

That night after closing up, Hill told Joan that the performing career of J. D. Harrison was over. "How can I file for a waiver regarding a lasegrapher from another union when J. D. Harrison isn't a member of any other union?"

Joan smiled wryly. "I guess it's not worth the risk of putting the Invisible Man on this one."

"Indeed not," Hill said. "Still, I'm going to miss you. You're much better at roga than that Darris princess who tramped in here a few months—"

She didn't really *hurt* him when she jabbed him in the stomach.

Joan and Hill left The Teapot Dome at just past 3 A.M. Sunday. Hill said he had just about enough time for a quick nap before leaving for Mass; on weekends—between his religious duties and his work at the Dome—he got most of his sleep in the afternoon.

It was a fifteen-minute taxi in Hill's skymobile from the club to his apartment. But while they were driving on Monica Boulevard, three blocks before Van Ness, a figure in a flying belt stooped on the vehicle's roof, rapped "Shave and a Haircut," then flew half a block ahead and waited for them to pull over.

It was the Invisible Man. Hill and Joan got out to talk to him.

"You look exhausted," Hill said.

"I just flew in from Newer York," he answered, "and boy, are my arms tired! But I had to get back to you in time, and couldn't risk any other type of travel for this one."

"Are you that hot?" Hill asked.

"No, you two are. And the simple fact that I know you is enough to get me a microwave job if I'm not careful." The Invisible Man took a deep breath. "The Monitors have your apartment staked out, Hill. And they've got a warrant naming both you and Joan Darris."

"Why didn't they pick me up at the Dome? Or right here?"

"Because the Monitor who got himself picked for the job of arresting you is one of the friars. He arranged this time to let me warn you. You know who it is, Hill."

"Yes."

253

"I was in Newer York, on business, when he called me. He said he'd hold things up until I got back."

"But how did they know *I* was here?" Joan asked.

"There's been a top-level search for you—and that means a linkup of every data bank the Federation has access to. They started by asking everyone who'd answer anyone else who you've spent any time with since your return to Earth. Your D.I. at Buffum—McDonough, I think her name is—mentioned you'd taken her to a mocha house where she watched you play roga. But she couldn't remember which of the twenty houses on Sunset it was. So they checked with the union. A waiver for the Dome was on file since last July."

"You say we're hot," Hill said. "Can you cool us off?"

"This is too much even for me, Hill. Brainprints and exit permits are easy. Chopping twelve centimeters off height, changing you from a mesomorph to an ectomorph—so you wouldn't fit the computer profile they've got on you—I can't manage. They've got a type on Joan—from her Corps records—that's even tighter. It doesn't matter how you change hair color, skin color, clothing. You go anywhere near a skyport with an A.P.B. like this out on you, and you've had it."

"What do you suggest?"

"If you can keep hidden a couple of weeks until the *Joan Baez* departs on the sixteenth, Roland might be able to get you off Earth as baggage. But you can't go near anywhere—the Dome, Hasty-Tasty, the home of anyone you know—that you could be linked with. I've got two flying belts and the address of my emergency retreat—a cabin up north in Sinsemilla. Stay over the ocean below scanning range—say, under thirty meters altitude—and you might make it there a little after dawn. Stay there until Roland or I get back to you. And don't stick your heads outside. The place is stocked with everything you'll need."

"Anything else?"

"Pray, Hill."

Hill smiled. "It's what I do for a living, Brian."

Brian loaded his flying belt into Hill's skymobile; then they taxied back toward the Dome, where the Invisible Man had parked a skymobile with the flying belts for Hill and Joan. While they were putting them on, he gave them detailed directions to his cabin.

Hill said a blessing for his friend; there was an exchange of handshakes, back pats, and kisses of Christian brotherhood; then—

with a rev of engines and another "Godspeed!"—Hill and Joan leaped into the night sky.

There was something wildly romantic, by its very nature, in an escape by night air, Joan thought, and the very danger of it seemed to heighten her artistic sensibility. The clear, open star canopy overhead, the Pacific below, the flashing blue-and-red of Hill's anticollision lights off to her right, their headlong rush into the cold wind of the unknown exhilarated her with the same intensity she'd previously found only while composing, or that one time with Dr. Blaine at Camp Buffum.

When they'd jumped out of Los Angeles, Joan had felt exhausted from being up almost twenty-two hours, with only a short nap Saturday afternoon, but the necessity of piloting the belt at 300 klicks per hour without either splashing into the Pacific or, like Icarus, flying too high for their own good and—in her case—being caught by Federation scanners left no room for exhaustion. Joan felt that maintaining communications silence, signaling only by hand, added to the eerie feel of the experience.

They made only one short landing, just north of Cruzville, so that Joan could adjust the gain on her windfield; then they resumed their escape north, with radiant units on their belts at full power for the remainder of their three-and-a-half-hour flight.

Dawn was just breaking when they reached the Invisible Man's cabin in northernmost Pacifica, which was helpful in recognizing the roof configurations he had mentioned. They landed just past 7 A.M. Hill spoke the voice code that let them into the cabin; then he switched on the cabin's heat reflector to prevent infrared detection that anyone was using the cabin before turning on heat and lights.

The cabin represented the bare minimums of civilized life—automatic kitchen, holovision receiver, domestic computer, and one dead serving robot. Even the bathroom was rustic, not have any vibromassage or holy screen. "Goddess," Joan said to Hill "I feel I've just fallen back to the Stone Age."

Hill nodded. "It was like this at the seminary."

"How did you survive?" Hill said.

"It wasn't easy," Hill said.

After changing into packaged pajamas they found in the closet, there was the problem of who would sleep where; there was only one bed. "You take it," Hill said. "I'll take the floor."

"Don't be ridiculous, Hill," Joan said. "There is no way that I'm going to allow you to sleep on a cold, hard floor. You haven't slept much in almost two days. In case of trouble, you'll need to be in good shape."

"The same reasoning applies equally to you," Hill said. "There's only one bed, though."

"Which we're going to have to share," Joan said.

"Joan, I'm a celibate priest. I can't sleep with a woman."

"I said sleep, not fuck."

"Haven't you ever heard of wet dreams? Put me in next to you for a night and I'm liable to go off like a firecracker."

"I might enjoy that," Joan said.

"Don't tempt me wickedly, Joan."

"I was born into that religion, remember? So you come. Do you stop being a priest?"

Hill shook his head. "Celibacy isn't a requirement in itself for being a priest since the Church unified. My own vow of celibacy was a personal matter, because of my previous sin. Aside from that, we're not married, and anything I do with you is fornication."

"Hill, I'm so exhausted I can hardly see straight, so I don't know if what I'm about to say is going to make any sense. But I'm going to *try* so we can both get some sleep. One. Your celibacy, as far as I can see, was a requirement of your command here on Earth—which you didn't give up: it was just captured by the enemy, and we're escaping behind the lines at the moment. Two. Any God who wouldn't say that—how many years have you been running the church for the Touchables?"

"Eight years," Hill said.

"Any God who wouldn't forgive you after that—when you say forgiving is His main hobby—isn't Jolly Good or a champion of *any* sort of goodness, so far as I'm concerned. Since you say He is by nature Good, I wouldn't worry much about His mercy. Three. You spent half an hour talking about love and the Female Principle in both God and human beings, without once realizing that this is something you've never experienced *in corpore*. Maybe sex in marriage is the ideal for us—I suspect it is, but I don't know for sure. But I don't think it's a corruption of that good if people love each other in any way possible, just being as careful as possible to be honest—not violate promises, or hurt someone else intentionally. There's always the possibility, in any action, of hurting someone by accident—but that's the price you pay for being human and not omniscient. There's no such thing as risk-free human action, and if God required perfect obedience, He would shout a little louder instead of whispering all the time. Fourth and—I hope—last. You talk about the Tower of Babel, and the truths being taught by each religion. In my view, the Wiccens and the Hindus are closer to the truth than Christianity on this one. To your knowledge, was Jesus ever wrong?"

"Once," Hill said. "He predicted the end of the world in the lifetime of His Apostles."

"Once is enough to disprove a rule, Hill. Maybe not everything He taught was *ex cathedra* either. Now, will you climb in here so we can fuck, then get some sleep?"

"Joan, will you marry me?"

"No, Hill. I'm already engaged. But you can have any commitment from me that you want short of that. I'm not dated up for the next sixteen years."

Hill stood there for a moment shaking, then said, "God forgive me," and climbed into bed next to Joan.

They put their arms around each other, and kissed. Then Hill said something in Latin.

"What did you just say?" Joan asked.

"Grace," Hill said.

VII.

λ6400Å to 7600Å

Both Joan and Hill were too tired, that first time, for it to be much of an experience. Hill came the instant after he entered Joan, so overwhelmed was he by the warm sensation of being encompassed, and Joan simply held him in her arms until he had fallen asleep, his body racked by sobs. She fell asleep, still holding him, immediately after.

Joan awoke first, at a little past noon on Sunday. She slipped out from under his arm and head, tried to bring some circulation back into her own left arm, then washed, showered, and ordered the kitchen to make some mocha. When it was ready, she bent over Hill and awoke him with a kiss. Hill opened his eyes lazily. "Good morning," Joan said.

It seemed to take a moment for Hill to become fully awake, and there was a look of puzzlement on his face while he tried to place where he was and what exactly was going on. When a few seconds later he remembered, he smiled back.

"How did you sleep?" Joan asked.

"Like Lazarus," he said.

"What?"

Hill laughed easily. "Well. I slept well. I've never slept better in my life."

"No guilt feelings?"

He smiled and took a cup of mocha from her. "None. Either I'm so far gone that I've shut my inner ear to God's scolding, or He's so mad at me that He isn't talking to me anymore—or you were right. I think it's the last."

Joan sat down in lotus on the bed next to him, then picked up her own cup again. "Hill," she said, "my conscience isn't as clear as yours. By coming to you for help, I brought a terrible price down on your head—far more than I thought it would be. I didn't know when I came to you that you were a Touchable, and I should have gone elsewhere as soon as I found out. Because of me, you've lost your mission, your career—everything—and I can't even offer to marry you and make an honest man of you."

He laughed.

"I've always tried to pay my own way," she went on, "and I don't like imposing costs on others—especially someone I care about as much as you."

"How did you figure to 'pay' me when you came to me last week? You weren't planning to seduce me as a payment from the start, were you?"

Joan shook her head. "I was planning to compose a lasegraphic *Mass*. That's the reason I asked to attend. It's something I don't know anything about, and I'd have to learn the form before I can start playing with ideas. I can't just work from the inside on it, as I usually do."

"I didn't know that," Hill said. "You've surprised me."

"You're surprised I needed to do research?"

"I'm surprised that you were planning to compose a *Mass* for a religious belief you don't share. You should have told me. I would have said you could come today—not that either of us made it."

"I was planning it as a surprise," Joan said. "I guess it doesn't matter now."

"It matters more than ever, Joan. Compose your *Mass*."

"It will have to be awfully good to make up for what I've put you through."

"Look, sweetheart, I'm an expert on guilt—both theoretical and applied—so I'm going to tell you something that I want you never to forget. Nobody—except by force or fraud—*ever* imposes a cost

260

on someone else without his or her consent. If I didn't want to help you, I could have sent you on your way."

"You were under a religious obligation," Joan said.

"Which I chose freely to adopt, Joan. Nobody put a knife to my throat."

"I should have foreseen this, Hill."

"Weren't you the one just last night who was telling me that there's no such thing as risk-free human action?"

"But I might get you *killed*." She was silent for another moment. "It wouldn't be the first time I've done it, either."

"Confessions usually begin 'Forgive me, Father, for I have sinned.' Want to take it from there?"

For the next few minutes, Joan told Hill the story of the Touchable woman who had chosen to be raped and icked rather than turn her over to the Wolf. She told how she had tried to work it through by abstracting the events into her first vistata, but that she felt she'd never been entirely successful. She still felt it was her fault.

Hill sighed. "I've lost track of how many confessions I've heard, but this one takes the prize. I absolve you. Okay?"

"It's not as easy as that, Hill."

"Joan, you were *five years old.*"

"What does my age have to do with it?"

"My God, do you think you were sprung from the head of Zeus with the wisdom of the ages?"

"I *chose* to go with her, Hill, and I knew what I was getting into. If I hadn't, she wouldn't have been icked."

"One," he said. "Nobody ever knows what *might* have been. Two. *She* was using *you* as a hostage. The only thing that proves she was a good soul was that she repented it in time to save you. But it cost her own life to do it."

"But that's just the *point*," Joan said. "She was willing to give her life for *me*, and I'm not willing to do the same for *any*one."

"Ah, the real issue finally gets out. Are you accusing yourself of selfishness or cowardice?"

"Both," Joan said.

"Joan, if you think you're a coward—just because you're capable of fear—then you don't understand what cowardice is. If you're thinking of the sort of thing where a man in battle freezes, or runs away, then it just shows he was the wrong man for the job in the first place—or he was improperly trained. Each of us has things that we can face better than others, and nobody has the right to tell us that what we choose to avoid facing means we're cowardly. The very fact that you're confronting yourself now with this—that you found it necessary to confront it in your art—proves you're not a coward."

"It doesn't mean that when it comes down to it I'd do any better the next time."

"Joan, there's a fine line between 'thinking strategically'—doing battle only when the odds are reasonably on your side—and running away simply because you're scared. Fear is a survival mechanism if we don't let it get the best of us."

"It *already* got the best of me, Hill. I've been telling myself for half a year that the reason I went into the service was to stay on the right side of the law so I could save my mother. The *real* reason was that I was afraid to try evading the draft, be declared Touchable, and maybe get icked—I'd never have risked escape now if Burke wasn't so disgusting."

"Both reasons were 'real,' Joan—and both were equally valid. But let's put cowardice aside, for a moment, and look at selfishness. You came back to Earth—when you didn't have to—to try to save your mother's life. Greater love hath no woman. And you think you're selfish?"

"I haven't proved anything, Hill. Risk my life for her, yes. Give it up for her, no."

"I don't have an answer for you on that, Joan. You said last night that my command had been captured by the enemy, and we were behind enemy lines. What you failed to take into account was that it was *my* command. If I'd wanted to demonstrate to my parish what faith really is, I would have been conducting Mass for them this morning when they came to arrest me. I could have sent you up here alone. Instead, I tossed the job to my assistant, Father Gregory, to make some excuse for my absence."

"You're a Touchable, Hill. If they catch you, they kill you."

"I'm going to die someday anyway, Joan. So are you. So does every one of us—no matter how long medical science lengthens the road in between. So if you're selfish and cowardly, so am I. So were the Apostles, when it came down to going to the cross with Jesus. A few hours ago I had an opportunity to make a really great exit. Instead, I ran off to hide, and to go to bed with you. You want to know something else? I'd do it again, with no regrets."

"We're some pair of selfish cowards, you and I," Joan said.

"We are. Both stem from our love of the only life we know from experience—*bios*. The transition to *zōē* may be desirable, but it sure isn't smooth. We go out kicking and screaming. But so does a baby when it leaves the womb. Why should being born again be any different?"

"That doesn't answer the question of giving up your life to save someone you love."

"Joan, ultimately, none of us can save *anyone*. There are four possible outcomes, restricting ourselves to the either-or possibility of an afterlife. Case one. Biological life only—no afterlife. You sacrifice your life to save someone you love. You're dead, neither enjoying nor regretting your action, and the person you saved is left alive—regretting your death, we hope—until his own eventual death. Case two. You fail to sacrifice your life for the person you love, and he dies—again, no afterlife. You're alive—feeling rotten about your own cowardice and his death—and he's dead and not regretting anything. Eventually, you die too. Case three. A *zōē* afterlife as well as the *bios* life we know now. You fail to sacrifice your life to save another, who's now dead. Ultimately, any saving that's to be done will be done by the will of God—you can't save anybody except yourself, so far as *zōē* is concerned. So if God likes the person whom you failed to save, *he* gets into heaven—and maybe you don't. It's up to God's assessment of your ultimate value—which may or may not have anything to do with your other-directedness. Case four. You sacrifice yourself for another, he's alive and you're dead. If God likes you, you're into heaven—but the person you save is left in *bios*, with more opportunity to rape up his own chances of getting to heaven. Ultimately, you don't have any control. See what I mean? Looked at one way, the most *selfish* thing you could do—assuming an afterlife—is sacrifice your life to save another as soon as possible; but I tend to think God looks upon players who deliberately put themselves out of the game about as favorably as he looked upon the builders of the Tower of Babel: both are trying to gate-crash. So don't worry about it so much. If I'm right about God and heaven, then He may decide He wants a top-notch lasegrapher even if you're weak on the self-sacrifice question. And if I'm wrong, then when you die you'll be dead and there won't be anyone who can give you any grief about it. This is about as close to a no-lose situation as anything I can think of."

Joan smiled. "You're out of mocha," she said. "I'll get you a refill."

Hill smiled, took both cups and placed them on the floor, then grabbed Joan, pulling her under him. They kissed. "If you don't mind," he said, taking a moment to nibble her left ear, "I'd like a different sort of refill right now."

Their second time was much, *much* better.

The next days were like a honeymoon, with Joan and Hill making love so often, and in so many different ways, that they thought they would be wearing themselves out. But it never happened—the more energy they expended on each other, the more energy they seemed to have. Joan felt the same rush of endless power that she felt at the console, as if she had stuck her finger into a power outlet. There seemed to be no end to the flow of energy; but it also made her hair—what there was left of it—stand on end.

For once, Joan was appreciative of her time in the Corps—her sessions with Dr. Blaine in particular—because what she had learned to be used on those she didn't care about could now be directed to someone she did. She didn't feel any less disgusted at having been drafted—she felt anything she wanted to learn could have been obtained with her own selection of teacher with her own price negotiations—but she wasn't going to reject a learning experience regardless of how it had come about.

With this knowledge that even the worst of trials brought growth came a relaxation to the possibilities of the future—an acceptance of whatever was to come, good or bad.

For Hill, his time with Joan was being born again ahead of schedule. He realized that there was a price still to be paid for this joy. He knew that he couldn't live—technically or actually—in sin with Joan and expect the Church to allow him to remain a priest. But he accepted his choice with the same calm with which Joan accepted her time in the Corps.

By their second Sunday together in the retreat, there was a sense that they had been together always. They had begun by guiding each other by show-and-tell. Now the kindergarten was over, and recess was in progress.

When they made love, their hands and lips, fingernails and teeth, tongues and eyelashes, vagina and penis seemed to find the most ecstatic spot on the other's body on automatic. They brought each other to ecstasy many, many times, and in between, they lay in each other's arms—sometimes in a joining of bodies that required no motion or effort—and Hill felt that if the joining of two human bodies could be this blissful, then the joining of two spiritual bodies had to be something so great as to be unimaginable. He said so to Joan.

She laughed. "I don't know about you—or anybody else—Hill, but I don't know of *anything* beyond my ability to imagine."

"Is that right?" he said.

"Yes. I'll prove it to you."

"How?"

"Give me a few minutes to prepare."

She spent the next fifteen minutes organizing her thoughts—applying the same tension-and-release formulas she used in her lase-graphic compositions—then announced to him, "*Tactata and Genitata No. 1* by Joan Darris. The first six movements form the tactata, the last the genitata."

First movement—hands. Second movement—lips. Third movement—fingernails. Fourth movement—teeth. Fifth movement—tongue. Sixth movement—eyelashes. Seventh movement—vagina.

He was too drained at the end of her forty-five-minute performance to applaud. But when he finally could speak again, he just gasped and said, "You win."

That Sunday, while they lay in each other's arms after making love for the fourth time that day, Joan wondered aloud to Hill how she could ever bring herself to leave him for Wolfgang, even sixteen years from now. Hill answered her that life existed only in the present moment—that it was only in the present that any choice was possible—and that neither of them had any claim on the future. A parting between them—as between all lovers—was inevitable, whether through separation by choice or through one of their deaths, so it was best not to think about that parting at all, and just accept the joining as it was. "Besides," Hill said, "maybe sixteen years from now we'll both be so convinced of the rightness of what we're doing that we won't feel the necessity of restricting ourselves to the monogamous sexual pattern. Perhaps you, Jaeger, and I will form a *mènage à trois*; or perhaps we'll find a fourth and play bridge."

Joan laughed, and they found the energy to make love for the fifth time that day.

They shared a simple happiness, that week, that neither of them had even known before.

But the parting came sooner than either of them had thought. On Monday, January 11, early in the morning while they were asleep, naked in each other's arms, the Federation Monitors surrounded the cabin, broke in, and arrested both of them.

Since Joan was not yet a Touchable, they allowed her time to get dressed. But Hill they dragged out into the cold air naked.

As the Monitors dragged the naked man out the cabin door, Joan shouted to him, "Hill, I'm sorry!"

Hill Bromley smiled and shouted back, "I'm not!"

JOAN WAS TAKEN back to Charlotte Amalie, where she was placed under house arrest at Villa Olga. She was kept there for three days, with no visitors permitted nor any outside communication—not even with her lawyer. She had time to play over and over again every shaky decision she'd ever made in her life, and didn't even have her lasegraphic instruments to keep her company—they'd been left back at The Teapot Dome. She had no idea what had happened to Hill, or how the Monitors had found them. She even had time to worry about the Invisible Man.

Finally, on Thursday, January 14, Burke Filcher paid her a visit. He seemed extraordinarily cheerful. "Good Goddess," he said when he saw her. "You really did do a job on your hair, didn't you?"

"Did you come here to talk about my hair, Burke?" Joan said.

Burke told a robot to fetch him a cup of mocha. "Oh, I expect we have many things to talk about, Joan."

"Well, you're running this squatball game. Go ahead."

"That's what I like about you, Joan. I've beaten you—absolutely and positively demonstrated my power over you—and you still have the wherewithal to be sarcastic to me. You're quite a woman."

"Are you trying to butter me up? I can't see why you'd bother."

Filcher laughed, and accepted the mocha from the robot. "Come on and sit down," he said. "I have a proposition for you."

They took two chairs in the living room.

"First," Filcher said, "I want you to understand exactly what your status is at the moment. When you disappeared from here, you were listed with the Corps as A.W.O.L. That was all I needed to get the search I wanted. And all it will take is a word from me to Matri-

266

arch Graves to have the charge at your court-venereal be desertion. You've seen what it means to be a Touchable. I don't think you'd like it. Are you with me so far?"

"Yes."

"All right. Now that you've seen the stick, I'll bring out the carrots. I will have you honorably discharged if you'll marry me, Joan."

Joan's mouth opened, shocked.

Filcher smiled at the impact of his words on her. "It's about time I settled down and had some children. I can't think of anyone who'd give them a better genetic start—and if they take after you at all, they'll probably turn out to be little devils. Second carrot. I've looked into your background, a little bit, and discovered why you came back to Earth in the first place. I was curious as to what could bring you back when you obviously disapproved of the way of life here so strongly. And I wasn't wrong about you: coming back to have your mother reanimated is just the sort of melodrama I should have expected from you, and it was stupid of me not to have realized that once you lost your custody suit against your father you would have no further reason to subject yourself to our laws. So I spent the last day and a half negotiating with your father and Vera, and have struck a deal. They are willing to turn over custody of your mother's body to me, awaiting a surrogate body which can be your first pregnancy when we're married. In exchange, I have arranged to introduce legislation that will ease trade restrictions that have been limiting your father's business interests, and I have promised Vera that I will support her nomination for the Ladyship from the Concord in the next election. So not only do you get a husband, but you also get your mother back. But if you ever leave me, not only will your release from the service be cancelled, and the desertion charges reactivated, but I will put an end to your mother's reanimation. That's just to keep you cooperative, in case you have any more silly objections to living out my sexual fantasies. So there's my offer. What do you have to say?"

Joan chose her next words carefully. "I don't suppose you could work in a few extra items?"

"It depends. Try me."

"The man I was arrested with, Hill Bromley. What is his status?"

"You should address that question to Vera, not me. It turns out this Bromley is a Touchable—did you know that?—and as such, he'll be tried by Legos, Ltd. I believe the charge will be statutory rape."

"What?"

"What else could it be? He had unauthorized intercourse with a member of the Peace Corps. A second offense of rape—it will mean the ovens for him, I think. But the jurisdiction falls on the Upper Manor, and if you have any special pleading to do on that one, talk to your sister, not me. Anything else?"

"Would you consider St. Clive for a honeymoon—say, next spring?"

"What's so special about St. Clive in the spring?"

"That's when the St. Clive Competition is held. I'd like to enter."

Filcher shook his head. "You can put that idea out of your head right now. I'm not about to have my wife running around the system as an entertainer. You can play the laser for me, and perhaps to amuse our guests when we give a reception, but that's it. Now I want your answer, Joan. You've tried my patience as much as I'm going to let you. What do you say?"

"You've left me no choice, Burke. I accept."

"Marvelous!"

He got up and kissed her on the lips. "You won't regret this, Joan. You and I are going to have lots of fun together."

"Shall we settle the wedding details now?" Joan asked.

"Such enthusiasm! By all means."

"My custody suit against my father and Vera has really strained our relations," Joan said. "I'd like to go back and live with them at Helix Vista until the wedding to patch things up. It will be the best place to hold the wedding, anyway. Since you're probably eager, I suggest we make it only a few weeks from now. How does January twenty-seventh—a Wednesday—sound to you?"

"Why a weekday, Joan?"

"I don't want a large, formal wedding, Burke, and that will cut down on the attendance to a certain extent."

Filcher nodded. "It all sounds reasonable. I suppose you'll want to be traditional about this, and not sleep with me again until our wedding night?"

"Absence makes the heart grow fonder, Burke."

"All right, you've sold me the entire bill of goods. You may leave for Helix Vista this afternoon."

"Will you be coming with me?"

"Why should I?"

"Aren't you afraid of my running off again?" Joan asked.

"Not in the least. With your mother as hostage, I'm not worried at all about losing you. Aside from that, you're really not all that good at escaping. Did you really think the Monitors wouldn't find the false transponders you shipped back here—what was it?—one to this address, one to C.P.O., and one to your lawyers? I must admit, they were packaged cleverly, but you're an amateur at that sort of thing, Joan. Stick to the laser, where at least you have some talent."

"May I ask how I was tracked down?"

"The—shall we say—'countereconomist' whose cabin you were using wasn't all that hard to persuade into giving us your where-abouts—once it was made clear to him that not doing so would cost him his life. We traded the information for a guarantee of immunity. Oh, one more thing," Filcher said. "Your luggage, laser equipment, and a box of your hair were recovered by the Monitors. Now that things are all settled, you may have them back."

"I was planning to have my hair made into a wig," Joan said.

"Wonderful! Can it be ready by our wedding?"

"I'll see that it is, Burke."

"Fine." Filcher got up. "You're going to make a beautiful bride, Joan."

Joan stood up and smiled. "I plan to wear white."

Joan was greeted, upon her return to Helix Vista, by her father, brothers, and Vera, with the welcome given to the Prodigal Son. It was like her return nine months earlier from Ad Astra, only even warmer. No mention was even made of their custody battle.

Dinner that night featured an appetizer of quiche Lorraine.

After dinner, Joan asked Vera if they could speak alone in her study. Vera said, "Of course," and they took their mocha in there with them.

"Vera," Joan said, "you and I have had a lot of trouble with each other, and I think you know the reason as well as I. I must have been a constant reproach to you, because of my continuation of the laser. I think you know, now, that that part of my life is all over."

Vera nodded and sipped her mocha.

"We know each other pretty well, and because we do, we've al-ways known just what needs to be done to hurt the other one. We've both done a lot of that to each other. If you feel you have any com-plaint against me, I apologize for it now, and will try to make up for it. But I'm going to ask you for a favor, now, and if you grant it, it will wipe the screen clean between us. You asked me once if I could forgive you. If you do this for me, I can and will."

"What is it, Joan, that you want me to do?"

"I want you to drop the statutory-rape charge against Hill Bromley."

"You care about a Touchable—and a Christian priest, I'm told—so much?" Vera asked.

"He's a friend who helped me when I needed it, Vera. And you and I both know that the statutory-rape charge is a technical offense. If you simply list my release from the service—which Burke is arranging—from the date I went A.W.O.L., then he won't have slept with a member of the Peace Corps and there will have been no statutory rape committed."

Vera took another sip of her mocha. "All right, Joan. If this means so much to you, I'll do it. I have no desire to see you live with this man's life on your conscience."

Joan found tears squirting down her cheeks. "Lady bless you," she said. "Consider the screen wiped clean between us, Vera."

"Thank you, Joan." Vera sipped again. "It won't be very difficult to make arrangements with the Federation prosecutrix. There's no necessity for a statutory-rape charge to send this man to the ovens. Why, possession of a grafted penis is quite enough to do it; statutory rape was merely a charge of convenience, so that our relations with St. Clive wouldn't be affected. Grafted penis, false transponder, appearing uncloaked in public—yes, it won't be any problem at all. We can deal with him quite nicely without putting your conscience on the line."

Joan stared at Vera as if she couldn't believe what she was hearing. "Do you think that it was *my* feelings I was thinking about when I asked you to drop the charges?"

Vera looked genuinely surprised. "What else?"

"Vera, I'm talking about saving a man's *life,* not my *sensibilities.*"

"You were trying to get a full pardon?"

"Yes, of course."

"But Joan, that's quite impossible. I assumed you knew that when you brought it up. How could you expect me to let a known criminal off free? Simply for your convenience?"

"Have you no compassion?" Joan said.

"Joan, I don't understand this. I thought that was what I was *showing* to you when I agreed to drop the statutory-rape charge. But nothing I do is ever enough for you, is it? It wasn't enough that I saved you from the Touchable when you were five—I was supposed to have saved the other Touchable also. It wasn't enough that I consoled your father when our mother was deanimated—I was supposed to cut out a baby's brain to bring her back. And it's not enough for you that I'm bending a lifelong moral principle to allow you to have just that repugnant medical procedure done, to please you—I'm supposed to violate my oath of office to uphold the Law of the Land just so a felonious friend of yours can be let free to run wild again. What do you *want* from me?"

Joan looked at Vera, speechless, for what seemed an endless minute. She carefully examined her older sister's face. "You really *mean* everything you just said, don't you?"

"Of course I mean it!"

Joan inclined her head. Then she looked up at Vera and said, "I'm sorry I bothered you with this, Vera. I'll try not to misunderstand you again."

Joan got up to leave.

"About that statutory-rape charge—"

Joan thought for a moment. "Best to leave things the way they are," she said. "If Hill is to die, I think he'd want it to be for this."

"All right," Vera said.

Joan left Vera in the study and walked outside to the lawn, which was covered by a thick blanket of snow. Helix Vista's radiant units were off, allowing the snow to remain. Joan stood in the snow looking up to the star-broken sky, and shivered. She wasn't shivering only from the cold.

GIFTS FOR THE COUPLE began arriving at Helix Vista immediately, as news of the wedding got out. Society reporters on the holy networks were calling it the political wedding of the decade—one of the most interesting alliances in the Federation's history, linking Wendell's influence and the family wealth with Burke Filcher's extraterrestrial friendships and political shrewdness. There was talk of the beginning of a new dynasty, with Filcher parlaying his marriage into the Prime Minister's Mansion, with Wendell Darris returned to the House of Gentry in the next election—possibly as the next President—and with either Vera Delaney or Joan herself making a run for the Upper Manor and ending up as First Lady.

Teny Reich, a gossip reporter from the Paraversal Network, came by Helix Vista to interview Joan, and asked her what her feelings were about marrying "the World's Most Eligible Bachelor."

"It's the most exciting thing that I've ever chosen to do," Joan said, gushing and bubbling for the camera. "Burke has promised me lots of fun, and I'm sure he's right."

"What about your future in politics?" she asked.

"Well, Teny," Joan said, "my family background is firmly Libertarian, and I think you'll find me proving myself no different."

"Then you don't discount the possibility of running yourself?"

"The first rule in politics, Teny, is never to pin yourself down before you have to. So I'll just say that everyone will know what I've decided very soon now."

Regardless of the wedding date's being a weekday, the guest list began growing dramatically. Soon it was so large that the terrace on the roof of Helix Vista, where the wedding was to take place, was booked about 10 percent past the number of people the design limits of the house called for, and plans were made to seat the overflow in front of a giant holoscreen on the lawn, where the reception was going to be. To make way for the reception, the lawn dome was dismantled.

Wendell Darris sent a picturegram from St. Clive with his best wishes for the bride and groom. But he also apologized that he would not be able to return to Earth in time for the wedding—and Joan wondered whether Wendell's excuse about ship schedules was true or whether he might be jealous of her. Wendell did, however, arrange for Joan to have a pair of brooches made up at his expense from fire gems mined by his father, by the most expensive jeweler in Newer York, one for her and one for her Maid of Honor, Vera. In Vera's place, Kate Seymour was to perform the wedding.

The arrival of wedding gifts overloaded the ability of the estate's robots to find storage space, and one afternoon, Joan accompanied two of the robots into Helix Vista's basement to see if she could lend a human touch to the problem. The place was crowded to the maximum with every sort of thing she could imagine, and Joan wondered—from her experiences with Jews' and Christians' damning every hammer that hit a thumb and every skymobile that was slow starting—whether there was a basement like this in Hell, where such uncooperative items ended up when their lives were over.

But while she was rummaging around looking for a clear space, she found something that startled her so much that for a few seconds, she froze. At first she saw only a patch of red, then at closer look red fabric; then—when she finally got close enough—she saw that it was a Touchable's red cloak. She didn't need to be told that it was the same cloak that had been ripped off the Touchable woman who had been icked on the landing strip, and the same cloak that Vera had wrapped her in when she carried her home.

Joan looked at the cloak carefully and almost felt the ghostly vibrations calling out from it. When she left the basement, she put it in a box and hid the cloak in her bedroom.

The next day was a busy one for Joan. She started by going to downtown Newer York to be fitted for the wedding gown she would be wearing—the same gown Kate Seymour had worn when she married Zachary Darris. Then Joan stopped by the downtown Newer York post office, where she picked up another package. She went immediately from the post office to the jeweler, where she made her selection of the brooch she wanted for herself and for Vera. The jeweler was a little chagrined at her choice. "Ms. Darris," Mr. Rabinowitz said, "that brooch is absolutely *huge*."

"If you don't like it, why do you sell it?"

"It's for—well—some of our clientele with less-refined habits."

"I like it," Joan said. "That's the size and style brooch I want."

"You're the customer," the jeweler said, "and the customer is always right."

"I like that," Joan said. "Is it original?"

Joan smiled, on her way out, as the jeweler turned to another comman and spoke to him in Yiddish. She didn't catch all of it, but she had spent enough time with the Rubinsteins to understand "*goyisher* taste."

After her visit to the jeweler, Joan had lunch, then flew the family limousine into Forest Hills. She spent an hour in the vivarium, visiting her mother's cryonic capsule in the Hall of Preservation. She told the capsule everything that had happened to her, and tried to explain why she was marrying Filcher. Then she pressed her lips against the capsule and cried. "I wish you could be here to see this, Mom," she said. "It's going to be quite a show."

She spent that evening with her younger brothers back at home. Delaney wanted to know if the man she was marrying was the same Burke Filcher they'd told him about in school, who had negotiated the Rainbow Compact in Brooklyn, and in whose honor the name

273

had been changed to Rainborough. Joan told her brother that it was.

The next day, Jack Malcolm visited Joan. He began by delivering to her the package that had arrived for her at the Malcolm Institute. Joan thanked him, but put it aside unopened; she wouldn't be needing that transponder, now.

"So," Jack said. "Another Darris bites the dust—pardon me: Vera is a Delaney."

"I'm not giving up the laser, Jack."

"No? That's sure what it looks like."

"Appearances can be deceiving," Joan said. "As a matter of fact, I've already started making some sketches for a *Mass*. It's going to take some time, though—I don't want to rush this. I promised someone that this would be very special. I'll send you a draft a year from now."

"I sent your *Helix Vistata* to the St. Clive Competition," Jack said. "You've been accepted."

"Jack, I can't possibly tell you at the moment how much that means to me."

"I don't see why," Malcolm said. "You're not going."

"There's more than one way to skin a cat, Jack—though why anyone would want a skinned cat is beyond me. Don't write off my career yet."

Jack cleared his throat. "If you say so." He paused for a second. "Joan, why Filcher? He doesn't seem to be your type."

"Jack! Are you jealous?"

"Well, maybe a little. I always thought you'd marry a lasegrapher, at least."

"Burke is only my first husband," Joan said. "And I expect he'll be getting tired of me much more quickly than he imagines. You never can tell. Maybe about sixteen years from now you'll find me marrying again—the next time, a lasegrapher."

"Is it true you're engaged to Wolfgang Jaeger?"

"Jack," Joan said reproachfully. "Is that something it's proper to ask me a few days before I marry someone else?"

One more package arrived at Helix Vista addressed to Joan, but this was one she was sending to herself, containing her flying belt and Marnie hunting medallion. That evening, she was going on a family hunt with her father, Vera, Mark and the twins.

Stanton expressed surprise that Joan was joining them, because of her remarks after the custody hearing about people who hunted Touchables. "Dad," Joan said, "if I've learned anything in the last few weeks, it's that there's a very easy answer why people hunt Touchables—and I'm certainly not going to pretend that some Touchables don't deserve it. If I'm going to be happy on this planet, I might as well get used to the core of its cultural heritage right away."

The family hunting strategy, however, was wrecked when Nicque and Vicque cluttered up the air with a squabble as to which one of them would get first dibs on any boy they caught. While they were arguing, Mark was prevented from hearing a signal being picked up on his wristscanner, and by the time he could hear it, it was too weak to triangulate on. Everyone but Joan was chilly to the twins for the entire skymobile trip back to Helix Vista.

The weekend before the wedding, Joan decided to take her brother Zack, who had just turned fifteen, on a weekend jaunt to Hawaii with her. She felt it was her only chance to thank him for his kindness in sending her lasegraphic instruments to her while she was in the Corps. They spent Saturday the 23rd touring around Honolulu, and she took him to Molokai to the gambling casinos that evening. Zack seemed to be a whiz at velletrom, walking out with several hundred more auragrams than he'd come in with.

They stopped off at The Teapot Dome in Los Angeles on the way back, to pay her respects to Roland and Estelle, who were running the mocha house in Hill's absence. She explained to them everything she knew about Hill's status, and what his hopes were. Zack was surprised at what Joan told them, but he promised not to say anything. Before they left, Roland gave Joan the wedding present he had told her he was holding for her. When she saw it—and could hold it in her hands—she thought it was the nicest present anyone could have given her.

Estelle told Joan, before she left, that they would see her in Newer York the next day, for Hill's trial.

Vera had decided that she would sit on the case herself.

"Do you have anything to say before sentence is passed?"

It was a drama that had been played out in courtrooms throughout history. The prisoner in this case, a handsome, determined-looking Touchable man with red hair peeking out from his red-hooded cloak, stood in the dock. His attorney—a public defender appointed by the court—wore a lavender cloak. The prosecutrix, in her pink cloak, sat at the prosecution table at the left of the chamber. The jury of eight women and four andromen were in a box on the right side with a court recorder, a robot, just in front of them. The court clerk, in his lavender cloak, sat at a desk just below the judge's bench, watching an array of video monitors and wearing a headset that permitted the judge to speak to him privately.

The visitors' gallery was large and filled, as usual, with witnesses, spectators, and holovision technicians; several cameras were suspended at discreet—but strategic—points around the courtroom. Two burly-looking bailiffs, both in blue, stood in opposite aisles of the visitors' gallery, each with his legs planted apart and his arms folded across his chest, looking like eunuchs guarding a harem.

Her Honor Vera Collier Delaney sat at her bench, raised higher than anyone else in this chamber, the Legos, Ltd., corporate logo with its motto "Lex Scripta, Lex Terrae" prominently displayed on the seal in front of her. She wore a black cloak. An enormous holovision monitor above her showed, at the moment, a close-up of Hill Bromley.

The image on the screen cut to Vera. She looked nervous waiting for the prisoner's reply to her question. For the entire trial, which had lasted all of that day, Hill Bromley had stood mute, refusing to offer any defense whatsoever to the charge of rape brought against him. The image on the screen cut back to Hill Bromley once again.

Hill looked at the jury, looked at the prosecutrix, looked up at the huge monitor—now showing an encompassing view of the gallery that allowed him to see Joan, Estelle, Roland, and several disguised Touchables from his parish—then lowered his eyes to meet Vera's.

He did not say anything.

Vera wondered why the prisoner looked so calm, and why she was the one who was sweating.

Finally, she couldn't take it anymore. "I'm told you're a Christian priest," she said. "Aren't you even going to forgive me?"

Bromley smiled. "It is my job to forgive sins after they are committed, not during."

"You say that aloud," Vera said, "but inwardly, you're asking your God to damn me, aren't you?"

"God doesn't damn anyone," Hill said. "It's just that sometimes He can't prevent them from damning themselves."

"Can't? I thought He was supposed to be All-Powerful."

"He can do All Things that can be done. This does not include denying the laws of logic, to which even He is subject. Once He decided that we would have the free choice to do good or evil, He was stuck with it. If you are to be damned, it will be because you have erected your own barrier against His Good, and He will not trespass your boundaries. I suggest you stock up, though. It looks as if it's going to be a long winter."

"How can you moralize this way when you are guilty of violating your own standards?"

"Have you seen me offer a defense? What happens to me happens to me. I thought we were talking about saving *your* soul."

"You seem to forget that I'm the judge here, and you're the prisoner."

"If you think you're free to judge me, then do it. Your turn in the dock will come soon enough."

Vera saw the holovision director signaling her to speed things up; they were going to be behind for the promo.

Vera pressed a panel on her bench. "Court clerk will read the sentence."

The text appeared on the clerk's monitor board. He pressed a panel on his desk, swiveling it around to face the gallery, then in a professional-sounding baritone began reading from his monitor. "Thank you, Your Honor. Touchable Number 809-8PC-101 will be taken for a last shuttle ride on PanCord Skylines to the Federation Execution Facility at Detroit, Ontario. There he'll be given a sumptuous last meal courtesy of Chez Bernie's Restaurants. Then, at midnight Sunday, the thirty-first of January, he'll be taken into the fabulous Radarmatic Microwave Oven for his personal execution."

Hill stood absolutely still, and Vera wondered why she felt it was she who had just been sentenced.

"We're running a little late, today, so we won't have time to mention all our fine sponsors. Back to you, Your Honor."

Both bailiffs turned to face the gallery, uncrossed their arms, and began applauding wildly.

No one else in the gallery applauded.

After a few seconds of embarrassing silence, the director ordered the control room to cut in a prerecorded applause track and get the shot off the gallery immediately.

When the applause track was muted down again, the holy zoomed in on Vera, who said, "So Mote It Be!"

She banged her gavel.

The director ordered the control room to restart the applause track and cut to the promo. But it didn't happen. Instead, in the silence that followed the banging of the gavel, the holy zoomed in on Hill Bromley again.

277

Nobody knew why the control-room technician, a young com-man named Richard Dover, ignored his director's order. It cost him his job. But transmitted live to the satellite, and from there to millions of homes on Earth, there was a holy shot of Hill Bromley as he looked straight into the camera and said to them all, "Forgive them, Father, though they know *exactly* what they do."

THE QUESTION most likely to be asked of a guest who arrived at Helix Vista for the wedding was not whether he was on the bride or groom's side of the family, but on which side of the aisle he sat in the House. Just about half the political notables from the Lower Manor had decided to show up. The bridegroom thought it unlikely that a quorum could be managed unless the session was called for right here.

The politicos at the estate, the morning of January 27, were out-numbered only by the sky marshals trying to assist the ushers in seating those with reserved places on the terrace, and keeping those of lesser privilege off. They were not entirely successful: a large contingent chose to stand near the back—out toward the edge of the terrace, actually—rather than take their seats on the lawn and watch on the holoscreen.

Several floors down, Joan was being assisted by Vera and her Aunt Melentha in putting final touches on her attire. She was wearing both her grandmother's white dress and the wig of her own red hair. At a quarter to eleven—fifteen minutes before the wedding was scheduled to take place—Joan asked if she could be alone with Vera for a few minutes. Melentha said it was perfectly all right, and left.

When they were alone together, Joan took out a box and opened it. It was the two brooches, laden with her grandfather's fire gems, that had been made up for her and Vera. One of them—the one Joan was to wear—had the fire gems set into the pattern of the Darris family emblem, an ascending helix. Joan asked Vera to pin it on for her, and she did.

Then Joan took out the other brooch, with fire gems set into the Delaney emblem, a half-moon. As Joan pinned it on Vera, she said, "Let this be a symbol of my true feelings for you. You know the Craft much better than I do, but I've left a part of myself in here for you."

"As a hostage?" Vera asked.

"As a simple reminder," Joan said. "Just keep it close to your heart whenever you're thinking of me."

"That's very sweet, Joan. I'll wear it always." She leaned over and kissed Joan.

"I was hoping you'd feel that way," Joan said. She kissed Vera in return.

"Ready?" Vera asked Joan.

"Go on ahead," Joan said. "I'll be out in a minute."

As soon as Vera left, Joan took out a small bottle of oil and anointed herself for what was to follow.

But the oil she used to anoint herself was not Lovers' Oil, which was traditional for a wedding. Joan anointed herself with Rosemary. It was used for protection in battle.

The terrace on the roof of Helix Vista was arranged in concentric circles of chairs around the altar, which was set up—according to tradition—with a white-cloth-covered table on which stood a statue of Diana the Huntress, a censer of incense, a caldron and chalice, and four candles: two white ones, a Red Yoni, and a Golden Phallus. In front of this table were three circles joined together. Kate Seymour, in her green priestess robes, stood in the top circle, which had a pentagram inside. Burke Filcher stood in the left circle, with his best man—the Prime Minister of the Federation—just outside the circle to his left. Joan stood in the right circle, with her Maid of Honor, Vera, just outside the circle to her right.

"All join hands!" Kate Seymour ordered. All on the terrace did so.

She began by casting the circle, using—this time—not a black althame, but a wand of mistletoe. Then the flour girls cast barley flour around the couple, followed by Kate Seymour consecrating the ground within the circle with incense, water, and salt—representing fire, air, water, and earth. Kate Seymour then said to the couple, blessing each of them with her wand, "I purify you from all anxiety, all fears, in the name of Diana."

It was time for the priestess to close the circle and make her invocations:

279

"Hail to thee, Powers of the East! Come and be witness as we perform the ancient rites!

"Hail to thee, Powers of the South! Come and be witness as we perform the ancient laws!

"Hail to thee, Powers of the Waters! Come and guard our circle!

"Hail to thee, corner of all powers! Great Demeter, Persephone, Kore, Ceres! Earth Mothers and Fates! Great sea of glass! Guard our circle and bear witness as we perform our rite according to your heritage!"

The wedding proceeded, methodically and slowly, with Kate Seymour spreading blessings with Love Incense from the censer in front of the statue of Diana. She bound the couple together with cord. She drew hot spiced wine from the caldron and ladled it into the chalice. The couple both drank from it.

Finally, it was time for the vows. Vera handed Joan the ring for Burke, and the Prime Minister handed Burke the ring for Joan.

"Will you, Burke Filcher, according to the Will of the Goddess and the laws of Hudson Parish, take this woman to be your wife?"

"I will," said Burke Filcher.

"And will you, Joan, according to the Will of the Goddess and the laws of Hudson Parish, take this man to be your husband?"

"As I have been done by, I will."

There was a murmur in the crowd; Joan had rewritten her vows unexpectedly.

Kate Seymour looked even more startled, but it was not because of what Joan had said. She was closest to the censer of incense, and she smelled it first.

The incense smell had changed, somehow, from Love Incense to Dragon's Blood.

She tried to ignore an omen that should not have been ignored. There were just too many people here to stop now.

"Then in the Name of the Mother of all Mothers and the World Federation—"

Nobody ever heard the rest of that sentence, if indeed she ever finished it. At the precise instant that Kate Seymour said the word "Federation," a deep roaring commenced, drowning out even the High Priestess's amplified voice.

The sound was enormously loud, and so low that all those present could feel the subsonics shaking them. Then, as it continued, the sound began to get louder and louder and louder as the vibrations found the natural harmonic of the house, and began to use it as a gigantic amplifier.

The entire house began to rumble, as if before an earthquake.

Kate Seymour was a trouper. She managed to shout above the roar and ordered, "Don't you dare panic! There is safe evacuation for everyone here if you do exactly as I say!"

She spoke into her wristphone and ordered Helix Vista's domestic computer to engage the emergency escape chutes from the terrace roof to the lawn, seven stories below.

It took almost ten minutes for everyone on the terrace and inside the house to slide down the chutes to the lawn, while the rumbling of the house became louder and louder and louder; but—many said that it was because of the protection of the Goddess—everyone was evacuated from the house, and standing well clear of it, when the vibrations and sympathetic harmony finally completed their work, and Helix Vista collapsed into rubble.

As the house collapsed, the amplifier effect cut off and it became possible to track down where the sound had been coming from.

A robot was standing in what was left of the Tiger Pit in the former location of the lawn dome. It was holding a bass fortissimo aimed at the house.

Nobody ever was able to find out much more than that the robot said it had been following orders it had received from Helix Vista's domestic computer. But nobody could ask the domestic computer if that was true, since it had been destroyed with the house and was now buried in the rubble.

Burke Filcher was a determined man. He wasn't going to allow a little thing like a house collapsing to halt his wedding. He asked Kate Seymour to complete the ceremony on the lawn, with everyone standing around in a single large circle; then he said to the assembled guests that he knew they wouldn't mind if he and his new bride didn't hang around, since there couldn't be a reception anyway. He and Joan got into his limousine and, escorted by a contingent of flying-belted sky marshals, flew off to Soleri Skyport, where they caught a privately chartered Federation shuttle back to Charlotte Amalie. His plans included spending their first night as man and wife at his estate before they took a private yacht—lent to him as a wedding present by his best man—to Ad Astra for a two-week honeymoon.

They spent the rest of that day at Villa Olga on their private beach; then he took Joan out for a romantic dinner and dancing at a club on the other side of Isle of Persephone.

They returned to his estate at 10 P.M.

Burke once again put on the silk pajamas that Joan had given him for Yule, and Joan put on a black-lace nightgown that Kate Seymour had given her for the occasion. Joan spent half an hour in the bathroom, freshening herself up; then Burke went in and cleaned his teeth before coming out to meet Joan.

When he came out of the bathroom, though, Joan was holding a laser gun on him. It looked as if it had been jury-rigged—indeed it had, from a very special LCAA MARK 800B—out of a chromatic laser. Joan had a power pack slung over her shoulder, and an extra gun on her hip.

"What on Earth do you think you're doing, Joan?" Filcher said.

"You told me I should stick to the laser, Burke," she said, "but you didn't want me entertaining with it. Well, am I entertaining you?"

"What—"

"I'm going to rape you, Burke."

"That's impossible."

"Is it? You told me that the essence of rape is trespass. Well, I can't be sure if I'm trespassing you—since I'm just returning a compliment you once paid me—but I'm going to try. Now listen to me carefully. I have this thing rigged either to deliver a continuous pulse at eighty-six watts—including a deadly line in the infrared—or, by switching from direct feed-in to capacitance, to give you bursts of power ten times that. My first shot will be at your family jewels."

"You've just sentenced your mother to death," Burke said.

"I don't think so. You're going to turn over custody of her body to me, all nice and legal, by the time we're through."

"You'll never get away with this!"

"I will."

Burke Filcher was not a stupid man. He knew if he could get a mirror behind him, Joan would not be able to shoot without risking a bounce-back to herself. He made a dash to get in front of his bedroom mirror.

He didn't make it. Joan shot directly into the mirror and landed a short, continuous pulse of the laser reflected into his behind.

Filcher yelped as the shot hit him, and the pain caused him to lose control. His bowels and bladder cut loose at the same time, making an utter mess of the silk pajamas.

Joan laughed; this was something she had not expected. "I like your *Scatata in Fifth*, Burke. It has a wonderful first movement. No, keep your hands at your sides, where I can see them."

282

"Are you going to allow me to clean up, now that you've had your fun?"

"Fun was never my intention, Burke. Nor was revenge—though I'm gratified that your accident provided me some. I'm doing this to save lives I can't save any other way. You're about to make a phone call to the Federation First Lady. Tell your computer to get her—now—or it'll be five years before you'll have anything to fuck with again."

"You *must* allow me to clean up before I call her."

"I must nothing! Call or lose it, raper!"

He ordered the domestic computer to call the First Lady. While the connection was being made, Joan told him exactly what to say, and assured him that if he did not do as he was told, the First Lady would be witnessing his assassination.

"If you kill me, you'll be dead too," Filcher said.

"That's a price I'm willing to pay, if I have to, Burke."

Joan stood out of range of the camera pickup, holding the laser pointed at Filcher's crotch. About another minute later, the domestic computer announced that it had the First Lady ready now.

"Burkie, darling!" the First Lady gushed. "I never expected to hear from you tonight!"

Joan had seen the First Lady on the holy, but somehow she seemed even more stunningly beautiful without her usual makeup, allowing her silken blond hair and large blue eyes to dominate.

"How are you tonight, Madam First Lady?" Burke said.

"Oh, you're not going to go all formal on me just because I'm First Lady, now, are you? I remember a time when you weren't *formal* with me at all. Or have you had so many other women that you don't remember?"

"How could I ever forget, Devereux?"

"That's better. Burkie, is there something wrong with your pajamas?"

"Hmm? Oh, I'm afraid my bride spilled some pineapple juice on me."

"Really? For a moment I thought you'd had an accident in your pants!"

"You're still a cat, love. Would I be standing in my bedroom talking to the First Lady—in the middle of my honeymoon—with scat in my pants?"

"You never did have an appreciation for my sense of humor, Burke. What's so important that you had to tear yourself away from your bride?"

"I've just received a picturegram from Wendell Darris, Madam First Lady—"

"It's still 'Devereux,' darling," she said. "I'm not mad at you."

"Devereux. He tells me that a certain Touchable we've just condemned to the ovens is one of St. Clive's best-loved missionaries. I'm afraid if we go through with it, we're liable to be pushed back twenty years in our economic dealings with them."

"Oh, dear!" the First Lady said. "Well, we certainly can't have that over one Touchable."

"They say if we pardon him, they'll accept him back into St. Clive with a minimum of publicity to embarrass us. If we move fast, we can have him on a ship to St. Clive tomorrow."

"I'll order a full pardon immediately," the First Lady said. "What's his name and number?"

"The name is Hill Bromley," Filcher said. "Sweetheart," he said to Joan, off screen, "what did the Facility in Detroit say the number was?"

Joan said, "It's 809-8PC-101."

Burke repeated it.

"My computer got that, darling," the First Lady said.

"Thank you, Devereux. If you'll have him released tonight, I'll take care of the rest."

"That's sweet of you, Burke—and so is your erection. Is that in honor of me, or your bride?"

Burke looked down; he had been so nervous that he hadn't even noticed that his penis had climbed out his pajama fly. "Just a salute to the First Lady," he said quickly, as it shriveled up.

The First Lady laughed. "This has been some day for you, hasn't it, darling? I heard about the debacle at your wedding. I do hope you and your lovely bride can visit me as soon as you get back from your honeymoon. Perhaps it will change your luck."

"Thank you, Devereux," he said.

"Good night, darling."

"Good night, Madam First Lady."

Burke stood at full attention until the image faded out.

Joan couldn't restrain her laughter any longer. "Bravo," she said. "That took guts and fast thinking, Burke. I compliment you."

"Why don't you go ahead and shoot?" Filcher said. "When she finds out the truth, my political career is over. And that bitch is the worst gossip in the Federation."

"That's the rape I intended to commit on you, Burke. Perhaps now that you're out of politics you might let your natural talents predominate and do something useful, for a change. You've been wasting yourself terribly."

"Small consolation," he said. "I suppose you realize that this is going to mean an annulment of our wedding?"

Joan laughed again. "That's what I like about you, Burke. You're standing with your pants full of scat, with me holding a laser on you, and you still have the wherewithal to be sarcastic to me. You're quite a man. Don't worry about me. I don't consider us married, anyway. I've never acknowledged any agreements I've made with you or the Federation to be binding on me—legally or morally—since they were made under duress. I've simply been waiting for the most strategically advantageous time to make a move. You can't say I didn't warn you."

"Do I get to clean up now?"

"I'm really sorry, Burke, but no. I can't risk that. We'll take care of my mother's custody now."

Joan had a prepared change-of-custody agreement brought up onto Burke's computer terminal, and held the laser on him while he took a light pen and signed it. She had an independent computer notarize the agreement, and filed it with the Forest Hills Vivarium's computer.

"How can you consider that agreement morally binding," Filcher said, "since you made me sign it under duress?"

"Morally binding, Burke? I'm saving my mother's *life*. This isn't a legal agreement, but a payment of ransom. You're free to try to cancel it because it was made under duress. You'll find, however, that the loot will be missing."

Finally, she told him to stand at the foot of his bed, with his back to her. She pulled out a small gun. "Are you going to kill me?" he asked.

"I'm just putting you to sleep for twenty-four hours," Joan said. "It's been fun knowing you, Burke. Look me up sometime. You'll find me listed under 'human race.' "

She shot him with a tranquilizer dart, then waited until he had collapsed onto the bed and she was sure he wasn't shamming unconsciousness.

Then she got out of the bedroom fast. It stank to high heaven.

She still had a very busy night ahead of her.

JOAN WAS PACKED and ready to leave Villa Olga at midnight, when the taxi she'd phoned for arrived. She had already called ahead to order the Forest Hills Vivarium to prepare her mother's capsule for immediate travel, and had given Zack the go-ahead to pick up his mother—and his own luggage—and catch the next shuttle up to Virginia Station. Zack had said that getting away from the Nova Cancy Hotel had been no problem at all, since Gramps was down the hall with his younger brothers and Stanton was spending that night at Vera's house on Earth Street.

Before the taxi's arrival, Joan had weighted down her jury-rigged laser gun and had given it a decent burial in the Caribbean. The Sword of Goddess had performed its jury duty well, Joan thought, redeeming itself from its one unintentional sin. She hoped it found a pleasant resting place in Neptune's Kingdom, and would never find a shelf in Hell's Basement.

She loaded her luggage and laser instruments into the taxi, then took a moment to make sure she hadn't forgotten anything. Joan had decided to take with her no wedding present except Wendell's brooch—the ascending helix formed out of her grandfather's fire gems. No, there was nothing she wanted from this planet anymore.

She didn't even bother to lock up when she left.

The rendezvous took place in Virginia Station at 5 A.M., Thursday the 28th. Joan's younger brother Zack was there, with Eleanor safely awaiting transfer to the torchship. The entire Roland Church ensemble was there. And Hill Bromley was there.

Joan practically broke Hill's neck when she hugged him.

Everyone was exhausted, but nobody wanted to sleep. There would be time enough for that on the voyage: Roland Church had bought first-class passage for all of them, including Zack, who jumped at the chance to leave Earth. "I'll pay it back at first chance, Roland," Zack told him. "All of it."

Roland smiled. "Don't pay it back, friar. Pay it forward. As an old friend of mine says, 'Everything that goes around comes around.' "

There was no problem in obtaining valid exit permits for anyone; though Joan had to sign Zack's as his legal guardian, and there wasn't a brainprint that Federation security had the slightest interest in. Just before boarding, Joan made a phone call to a computer on Earth that would be monitoring the Legos, Ltd., courthouse agenda. It would do the rest. Then she forgot about Earth and looked out to the stars. *De Profundis ad Astra*, she thought. She had certainly plumbed the depths. Now was the beginning of her voyage to the stars.

They all boarded the torchship at 8 A.M., and spent the next hour getting settled in their stateroom. Joan and Hill were sharing one stateroom, and Zack was bunking with the vampish percussionist of the band, Phoebe Norton. Joan thought Zack would enjoy the voyage.

At 10:30 A.M., the torchship *Robert A. Heinlein* departed Virginia Station for its nine-day voyage to St. Clive, Deep Heaven. Joan doubted that there had ever been a happier departure in history.

When Burke Filcher phoned Vera Friday evening, the 29th, and told her what had happened, she was furious. "Then the bitch *was* behind the destruction of Helix Vista!"

Filcher nodded. "I'm afraid that's not all she's managed, my dear. With her went my political career, your mother, the Darris family name here on Earth, any chance that you might have had for a seat in the Upper Manor, that Touchable priest who sassed you on the holy, and possibly Wendell's ambassadorship as well. Not bad for a few days' work—and we can't touch her. The *Heinlein* is registered out of Ad Astra."

"Can we extradite?"

"Are you joking? Once the King of St. Clive finds out how Joan saved one of his missionaries from the ovens, he'll probably knight her."

"We can't let her get away with this!" Vera said.

"Vera, she's *gotten* away with it. There's nothing we can do."

"Can't we at least have her court-venereed and declared Touchable? At least we can make her *persona non grata* on Earth."

"I don't think she has any desire ever to come back to Earth," Filcher said. "Aside from that, she's a civilian now."

"You could ask the Corps to rescind her discharge."

"To what end? The Corps won't conduct a court-venereal without the prisoner being there in the flesh. Besides I'm out of office now."

"Do we have anything else we can prove?" Vera asked. "Some charge that doesn't depend on her being in the Corps?"

"Well," Filcher said, "we *did* catch her transporting false transponders."

"That's enough for me," Vera said. "I can issue a court order declaring her Touchable *in absentia* on 'Interplanetary Flight to Escape Felony Prosecution.'"

"If it will make you happy, Vera. But don't count on my testifying beyond next month. I'm going to be leaving Earth myself."

"For where?" Vera asked.

"For Daedalus, probably. I heard whispers of 'Old Scatbottom' a few times too often when I resigned from Commen this morning. If I'm going to begin a new life, it will have to be someplace where everybody is given a clean start. Nobody cares what your background is in a mining camp."

"You, as an asteroid miner?"

"Oh, I think I can manage at least an administrative position. I'm not completely without friends in the habitats."

Vera thought about it for a few minutes after they disconnected. Then she got on the phone to the Federation prosecutrix and told her to prepare her case from evidence that would be supplied by Burke Filcher and the Monitors. She scheduled the trial of *The World* v. *Joan Darris* for Tuesday, February 2, at 10 A.M. in her courtroom.

When Vera came into her office on Tuesday morning, she gasped. There was a Touchable's red cloak laid out on her desk, and her message indicator was flashing. She went to it and retrieved the message. It said:

> Vera:
> Do as you would be done by.
> Joan

Vera called in her law clerk immediately. "Ted, how the rape did this get in here?"

"Your Honor? A robot brought it half an hour ago. Isn't it evidence?"

"Uh, no," Vera said.

"You look pale, Your Honor. Can I get you something?"

"Uh, no. Yes. I could use a cup of mocha."

"Coming right up."

Ted left.

You're not going to get away with this, Vera thought. And as if in

288

deliberate emphasis of that thought, she went to her handbag and took out the fire-gem brooch Joan had given her. She pinned it to her blouse.

Vera was wearing the brooch under her black cloak, at noon, when she banged her gavel and said, "So Mote It Be!" She had found Joan guilty of Felonious Flight and had sentenced her immediately. Then Vera went back to her chambers, sat down at her computer terminal, and entered her Legos, Ltd., code. She informed the Federation Bureau of Immunity that henceforth, the brainprint of Joan Seymour Darris should be filed under "Touchable."

Vera was still wearing the brooch when she went to lunch.

On the last night of the voyage to St. Clive aboard the *Robert A. Heinlein,* Joan and Hill returned to their stateroom after a night of dinner, celebration, and dancing. "Hill," Joan said, "do you have any thoughts about what sort of place we should get in Cair Paravel?"

"You mean what sort of place *you* should get," he said.

"You mean you want to preserve appearances?" Joan said. "That's not like you, Hill."

"No, it isn't," he said. "And that's precisely why this will be our last night together, Joan. As soon as we got into a reasonable time-lag range, earlier today, I had a long conversation with my bishop. He's going to allow me to remain in the Church. As a priest. And priests can't live in sin, Joan. Since you're engaged, that's what it would be. Unless you've changed your mind about marrying me?"

Joan shook her head slowly. "I made a promise."

"I understand. So have I."

Joan asked the next question after a pause. "Do you know where your next assignment is going to be?"

"I asked for something interesting," he said. "I'm going to return the favor an old miner once did for me. I've been assigned to a mining camp in Daedalus."

"You will be able to be there for the St. Clive Competition, won't you?"

"I can't promise you that, Joan. But I will promise to be there, no matter what, for the premiere of your *Mass.*"

Joan got up and put her arms around him. He hugged her back. Then she smiled. "Wolfgang made me promise not to live the life of a nun. I want to know. Have I?"

Bromley laughed.

"I think I could love you, Hill."

He wiped a tear off her cheek. "Tonight will be your only chance to," he said.

It was dark on Earth Street as Vera got out of her skymobile and began walking from the landing strip to her house. She was still wearing the brooch Joan had given her, and—perhaps it was the sort of almost-posthypnotic suggestion one finds it impossible to ignore—she had found it almost impossible to get Joan off her mind in the two weeks since she had declared her sister Touchable. There was very little satisfaction in it, she thought, with Joan far removed from the place where she could be touched. She heard the distant whine of a flying belt, and it made her wonder how many Touchables she had sentenced to be hunted in the almost nine years she'd been on the bench.

She was going to have to go hunting with Stanton soon again, she thought. He still hadn't seemed to recover from the collapse of Helix Vista. Perhaps things would be better when the architects had finished their new designs and he could begin reconstruction.

The whine of the flying belt became louder.

It seems to be very close, Vera thought. Was there a hunt going on right in her neighborhood? Perhaps, if she got suited up in time, they'd allow her and Stanton to join—

Suddenly, a beacon of light from a flying belt hit her, and a man in leather dropped down only a few feet from her. "Hello," Vera said. "Having any luck tonight?"

"Not until now," the man said. Vera thought he looked somehow familiar, but couldn't place him. He was wearing the flying belt and standard Marnie hunting apparel—black leather jacket and pants, high leather boots—but he was not wearing a Marnie's helmet with its official hunting medallion. The man was short by current standards, only about five feet eleven inches. His face was long, unshaved, and rattish, with sharp nose and pale-but-mottled skin. His black hair was greasy and unkempt.

"Have we hunted together?" Vera asked.

The man laughed. It was not a pleasant sound.

"Why are you looking at me that way?" Vera said. "And when it comes right down to it, where's your medallion? I'm a judge. If I report you, you could have your license pulled for not wearing it."

"If you're a judge," the man said, "then I'm the First Lady. Now, are you going to jaw all night, or shall we get down to it?"

"What?"

"Take 'em off," he said. "Do you expect me to do all the work?"

"Are you crazy? Are you under the impression that I'm a Touchable?"

"That's what the scanner says, Your Ladyship."

"You're insane," Vera said. "You'd better read it again."

"Anything to please you, Your Ladyship."

The man scanned Vera again, and waited for the Federation computers to reply. "See?" he told Vera, showing her the reading on his wrist. "Now, take off your clothes, before I get nasty. You sure manage to dress up nice—I have to give you that."

"There's been some terrible mistake," Vera said. "The computers have made an error!"

"Computers don't make errors, Your Ladyship. That's the first thing they teach you in school. You look like you went to school, so you must know that. Goddess, you're beautiful!"

The man went up to Vera and began taking off her outer coat.

"Stop it!" Vera said. "I'll scream!"

"You do and I'll belt you one," the man said. "Do you think I want everyone and his brother muscling in on my catch?"

"Help!" Vera shouted. "Isn't there anyone who—"

The man backhanded Vera hard across the face, knocking her to the ground.

He didn't bother undressing her more than he had to—opening her coat, unfastening her skirt, pulling down her panties.

"Don't," Vera said. "Please don't!"

The man unzipped his fly and released his erect penis. Then he took some grease off his hair and spread it onto his organ.

He forced his way in.

It didn't take very long. He came in about a minute.

"I'll report you," she said. "You've just raped a judge. I'll report you!"

"Sure you will. Hey, that's a nice piece of jewelry. You don't mind if I take it, do you?"

He dropped it into his pocket.

Suddenly, he noticed that the reading his wristscanner was getting from Vera had changed. "What the rape?" he said. "You were telling the truth!"

"I'll report you!" Vera said. "I may even declare you Touchable myself!"

"You're a little late on that," the man said. "So I think you'll understand why I'm not about to leave any witnesses."

"No, you—"

291

The man pulled Vera to her feet. He waited just a moment, to allow her to appreciate the full impact of what he was about to do. Then, exactly as they'd shown on *Red Hunt* every week for the past twenty years, he smashed Vera's nose into her head, propelling a bone splinter up into the brain.

She was, in the only important respect, dead—her brain swelled irreparably against her braincase—when she was found on the street, fifteen minutes later, and an ambulance called for her. But since the paramedic team from Golden-Sky General Hospital found an organ-donor card in her wallet, Vera Collier Delaney was placed into controlled hypothermia as soon as they reached the hospital.

Her body was still intact, waiting at 4 degrees Celsius, when Stanton Darris learned of her death.

VIII.

λ 2970Å

"She's awake again."

"May we see her now?" Joan asked.

"Goodness," the nurse, a young woman, said, "there are so many of you! I'm afraid it might be too much all at once. Why doesn't just one of you go in first, and if it's not too much of a strain, then the rest can come in by pairs?"

"Go ahead, dear," Grandma Collier said to Joan.

"But shouldn't one of you—"

"There's no one your mother will want to see more," Stanton said.

Grandpa Collier, Wendell, and Joan's seven brothers all agreed.

Joan followed the nurse along the guideline in the tube of the Cerebral Wing in City of Joy Hospital, and floated into the C.C.U.

Eleanor was wrapped in a netting that prevented her from floating around the room, and was wearing a large helmet that would have been much too heavy for her if she had not been in zero gravity. The scars Vera's body had sustained had already been healed.

Joan looked at her mother, and tears began welling up in her eyes, refusing to break away. She found she couldn't speak.

Eleanor could. "I don't think I really believed any of it until now," she said. "You've grown up to be gorgeous, Joan."

"Mom," Joan floated to the netting and, with some difficulty, managed to hug and kiss her mother.

"There, there," Eleanor said, "why all the tears? It seems like just yesterday that I saw you." Eleanor reached her finger up to Joan's face and brushed away a tear from the corner of one eye.

Joan could almost not help laughing. "For me it's been almost six years," she said.

"Really? Anything interesting happen?"

"I'm not sure you'll believe me when I tell you. Mom, how do you feel?"

"There's a slight earache that the doctors tell me will take another week to go away. Aside from that, I feel fine."

"I like your new hat," Joan said.

"It's the latest model," Eleanor said.

"Mom, there's something I have to tell you. I'm not sure this is the proper time, though."

"Joan, if it's about Vera, you don't have to say anything. I already know."

"You know what?" Joan asked.

"I know that you gave her the transponder with your brainprint in it, disguised in a brooch."

Joan opened her mouth, and immediately had to close it to prevent a globule of saliva from breaking away.

"But how— Who told you? Who *could* have told you?"

"Nobody told me," Eleanor said. "I seemed to figure it out while I was in the half-dreamy theta state just before I woke up. The surgeons tell me that a section of my brain's left hemisphere had suffered from cryonic burning—the perfusant had failed to reach it— so they decided to take that part of Vera's brain's left hemisphere and put it back in; they said they were able to reduce the swelling considerably. I have Vera's memories—most of them dim and distant, but I can remember the last year of her life almost exactly. I remember her arranging to have you drafted. I remember her refusing to allow me to be revived. I remember your giving her the brooch just before your wedding to Burke Filcher, and I remember a conversation Vera had with him by phone a few days later. I remember her finding the Touchable's cloak on her desk with the

294

warning from you, I remember her having you declared Touchable, and I remember the Touchable who raped her and killed me—I mean her. I seem to remember Vera's death far more clearly that I remember my own. I think my last days might have been imprinted most strongly in the section of my brain that was left out—I hardly remember my performance at the pyradome. I remember almost everything, though. The doctors told me about holographic storage of information in the brain."

"The brain stores information like a hologram?" Joan asked.

"Yes. The whole is in every part—it's just that it becomes hazy and shallow if it's not connected to the rest of the whole. Now I know what is meant by the old saying 'The macrocosm is in the microcosm.' "

"Maybe the whole universe is that way, Mom. Possibly that's why God is called holy. Are you telling me that Vera is still alive?"

"I don't know how to answer that, Joan. I know that I'm Eleanor, not Vera. But it's as if Vera were standing just behind me, close enough that I can feel her touching me and close enough that I can hear her. But I'm in complete charge."

Joan hesitated a moment. "Mom . . . if there's any part of Vera in you, I'm not going to apologize to her for what I did."

Eleanor nodded slowly. "You don't have to, Joanie. You just held up a mirror as a shield against Vera. She fired the laser bolt, and it was her own fault that it got reflected back to herself."

"You're not angry with me?"

Eleanor ran her hand over Joan's cheek. "I'll never be angry with you, Joan."

"Uh, what about Dad?"

Eleanor smiled, and for a moment she wore a wicked expression that Joan associated much more strongly with Vera.

"Your father and I are going to have a long, *long* talk," Eleanor said.

Eleanor's homecoming to her grandparents' house in Tolkien Valley was a grand party with her entire family. She was shocked to find out that the Colliers now allowed liquor in their household, though they still wouldn't touch a drop of it themselves.

It was the sort of party Eleanor had always tried to avoid on Earth: everyone talked about things that he or she *cared* about. She found herself involved in a conversation with Wendell when she'd asked him how he felt about being forced to resign as ambassador.

"It's the best thing that ever happened to me," he said. "I was getting a little sick of playing the role of intellectual guerrilla in that Grand Guignol back on Earth."

"Intellectual gorilla?" Delaney asked. "You mean like *Hello, Joe*?"

Wendell laughed. "Not the sort of gorilla with hair on his arms, son—though I must admit that most guerrillas have been pretty hairy. A *guerr*illa is someone who makes raids into enemy territory, plants explosives, then retreats into the night. That's what I was trying to do in politics. Plant an explosive concept in the enemy camp, then retreat into the night. I'm not sure it did any good, though. The people I was trying to infect seemed to be the least-susceptible ones around."

"What are your plans now?" Joan asked.

"I'm going to be running the Astran office of Darris Investments. My father had the right idea of where the future was. I sometimes wonder why he ever returned to Earth."

"Didn't he ever tell you?" Stanton said. "He says a witch cast a spell over him, and he had to marry her."

"That's Mother's version of it," Wendell said, "not Father's."

"By the way," Joan told Wendell, "did I mention that I just received a picturegram from Hill Bromley?"

"Really? I thought he had gone to that mining camp."

"He did, but that doesn't mean they don't have phones there. You know who he said is the best tenor in his church choir?"

"Who?"

"Burke Filcher," Joan said.

Wendell laughed. "That figures. Though from what you told me, he came pretty close to singing soprano."

"Can I try it now?" Joan asked.

"Let Zack try it first," Wendell said. "I seem to be getting a stronger signal from him."

Zachary Armstrong Darris II stood in front of the Direct Emoting Console and concentrated his thoughts on the fire gems inside, using the same technique he'd used playing velletrom. "I'm getting something," Wendell said, "but the emotions are all jumbled together. Just noise."

"I can't seem to tell them apart," Zack said.

"May *I* try it now?" Joan asked again.

"Might as well," Zack said. "I'm not getting anywhere."

Joan placed her hands on the console, and began to think.

"It feels like a scale," Wendell said. "Starting very heavy and depressed, and moving toward joy."

"That's exactly what I was trying to do," Joan said.

"Have they decided whether the aliens on Lucifer used them like this?" Zack asked Wendell.

Wendell shrugged. "They might have, but it's thought they were primarily telepathic relays."

"I'm going to try a coloratura now," Joan said.

She began to concentrate on the fire gems, and tried to pick out the sequence of the *Resurrection Vistata*.

After a few minutes, Wendell was crying too hard, and she had to stop.

The King and Queen of St. Clive declared the official opening of the St. Clive Lasegraphic Competition on Joan's birthday, April 15, but she wasn't scheduled to play until the next day. Joan floated in the audience in the upper hemisphere of the new Wolfgang Jaeger Sphere, in a cage just a few meters away from the cage that held the King and Queen themselves. In the cage with her were her mother and Jack Malcolm.

The competition was tough, Joan had to admit. Two compositions in particular were good enough that she worried about them—*The Magonia Vistata* composed by Gregor Laseroff and *Diurne in Seventh* by Julia Davidson.

The next afternoon, Joan floated downstage with her mother and Jack, waiting to go on. "I wouldn't mind so much," Joan said, "if only the sweat would *go* somewhere."

Jack smiled. "You'll be fine. Stop worrying about it."

She smiled back at him. "I wish Wolfgang could have been here to see this," Joan said.

"He will be," Eleanor said.

"What? You mean he will be when I show him the recording, fifteen years from now."

"I mean that he'll be here *today*," Eleanor said.

"Mom, he's in a cryonic capsule in Ad Astra."

"Do you think I don't know that?" Eleanor said. "But it won't prevent him from being here—he'll zero right in on your thoughts."

"What do you mean, Eleanor?" Jack asked.

"Astral travel," she said. "I did quite a bit of it while I was frozen."

"You're not serious."

"I remember it quite distinctly. Oh, the doctors told me that it was just dreams I was having while I was being revived. They didn't believe me. That's why I haven't mentioned it before. But I *know*."

"Mom, do you think he'll make it back from wherever he is now?"

"Yes, Joan."

"You shouldn't make promises like that, Eleanor," Malcolm said. "Wolfgang's brain is very old. There's no guarantee that it will be able to be revived."

Joan shook her head—which in free fall caused her body to shake the other way. "Wolfgang's brain was as young the day his heart stopped," she said, "as the day he first sat down at a console. If that's all that's preventing him from coming back, he'll make it."

She loved the lights.

She began by playing a piece she had not written but that had never had a premiere.

It was a happy little dance. A blue figure-8 warbled and squiggled its way across the dome and around the edge. It turned somersaults and cartwheels. It metamorphosed into different shapes and sprang back again. It shrank down to a pinpoint, then rebounded into a giant. When it had finished, a red figure-8 repeated the dance the blue one had done, while the blue now weaved in and around the red figure's dance like a dog running around and between its master's feet.

When the red figure had finished its exposition, a green figure-8 began the dance still again, while the red began its own embellishments. The pattern continued with a violet figure doing the dance, then embellishing; then a yellow; then an indigo; then an orange; then the blue once again, while each of the other figures now weaved into, out of, and around the blue in a sprightly, contrapuntal moving design.

Applause thundered into the Avocado Pit from all directions, as Joan Darris finished playing *Fugue in Blue* by Vera Collier Delaney.

She lowered the glowing again, and began to play. She was a little frightened at first, but sensed a personality she recognized floating behind her. Her mother had been right. Of course Wolfgang would be here.

It was an exercise in rising spirals. It began with a theme of Chaldean orbits, but this was much too stiff and limiting to be allowed to continue for long—it was interrupted by a merry waltz of blue sparks and red, an echo of a friend's voice.

It spoke of the passage of the seasons, each one with a memory of the past and a promise of the future. It spoke of the marriage of the line and the circle. It spoke of paths to a place higher up and farther in. It promised that those beings who lifted themselves up with the left hand would be pulled up by the right.

After a cadenza that consisted of the destruction of a spiral, another resurrected anew, it seemed an inevitable outgrowth of what had come before. It began moving slowly, then raced around faster and faster and faster, until she was surrounded by an immense spiral rainbow.

When *The Helix Vistata* was over, and Joan had raised the day glowing, she didn't notice the thunderous ovation at first. She didn't see the King of St. Clive unstrapping himself from his pallet, leaving his cage to join her in the Avocado Pit.

She was still listening to the lights. She knew they had always been telling her something, but now she understood what they were saying.

And above all, she knew that she had fulfilled a promise she had made to herself. She knew that she had told the colors how to make a rainbow.

Written in Long Beach, California,
and San Antonio, Texas.
Completed December 25, 1981.

Author's Acknowledgments

SCHULMAN'S SECOND LAW: The number of people to whom an author wishes to dedicate a book will exceed the number of books that author writes.

(SCHULMAN'S FIRST LAW: Books will exceed bookshelving.)

So while this, my second novel, is lovingly dedicated to my parents, there are people who inspired this one to whom I would be dedicating it—if my parents weren't overdue from my first novel.

Hence these acknowledgments—a cheap way out.

To the pioneers, then and now, at Laserium: Ivan Dryer, who will (if he accepts my nomenclature) someday be called the Father of Lasegraphy and who stintlessly spent many hours helping me understand it; to Charles McDanald, Laserium's co-founder; to Laser Images, Inc., President, Sam McGee, and choreographer John Tilp; to Gene Partyka, Danny Sofer, Brian Samuels, Glenn Thomas, and Ned Madden, who also lent me expertise; and to Laurie Plainer, the blond laserist who told me her favorite book was *The Fountainhead*, and who dreams about the dancing lights.

Also to the Mother of Lasegraphy, Dr. Elsa Garmire, whose 1970 demonstration at Caltech inspired Ivan Dryer to begin commercially exploring this new art form.

To editor F. Lanier Graham and the contributors to *The Rainbow Book* (Vintage Books, 1979), who gave me endless metaphors to play with; to Andrew Kagan for an article on Laserium in the March, 1978, issue of *Arts* magazine, which reinforced my own notions on theory while I was doing my initial brainstorming; to Barney Kaelin, who defined visual music for me; and to all the other independent laser artists (and video artists, too) whom I couldn't find the time to interview, but who are doing important work in this field.

To my Wiccen Friends (who I think would rather have me leave them unnamed) who lent me insight into the Craft.

To Gerard K. O'Neill, Jerry Pournelle, G. Harry Stine, and Thomas Heppenheimer, who—both in print and in person—helped me out with redesigning the solar system; to Theodore Karp, whose *Dictionary of Music* was indispensable (along with my father) in making musical theory clear to me (I hope!); and to Susanne Langer, whose *Philosophy in a New Key* lent me fresh insight to the nature of art.

To my friends in the Los Angeles Science Fantasy Society ("De Profundis Ad Astra") and the C. S. Lewis Societies in Southern California and New York, who have always been ready with a fresh idea and a new insight.

To Timothy Leary (was he the one whose cow started the Chicago fire?), Robert Anton Wilson, and all those who want the human race to SMI^{2}LE.

To Durk Pearson and Sandy Shaw, who told me how to increase my intelligence so I could write this book. (Did it work?)

To my friends Virginia Jacobs, Alan Brennert, Victor Koman, Richard Kyle, Barbara Branden, Walter Bilinski, L. Neil Smith, and Sam Konkin, who lent me knowledge, food, and moral support; to Alan Ackley, Janice Allen, Paul Ford, David Friedman, Marggy Garron, Ken Gregg, Melinda Hanson, Keith Kato, Robert Le-Fevre, Sue Martin, Wendy McElroy, Sandy McIntosh, Susan Monahan, Sharon Presley, Lowell Ponte, Jeff Riggenbach, James Sadowsky, Chris Schaefer, Andy Thornton, Sheila Wymer, and Bernie and Teny Zuber, who also lent me knowledge, expertise and other worthwhile things; to Harlan Ellison, who probably saved my life by sitting in a pyramid and writing stories a few years back; and to Michael Grossberg, who made me so mad with his bad review of my first novel that I had to write this one to prove him wrong.

To Robert A. Heinlein, who is wrong about H. G. Wells's being possibly the greatest science fiction writer of all time—*you* are, sir—and to C. S. Lewis, Ayn Rand, and J. D. Salinger, the other three logographers who taught me almost everything I know about my art.

To Joel Gotler, my agent, who believed in this book when nobody else did; to Simon and Schuster editor John Herman, who fought the good fight; and finally, to my saintly editor, Larry Freundlich, who kept the wolf at the door at bay while he waited, and waited, and waited . . .

J.N.S.

APPENDIX I.

APPENDIX II.

Appendix I.

SOME RAINBOW CADENZAS

There are three usual reasons for a novel to have an Afterword.

The first usual reason is that the author is long-dead, which puts the book in the "classic" category, at which point the Teacher's Unions demand a piece of the action, and the publisher appeases them with an Afterword.

The second usual reason is that a still-living author—insecure about whether the novel has made its point—tacks on an Author's Afterword to make sure a reader has gotten the message.

The third usual reason is that even though the author is regrettably still alive—and might possibly still embarrass those academics who have staked their reputations on saying that this author is the reincarnation of Thomas Hardy—the book is being taught in high schools or colleges, and the Afterword is supposed to provide the test questions.

I'll admit to the second reason, but I decided I also wanted multiple Afterwords to The Rainbow Cadenza *for a fourth reason: I am genuinely passionate about various themes I wrote about in my novel, and their are experts who—given a chance to improvise their own nonfiction "cadenzas" on my fictional themes—might shed some additional light on each of them.*

Since I organized my novel around the seven colors in a rainbow plus an invisible ultraviolet, the light that will be shed on these topics will be rainbow-colored as well: there will be eight of them—one for each color, and one for ultraviolet.

If you are reading these words before you've read my novel, please read my novel first. As a matter of style, these "cadenzas" are placed after the novel since there's no point playing riffs until you've seen the theme. If I thought everything I wanted to say could be said in nonfiction, I would have written a textbook, not a novel. But a novelist is likewise wary of losing dramatic pace with technical discussions, so having some nonfiction follow the fiction is my attempt to let you have your cake and eat it, too.

For the record, let me say that while I would not be at all opposed to this edition of The Rainbow Cadenza *being used for classroom discussions of these—and other—ideas, I do request that teachers refrain from paying me the compliment of placing my novel on any mandatory reading lists.*

When I was in school, having a book assigned to me made sure that either I would avoid reading it or, if I forced myself, that I would hate it. I went so far as, in class, to read books I freely chose from the library hidden behind the covers of the assigned book.

Even though I know it's irrational, I still hate the books I was assigned. Any author with strong opinions will find enough readers to dislike his or her books without being hated for being made compulsory reading.—JNS

VIOLET
HOUSE OF THE LASER
by Ivan Dryer
Chairman
Laser Images, Inc.

Joan Darris sees her first lasegraphic performance at the "pyradome" named the "McDanald Media Temple," studies at the "Dryer School of Lasegraphy," and performs zero-gee recitals in "Garmire Cathedral." These names for future lasegraphic institutions harken back to the early history of the LASERIUM concerts produced by Laser Images, Inc., of which Ivan Dryer was the pivotal founder and is currently Chairman.

LASERIUM and The Rainbow Cadenza *are converging into a multimedia "READ THE BOOK—SEE THE LASER" event with the Fall, 1986 premiere—in multiple North American cities and London, England—of "LASERIUM Presents The Rainbow Cadenza." This will be an all-classical-music LASERIUM show which will allow readers who enjoy my depiction of lasegraphy in* The Rainbow Cadenza *to experience the excitement of a live laser concert for real.*

To celebrate "LASERIUM Presents The Rainbow Cadenza," Ivan Dryer wishes to make LASERIUM Discount Coupons available to readers of this book. For a listing of current LASERIUM locations, and discount coupons where available, send a Self-Addressed, Stamped Envelope to:

"LASERIUM Presents The Rainbow Cadenza"
Laser Images, Inc.
6907 Hayvenhurst Avenue
Van Nuys, CA 91406.

Here Ivan Dryer gives a brief history of the beginnings of LASERIUM, and lets fly his own imagination about additional forms of entertainment to which we can look forward.—JNS

In the summer of 1956 an aspiring young astronomer joined the staff of the Griffith Observatory and Planetarium in Los Angeles. Fourteen years later, I was still aspiring—but to be a filmmaker—and was then introduced to a laser for the first time. I had gone out to Caltech to film the off-hours artwork of laser physicist, Elsa Garmire. When the laser turned on so did I. I immediately knew where and what to do with it.

Within a month, in December, 1970, a simple demonstration was given by the two of us to the Observatory staff. It would be for a one-hour live show with alternately filmy and neon-like laser patterns projected among the stars of the Planetarium sky. It would be called LASERIUM ("House of the Laser"). The staff people liked what they saw... but not enough. This was entertainment, not science. We were outsiders. The banks felt somewhat the same way. A one-hour show of abstract patterns of light with music? No story, no characters—no track record? No dice.

Three years later, a one-watt Krypton laser was borrowed for another demonstration at Caltech. Over a hundred people were invited. Only two showed—but they were the new Director and Head Lecturer at Griffith Observatory. A permit was issued for a test run, beginning with our world premiere on November 19, 1973.

My new partner, Charles McDanald, and I finished building and installing the Krypton laser projector at 5:00 a.m. the morning of the premiere. At 8:00 a.m. I appeared on a local TV show, and at 11:00 a.m. we held our press preview. It was also our first rehearsal, and it was terrible. Nonetheless, that evening 700 people came to see what this LASERIUM was about.

At the conclusion of our four-week test period we were turning away 500 a show. (So much for the banks.) Since then, approx mately thirteen million persons worldwide have experienced one of what now number twenty LASERIUM shows, featuring rock, classical, jazz, and synthesized music, alone and in combination.

Because the laser colors (red, yellow, green, and blue) are so pure, the images appear three-dimensional and seem to be almost alive. The essentially abstract nature of LASERIUM allows the audience to participate with their imaginations in helping create their own experiences. That, combined with the element of a live performer responding to audience feedback, makes for a lot of repeat customers—the LASERIUM experience is always unique.

Arts Magazine proclaimed in 1978 that "within LASERIUM...lie seeds of what will become the high, universally acclaimed visual art of the future." While *The Rainbow Cadenza* is certainly an heir to that statement, I have always considered our shows as entertainment, mass entertainment, "environmental" entertainment.

It is my opinion, and my dream, that future entertainment forms will build on LASERIUM's environmental, essentially abstract approach. With the advent of the scale, diversity, and technological quality that home entertainment will offer in the next decade, the public will be coaxed to leave their personal media centers primarily for spectacles that are unreproducible at home.

The first wave of the "new entertainment" will be manifest in "Multi-media Palaces": large movie theaters outfitted with huge screens, lasers, and large-frame film projectors, as well as side screens, slide projector arrays, pyrotechnics, smoke, fog, the kitchen sink!

Next will come the "Media Temples," state-of-the-art domed multi-media theatres such as our Pyradome design, featuring all of the above and more. But even these will fall short of the promise of Holography: laser-generated, true 3-D images.

Sometime in the next 30 years someone is likely going to come up with the technology to produce the "Holos": three-dimensional objects projected in mid-air, with such apparent solidity and resolution of detail that they seem to be "The Real Thing." Hooking their Hologenerators to their then vastly powerful desk-top computers, people would be able to synthesize any person, and re-create any event at any place they desire.

What we're talking now is the creation of new realities, indistinguishable from the old one we now share, at least in their verisimilitude. We can only surmise what would be the impact on our social structure and institutions.

In my view, the ultimate environmental entertainment would be the Holo-sphere, a huge experience sphere in Space at near-zero G. You jump away from the slowly rotating perimeter toward the weightless center. You fly, unfettered (an ancient dream in itself). The Hologenerators are activated, each responding to telemetered feedback from you and your fellow Holonauts.

As your thoughts go, so do the images forming around you: you soar among the mountains of the moon, into the clouds of Jupiter, and through the rings of Saturn. You journey beyond the edge of the galaxy to view its immense pin-wheel filling the sky. You venture into its central black hole, into another universe? If you so will it—it is anything you want it to be. (As real as the chair you're sitting in now.) How do you get back?

Do you want to?!!

INDIGO
NEW WINE IN AN OLD BOTTLE
by Wendy McElroy

Wendy McElroy is editor of the book Freedom, Feminism and the State—*an anthology of feminist writings—editor of the magazine* The Voluntaryist, *a former Reichian clinical therapist, an activist in the Anti-AntiPornography movement, a popular libertarian lecturer, and an author who has published prose in* The Journal of Libertarian Studies *and* Reason *as well as poetry in* The Magazine of Fantasy & Science Fiction. *Here she contrasts the feminist struggle for women's freedom and self-realization with the continuing paternalism which is marketed to women in the guise of "women's power."—JNS*

In the war between the sexes, the bodies of women are the battleground. When feminists of the '60's cried "the personal is the political," they pointed to the control of biology as the key means of politically repressing women. Through birth control and abortion laws, the restriction of pornography, the licensing of marriage and divorce, the government declares a woman's body to be state property. *Be sexual*, it agrees, *but on our terms. Be a woman, but follow our blueprint.*

The women in J. Neil Schulman's *The Rainbow Cadenza* know what it is to be state property, for this book carries the war over biology to its ultimate, hideous conclusion...the drafting of women for sexual service—three years of what Joan Darris, the heroine, calls "continuous rape."

"Is that such a bad deal?" asks Burke Filcher, the novel's main villain a/k/a a main politician. After all, in this rainbow world, men vastly outnumber women, and uncontrolled rape could easily shred the tender web of social harmony. Surely it is more civilized to issue quotas of sex to men who need it and, thus, take rape out of the street and into the political process where it belongs.

To draftees unable to follow this logic, Burke expands: "[L]ook at the bargain ...immediately after the service, you are one of the prime beneficiaries of that peace and prosperity—one of the privileged ruling class." And Burke is telling the truth.

Through serving the state, women gain status and access to powerful positions through which they too can enforce laws institutionalizing rape. Vera Delaney, for example, uses the position of judge to prematurely conscript her sister, Joan, into the Corps. Is this such a bad deal?

For better or worse, it is merely new wine in an old bottle. The state has always regaled women with the advantages of being controlled. Marriage laws protect purity. Abortion laws protect the family. Women need protection from falling into sin through weakness. This is one expression of the madonna/whore approach to women. Women are pure, but only so long as the sexual animal pacing within is tightly chained.

Of course, *The Rainbow Cadenza* chains this beast on a different leash. Instead of passing laws to hold women back from the steaming sexual abyss, Schulman's society commands—jump or be pushed! Instead of using a woman's innocence to measure her worth, it merely flips through her service record.

Schulman's ideal woman is a state whore who pledges allegiance to the state by placing her left hand over her ovaries. The measurement changes but the standard lingers on. Sex.

This standard is cemented into society by those old fellow travellers, church and state. *The Rainbow Cadenza* unveils a state-sanctioned religion (Wicce) which worships a goddess and ritually welcomes corpswomen back from the service and into "the world of men." It unfolds a state which introduces draftees to be raped with the chilling words: "Greetings from the First Lady of Earth. You are hereby ordered to report to a physical examination to determine your fitness to serve…"

Consider the paradox. Both church and state ostensibly enshrine women, yet Joan Darris is being systematically, officially raped every day. How can this be? Let's add one more fact to the equation: the women with power are those enmeshed in the church or state institutions; the women enshrined are those who obey. They may indeed have power. They do not have freedom.

Joan Darris will not obey. She does not want to be enshrined or privileged. "I think if there were a button here," Joan tells Filcher, "and by pushing it I could blow up this planet to avoid subjecting myself to the next three years [of service], I wouldn't delay pushing it for a second."

After lighting his pipe and pronouncing Joan a "pretty prosecutrix," Filcher takes a puff and comments on how small a price is the sexual draft compared to a military one. "You are completely free from this price," Joan observes. "Is that fair?"

"Life is rarely fair, my dear," Schulman's villain responds, "especially when the needs of a world are involved."

Here is the hunger of feminism: women must be the legal equal of individual men; and all individuals must be respected.

But *The Rainbow Cadenza* is not essentially a political novel and to paint it as such is to lose much subtlety. It is a novel about individuals—primarily Joan Darris—who refuse to obey. The state is merely one and perhaps not the greatest enemy of the individual.

Joan must say "no" to much more than a state committee. To preserve the spark which defines her, Joan must say "no" to both family and culture. What could possibly be worth this struggle?

She loved the lights… When the dance was over, she did not understand what, or how, or why, but she knew the lights were telling her something, if only she could understand them. She knew she had to find out what the lights were telling her, and more: though she was not yet five years old, Joan Seymour Darris made a promise to herself that someday she also would tell the colors how to make a rainbow.

Someday Joan will be a lasegrapher and the lights will dance from her fingertips. Now, she must fight for the rainbow against a woman who loves and hates it… Vera Delaney.

Vera can never forgive Joan for conquering the lights which she herself can neither conquer nor abandon, but must hunger after. Joan is the mirror of Vera's failure.

Eleanor is the reason for it.

Vera is Eleanor's parthenogenic daughter, with all forty-six chromosomes taken from the mother. She is such a true genetic duplicate, and Eleanor has aged so little, that they are often mistaken for each other. This pleases one of them.

The relationship between Eleanor and Vera is easily the most intriguing one in the book. In this nightmare version of My Mother/My Self, Vera does not even possess her own genetic pattern. When Eleanor advises her to expand horizons and find herself, Vera spits back:

> *You tried them all. Dance, music, painting, sculpture... if you couldn't find yourself that way, neither can I. Besides, I'm not looking to find myself. I know what I'd find. You.*

To become herself, Vera must destroy her mother. To live with herself, she must destroy Joan. She is a fascinating failure at both. Even after shelving Eleanor in cryonic suspension, Vera is not free. There is no Vera for her to grow into. There is only Eleanor, in whose bed Vera sleeps, in whose identity Vera settles like a cat.

Through a sharp plot twist, Vera, in turn, is stripped of her stolen persona and destroyed, allowing Eleanor to live again, her brain within Vera's body. One must die if the other will live for there is only one identity.

But Joan possesses the inestimable benefit of a unique genetic pattern and does not have to destroy others to be herself. She eliminates Vera as a matter of self defense and justice to her mother. Although much could be made of the Joan/Vera conflict being symbolically a daughter/mother one, this dilutes the sharp purity of the battle between Vera and Eleanor. Even Freud admitted, "sometimes a cigar is just a cigar."

Sometimes Vera is just Vera. How ironic that the only person by whom she may have been perceived as thoroughly herself destroyed her. Vera is a tragedy. And *The Rainbow Cadenza* is a triumph in at least this area... it understands women.

BLUE

SEX SELECTION: SOME PREDICTIONS BASED ON PRESENT TECHNOLOGY

by Ronald J. Ericsson, Ph.D.
President
Gametrics Limited
Colony (Wyoming) Route
Alzada, Montana 59311

The Dr. Ronald Ericsson referred to in The Rainbow Cadenza *as a pioneer of sex-selection technology actually exists: his patented process, made available in clinics by his company Gametrics Limited, has permitted thousands of families around the world to select the sex of a child.*

Dr. Ericsson, also the co-author of Getting Pregnant in the 1980's, *makes here a powerful case for the human right of absolute freedom in reproductive options, and demonstrates that only such free choice can avoid the disastrous gender imbalance which I show politics causing in* The Rainbow Cadenza. *Readers who wish further information on selecting the sex of a child may write to Gametrics Limited at the above address.—JNS*

Gametrics Limited has the only biotechnology to preselect for males with a high degree of accuracy. Couples that have used this method number into the thousands, and 80% of those who conceived had boys.

311

This method isolates Y sperm (which produce boys) by allowing sperm to swim downwards into a vertical column of human serum albumin. It has proven to be effective when used by gynecologists throughout the world. A somewhat similar, but more complex, method to preselect for girls (preselected sperm artificially inseminated in conjunction with the hormonal induction of ovulation) has provided positive, but as yet limited, results.

The above methods to preselect sex of children, which I researched and invented, have received worldwide recognition. The scientific and medical communities accept this research to be reliable and repeatable. Gynecologists in clinical practice now acknowledge sex preselection as a reproductive choice available to their patients.

The reality of sex selection on a clinical basis has brought out concern over the possible imbalance in the sex ratio. Sociological research of two decades ago clearly showed a preference for a first-born male. Present-day sociologists, demographers, bioethicists, and reporters voice concern over the "impending" male preference, now that a methodology can change a desired choice into reality.

But, is the desire for a first-born male going to be fulfilled?

It would seem not, for several reasons.

First, the attitudes about male preference have changed a lot in the past twenty-five years. Second, couples who use our method to produce a son almost always choose to do so only after having had one or more daughters. Less than one out of every 100 couples seek a sex-selected, first-born son. When the furor dies down—or the smoke clears, or call it what you will—over sex selection, then rational thoughts will prevail. The majority of couples, in developed countries, wish to restrict the number of children and would, given the opportunity, like to have at least one child of each sex.

It comes as a jolt to the image makers and keepers of statistics that 52 percent of the requests we receive for a sex-selected child are for girls. This percentage runs contrary to their dogma and personal bias. They do not like to believe that such a high percent of couples would seek a daughter. This high desire for girls runs counter to their predictions of biological disaster due to an imbalance of the sexes.

My granddaughter, Marie, is aged three. When she reaches the age when most women bear children, sex selection will be no more controversial than microwave ovens are now.

I have been accused of opening Pandora's box. Instead of opening Pandora's box, we have stimulated many scientists and institutions to initiate research in the field of male reproductive biology. The success-is-contagious syndrome is definitely at work here. None of the critics, however, go so far as to criticize anything that improves the quality of life. The preselection of X and Y sperm is only one of many facets of this field of research. Nobel prizes are awarded to discoverers of antibiotics and other breakthroughs that enhance people's lives. The field of male reproduction has now been primed, and the public will soon be the recipients of this research.

We of the modern world frequently get caught up in our own hype. Particularly, the successes in the fields of electronics and computers have given us the impression that comparable results should be forthcoming in medicine. Organ transplants, artificial hearts, test-tube babies, and the like get considerable media attention. It should be remembered that even though the media hypes these as breakthroughs, the numbers and successes are few. To work out a system whereby the human female can conceive from a sex-preselected sperm with a reasonable degree of efficiency is no small task indeed.

All countries, except the People's Republic of China, allow couples Free Choice in parenthood and number of children. It should remain the right of couples to have a sex-selected child. World population increase has been a major concern of governments for a number of decades. A lot of children born are the direct result of their parents seeking a child of one sex. To eliminate unwanted children would be effective family planning and, in part, sex selection serves this end.

I do not forsee a large imbalance between the sexes due to the widespread use of sex-selection technology. Nor do I forsee that a high percentage of couples will use such technology, particularly for the first born. I do forsee more clinical use of technology whereby sperm are preselected to reduce the incidence of conceiving a genetically handicapped child.

Finally, I am certain that this field of male reproductive biology will expand rapidly within the next two decades, and yield positive results beyond our present knowledge.

GREEN
TWO ADVOCATES OF REASON: AYN RAND
AND C.S. LEWIS
by Brad Linaweaver

Brad Linaweaver is a libertarian writer whose science fiction novella, "Moon of Ice," was praised by Robert A. Heinlein and a final nominee for the 1983 Nebula Award. He has also published nonfiction on political topics in The New Guard.—*JNS*

Some things just don't go together: such as Count Dracula and communion wafers, or Turkish coffee in an Armenian restaurant. Another culinary unlikelihood, certainly indigestible as the foregoing, would be the philosophical alignment of Ayn Rand and C. S. Lewis. In what conceivable manner could a fire-and-brimstone Atheist and a High Church Christian find common ground? It takes a novel as unusual as *The Rainbow Cadenza* to provide an answer, and a tasty one it is.

At this point, it is appropriate to congratulate Schulman on his presentation of an intellectual issue in a novel, thereby violating one of the sacred rules of modern-formula-crap-fiction. He dares interrupt the narrative flow for the expression of mere ideas! The dialogue between Hill Bromley and Joan Darris, in which the Rand/Lewis matter comes into focus, is the sort of exchange one might expect from intelligent people, but the High Priests of the modern novel decree that all must be copied from real life—except interesting conversation which, apparently, they've never heard.

The differences between Rand and Lewis are many and obvious; the similarities, however, are essential: as Schulman has Bromley say, "There were two main exponents of rationalism in the twentieth century..." and then, having identified our heroes, goes on to praise their mastery of deductive logic and admirable talent for "creating metaphors to explain abstract philosophy."

Here let Rand and Lewis speak for themselves. In her book, *Philosophy: Who Needs It*, Rand makes this point: "Now ask yourself: If you are not interested in abstract ideas, why do you (and all men) feel compelled to use them?"

Words from the same universe belong to C. S. Lewis, writing in his book, *God in the Dock:* "Human intellect is incurably abstract." Neither had much use for the anti-intellectualism so in fashion in this, the most timid of all ages. Both realized that pragmatism is only useful for dealing with means, *but provides no guide whatsoever for ends.*

Whatever their differences, neither would appreciate the minds that have taken over much of science fiction—supposedly a literature of *ideas*—with one guiding principle directing their every move: "Whatever you do, DON'T PREACH, DON'T HAVE A MESSAGE, DON'T TELL YOUR READERS *ANYTHING*—ONLY SHOW THEM." Anyone acquainted with abstract reasoning knows that some things cannot be "shown," but only "told." And nobody, but nobody, could weave a tapestry of fiction that performed both tasks better than the feisty lady from Russia and the patient gentleman from Ireland.

Schulman identifies the epistemological distinction that led Rand and Lewis to different metaphysical country. Rand denied that emotions could be tools of cognition; Lewis insisted that they were legitimate guides. Surely thinkers inhabiting such different premises would not enjoy the same view from their picture windows, except that they often did! As Bromley tries to explain to Darris, morality was an area where *this* Atheist and *this* Christian shared, at the very least, an emotional affinity.

They saw the same Evil. Look at the villainous bureaucrats of N.I.C.E. in Lewis's *That Hideous Strength*, or their counterparts in charge of Project X in Rand's *Atlas Shrugged*. These writers frequently observed that evil is an *emptiness* that can only be temporarily filled by draining the good. Compare the views of Ellsworth Toohey in Rand's *The Fountainhead* to those of the Demons in Lewis's *The Screwtape Letters*, or the description of Hell as "smaller than one pebble of your earthly world" in Lewis's *The Great Divorce*. From the same book we have this statement about the good: "But it will not, at the cunning tears of Hell, impose on good the tyranny of evil." Sounds like Rand's *sanction of the victim* in *Atlas Shrugged*, doesn't it? And Lewis: "Every disease that submits to a cure shall be cured: but we will not call blue yellow to please those who insist on still having jaundice...." Aristotle would be pleased.

Yet their art was hardly limited to morbid dissections of wickedness. In portraying the good, there were surprising convergences as well. Compare the description of John Galt in *Atlas Shrugged*, his face without pain or fear or guilt (remember?), to the suggestion of what salvation really means in Lewis's *Till We Have Faces*.

The cleverness of what Schulman has done is to realize that "Saint Clive" Lewis's approach to Christianity was original enough (or old enough, if you prefer) to merit its own sect in the future. The modest Lewis would be put out by this, no doubt, but Saints don't decide their own Sainthood...outside of Rand's Objectivism.

Lewis proved that a belief in the supernatural does not have to violate the Law of Identity. A is A, even among ghosts. Rand's assertion that the universe is not a haunted house is beside the point. Kant's irrationalism derives no comfort from either proposition.

J. Neil Schulman is not playing a game in semantics by raising this topic. Lovers of liberty sometimes forget that where a person begins (in his head) is less important than where he ends (as your neighbor). Rand and Lewis would have made good neighbors.

Rand's egoism may have been strident, but it was always high-minded, never simple self-centeredness. She worshipped integrity. It was not her fault that manipulators twisted her ideas from *The Virtue of Selfishness* into an odious formula for Winning Through Intimidation. Can you imagine a face without guilt intimidating its way through life? Rand deserved better than this.

As for C. S. Lewis, he was the Christian who, in one of his most powerful works of fantasy, has a demon describe the underside of modern democracy as, "...slavery is restored, and the individual is told that he has really willed (though he didn't know it) whatever the Government tells him to do." This is also the Christian who wrote, "...it is better to love the self than to love nothing."

Ayn Rand and C. S. Lewis were honest individualists in a despicable period of rampant collectivism. *The Rainbow Cadenza* tells us, and shows us, that if there is any hope left in the future, these two will have helped provide it.

YELLOW
FEMINISM, AUTONOMY AND LIBERTARIANISM
by Sharon Presley, Ph.D.

Sharon Presley received her doctorate in social psychology from the City University of New York, where her mentor was the late Stanley Milgram, author of the classic Obedience to Authority *that documented the famous experiments in which the majority of ordinary people were willing—on the authority of only a lab-coated "researcher"—to give supposedly painful electrical shocks to an experimental subject (actually another researcher faking being shocked). Dr. Presley is currently conducting her own research on the other side of the coin:* resistance *to authority, particularly among women.*

A libertarian activist for many years, Presley is former National Coordinator of the Association of Libertarian Feminists, and this afterword is a revised version of a discussion paper she wrote for the A.L.F.—JNS

> "The right to vote, or equal civil rights, may be good demands, but true emancipation begins neither in the polls nor in courts. It begins in woman's soul."
> —Emma Goldman in "The Tragedy of Women's Emancipation"

If a woman said to you, "I want to be free from the domination of men," but turned to a tyrannical husband not only for financial support but for decisions about her own personal and social life, you would undoubtedly consider her inconsistent. Yet that is what many feminists are doing on a political level. They say they want to be free of the domination of men, but ask for favors and handouts (for example, government day-care centers) from a government of men. They say they reject the authoritarian ways of thinking and acting that have characterized men throughout history, but turn around and advocate the same old authoritarian methods that men have always used—compulsory taxation and more government controls.

But there is a non-authoritarian alternative—a philosophy that not only has goals compatible with the psychological goals of feminism but methods *more* compatible with these goals than the alternatives usually touted by feminists. That philosophy is libertarianism.

Some libertarians advocate a strictly limited non-coercive government; others are anarchists. Some advocate voluntary communism (communal ownership of

315

the means of production), others are individualists and advocate a totally free market (as distinguished from the corrupt State corporate capitalism that we now have). But what unites them all is the belief that all social interactions should be voluntary, that no one has the right to rule another, that individuals have the right to live their lives as they see fit so long as they don't initiate force against others.

Feminists want women to be free psychologically—free of the domination of men, free to control their bodies and psyches as they see fit. Libertarians want *all* individuals to be free—politically as well as psychologically—free to make their own decision about their own lives independently of the coercive domination of others.

Libertarians believe that we can't achieve a non-authoritarian society by authoritarian methods. If our goals are personal autonomy and individual freedom, we can't achieve these goals by taking away individuals' rights to choose for themselves. A feminist advocating anti-obscenity laws is no better than a conservative advocating anti-abortion laws. If we pass laws that force our values on others, we are no better than men who have forced *their* values on us through legislation. We merely substitute our tyranny for the tyranny of men.

Libertarians refuse to play political power games. They want to get rid of laws, not to pass them. They are not interested in stopping people from smoking pot, from having abortions or having babies, *or* from spending their money as they see fit. Libertarians just want to leave people alone.

Libertarians would remind conservatives who wish to deny a woman's self-ownership of her own body by restricting abortion that, as Schulman portrays, a State powerful enough to prevent abortions is also powerful enough to *force* abortions. Once the right of self-ownership is denied, the State is the new owner of a woman's body. Likewise, libertarians would remind liberals that a State powerful enough to tax for domestic programs is also powerful enough to tax for foreign adventures.

Feminists are fond of saying, "the personal is the political," but have often failed to see some of the levels on which that is true. They have not carried feminist philosophical premises to the logical political conclusions. They have not been willing to recognize that power over others is as destructive on a political level as it is on a personal level—nor is it in any way necessary.

Feminist psychiatrist Jean Baker Miller, M.D., in her insightful book, *Toward a New Psychology of Women*, declares that women who have power over themselves do not need power over others. "In a basic sense," she writes, "the greater the development of each individual the more able, more effective and less needy of limiting or restricting others she or he will be."

But the alternatives that many feminists advocate—Liberalism or Socialism or Marxism—are just variations on the same familiar theme: power over others. Taking decision-making out of the hands of individuals and putting it into the hand of a centralized, bureaucratic State. Liberals may let a woman have an abortion (government-regulated, of course), but think they know better than she does how to spend her money and will take it by force. What they are advocating is the worst sort of paternalism. Some even want to equalize the oppression by having a Compulsory National Service for women as well as men. As *The Rainbow Cadenza* demonstrates with a *reductio ad absurdum*, this isn't gaining equal rights but perpetuating slavery—equal or not.

Socialists think they'll make us free by doing away with the power of business monopolies by substituting one big monopoly instead—the government. As Lenny Bruce once said, that would be one Big Telephone Company—and even the government finally had to admit that *this* didn't work very well.

Marxists are no better: they have party structures that are every bit as centralized and authoritarian as the ideologies they criticize.

All are based on the same authoritarian model as the patriarchal family. Decision-making is centralized in an authority figure—in one case, the father; in the others, the politicians, or President, or central committee. Involuntary means are used to induce obedience—either psychological or cultural pressures or the threat of physical force. The rationale for the role-behaviors is essentially the same—that it serves "the good of the whole," whether it be the family or society.

When someone else controls the power and the money, there are always strings attached. What the government finances it controls. There is no historical basis for assuming that government is suddenly going to be any different with a new crop of politicians. The system is inherently authoritarian and no Liberal palliatives or Socialist edict can change it in any basic way.

Feminists, because of their acute awareness of the destructiveness of authoritarianism, should be eager to join with libertarians in exploring non-authoritarian, non-coercive alternatives to government. We are learning to break free of patriarchy politically as well as psychologically. We don't need it either way.

ORANGE
REFLECTING ON THE HUMAN SOUL
by Michael Grossberg

Michael Grossberg is the film/theater critic for the Columbus (Ohio) Dispatch. *In 1981, he founded the Libertarian Futurist Society which sponsors the Prometheus Awards and which publishes the newsletter* Prometheus, *121 McKinley Street, Rochester, NY 14609. Grossberg is also Executive Director of the Free Press Association, a national network of journalists, and has reviewed fiction for* Science Fiction Review, Reason *magazine, and other publications.—JNS*

> "If anything is sacred the human body is sacred."
> —Walt Whitman, "Children of Adam"

Much of the sexuality in *The Rainbow Cadenza* deeply disturbs, shocking readers with its graphic intensity. Yet this unusually adult coming-of-age novel, boasting some of the most scatological material to be found this side of Krafft-Ebing, arguably has no gratuitous sex scenes. Instead, J. Neil Schulman integrates his disquieting eroticism into a complex narrative about a future Earth where birth control advances have had a radical and damaging effect on human relationships, sexual equality, and personal rights.

Given the development of such an unbalanced society, the novel's often perverse sexuality should not surprise us. After all, the sexual act is a mirror. In reflecting consciousness and character, it offers a highly revealing glimpse of its participants' humanity (or inhumanity). At its best, of course, the sexual act can be a deeply satisfying expression of romantic love and spiritual intimacy, or at least a mutually enjoyable experience between consenting adults. At its worst, the sexual act can be perverted into a neurotic and symbolic act, communicating hostility instead of affection, revenge instead of respect, dominance and submission instead of acceptance, anger and rage instead of bona fide sexual passion. All this, and more, can be found in the diverse sexuality of *The Rainbow Cadenza*, a morality play in which those who allow themselves to be corrupted by power lust soon find their sexual lusts corrupted as well in the inevitable workings of karmic justice.

If, as the historian Lord Acton observed, "power corrupts and absolute power corrupts absolutely," then, as Schulman shows, power also perverts, and absolute power perverts not only sexuality, but every other dimension of family relationships and community life. Joan Darris's heroic quest to free herself from authoritarian patriarchy is no more and no less than an act of self-assertion and self-defense against legalized rape—and rape, the ultimate obscenity, *is* shocking and must continue to be so in any civilized society.

According to the conventional Judeo-Christian morality that unfortunately still casts its bleak anti-sexual and anti-rational shadow over our age, what is shocking is not the violence which objectively defines the so-called sexual act of rape, but such socially defined perversions as heterosexual or homosexual sodomy, which are stigmatized as "unnatural" in part because of their presumed statistical infrequency. Schulman, on the other hand, is wise enough and tolerant enough to understand that true perversion has little to do with the type of sexual act engaged in, but everything to do with the consciousness and intent of those who engage in it—and especially with whether their acts are voluntary or coerced.

The Rainbow Cadenza dramatically conveys the anguish and needless suffering caused by authoritarian personalities and authoritarian politics, ranging from illicit or socially sanctioned isolated acts of sadistic sex to the impersonal institutionalized violence of a future military draft that forces women to "make love, not war." In so doing, the author brilliantly communicates one of his major themes: that rape is not the only form of "rape" worth opposing. Any infringement of individual liberty constitutes a kind of rape, no less vivid and violent for being non-sexual. With "the emperor's new clothes" stripped away by Schulman's insight, every coercive intervention, private or public, is revealed to be an aggressive act of dehumanization and humiliation by one individual, or group of individuals, against other individuals—most often, predictably, the weak, the poor, and the powerless. Such violations of the human spirit can and do warp an individual, a family or an entire society. And the destructive results may take generations to abate, as the neuroses and sins of mothers and fathers are visited upon their daughters and sons.

Vera's abusive and exploitative relationship with her younger sister may be "far more brutal, and far more hideous" than some readers may wish to see, but it remains a chillingly accurate portrayal of the devious lengths to which some people will go to inflict on others the buried primal pain that they can not permit themselves to feel. By writing with such white-hot radiance that he overcomes the reluctance of even the most squeamish reader to emphathize with Joan's persecution and humiliation, Schulman illuminates the repressed childhood traumas and complex subconscious motivations that warp human rationality and may provide the neurophysiological underpinnings of authoritarianism.

In *The True Believer*, Eric Hoffer described the authoritarian personality as one which emerges out of profound frustration: the inability to live one's own life creatively finds some small compensation in the struggle to control, or sabotage, the lives of others. Vera's lifelong struggle against Eleanor and Joan (and against herself) is a compelling re-creation of the authoritarian personality. Schulman's portrait of evil is filled with tragic understanding, but imbued with a righteous justice rather than a false mercy. There is no excuse for the kind of hidden cruelty in child rearing—exemplified in Vera's treatment of Joan—that appears to be a major antecedent of our society's widespread violence and child abuse.

None of this is to claim, simplistically, that sadistic sex and poor toilet-training, alone, lead to the kind of coercive political systems in which, as Ringo Starr once observed, "everything the government touches turns to shit." No need to go that far to acknowledge the implicit truth in Schulman's multigenerational family saga: that there are intimate ties between the psychological traumas of childhood and the petty (and not so petty) tyrannies of adulthood.

The Rainbow Cadenza is a psychosexual thriller that breaks new ground in unveiling the hidden roots of oppression within the maturation process. By projecting a future in which parents can generate virtually identical genetic copies of themselves through parthenogenesis or cloning, Schulman throws into stark dramatic relief the ongoing struggle of children to separate and individuate from their parents, as well as the less natural struggle of some parents to live through their children, pressuring them to live selflessly—without a Self. Joan's successful quest to find herself, and Vera's similar but aborted quest to escape the fate of becoming Eleanor's "carbon copy," serve as a symbolic future microcosm of the two basic alternatives facing humans today as in every generation: to grow from dependent childhood to independent adulthood, or to fail to grow up at all, never experiencing full individuality.

Why do most people submit to unjust authority, following orders all the way to the concentration camp, or worse, following orders to send others to one in their place? And why do other people resist authority? What are the connections between psychological repression and political repression? Even in the late twentieth century—by no accident, the century of both total war and the totalitarian State—these very much remain open questions, despite the intriguing non-fiction speculations of Wilhelm Reich, Stanley Milgram, Arthur Janov, Stanislav Grof, Nathaniel Branden, Peter Breggin, and Thomas Szasz. By tying together the personal and the political in his fiction, Schulman communicates fascinating pre-scientific insights that shed light on this dark phenomenon. By linking Joan Darris's struggle for political freedom to her struggle for personal liberation, Schulman hints that the shortest distance between authoritarianism and a fully free future may not be a straight line but a spiral—a fusion of the political and the personal based on the recognition that any successful revolution for freedom must be accompanied, if not preceded, by a revolution in consciousness.

Schulman's projected 22nd century world may be more prosperous and peaceful—and, even, in some ways, "freer"—than our own, but, Schulman asks, at what psychic cost? He answers that question by balancing his exploration of sexuality with an exploration of the creativity involved in developing the art form that gives his novel its name. Like sex, art is an arena in which one's deepest values—and deepest value-conflicts—can be spotlighted. Focusing on both sexuality and creativity, Schulman succeeds in exposing the devastating consequences of authoritarianism in that most personal of all realms: the human body/spirit. The result is a startlingly original novel of ideas in the best tradition of romanticism that goes beyond traditional romantic subject matter to embrace a rainbow of diversity, from the depths of sexual perversion and blocked artistic accomplishment to the heights of romantic ecstacy and creative self-expression.

Like Whitman, Poe, Dos Passos, Rand, Kesey, and Delaney, Schulman's passionate commitment is to self-expression, self-discovery, and self-fulfillment, no matter what the authoritarian obstacles. His novel thus lies squarely within the mainstream of the often misconceived and minimized American literary tradition, which in its dazzling variations has always embraced the struggle for individuality as its central theme. If America is uniquely the culture of the "self-made man"—a popular colloquialism quite properly born on these shores—then American literature is the story of individuals creating and re-creating themselves. That is one reason, I suspect, why so much popular American literature is science fiction—preeminently the modern genre of secular transcendence and unchained human potential—and why so much of that fiction of the future explores themes of individualism and libertarianism, the ethics of the future and the politics of full-fledged adulthood.

Many libertarian novels have dramatized the more visible social consequences of authoritarianism, showing how coercive government intervention destroys prosperity, sabotages peace, and sacrifices civil liberties. Schulman's novel dramatized authoritarianism's less visible consequences for the individual, showing how the State's institutionalized aggression warps sexuality, saps creativity, perverts relationships, weakens families, and replaced the benevolence and sympathy that healthy human beings naturally feel for each other with an insidious "every man for himself" attitude that is the inversion of true individualism. Such harmful personal crises may be less obvious than the war, mass murder, monopoly privileges, recurrent depressions, and runaway inflations brought about by the State throughout history, but they are no less significant, for such psychic wounds eventually dissolve the voluntary social bonds which sustain civilization itself.

The Rainbow Cadenza is a passionate testament to the sacred importance and irreplaceable value of every human being—the ultimate foundation of individualism and individual rights. Schulman's genius as a novelist lies in the way his story makes us feel the scars on the soul that result when individual rights are violated and human dignity is raped.

In recognition of Schulman's talent and insight, the Libertarian Futurist Society chose *The Rainbow Cadenza* from a field of 25 nominated novels as the winer of the 1984 Prometheus Award, a privately minted "Hayek Half" gold coin. Novelist James Hogan, 1983 Prometheus winner for his own *Voyage From Yesteryear*, presented Schulman with the award before an audience of more than 2,000 people at the 42nd World Science Fiction Convention in Anaheim, California. Appropriately enough, considering its similar focus on the fight for civil liberties in an authoritarian society, *The Rainbow Cadenza* won its award in the same year that Ray Bradbury's civil libertarian masterpiece *Fahrenheit 451* and George Orwell's anti-authoritarian classic *Nineteen-eighty-four* were inducted into the Prometheus Hall of Fame honoring outstanding pro-freedom fiction of the past.

Winning the Prometheus Award was a well-deserved honor for *The Rainbow Cadenza*, which not only powerfully portrays the evils of authoritarianism, but also offers its readers an inspiring example—through the character of one of literature's most memorable heroines—of the vast potential that freedom, and the thirst for freedom, can unleash in the human spirit.

Joan Darris loved the lights so much that she created a rainbow. Schulman loved liberty so much that he created *The Rainbow Cadenza*, a cautionary tale with a timeless message we ignore at our peril: "*Warning: Coercive Government May Be Hazardous to your Health.*"

THE DRAFT IS SLAVERY
by Paul Jacob

Paul Jacob is a young man uniquely qualified to write about the draft: several years ago he refused to register for the draft, made his refusal public knowledge, and went underground to remain free to deliver anti-draft speeches. After two years on the run, he was arrested by Federal authorities who were laying in wait when he returned home briefly to see his wife and, for the first time, their newborn baby.

Paul Jacob was convicted of violating the Selective Service Act, which is a federal felony, and sentenced to six months' imprisonment (now completed) and four-and-a-half years' forced "community service"—precisely the involuntary servitude to which he morally objects.

At the time I requested this afterword, Jacob was in solitary confinement at a federal prison in Dallas.—JNS

Not so many years ago, young men were drafted to kill and be killed in the swamps and jungles of Vietnam. In a fit of refreshing sanity, many Americans kicked and screamed, rebelled and resisted, and worked very, very hard to end this brutality.

Yet in the angry furor over the stupid, useless, and horrible war in Vietnam, few people stopped to consider the principles on which conscription—*for any war or any reason*—must rest. The draft was fought and ended largely because it enhanced that particularly unjust war effort. Today, the justice of conscription is often judged by the military policy that calls for it rather than on its own.

Even beyond the fatally uncomfortable fact that a draftee in the military may be forced to murder or may be murdered for a cause he or she does not believe in, conscription is, in its essence, a mighty wrong. Regardless of the reason, the draft is slavery. It is slavery in the very same way that dragging Africans across the ocean and forcing them to work in the cotton fields of the South was slavery. It is forced labor.

Indeed, rarely is any argument made that the draft is anything but slavery; however, the draft has been camouflaged for so long in talk of patriotism and paranoia that the issue of slavery is usually merely avoided. The definition of slavery is not altered by whether it is used for war or agriculture, by politician or plantation owner.

A favorite defense for the draft is that the individual has a duty to serve the government when called. This service is what the citizen "owes" the state. Implied is both that the individual incurs a debt to the government simply by being alive and, further, that the amount of indebtedness is ultimately the individual's entire being: his body, his labor, and his life.

If government has a right to conscript the people, then the government, in fact, "owns" the people. Such an idea must constitute a cold, hard slap in the face to those whose history books contain the Declaration of Independence and the Bill of Rights, proclaiming individual freedom by birthright and limiting government to the protection of that right.

Thomas Jefferson wrote in the Declaration of Independence that all men have "unalienable rights, that among these are life, liberty and the pursuit of happiness. That to secure these rights, governments are instituted among men, deriving their just powers from the consent of the governed." More simply, individuals own themselves. And their lives are their own, thus they should be free to live as they choose. The individual is the sovereign power that creates government; government is not a sovereign "owner" or master, but the servant of the people. To argue otherwise is like maintaining that cars and refrigerators have a claim on the life and labor of the people who made them. For in like manner, people made government.

Even without the clear message in the Declaration of Independence and the freedom proclaimed in great political writing throughout history, it seems self-evident that for a man to force his neighbor to work for him is gravely unjust. The injustice of this act is not removed if instead of one man enslaving his neighbor it becomes many men and women behind the cloak of government enslaving their neighbors.

Government is nothing more than an instrument of men and has no claim on any individual save that he not injure his fellow man. The individual certainly does not owe any person or any government his life. No matter how loud the cry of "necessity," no matter how cleverly conscription is disguised, no matter how equally applied, the draft is nonetheless slavery. It is wrong.

It is no coincidence that all totalitarian states—from communist to fascist military dictatorships—use conscription. In fact, many of these governments are ushering in a new age of conscription where not only are soldiers drafted but also other workers. Truly, if the state owns the people (as totalitarian governments invariably believe), thus drafting them for war, then nothing prevents the draft for other purposes.

Unfortunately, the very reasoning found in these "evil empires" has emerged countless times in the U.S. Congress in bills calling for a mandatory "national service." Enslaving people into the military has engendered great opposition, so certain draft adherents are proposing not an end to slavery but slavery toward new ends.

Yet, whatever the purpose of a draft or the nature of the work draftees will perform, it will inevitably lead to serious harm. The work they are to do—soldiering, teaching, bridge-building or hospital work—will be despised for the obvious reason that it is not of their choosing. The goal of their labor is historically shown to be more likely for evil than for good because, once enslaved, they have lost control over both their government and themselves.

Napoleon used the draft to scatter death and destruction across Europe, and a century-and-a-half later, conscription was indispensable to Adolf Hitler in doing similarly in even more gruesome fashion. Perhaps less horrible, but only in comparison, are two modern, "peaceful" examples. Vietnam has drafted thousands and sent them to labor in the Soviet Union to pay war debts, and Poland, during periods of worker unrest, has drafted those workers into the army and ordered them to perform their factory work.

Army General John A. Wickham, a member of the Joint Chiefs of Staff, said in praise of American soldiers, "They follow orders and they die." Whether drafted for war or for any other purpose, this statement sums up the distressing fate of the conscript. When human beings lose the power to decide the destiny of their own lives, when they are relegated from pursuing their own happiness to merely following orders, then they do die. If the death is not a permanent physical one, it is certainly a death of the human spirit—a death of the soul.

ULTRAVIOLET
REMARKS UPON ACCEPTING THE 1984
PROMETHEUS AWARD
by J. Neil Schulman

The following is the text of my remarks following my acceptance of the Prometheus Award on August 31st, 1984 at the 42nd World Science Fiction Convention, LACon, in Anaheim, California.—JNS

Science fiction stories are about ideas—and the ideas that people have determine what sort of world they will live in.

I wrote *The Rainbow Cadenza* to destroy an idea by reducing it to absurdity. The idea is: the rights of the individual should be sacrificed when the greatest good for the greatest number demands it. This idea is the justification for every violation of human rights on this planet today.

What I did in *The Rainbow Cadenza* was to take the sixties' slogan, "Make Love, Not War," at face value. I show what sort of lousy world we'd have if—in the name of "the greatest good for the greatest number"—people stopped demanding that young men be drafted to Make War, and instead demanded that for three years young women be drafted to Make Love.

I hope this logical absurdity horrifies you even while you smile. If it doesn't horrify you, I wrote *The Rainbow Cadenza* to show why it should: my young draftee is a woman whose artistry with lasers can make rainbows of hope. If it does horrify you, I wrote *The Rainbow Cadenza* to show why drafting *anyone* to Make War should horrify you even more.

Above all, I wrote *The Rainbow Cadenza* because each artist—in *whatever* medium—has a powerful weapon to fight what Thomas Jefferson called "every form of tyranny over the mind of man," and nobody had to draft me for that. I volunteered. Thank you.

Appendix II.

A GLOSSARY OF
THE RAINBOW CADENZA

by J. Neil Schulman

As with afterwords, there's something almost sinful about an author putting a glossary at the end of a novel. It suggests that an author feels, due either to the author's own failure or to the reader's, that the novel can't be understood without further clarification.

I don't believe this to be true about The Rainbow Cadenza.

Some terms, institutions, or situations I invented for the novel may not be clear at the beginning, but I promise that if a story point hinges on something being clearly understood, I'll have told you in time. As a matter of fact, I strongly suggest you avoid looking at this glossary until after reading my novel, since I reveal important plot points here which might ruin the suspense for you.

Then why have a glossary at all?

My reason for writing a glossary is that not everything I wanted to tell about the times and places I've taken you could be catalogued within the dramatic confines of my story. And I hope your reason for reading this glossary will be that I have intrigued you enough that you want still more explicit details about the times and places you've just visited.

In the following, I have attempted to give definitions and encyclopedic background relating to terms found in The Rainbow Cadenza. *Those terms I Invented are marked (I); those to which I gave New Meanings are marked (N); and those which are Already In Use, either as accepted terminology or in the writings of other authors, are marked (A). CAPITALIZATION indicates a reference to another HEADING for additional information—JNS*

ABSOLUTE POWER: (N) The maximum power output of a CHROMATIC LASER instrument. For Joan's LCAA MARK 800B, this is 86 Watts. A LASEMEISTER will warn a student that "Absolute power corrupts absolutely." This is not a restatement of Lord Acton's political dictum, but a practical warning for the student to connect the chromatic laser's POWER DAMPERS. The engineering oddity by which the same type of power connector is used from wall outlet to a CONSOLE and between a console and an LCAA chromatic laser is due to the nature of FIRE GEMS in the LCAA chromatic laser, which periodically need to be retuned by running absolute power through them. Compare with FULL POWER.

ACHROMATIC: (N) Without color: colorless. A lasegraphic composition not based on color DIALECTICs, equivalent to "atonal" music, which has no harmonic dialectics.

ACUTE: (N) Cute, sexy—a slang meaning returned to the full root.

ADAMINE: (I) Brand-name for drug which, when taken by a man, inhibits his female-producing gynosperm, allowing his male-producing androsperm the only chance to fertilize an ovum. Any resulting pregnancy would be for a male child. Compare EVELINE.

AD ASTRA: (N) Latin, literally "to the stars." Cluster of FREE-SPACE HABITATs, population 50 million, situated in the LaGrange Two orbit, behind Earth's moon. This strategic location, shielded against direct view from Earth by the moon, was primarily responsible for the habitats' victory in the WAR OF COLONIAL SECESSION.

ADOPTION: (N) The marriage of a senior ANDROMAN to a junior andro-man, who becomes the senior androman's WARD.

ALAMO CITY: (N) New name for San Antonio, Texas. Places named after saints have been renamed because of unpleasant connotations to the anti-Christian culture in the Federation.

A.M.: (A) Amplitude Modulation in LASEGRAPHY, by which projected forms are made larger or smaller. Usage derived from LASERIUM.

ANDRECOLOGY: (I) Medical specialty dealing with the problems of ANDROMEN.

ANDRO: (N) From root for male: ANDROMAN, or relating to andromen.

ANDROID: (N) Relating to ANDROMEN.

ANDROMAN, ANDROMEN: (I) Literally, "male-man." A socio-political designation in the Federation referring to males whose sexual preference does *not* include women as partners and usually, but not necessarily, includes other males: a resolved celibate could choose to be classified as either androman or comman. Only andromen may stand for election to a LAVENDER Seat in the Upper Manor, or vote in elections for Lavender seats. Compare COMMAN.

ANKH: (A) An ancient Egyptian life symbol used as insigne for the rank of MISTRESS in the Federation Peace Corps.

ANTI-PRECIPITATION FIELD: (I) Weather-control barrier against rain, snow, sleet, hail, etc. Compare CLOUD FACTORY.

ANTITHESIST: (I) Musical instrumentalist in a ROGA band who plays the Antithesizer, which counters visual imagery with melody. See DIALECTIC.

ARTICLES OF FEDERATION: (N) The constitution of the WORLD FEDERATION, enacting a republican World State.

AURAGRAM: (I) One gram of gold, in coin or money substitute. The money of the WORLD FEDERATION.

AVOCADO PIT: (N) The geometric core of a zero-gravity CATHEDRAL, where the lasegrapher performs. Derives from TIGER PIT.

BASS FORTISSIMO: (I) See FORTISSIMO.

BELT: (A) A powered, individual FLYING BELT: a sky belt.

BELTANE: (A) May Day. A legal holiday in the Federation. Also, a WICCEN holiday celebrating the MAIDEN GODDESS' Coming of Age.

BELTER: (A) A person who flies a sky belt.

BETWEEN A METEOR AND THE MOON: (I) Slang equivalent to "between Scylla and Charybdis" or "between a rock and a hard place."

BIRTH-RECORD PRINTOUT: (N) Birth certificate.

BLUE: (N) Official designation, in Federation color-code, signifying a COMMAN or commen. Blue is included in the clothing design of commen to differentiate them from andromen, and is the color of the seats in the HOUSE OF COMMEN.

BLUE JAY: (N) Ragging term used by andromen referring to a COMMAN. Compares with "Lav," ragging term used by commen referring to an androman.

BOH: (I) Slang term for Bohemian in period following WAR OF COLONIAL SECESSION, comparable to beatnik, hippie, or punk.

BOOSTY: (N) Teenage slang in AD ASTRA, referring to a person who provides an ego-boost. Also, slang for high on COCA MOCHA. See also COKED TO THE MOKE.

BRAINPRINT: (I) A registered recording of a person's PRIMARY NEURAL MODULATION, kept on file by the FEDERATION BUREAU OF IMMUNITY. See also SCANNING and NINTH AMENDMENT.

BRUSHFIRE WAR, THE: (I) A thirty-year-long period of limited wars, in the early Twenty-first Century, which led to the gender imbalance, great socio-political changes on Earth and, consequently, the Federation.

BUTCH: (A) Very masculine. Originally a term used by male homosexuals to denote the more-male role in a relationship, later in general use in the Federation as a generic term of approval.

CABINET: (A) The government of the WORLD FEDERATION, chaired by the PRIME MINISTER, and comprising the Ministers of each Federation Ministry.

CADENZA: (A) Italian for "cadence." Derived from classical music, lasegraphic term referring to a virtuoso passage in a composition—often composed by a performer—in which a performer gets to stretch instrumental technique to the limit. Compare with RIFF.

CADETTE: (N) Female cadet: Cadette Corporal in the Federation Peace Corps. See CORPORAL.

CADILLAC DE SADE: (I) A large, gaudy skymobile named for the Marquis de Sade (1740-1814), an author popular among Marnies in the Federation for his explication of the use of pain (hence the term "sadism") to increase sexual pleasure. They are invariably piloted by rich show-offs with rude manners. If a skymobile cuts you off, it's probably a Cadillac De Sade. Compare Cadillac De Ville, the equivalent automobile.

CAIR PARAVEL: (N) Capital city of ST. CLIVE habitat, named for the capital of Narnia in C.S. Lewis's *Chronicles of Narnia*.

CALDRON, THE: (N) Earth slang for Hell or Hellish place, derived from WICCEN usage.

CANAVERAL SKYPORT: (N) Space port at Cape Canaveral.

CANNABIS: (A) The female hemp plant and derivatives: marijuana. Completely legal in both the Federation and the habitats.

CANNABIST: (I) A person who sells or serves marijuana or hashish, particularly in a CANNABISTRO. Derives from CANNABIS.

CANNABISTRO: (I) Combination of CANNABIS + bistro. A bar where marijuana or hashish is sold or served.

CAPOTE: (A) Literally French for "hood," it refers to a hooded cloak. Lavender capotes are worn officially or formally by andromen in the Federation, in honor of a RENAISSANCE author they particularly admire. In the Federation the hood is optional and the term refers to any cloak. See CLOAK, CLOAKED.

CATHEDRAL: (A) Literally "DOME," refers not only to a place of worship but also to a MEDIA TEMPLE.

CENTIGRAM: (A) One-hundredth of a gram: in the Federation, one-hundredth AURAGRAM: cent.

CEREBRAL ABORTION: (I) Procedure performed on a premature fetus whereby only autonomic functions of the undeveloped brain are permitted to continue. In the procedure of cerebral abortion, an embryonic human has its cerebral cortex chemically inhibited to prevent even prenatal personality formation, and after induced parturition at sixth months of development, the forever-mindless infant has a RADICAL LOBOTOMY performed, so the body may be artificially grown to maturity without any personality formation whatever. When the fetus grows into an adult body, there will be "no one at home," leaving the body free to have a genetically-compatible, cryonically preserved adult brain transplanted into it, making a whole person once again. In the Federation, the term is also used as school slang for "stupidity."

CHACUN A SON GOUT: (A) French, literally "Each to his taste."

CHAIRISTIC HEURONOMY: (I) The study of problem-solving leadership, a subdiscipline of Motivational Studies (see QUADRIVIUM) at UAANP. Also slang for a cushy, but useless, figurehead position.

CHALDEAN: (N) Period of lasegraphic development which developed most of lasegraphic form, sometimes at the expense of spiritual freedom. Equivalent to baroque period in classical music. Derives from Chaldeans, ancient astronomer-priests who built the Tower of Babel, an attempt to open the gates of Heaven by the ritualistic forms of worship, rather than spiritual content of worship. Compare NASCENT PERIOD, SYMBOLIST PERIOD, IMPRESSIONIST.

CHAUVINISTS: (N) The Chauvinist Party in the Federation. Originally a party concerned with national, provincial rights, later a party indistinguishable from its opponent LIBERTARIAN Party.

CHRIST: (N) In Federation usage, a horned god or devil. Used as a mild exclamation.

CHROMATIC LASER: (I) A laser instrument capable of emitting a full visible spectrum, by extension: the lasegraphic instrument. Contrasted with monochromatic lasers.

CIVILIZATION AND ITS DISCONTENTS: (N) A commercial chain store in the Federation boasting that it sells "the contents of civilization on DISC" but, as a play on the title of Sigmund Freud's seminal essay of that title, conceding that all such contents are the unending bitchings of a bunch of malcontents.

CLASSICAL LASEGRAPHY: (I) LASEGRAPHY performed in silence, relying on internal themes rather than being choreographed to music. Compare with ROGA.

CLEAVAGE: (N) 1/10th of a DIVISION in the Peace Corps, comprising 4,500 women, segmented into 10 DICTERIA.

CLOAK, CLOAKED: (A) Formal or official dress in the Federation, one style of which is the CAPOTE worn by ANDROMEN. Formally, COMMEN wear BLUE cloaks, andromen wear LAVENDER cloaks, WOMEN wear PINK cloaks, judges wear black cloaks, and TOUCHABLES are legally required to be cloaked in RED while in public.

CLONE: (A) A sociological, as well as biological, designation in the Federation. A human deriving from a single cell from one parent only, so that the resulting child is an identical genetic twin of that parent. The process is used by ANDROMEN to reproduce themselves, implanting such cells into a HOST MOTHER for the pregnancy. Compare with PARTHENOGENESIS and TWIN.

CLONE-FATHER: (N) The single parent of a CLONE child.

CLONING, TO CLONE: (A) Not only to produce a CLONE, but to reproduce a replacement part of a body by cloning in vitro.

CLONERAPER: (I) An ANDROMAN who rapes his CLONE. Also an emphatic insult equivalent to current usage of "MOTHERFUCKER."

CLONERAPING: (I) Emphatic verbal intensifier, in the Federation, indicating the displeasure of the user.

CLOUD FACTORY: (I) Weather control device which produces precipitation. See also ANTI-PRECIPITATION FIELD.

COCA DRINKER: (N) A drinker of COCA MOCHA, also implying a *BOH* or ROGA aficionado. See MOCHA HOUSE.

COCA MOCHA: (I) A hot beverage comprising coffee, cocoa, and cocaine. The caffeine and cocaine are in small enough amounts to provide an equivalent boost to coffee or tea, beverages which it has largely supplanted. Its ritualistic properties associated with bohemian culture are all out of proportion to its actual biochemical effects.

COKED TO THE MOKE: (I) Slang used by ROGA players and aficiorados. High on COCA MOCHA—feeling good. BOOSTY.

COLONIAL WAR: (I) THE WAR OF COLONIAL SECESSION. Used largely on Earth to avoid having to remind themselves that they lost.

COLONIES: (N) The FREE-SPACE HABITATS. Used in the Federation only, since its usage is inflamatory in the habitats.

COLORATURA: (N) Derived from opera: coloration. In LASEGRAPHY, a LEITMOTIF based on color DIALECTICs.

COLOR-BLIND: (N) With regard to LASEGRAPHY, equivalent to being tone deaf to music.

COMIC DISC: (I) A DISC containing cartoon material, equivalent to comic book.

COMMAN: (I) Common Man. Socio-political designation in Federation for a male whose sexual partners include women. The term does not exclude ambi-sexual males who choose other male sexual partners as well. A legal prerequisite to standing for the HOUSE OF COMMEN, voting in elections for the House of Commen, or visiting the DICTERIA. See ANDROMAN and WOMEN.

COMMEN: (I) More than one COMMAN. Also the Federation Lower Manor, the HOUSE OF COMMEN.

CONCORD: (N) The NORTH AMERICAN CONCORD.

CONFUCIUS: (N) A FREE-SPACE HABITAT built by the Chinese.

CONGLOMERATE: (N) The largest segment of the Peace Corps, comprising 450,000 women. 1/10th of Corps, divided into 10 CORPORATIONS.

CONSCRIPTION: (A) Compulsory national service, usually but not always in the military. It might have been forbidden in the U.S. Constitution if it hadn't first been put into common use in France six years after the U.S. Constitution was drawn up; it might have been later interpreted by the U.S. Supreme Court as forbidden by the Sixteenth Amendment ban on "involuntary servitude" if conscription hadn't first been used in the United States during the Civil War, a war which we're told was fought to *abolish* slavery.

CONSOLE: (N) A lasegraphic keyboard and, by extension, the CHROMATIC LASER instrument itself.

CONTROLLED HYPOTHERMIA: (A) Medical procedure used for preparing a patient for CRYONIC SUSPENSION by reducing body temperature without freezing damage.

COPYRIGHT: (N) No longer referring just to rights protection of writing, music, maps, etc., but refers primarily to laws relating to CLONING and PARTHENOGENESIS.

CORPORAL: (N) Ranks in Peace Corps, starting with Cadette Corporal, equivalent to buck private in the military (insigne Virgo); then to Second Corporal, equivalent to private in the military (insigne gold YONI); then to First Corporal (insigne silver yoni), with ranks ranging (by number of yoni) between corporal in the military to sergeant. The term literally classifies the women in the DICTERIA as "bodies"—and bodies which are in no sense "private."

CORPORAL JOAN-OF-ARC: (N) Dr. Blaine refers to Joan Darris this way, comparing her to the French heroine Saint Jeanne d'Arc (circa 1412-1431) known for her unyielding fortitude. However, since the French term for rainbow is *arc-en-ciel*—arc in the sky—his name for Joan is truer than he imagines. Joan later becomes a "Jeanne-d'Arc-en-ciel" when she one-ups Jaeger's RAINBOW CADENZA.

CORPORATION: (N) In Peace Corps, 1/10th of a CONGLOMERATE comprising 45,000 women segmented into 10 DIVISIONS.

CORPS, THE: (N) The WORLD FEDERATION PEACE CORPS.

COURT-VENEREAL: (I) A trial for, or to try, a member of the Peace Corps. Literally "Court of Venus," the Goddess of Love. Derives from court-martial: "Court of Mars," the God of War.

COURT-VENEREED: (I) Past tense of COURT-VENEREAL.

C.P.O.: (I) Corps Post Office. The internal mail system of the Peace Corps.

CRONE: (A) The third aspect of GODDESS in the WICCEN trinity of MAIDEN, LADY, AND CRONE, largely an exclamation equivalent to "God" or "Christ" today.

CROSS, VENUS: (A) The traditional symbol for woman, used as an official insigne in the Peace Corps signifying the rank of MATRIARCH.

CRYONIC SUSPENSION: (A) The process whereby a human being is preserved at below-freezing temperatures, usually until medical treatment can be accomplished. In *Rainbow Cadenza*, this is accepted medical procedure following CONTROLLED HYPOTHERMIA, and the "DEANIMATED" person is preserved in a VIVARIUM.

CRUZVILLE: (I) City in PACIFICA PARISH, NORTH AMERICAN CONCORD, originally Santa Cruz, California. See ALAMO CITY.

CURFEW: (N) In Federation, refers to sunset, the point at which TOUCHABLE hunting becomes legal for the night. Certain Touchables—such as mothers with small children—are allowed immunity for the night so long as they are in designated ghettos by curfew. See VAGINATOWN.

DAEDALUS: (N) A FREE-SPACE HABITAT in the asteroid belt but which has long-term plans to migrate to the orbit of Jupiter, where its main industry would be commercial exploitation of the Jovian moons and the gas-mining of Jupiter itself. The farthest out of the habitats, it is noted for its wild frontier mentality. Named for mythic hero, father of Icarus—see ICARATE.

DANCE CARD: (N) In the post-BRUSHFIRE WAR period, a record of a woman's compliance with the EQUALIZATION-OF-SEX-OPPORTUNITY LAW. By Joan Darris's time, usage has reverted to its original meaning of a card at a social function whereby partners make appointments for dances—only *men* now keep the card.

DAYGLOW, DAYGLOWING: (N) From Dayglo. In lasegraphic usage, refers to the phosphorescent black light used in a dome to keep light levels comfortably low during entry and exit.

DEADER: (N) A recorded BRAINPRINT taken from a person now deceased. Compare LIVE and ICICLE.

DEANIMATE: (I) Not moving. Frozen in CRYONIC SUSPENSION, but not permanently dead.

DEASIL: (A) Clockwise.

DEEP HEAVEN: (A) Term used by C.S. Lewis in the "Ransom" trilogy for outer space beyond the orbit of Earth's moon. Usage adopted in the ST. CLIVE habitats.

DEMIMONDE: (N) In a zero-gravity CATHEDRAL, there are opposing domes, with laser images duplicated "upper" and "lower." The "lower" dome (with reference to the lasegrapher's attitude) is the demimonde. Also play on French term for Underworld.

D.H.: (I) DEEP HEAVEN.

DIALECTIC: (A) Literally "through words," it refers to the logical process of contrasting a statement (thesis) with a contrary statement (antithesis) and integrating both statements into a new statement containing both (synthesis). In the dialectical materialism proposed by Hegel, a political thesis finds its realization

331

in its antithesis, but to avoid the excluded middle in Aristotelian logic, this would require a shifted context, bringing in at least one new dimension to those considered in the original statements. In LASEGRAPHY, dialectic refers to a LEITMOTIF countered by another leitmotif, creating psychological tension, then releasing tension by resolving into a third leitmotif encompassing the first two. By the tension dialectic theory that Wolfgang Jaeger used, the basic human tension is doubt about survival: the tension of sowing released by reaping, the tension of hunting released by the kill, the tension of hunger released by eating, the tension of sexual arousal released by orgasm; and the eschatological dialectic of human existence—as symbolized by an ascending spiral—is represented by genetic reproduction: one parent's genetic code as thesis, the other's as antithesis, the child's as synthesis. In this theory, all forms of art and music derive their fundamental biological power from applying cognitive dialectics within a defined context of willingly suspended, or suspenseful, disbelief: as examples, in painting, *trompe l'oeil*; in poetry, oxymoron; in drama, plot; in music, melody; in dance, kinesics.

DICHROIC: (A) Literally, "two colors." Relates to dichroism, the property of a crystal, mirror, or filter to pass only one of two spectral lines: dichromatic. Dichroic filters are used in CHROMATIC LASERs to separate out spectral lines before further modulation or re-mixing.

DICHROIC SCALE: (I) THE THIRTY-SIX-COLOR SCALE of LASE-GRAPHY. Should have been "diachroic scale" for "through colors" in comparison to "diatonic" for the scale in music, but the term "DICHROIC" was already in use by lasegraphers to refer to filters in their laser instruments.

DICTERIA: (A) Originally the state-run houses of PROSTITUTION in ancient Athens, the term was adopted by the Federation Peace Corps for the network of hotel-like facilities where CORPORALs provide sexual services to COMMEN.

DICTERIAL: (I) Referring to the DICTERIA. Usage comparible with "military," since this is the primary function of the Peace Corps.

DICTERIAT: (I) Comb. DICTERIA + secretariat. The primary administrative unit of the Peace Corps (1/10th of a CLEAVAGE, comprising 450 women, divided into two TROOPs) and, by extensions, the singular for dicteria and the actual building where CORPORALs service COMMEN.

DIFFRACTIONS: (A) A kaleidoscopic duplication of LASER imagery by passing the beam through a HOLOGRAPHIC plate. One of the three basic types of laser image, along with RAW SCANS and LUMIA. See also SCANNING, LASEGRAPHIC.

DIRECT-EMOTING CONSOLE: (I) An experimental device which uses FIRE GEMS to modulate and transmit psychic impulses from one person to another. Joan realizes this could be the logical next art form after lasegraphy.

DISC: (A) Any flat, circular medium which can record, store, or play back information signals, whether visual, aural, mechanical, or in language.

DISCOTHEQUE: (N) A place where DISCs are read: library.

DISNEY: (N) One of the cylinders in AD ASTRA—a city.

DIVISION: (N) In the Peace Corps, 1/10th of a CORPORATION, comprising 45,000 women segmented into 10 CLEAVAGEs.

DOME: (A) See CATHEDRAL, LASERIUM, MEDIA TEMPLE.

DOMESTIC COMPUTER: (I) A computer used in a residence to run the household.

DOUBLE READING: (I) MONITOR jargon for getting the same BRAIN-PRINT reading from two different persons. A sure indication of illegal activity, since all brainprints are discrete.

DOVES: (A) Insignia of peace used in Peace Corps by the rank of MATRON.

DRAFT, THE: (A) See CONSCRIPTION.

DRYER, IVAN: (A) (1939-   ) First person to record a lasegraphic composition in a film titled *Laser Image* (1970), and in 1973 pivotal founder of Laser Images, Inc., a commercial entertainment and special effects company which produced NASCENT-PERIOD concerts, usually in planetariums, under the trademarked name LASERIUM. When last heard of, Chief Holographer on the *Crystal Odyssey*, first torchship sent out to explore the Alpha Centauri Star System.

DRYER SCHOOL OF LASEGRAPHY: (I) Institute of lasegraphic studies in NOVA PAULUS, AD ASTRA, associated with the UAANP, of which Wolfgang Jaeger is the Dean. Named for IVAN DRYER.

DUMBJOHN: (A) A derisive term for a new cadet in a military academy, later was combined with the prostitute's term of a customer—"john"—as a derisive term used by a CORPORAL in the Peace Corps for a visiting COMMAN, and—by extension—all stupidity.

EARTH STREET: (I) A street in a fashionable section of NEWER YORK, in a location where—before the RAIN OF TERROR destroyed it—Greenwich Village used to be.

EFFETE: (A) Sickly, decadent. A term of praise in the Federation.

ENTROPIC: (N) In lasegraphic usage, the descending color-scale: literally means "turning into the circle." Compare to EXTROPIC.

EQUALIZATION-OF-SEX-OPPORTUNITY LAW: (I) A law in the post-BRUSHFIRE WAR period, requiring women to include a minimum number of "sexually deprived" males as their sexual partners. A follow-up to the MINIMUM-SEX LAW.

ERIKA BLAIR: (I) A woman whose parents named her after Eric Blair.

(1903—1950), an ancestral kinsman of hers who wrote under the penname George Orwell.

EVELINE: (I) Brand name for a drug taken by a woman that counters the effects of ADAMINE, sterilizing androsperm and reactivating gynosperm, ensuring that any ovum fertilized will produce a girl.

EXTRATERRESTRIALITY: (N) A legal term in the Federation: extraterritoriality with regard to the habitats.

EXTROPIC: (I) The ascending color-scale in lasegraphic usage, literally means "turning out of the circle." Also, by extension, neg-entropic in thermodynamics. Compare to ENTROPIC.

FAKE OR FALSE TRANSPONDER: (I) An IDENTITY TRANSPONDER which transmits a recorded BRAINPRINT, thus covering up the actual brainprint of the wearer.

FALSE BRAINPRINT: (I) A BRAINPRINT reading that does not correspond to the actual brainprint of the person from which it's been read.

FAMILY CIRCLE: (N) A family coven, in a WICCEN family. Also the accepted usage of an extended, as opposed to nuclear, family.

FEDERATION: (N) The WORLD FEDERATION.

FEDERATION BUREAU OF IMMUNITY: (I) A bureau of the Federation charged with recording and keeping categorized BRAINPRINTs, equivalent to the fingerprint files kept in the United States by the FBI, an organization whose initials it shares.

FEDERATION PEACE CORPS: (I) The WORLD FEDERATION PEACE CORPS.

FEDERATION SPACE CORPS, THE WORLD: (I) The only military of the WORLD FEDERATION, since the individual PROVINCEs of the Federation are expected to provide the land and sea forces. Since the Colonial War, its function is largely to maintain a space perimeter between Earth and the habitats. It also provides security to VIRGINIA STATION and other space platforms in Earth orbit. Compare with MONITORS.

FERROFOAM: (I) Originally a brand-name for foamed steel—an actual product experimentally produced by NASA—it later became a generic term.

FIRE GEMS: (I) Crystals found in the asteroid belt with odd electromagnetic properties, found also to modulate, amplify, and transmit psychic impulses. Not known whether they are natural crystals or synthetic artifacts—see LUCIFER—they are nonetheless used in the best CHROMATIC LASERs and, later, in DIRECT-EMOTING CONSOLEs.

FIRST CORPORAL: (I) See CORPORAL.

FIRST LADY: (N) A LADY elected by vote of the Ladies in the HOUSE OF GENTRY, the First Lady is Head of State in the World Federation, Commander-in-Chief of the Peace Corps, and Chief Justice of the World Federation. Compare with PRESIDENT and PRIME MINISTER.

FLYING BELT: (A) A turbine jet worn as a backpack allowing individual flight. Bell Laboratories experimented with them in the 1960's, but fuel limits only allowed several minutes aloft. See also GENERAL ELECTRIC JOOB FLYING BELT.

F.M.: (A) Frequency Modulation. In lasegraphy refers to the scanning frequency of the mirrors in a CHROMATIC LASER, which determines the shape of a laser image. Usage from LASERIUM.

FOREST HILLS VIVARIUM: (I) A VIVARIUM in Forest Hills, a township of New and NEWER YORK.

FORTISSIMIST: (I) An instrumentalist who plays a FORTISSIMO.

FORTISSIMO: (N) From Italian, literally "very loud" in music, refers to a turbine pipe organ used to accompany ROGA: it is always very loud. In the high range this is a tenor fortissimo—about equivalent to a six-stringed guitar—and, in the low range, a bass fortissimo—with a range from subsonic lows to the highs of a bass guitar. The name derives from usage of piano, originally pianoforte: soft-loud.

FREE-SPACE HABITAT: (A) Term used and described by Gerard K. O'Neill (see O'NEILL) in his book *The High Frontier* for a manufactured habitat in space orbit at a LaGrange point. The cylindrical habitats in *The Rainbow Cadenza* are based on O'Neill's Island III design. Also called an "O'Neill Colony."

FRIAR: (N) In ROGA slang, brother.

FUCK: (A) In Federation usage, this means *only* to engage in sexual intercourse, and the usage is standard rather than vulgar. All the vulgar usages have been replaced with terms referring to rape and clone-rape. I got the idea for this change of usage from Ira Levin's novel, *This Perfect Day*, where the term fuck likewise has been replaced in vulgar usage by the word "fight."

FUGUE: (A) Akin to the fugue form in classical music, a composition in LASEGRAPHY which states a theme in a tonic color, then repeats it contrapuntally a fifth color above, and so forth. Vera Delaney's *Fugue in Blue* is in the third EXTROPIC key.

FULL MATRON: (I) A rank in the Peace Corps—insigne the "N.D. CIRCLE OF PEACE"—which commands a CLEAVAGE of 10 DICTERIA.

FULL POWER: (N) The standard power output of a CHROMATIC LASER in performance at the PYRADOME: 1.72 watts. Compare ABSOLUTE POWER.

GAYLORD: (N) An ANDROMAN elected to a LAVENDER Seat as a junior senator in the HOUSE OF GENTRY by vote of the andromen in a Federation PROVINCE. The term is for six years. In addition to sitting in the House of Gentry, which convenes for only two months out of the year, a Gaylord is also Governor of his province, an office equivalent—in the NORTH AMERICAN CONCORD—to the old office of President of the United States. Term derives from a given name of landed gentry in the American South, from later slang term referring to gentrified "gay" homosexuals, and from the upper house of the British parliamentary system being the House of Lords.

GENERAL ELECTRIC JOOB FLYING BELT: (I) A FLYING BELT, on file with the jet-engine division of General Electric, practical when tokamak nuclear fusion becomes portable and safe.

GHETTO: (N) 1. The VAGINATOWN ghetto.   2. Any temporary gathering place of TOUCHABLEs.

GLOWING: (N) DAYGLOWING.

GOD: (A) Supreme Deity, often thought of as male, in the Judeo-Christian tradition, often called the Lord. In Christianity also sometimes the First Person of the Holy Trinity of Father, Son, and Holy Spirit. Also a mild exclamation used in the habitats.

GODDESS: (A) Supreme Deity, female, in the WICCEN tradition, often called the LADY. Also the Wiccen Trinity of MAIDEN, LADY, AND CRONE. Also a mild exclamation used in the Federation.

GOVERNOR: (A) A male tender of children, equivalent to governess. In common usage the term has supplanted the political meaning of provincial governor, who is usually referred to as the GAYLORD.

GRAM: (N) In the Federation, synonym for AURAGRAM, one gram of gold, and a unit of money.

GUBERNATORIAL: (A) Referring to a governor and his duties.

GYNE: (I) An act of GYNUFLECTION: salute.

GYNUFLECT: (I) To perform A GYNUFLECTION.

GYNUFLECTION: (I) A gesture of courtesy, combining the curtsey and genuflection, used in the Peace Corps as a salute. Combines "genuflect" with the root "gyno-" meaning female.

HABITAT: (A) FREE-SPACE HABITAT.

HALF-SISTER: (N) A sister with whom one has one of two parents in common. This may not be categorically useful since—if one's entire genetic code is derived from one parent—a half-sister may have as much in common with one genetically as a full-sister would normally.

336

HALL OF PRESERVATION: (I) A ceremonial area in a VIVARIUM allowing family and friends spiritual communion with their cryonically preserved loved ones.

HARD LIQUOR: (A) Distilled liquor in its pure form, prohibited from being served or sold retail in the Federation. Liquor may only be legally served or sold in the Federation in a cocktail. Beer and wine are legal for service and retail sale.

HAREM: (N) In the Peace Corps, the smallest unit, 1/5th of a SORORITY, comprising 9 women and commanded by a Second Corporal.

HARLEM LAKE: (I) A lake in NEWER YORK, where the old Manhattan neighborhood of Harlem was before a meteor in the RAIN OF TERROR destroyed it and created a giant crater, later filled in with water to create a lake.

HAWKS: (N) Robot flying belts used by a MARNIE in SCANNING for TOUCHABLES.

HELL'S BASEMENT: (I) The place where all damned, inanimate objects end up, when cursed to Hell.

HER LADYSHIP: (N) Form of address for a LADY in the HOUSE OF GENTRY.

HIS EXCELLENCY: (N) Form of address of a Member of the HOUSE OF COMMEN.

HIS GAYLORDSHIP: (I) Form of address for a GAYLORD in the HOUSE OF GENTRY.

HOLODRAMA: (I) A dramatic play in motion holograms: movie.

HOLOGRAM: (A) A photographic plate produced by holography.

HOLOGRAPHIC: (A) Relating to holography, the process of aiming a split laser beam—half a reference beam and the other half an incident beam bounced off an object—at a photographic plate, to produce a true three-dimensional photograph of that object. Holographic plates have the property of distributing the recorded visual information in diffracted microcosms of the entire image, so that if a holographic plate is cut in half, the entire image remains (though with less information density) and the same is true if each is halved again, and so forth until the information density is too thin to overcome background noise. Current theories of the human brain suggest that holographic distribution of information is one of the ways the brain stores information, as well as specific information stored in a particular brain location. As well, it has been suggested by physicist David Bohm that the entire universe as we know it might store information holographically, suggesting that the universe might be a single conscious entity (God or Goddess) or at the very least a "holographic" record of the entire universe accessible by the human brain—thus explaining precognition and clairvoyance. Contemplating holography, I came up with the same theory about the universe before I'd heard of Bohm's formulation, which suggests that his theory of distributed information might be true.

HOLOSCREEN: (I) A HOLOVISION screen, generally used for holovision reception, as a simulator of LASER projection, and for the visual component of telephone usage.

HOLOVISION: (A) HOLOGRAPHIC 3-D television.

HOLY, THE: (I) Slang in the Federation for HOLOVISION, equivalent to HV in the habitats, used for its irreverence to Judeo-Christianity. The irreverence backfires when Hill Bromley gets the last word in his trial broadcast.

HOLY GUIDE: (I) A listing of HOLOVISION programs available for recording that day.

HOLY NETWORKS: (I) HOLOVISION producers who share programming among themselves.

HOOP DOGS: (I) A frankfurter shaped into a toroid circle—like a doughnut—and served in the Federation on a bagel. It's popular in the Federation because it replaces the phallic hotdog with a female symbol more acceptable to a WICCEN culture. I came up with the idea of a toroid frank before I wrote *Rainbow Cadenza*, reasoning it would be served on an English muffin, and sauerkraut could be dumped into the hole. When I told the idea to a friend, Samuel Edward Konkin III, he christened it the Hoop Dog.

HOST: (A) A HOST MOTHER.

HOST MOTHER: (A) A woman who bears a child not conceived from her own ova. Not to be confused with a surrogate mother, who is contracted to have her own ovum impregnated by a father, bears that child, and then relinquishes legal claim to a child of which she is the true mother. I got the usage from Heinlein.

HOUSE OF COMMEN: (I) The Lower Manor of the bicameral legislature of the republican WORLD FEDERATION, seating commen elected one from each parish for a six-year term by vote of the commen in that parish. Jurisdiction includes appointment of ambassadors to the habitats, domestic relations between provinces, administration of the MONITORS and FEDERATION SPACE CORPS, and the passage of legislation along with the HOUSE OF GENTRY. Elects the PRIME MINISTER of the Federation, who—as Chairman of the Cabinet—is Head of Government. Name derives from the lower house in the British parliamentary system, the House of Commons. Form of address for a Member of the House of Commen is "Your Excellency," and abbreviation for a member is M.H.C.

HOUSE OF GENTRY: (I) The Upper Manor of the bicameral legislature of the republican World Federation, seating one LADY elected to a PINK Seat by vote of the WOMEN of each PROVINCE as a senior senator from each province, and one GAYLORD elected to a LAVENDER Seat as a junior senator and provincial governor by vote of the ANDROMEN of each province. Gaylords and Ladies stand for election as running mates from each province, and are jointly elected—or defeated—for a six-year term. Form of address for an elected Lady is "Your Ladyship," while form of address for an elected Gaylord is "Your Gaylordship." The Ladies in the House of Gentry elect the FIRST LADY of the Federation, who is Head of State of the Federation, Chief Justice, and Commander-in-Chief of the Federation Peace Corps, and the Gaylords in the House of Gentry elect the PRESIDENT of the Federation, who is Chief Executive Officer. The Upper Manor provides the Judiciary of the Federation, by monopoly grants to private JUDICIARY FIRMS charged with administering the laws passed by the Federation legislature.

HOVERCART: (I) A small hovercraft supporting a pushcart.

HUDSON CORRIDOR: (I) The Hudson River Air Corridor, largely following the Hudson River, designated as a highway for SKYMOBILE traffic.

HUDSON PARISH: (I) PARISH in the NORTH AMERICAN CONCORD comprising most of New York State, New Jersey, and New England.

HUNTING: (N) SCANNING for a TOUCHABLE performed by a MARNIE.

HUSBAND: (N) Not only a COMMAN mated to his wife, but also an ANDROMAN mated to his WARD.

HV: (I) Slang for HOLOVISION in the habitats.

ICARATE: (I) To drop to one's death out of the sky. From the legend of Icarus who—with his father Daedalus—escaped from Crete by flying away with wax wings, disregarded his father's advice to keep low lest his wings melt, and consequently plunged to his death. In the Federation, this is also a sexual perversion performed by MARNIEs on TOUCHABLEs: taking them for a "flying fuck" then dropping them to their deaths.

ICICLE: (N) A recorded BRAINPRINT taken from a person now in CRYONIC SUSPENSION. Compare with DEADER and LIVE.

ICK: (I) Children's slang for "to ICARATE," derived from the likely condition of the icarated corpse. Used as a rude suggestion of what one can do to oneself.

IDENTITY TRANSPONDER: (I) A tiny radio transponder implanted near the spinal cord to read PRIMARY NEURAL MODULATION, its outgoing signal amplified with power provided by body heat, which when scanned returns a BRAINPRINT signal. See SCANNING.

I LOVE LUCIFER: (I) A situation comedy on HOLOVISION involving the stupid antics of the humanoid aliens on the planet LUCIFER, before the residents clumsily blew it up creating what is now the asteroid belt.

IMMUNITY: (N) Privilege granted by the government to avoid a cost previously imposed on everyone. Sophisticated government always hides its actions by first imposing an "equal" cost on everyone, then selectively granting immunities, thus creating a privileged ruling class. Those who make the rules *always* win the game. In the Federation, refers specifically to the immunity to rape granted to everyone but TOUCHABLEs and NONPERSONs.

IMPRESSIONIST PERIOD: (N) The lasegraphic period following the SYMBOLIST period, created by Wolfgang Jaeger's use of COLORATURA in *The Rainbow Vistata*. Followed by Expressionist Period, created by Joan Darris when she incorporated ROGA DIALECTICs into *The Helix Vistata*.

INHABITANT: (N) Resident of the habitats.

IRRADIATION SEALER: (A) The process was developed years ago by the U.S. Army Natick Laboratories. A device which hermetically seals food in plastic then irradiates it, killing all bacteria in the food: perfect food preservation, without chemical additives or refrigeration. Coming soon to your neighborhood, nuclear accidents notwithstanding.

IRISHLAND: (I) A misnomer for Ireland—a land where the Northern Irate fight among themselves, giving the English stomach ulsters—in a time when territorial disputes leading to civil war are largely forgotten.

ISLE OF ARTEMIS: (I) New name of St. Croix, Virgin Islands, in the Federation. See ALAMO CITY.

ISLE OF PERSEPHONE: (I) New name of St. Thomas, Virgin Islands, in the Federation, and the World Capital District. See ALAMO CITY.

JOAN BAEZ, THE: (N) Thermonuclear torchship named for anarchist folk singer (1941–   ) once married to a draft resister named David Harris.

JOYNETTE: (I) A manufactured cigarette mixing CANNABIS and tobacco. Combines "joystick," "joint" and "cigarette."

JUDICIARY FIRM: (I) A nominally private corporation, administered by the HOUSE OF GENTRY, granted the business of trying cases based on laws passed by the Federation legislature. Though private, judges are "Officers of the Upper Manor," in the same way that attorneys in private practice are "Officers of the Court."

JUPITER MOON, THE: (N) A thermonuclear torchship named after a song performed by the rock group, The Weirz.

KAMA ROGA: (I) Literally "love roga."

KEYBOARD: (N) A lasegraphic console.

KIBBUTZ: (N) The FREE-SPACE HABITAT built by Jews who felt that God's promise was for living space, not turf surrounded by enemies.

KINESIS: (N) Literally "movement," refers to psychokinesis in the game of VELLETROM.

KING ELWIN: (N) First monarch of ST. CLIVE and First Cardinal of the MERE CHRISTIAN CHURCH. Name is taken from Elwin Ransom in C.S. Lewis's "Ransom" trilogy.

LADY: 1.(A) Second aspect of GODDESS (used with "the") in the Wiccen trinity of MAIDEN, LADY, AND CRONE. 2.(N) A woman elected to the PINK Seat in the HOUSE OF GENTRY.

LAKE KINGSTON: (N) Name in time of Helix Vista for Mirror Lake, Kingston, New York.

LARIAT: (N) See SQUATBALL.

LASEGRAPHER: (I) A composer and/or performer of LASEGRAPHY.

LASEGRAPHIC: (I) Relating to LASEGRAPHY.

LASEGRAPHY: (I) The visual music form produced by projecting abstract moving, colored LASER forms onto a screen. Incorporates both CLASSICAL LASEGRAPHY and ROGA. All lasegraphy commercially performed today is NASCENT PERIOD proto-roga.

LASEMEISTER: (I) A master of LASEGRAPHY: teacher.

LASER: (A) Acronym: Light Amplification by Stimulated Emission of Radiation. Photons are excited by pumping, then drop a quantum energy level all at once, shooting out photons in spatial coherence: a quantum-mechanic light-orgasm. Among lasegraphers, laser is short for CHROMATIC LASER.

LASERIUM: (A) Literally, "House of the Laser." LASERIUM or Laserium is a trademark of Laser Images, Inc., for their laser concerts. The lower-case "laserium" in *The Rainbow Cadenza*, used as a generic term for any dome where lasegraphy is performed, is an extrapolation to far-future time when the trademark has expired, and is not intended to deny or weaken the LASERIUM trademark: it must not be used elsewhere.

LAVENDER: (N) Official designation, in Federation color-code, signifying an ANDROMAN or andromen. Lavender is included in the clothing design of andromen to differentiate them from commen, and is the color of the seats held by GAYLORDs in the HOUSE OF GENTRY.

LAVENDER DEPARTMENT: (I) That part of a department store providing clothing and accessories to ANDROMEN.

LAVENDER SEAT: (I) A seat in the HOUSE OF GENTRY belonging to a GAYLORD.

LAW DISCS: (I) Law texts on DISC.

LAZAK: (I) A commercial name for "easy viewing" LASEGRAPHY played in stores, elevators, waiting rooms, and DICTERIA Hospitality Suites. Derives from Muzak.

LCAA: (I) Lasegraphy Company of Ad Astra.

LCAA 1600: (I) A commercial model of lasegraphic console.

LCAA MARK BOOB CHROMATIC LASER: (I) Joan's first laser instrument, with its deadly spectral WOLF in the infrared, later used by her as a weapon she thinks of as "The Sword of Goddess."

LCAA MARK 800B CHROMATIC LASER: (I) A later model of laser instrument, owned by Joan, without the "wolf" problem.

LEASE, THE: (N) In AD ASTRA, the explicit social contract—which all inhabitants or visitors must sign, have a guardian sign for them, or leave—by which one agrees to answer for all liabilities which impose costs or damages on the life, liberty, and property rights of all others. This avoids Hobbes' "war of everyone against everyone" that Rousseau argued the social contract of government was supposed to prevent, without the necessity of imposing government on any individual without that individual's consent. Statist thesis: without a social contract, there would be chaos. Anarchist antithesis: imposing a contract on a person without that person's consent is self-contradictory, since the concept of "contract" requires free, individual consent. Synthesis: the Lease: contractual consent is unanimously achieved, *individually*, from all persons *before* they are allowed to make further contractual arrangements to live in a place, whether that contract is to buy, lease, or rent property, or to purchase food, or to buy air. You don't want to sign? "*Your* right, sir or madam: but *we* are not willing to take the risk of allowing you on *our* property unless you sign the Lease or find a guardian to sign for you." Other of the habitats have similar contractual arrangements, including ST. CLIVE, which—though a constitutional monarchy—uses a similar document for all matters not involving pomp and circumstance. The idea of the Lease is derived from the General Submission to Arbitration contract explained in my novel *Alongside Night*, and "proprietary community" theories that say if it works in a condominium or shopping center, it would work everywhere else.

LEGOS, LIMITED: (I) JUDICIARY FIRM granted monopoly by the HOUSE OF GENTRY of all matters involving TOUCHABLEs and/or MARNIEs.

LEITMOTIF: (N) In LASEGRAPHY, literally—as opposed to figuratively in German opera—a "leading theme in motion."

LENIN: (N) FREE-SPACE HABITATs built by the Soviet Union, but INHABITANTS decided the state had "withered away" after secession in the Colonial War, and declared themselves anarcho-communists.

LENINITES: (N) Residents of LENIN, still *very* Russian.

LESBIAN: (A) In the Federation a female who, for religious reasons, refuses to engage in sex with men. The only sects granted conscientious objector status to UNIVERSAL SERVICE.

LEWIS, C. S.: (A) Clive Staples Lewis. See SAINT CLIVE.

LEX SCRIPTA, LEX TERRAE: (N) Latin, literally "The Written Law, the Law of the Land." As motto of LEGOS, LTD., it means "The Written Law, the Law of Earth."

LIBERTARIANS: (A) The Libertarian Party in the Federation. Originally a party that fought for and won a common, hard money for Earth, and absolute free trade between Federation provinces, later a party indistinguishable from its opponent CHAUVINIST Party. Not to be confused with real libertarians, who stay out of party politics.

LIEUTENANT MATRON: (I) A rank in the Peace Corps, designated by the insigne of the Palladium Dove, which commands a DICTERIAT.

LIGHT PENMANSHIP: (I) The study of writing with a light-emitting pen on a computer monitor.

LISSAJOU: (A) Any of solid shapes produced by crossing an X-axis with a Y-axis. In SCANNING, LASEGRAPHIC, the basic image.

LIVE: (N) A recorded BRAINPRINT taken from a person still animate. Compare with ICICLE and DEADER.

LOCAL 47: (A) Los Angeles Local of the American Federation of Musicians, later the Los Angeles local of the World Confederation of Lasegraphers.

LOWER MANOR: (N) The lower house in the Federation's bicameral legislature, the HOUSE OF COMMEN.

LUCIFER: (A) The theoretical missing "fifth" planet between Mars and Jupiter predicted by Bode's Law, where the asteroid belt now orbits. The name Lucifer was used for this theoretical planet by Robert A. Heinlein in *Space Cadet*, where he also suggested the idea that nuclear weaponry blew up the planet.

LUMIA: (A) A LASER image produced by passing the laser beam through an interfering medium to produce a gossamerlike projection: an interference pattern. One of the three fundamental types of laser image, along with Raw Scans and Diffraction Patterns. See DIFFRACTIONS and SCANNING. LASEGRAPHIC.

MAIDEN: (A) First aspect of the WICCEN trinity—GODDESS in her youngest form. See below.

MAIDEN, LADY, AND CRONE: (A) The WICCEN trinity of GODDESS in her Three Aspects—young girl, woman in full flower, and aged dame. Also a slang exclamation in the Federation equivalent to "Jesus, Mary, and Joseph!"

MAKE LOVE, NOT WAR: (A) Used as an anti-Vietnam War slogan by 1960's hippies who didn't expect to be taken literally, later used as the motto of the Federation Peace Corps, which did.

MANHATTAN BOULEVARD: (I) New main boulevard of Manhattan, dividing the city from the Battery to the Bronx, after Manhattan was razed by the RAIN OF TERROR in the WAR OF COLONIAL SUCCESSION.

MARNIE: (N) A member of the Marnies, the semi-official organization—

combining aspects of the Chamber of Commerce, the United States Marines, the Hitler Youth, the Hell's Angels, the Civil Air Patrol, and the Boy Scouts—licensed by the Federation to hunt TOUCHABLEs, and to rape them when they catch them (see RAPE, LEGAL DEFINITION OF IN THE FEDERATION). Marnies wear leathers reminiscent of motorcycle gangs, crash helmets, official medallions with their hunting license, and hunt by SCANNING while wearing FLYING BELTS. Hunting is legal only at night, except in official ghettos prohibited by law (see VAGINATOWN), and hunting is forbidden on legal holidays. COMMEN, ANDROMEN, and WOMEN veterans may all join the Marnies. A Marnie had better be damn sure the person he or she rapes is a Touchable: a mistake will not be forgiven, and the Marnie—if convicted—would become a Touchable, also. Other offenses which could result in fine or suspension of hunting privileges: daylight hunting, exposing children to observation of sexual violence, murder of a Touchable who has not resisted, or icarating a Touchable (see ICARATE) causing damage to a citizen's life or private property. Marnies are tried by LEGOS, LIMITED, and final appeal of all cases is to the FIRST LADY. Name either derives from Alfred Hitchcock movie *Marnie* about woman obsessed by color RED, or from anagram of "Marine."

MARSUPIAL CLUB: (I) Private club in the penthouse of the LEGOS, LTD., courthouse frequented by judiciary and legal personnel. The name implies that Legos, Ltd., is a kangaroo court, an "in" joke that proves that no one is worried about this idea being taken seriously.

MASSIVE: (N) In ROGA slang, equivalent to current heavy or heavy-duty.

MATRIARCH: (N) In the Peace Corps, ranks equivalent to General in the military. Matriarchs command DIVISIONs (insigne is one Venus Cross), CORPORATIONSs (insigne is two Venus Crosses), and CONGLOMARATES (insigne is three Venus Crosses). The SUPREME MATRIARCH, equivalent to a Five-star General, is the administrative commander of the Peace Corps.

MATRON: (N) In the Peace Corps, a rank equivalent to Major or Colonel in the military.

MAY EVE: (A) The last evening of April, before BELTANE. A WICCEN holiday and a legal holiday in the Federation.

MEDALLION: (N) A MARNIE's license, worn while hunting.

MEDIA TEMPLE: (A) IVAN DRYER's term for a multimedia palace.

MERE CHRISTIAN: (A) Term popularized by C.S. Lewis, in his book *Mere Christianity*, which promotes the idea that with Christianity under seige by atheism and agnosticism, Christians had better focus on the "merely" Christian doctrines common to all, rather than fighting among themselves in doctrinal disputes. Later used to refer to a member of the MERE CHRISTIAN CHURCH.

MERE CHRISTIAN CHURCH: (I) An umbrella organization of the loosely-affiliated remnants of the Roman Catholics, Anglicans, Church of Ireland,

Presbyterian, Methodist, Eastern Orthodox, Lutheran, and several dozen other Protestant and Catholic sects, who—disgusted with Earth when the Federation passed the sexual draft law—built the ST. CLIVE habitats and emigrated there en masse. The head of the Church is the First Cardinal, also hereditary Monarch of St. Clive, who is considered to wear "the Shoes of the Fisherman" by the Catholics in the Church, but whose authority is not binding on the affiliated Protestant churches. To avoid doctrinal disputes ranging back hundreds of years, each of the affiliate churches is free to maintain its own ceremonial, doctrinal, and organizational customs. In both doctrinal and secular matters, the Church is completely laissez-faire: the reigning King of St. Clive is rather High Church in his ceremonial ideas, but this isn't binding on anyone but the immediate Court. As to Saints, theoretically the First Cardinal is empowered to name them, but the only person canonized since the formation of the Church is Clive Staples Lewis.

MERLINO CHROMATIC LASER: (I) A hand-made CHROMATIC LASER instrument produced by members of the Merlino family, master craftspersons in the IMPRESSIONIST PERIOD. Wolfgang Jaeger plays one.

METRONOME: (N) Ticker: lasegraphic slang for heart.

M.H.C.: (I) Member, HOUSE OF COMMEN. A COMMAN elected by vote of the commen in a PARISH to a six-year term as a representative in the Lower Manor of the Federation legislature. Form of address is "Your Excellency."

MICHAEL COLLINS, THE: (N) A thermonuclear torchship named for Michael Collins (1930-   ), the third man in the Apollo 11 moon mission—the one who *didn't* get to set his feet on the moon.

MICROWAVE JOB: (I) Slang in the Federation for being executed.

MICROWAVE OVENS: (N) No longer just the harmless kitchen appliance, but the Federation's high-powered execution chamber which destroys a victim's brain in the first instant, boils the victim's blood a split second later, then explodes all the victim's cells, leaving no genetic material intact which could be cloned. When the Federation kills you, it wants to make sure there isn't enough left of a brain for even *part* of the person to be saved. Like all forms of state execution, it is theoretically humane to the person being executed (though who can argue?) and gruesome to the maximum for everyone else. The exploded remnants are then cremated in a conventional oven.

MIDSUMMER: (A) MIDSUMMER SOLSTICE. Used to distinguish from the YULE SOLSTICE, which is often called just "Solstice."

MIDSUMMER SOLSTICE: (A) The summer solstice, a WICCEN holiday and a legal holiday in the Federation.

MINIMUM-SEX LAW: (A) A law passed in the post-BRUSHFIRE WAR period—based on the precedent of minimum-wage laws—which required a minimum number of sexual encounters per week by every woman. It didn't work, resulting in a further complication: see EQUALIZATION-OF-SEX-OPPORTUNITY LAW. The idea was suggested once as a theoretical exercise in a post-class drinking session with libertarian economist Murray Rothbard, to see if there were any laws at all which the drunken male anarchists at the table would favor. I doubt any of us remember who said it first but I'm willing to bet it was either Rothbard or Samuel Edward Konkin III.

MINISTRY OF PEACE: (N) The Ministry running the Federation Peace Corps, equivalent to the Department of Defense today. The SUPREME MATRIARCH is by custom the Minister.

MINISTRY OF UNIVERSAL SERVICE: (I) The Federation's draft ministry, actually a sub-agency of the Peace Ministry.

MINNEANOVA: (I) One of the twin cities in AD ASTRA's first two cylinders, named after the twin cities of Minneapolis and St. Paul. See NOVA PAULUS.

MISTER DUMBJOHN: (A) DUMBJOHN.

MISTRESS: (N) A rank in the Peace Corps, designated by the insigne of the silver ANKH, which commands a TROOP.

MOCHA: (N) COCA MOCHA.

MOCHA BREAK: (I) Equivalent to a coffee break.

MOCHA HOUSE: (I) A club where COCA MOCHA is served, often in combination with live ROGA, initially hang-outs for *BOHS* during the early post-Colonial War period.

MOLLY MONOCHROME: (I) A one-color lasegraphic composition, similar to the song *Johnny One Note*. In lasegraphic slang, a composer with only one good idea, endlessly repeated.

MONICA, MONICA BOULEVARD: (I) New names for City of Santa Monica, California and Santa Monica Boulevard in Los Angeles. See ALAMO CITY.

MONITORS, THE: (N) The central police organization of the World Federation. Compare with FEDERATION SPACE CORPS.

MOTHERFUCKER: (N) Not a vulgarity in the Federation Peace Corps, but an expression of rough endearment for a commanding officer, equivalent to "the Old Man" in the military. No longer a charge of incest, but "the Mother to the Fuckers." See FUCK, RAPE.

MURDOCK PRIZE: (I) A journalistic award for news and literature in the Federation, equivalent to the Pulitzer Prize today. Named for Rupert Murdoch, the news magnate who's the direct descendant of Joseph Pulitzer's "give the people what they want" philosophy.

M.U.S.: (I) MINISTRY OF UNIVERSAL SERVICE.

MY GOD: (A) In the habitats, a mild exclamation. See MY GODDESS.

MY GODDESS: (I) In the Federation, a mild exclamation. See MY GOD.

NASCENT PERIOD: (I) The earliest period of proto-lasegraphy, wherein laser images were choreographed to music. The period we're in as of this writing.

N.D. CIRCLE OF PEACE: (N) The letters "N" and "D" in semaphor, overlaid into the Nuclear Disarmament "Peace Sign" of the nineteen sixties, and later enacted by the Federation. An insigne for a FULL MATRON in the Peace Corps.

NET, NETS (N), NETMAN (I): See SQUATBALL.

NEVER AGAIN: (N) Alternate name, used in the habitats, for Jewish Holiday *Yom Hashoah*, "Day of the Fire," commemorating the Holocaust.

NEWER YORK: (I) The reconstructed city of New York, after the devastation of the RAIN OF TERROR.

NIGHTSTALK: (N) A TOUCHABLE hunt.

NINTH AMENDMENT: (N) One of the Bill of Rights in the ARTICLES OF FEDERATION, providing that BRAINPRINT registrations may not be used for personal identification.

NO GLOW: (I) ROGA slang meaning easy. Equivalent to "No sweat," it's a pun on "sweat" and "glow" in a dome.

NOM-DE-LASEGRAPHIE: (I) In French, literally "lasegraphic name." Usage equivalent to *nom-de-plume*: pen name. A name taken professionally by a lasegraphic performer.

NONPERSON: (N) A person not transponding a BRAINPRINT in the Federation. Such a person has no legal rights whatsoever, and it is legal to do anything to them including enslave or kill them. This category exists to prevent TOUCHABLEs from surgically removing transponders. See SCANNING.

NONSMOKING SECTION: (N) A section designated for either smoking or refraining from smoking, but where it is not compulsory to smoke. See SMOKING SECTION.

NORTH AMERICAN CONCORD: (A) A State comprising the territories of the United States, Mexico, Canada, and Cuba, later a PROVINCE in the World Federation. The idea was proposed in earnest—sans Cuba—by Ronald Reagan. The demarcations into parishes are loosely based on a proposal by Gore Vidal to restructure the United States into several larger provinces.

NOVA CANCY HOTEL: (I) A hotel chain in the Federation where "there's always room for one more.," This contradicts the name of the hotel chain, which promises "No Vacancy."

NOVA PAULUS: (I) Literally, "New Paul." One of the twin cities in AD ASTRA's first two cylinders, named after the twin cities of Minneapolis and St. Paul. See MINNEANOVA.

O'NEILL: (N) A FREE-SPACE HABITAT named for Princeton physicist Gerard K. O'Neill, Ph.D. (1927-   ), advocate of habitats situated in the LaGrange Points. O'Neill's proposal was later adopted by the L-5 Society, which promised to disband as soon as they could meet in a habitat at the LaGrange-5 orbit site for which their organization was named. This they did, but the habitat was later destroyed in the WAR OF COLONIAL SUCCESSION, at a cost of five million lives.

ONTARIO: (N) PARISH of the NORTH AMERICAN CONCORD, now includes Michigan.

OVAFIED: (I) Past tense of ovafy: to give ovamony—to swear out evidence. Feminine for "testify," under the theory that the term "testify" originated in ancient times when men could swear by their testicles and women, having no testicles, could not swear out evidence. The etymological case is tempting but by no means conclusive.

OVENS, THE: (N) The execution facility in Detroit, Ontario, combining execution in a MICROWAVE OVEN and followed by cremation of the remnants in a conventional oven.

OVER THE RAINBOW!: (N) From the song made famous by Judy Garland. In lasegraphie usage, a wish for a good performance, equivalent to the theatrical "Break a leg!" Also, by extension, a performance well done.

PACIFICA: (N) A PARISH in the NORTHERN AMERICAN CONCORD including territories bordered by the Rockies on one side and the Pacific Ocean on the other.

PALLET: (N) A couch to which one is strapped in zero-gee.

PARAGRAPH 23: (I) In the Peace Corps, equivalent to the U.S. military's famous Section 8: a psychiatric discharge.

PARISH: (N) A political division of PROVINCE, with territories equivalent to one of the larger United States or Canadian Provinces. The COMMEN of each Parish elect one Member to the HOUSE OF COMMEN.

PARTHENOGENESIS, PARTHENOGENIC: (A) Literally, "virgin birth." If Jesus was God's son, born by virgin birth to Mary, then a) either God chose Mary's genetic code because it was clean of sin and changed her female XX-chromosome to a male XY; or b) God impregnated Mary with a genetic code of his own choosing—possibly a HOLOGRAPHIC version of his own code or "logos"; or c) Mary had a XXY chromosome to begin with, so her parthenogenic child could be of either gender—or both? In the Federation, usage refers to Gynogenesis, a process by which an unfertilized ovum is made to reproduce, keeping the genetic information normally expelled with the polar body, thus producing a female child who is an identical TWIN to the mother. The child would theoretically be genetically indistinguishable from a CLONE, but in the Federation this issue in debated on the empirical evidence, since cloning is mostly used by ANDROMEN while woman who wish to twin use their own ova for parthenogenesis.

PATRON: (N) A male matron.

PEACE CORPS, THE: (N) The WORLD FEDERATION PEACE CORPS.

PENIS: (N) As well as the male genital organ, in the Federation Peace Corps, a derogatory term for a male, equivalent to calling a man a "prick."

PEOTOMY: (A) Surgical removal of the penis, a punishment—in addition to being declared Touchable—for a first offense of rape in the Federation. A second offense of rape—punishable by execution—would not seem likely, but it is not unheard of, considering the possibility that a penis can be illegally cloned and reattached (see CLONING, TO CLONE), or the offense may be sexual activity with a nonconsenting person that does not require a penis. See RAPE, LEGAL DEFINITION OF IN THE FEDERATION.

PHAETHON SPORTSTER: (N) A sporty skymobile in the tradition of the early Phaeton automobile.

PHOBIA DISCHARGE: (I) PARAGRAPH 23.

PIAGETIC: (I) Relating to the work of Jean Piaget (1896-1980), psychologist who mapped children's development of fundamental human perceptive and learning abilities according to age. Piaget theorized that if certain perceptions are not developed at a biologically-predetermined time, they never can be.

PIAGET TESTS: (I) Tests used by LASEMEISTER to map the abilities of a child to perceive motion, time, and speed, prerequisite to beginning lasegraphic training. See above.

PICKPOCKET TRANSPONDER: (I) An IDENTITY TRANSPONDER that can record a BRAINPRINT by mere proximity, and later transpond the recorded signal.

PICTUREGRAM: (I) A visual telegram.

PINK: (N) Official designation, in Federation color-code, signifying a WOMAN: the color of the working uniform of CORPORALS in the DICTERIA. Unlike BLUE and LAVENDER, pink is not required in a woman's clothing, since no one in the Federation confuses them with commen or andromen. Pink is also the color of a seat held by a LADY in the HOUSE OF GENTRY.

PINK-AND-POLISH: (I) Peace Corps slang: spit-and-polish. Well mannered corporals do not spit; but they do wear PINK and polish their nails.

PINK PANTHER, THE: (N) Named for the Blake Edwards movie. A ROGA club affording a showcase to new roga performers, and a separate CANNA-BISTRO to unescorted women who wish to keep it that way.

PLASTICE: (I) A sprayable plastic poultice.

POLICE SIREN: (N) A woman used as a secret agent or sexual decoy by the

MONITORS or previous police agencies. This usage derives from post-BRUSHFIRE WAR period, when police sirens were used to entrap rapists.

POLYANDRY: (A) Polygamous marriage where a woman has more than one husband, it could provide a non-coercive solution to the Federation's sex-ratio problems, if the ARTICLES OF FEDERATION did not prohibit it.

POLYURBAN: (I) Incorporating a mixture of lifestyles into a residential area.

POSTBELLUM: (N) In the Federation this means one thing: after the WAR OF COLONIAL SECESSION.

POWER DAMPERS: (N) The power transformer on a CHROMATIC LASER instrument.

PRESIDENT: (N) Chief Executive Officer of the WORLD FEDERATION, a GAYLORD elected by vote of the Gaylords in the HOUSE OF GENTRY. Compare with FIRST LADY and PRIME MINISTER.

PRIMARY NEURAL MODULATION: (I) That which is encoded in a BRAINPRINT recording: a mapping of a particular neural pattern which is known to be unchanged from birth to death, and is individually discrete for all brains, even those produced from identical genetic codes.

PRIME MINISTER: (N) Head of Government in the World Federation, a COMMAN elected by vote of the Members in the HOUSE OF COMMEN. Compare with PRESIDENT and FIRST LADY.

PRINCESS: (N) ROGA slang originating in ST. CLIVE: a term of honor or endearment, equivalent to "SISTER."

PROSECUTRIX: (N) In a rape trial today, the woman who testifies against her rapist. In Federation usage, a female prosecuting attorney.

PROSTITUTION: (A) *Not* what takes place in the Federation Peace Corps, since prostitution is *consenting* sexual favors granted for remuneration, and the corporals are draftees. Prostitution is illegal in the Federation—fornication is a nationalized monopoly—but completely legal in AD ASTRA and other of the habitats (not including ST. CLIVE). Prostitution should also not be confused with a currently existing system whereby women are kept as slaves—by threats and intimidation against which they feel powerless—by pimps or madams, and rented out for sexual favors to gain their masters money.

PROVINCE: (N) One of the States originally independent but now a division of the WORLD FEDERATION, among them the Union of Soviet Socialist Republics, the People's Republic of China, the United States of Europe, the South American Union, and the North American Concord. States, republics, or provinces in these once-independent superstates are now PARISHES in the Federation.

PYRADOME: (A) Laser Images, Inc.'s, design for a MEDIA TEMPLE combining the forms of a pyramid and a dome, scaled up in Newer York to the size of a Pharoah's tomb, and built on the former site of Saint Patrick's Cathedral, destroyed in the RAIN of TERROR.

QUADRIVIUM: (N) In medieval education, the upper division of the seven liberal arts, comprising the study of arithmetic, music, geometry, and astronomy, following the lower division called the trivium, comprising grammer, rhetoric, and logic. The University of Ad Astra at Nova Paulus (UAANP) makes a trivium of Language Arts (combining grammer and expression fundamental to all human and machine symbol systems), Logics (non-contradictory design of both deductive and inductive symbol systems), and Observations (the actual things you had better know if you're going to get along in the real world) prerequisite to admission, and teaches a Quadrivium consisting of Motivational Arts (getting your act together), Practical Arts (disciplines for manipulating the physical universe), Praxeology (the value-free study of human action), and Intangibles (everything we're not sure about yet).

QUEEN LUCY: (N) The reigning Queen, along with KING ELWIN, of ST. CLIVE. Name is taken from Lucy Pevensie, heroine in C.S. Lewis's *Chronicles of Narnia*.

QUICHE: (A) A custard pastry that real men don't eat today but which—in a society in which andromen are socially prestigious—has been reduced to universal junk food equivalent to pizza.

RADICAL LOBOTOMY: (I) The severing of the cerebral lobe of a human brain from the body, resulting in a brain without a body and a body without a brain. See CEREBRAL ABORTION.

RAINBOROUGH: (N) A borough in the City of NEWER YORK, and the new name for the Borough of Brooklyn, New York, so named because the RAINBOW COMPACT was signed there in Borough Park, one of the few neighborhoods undamaged in the RAIN OF TERROR.

RAINBOROUGH BRIDGE: (I) A bridge linking pedestrians and ground-traffic between the NEWER YORK boroughs of RAINBOROUGH and Manhattan, replacing both the Brooklyn Bridge and the Manhattan Bridge, destroyed in the RAIN OF TERROR.

RAINBOROUGH PARK: (I) New name for Borough Park, Brooklyn, so named because the RAINBOW COMPACT was signed there.

RAINBOW CADENZA: (I) Any of many cadenzas written by students of Wolfgang Jaeger to be performed in Jaeger's *Rainbow Vistata*.

RAINBOW COMPACT: (I) The formal peace treaty of the WAR OF COLONIAL SECESSION signed decades after the actual end of hostilities, ending mutual embargoes between the new World Federation and the habitats (excluding ST. CLIVE, not yet built). It was negotiated by Federation Ambassador Burke Filcher, signed by him on behalf of the Federation at a formal ceremony in Borough Park, Brooklyn with representatives from each of the habitats. The name derives from the rainbow which God used as a sign of his promise never to destroy the world again.

RAINBOW PAPER: (I) Paper that changes colors when heat is applied to it. A child's toy. Used with THERMOCRAYONS.

RAIN OF TERROR: (I) The devastating retaliation against the NORTH AMERICAN CONCORD (before it was a Federation PROVINCE), for its responsibility in launching the nuclear missile which destroyed the FREE-SPACE HABITAT, O'NEILL, at the cost of five million colonial lives. The retaliation consisted of meteors launched by mass-drivers from Ad Astra against three specifically-targeted cities in the Concord: New York, Montreal, and Mexico City. The devastation in those cities was close to total, with a cost to the Concord of thirteen million lives. The badly wounded Concord—and its allies terrified of further attacks against their own cities—immediately recognized the sovereignty of the habitats, and instituted the trade embargo which characterized the remainder of the Colonial War. The name was a natural homonym for the Reign of Terror in the French Revolution of 1793. See also WAR OF COLONIAL SECESSION.

RAMON RAQUELLO ORCHESTRA: (N) A ROGA band which took its name from the dance band in Orson Welles's 1938 radio adaptation of H.G. Wells's *The War of the Worlds*.

RAND, AYN: (A) (1905-1982) born Alissa Rosenbaum in Russia, American-immigrant novelist, playwright, screenwriter, and philosopher who perfected a rationalist school of metaphysics, epistemology, and esthetics which she called Objectivism. There is testimony by a former intimate that she *was* familiar with C.S. Lewis—enough to have marked up her copy of Lewis's *Mere Christianity* with exclamations against a logic leading to conclusions she hated—though she never mentioned Lewis in print. There is no corresponding evidence that Lewis was familiar with Rand.

RAPE: (N) A vulgar exclamation—equivalent in power to FUCK today—unless used in legal proceedings or in official ceremony. This double-standard of vulgarity is not unheard of, considering that "bloody" is vulgar usage as a common intensifier by the English, yet no one could fault the British Prime Minister from saying a speech, "those brave men who have died in this long, bloody war."

RAPE, LEGAL DEFINITION OF IN THE FEDERATION: (N) In the Federation, rape is defined as "non-consenting sexual activity or sexual activity otherwise prohibited by law." Since the sexual activity in the DICTERIA is considered voluntary—the CORPORALS have sworn an oath upon joining—and since sexual violence against TOUCHABLEs is mandated by law, these are not legally rape in the Federation. Only sexual violence against a non-consenting person (not Touchable or on duty the Peace Corps) is rape in the Federation. Any other sexual intercourse with a consenting partner not authorized by Federation law is statutory rape, and this includes sexual activity with minors and sexual activity with a corporal in the Peace Corps who is AWOL or a deserter, since she is government property and can't give her own consent; however a corporal in good standing may under the Universal Code of Dicterial Justice grant consent while off duty. It is the official position of the Federation that the Peace Corps *prevents* rape, rather than enacts it. If you find this whole set-up unlikely, then consider that property taken from a person without that person's consent is theft—unless it is taken by a government tax collector to hire police to protect us from robbers—and consider that taking another person's life is murder—unless it is taken by a government executioner to prevent us from being murdered—and consider that forcing servitude on another person is slavery—unless it is done by a government draft board to save us from those foreign enemies who would, if they conquered us, reduce us to involuntary servitude. Government never outlaws these crimes: it merely claims a monopoly on them—so why should rape be any different?

RAPER: (N) Rapist. Not only literally, but as an insult equivalent to "fucker."

RAPIER: (N) A polite euphemism for RAPE, equivalent to "heck" or "darn."

RAPING: (N) A vulgar intensifier, equivalent to "fucking."

RAW SCAN: (A) One of the three basic types of LASER image, along with LUMIA and DIFFRACTIONS. See SCANNING, LASEGRAPHIC.

REANIMATE, REANIMATION: (I) To revive from CRYONIC SUSPENSION. See DEANIMATE.

RED: (N) Official designation, in the Federation color-code, signifying a TOUCHABLE. Touchables are required to wear a red CLOAK at all times when in public. Since they are not permitted to own property, and would be raped every night if they stayed at a known permanent residence, they are virtually always in public, and for all-intents-and-purposes required to be CLOAKED.

RED HUNT: (I) A long-running HOLOVISION drama, involving members of the MARNIEs.

RENAISSANCE, THE: (N) The period in human history that has produced the greatest number of advances in the arts, technology, and science: now. In the Federation, the Renaissance is usually dated from the beginning of large-scale commercial television broadcasting at the end of World War II.

RIFF: (A) From usage in jazz and rock music, a chance for a performer to improvise a section of a composition. A CADENZA in ROGA.

RISING SUN: (N) A FREE-SPACE HABITAT built by the Japanese.

ROBERT A. HEINLEIN, THE: (N) A thermonuclear torchship named for the retired naval officer (1907-   ) who first described and named the torchship: a nuclear-powered, constant-boost spaceship.

ROBOTICS REVOLUTION: (A) The post-industrial period when high-level artificial intelligence became practical for home and office use, liberating humanity from most of its dull, repetitive work. In argument, Burke Filcher attributes the healthy Earth economy on Federation policies; Joan attributes it to the robotics revolution.

ROGA: (I) LASEGRAPHY performed with, or to, music, it is to CLASSICAL

LASEGRAPHY as jazz or rock is to classical music. It is associated with BOHemian culture and MOCHA HOUSEs, its aficionados speak their own slang, and its leading lights are as popular as rock superstars today. The origins of the term are lost in obscurity, but it is thought that the term derives from "rogue" lasegraphy—rogue because it departs from the classical lasegraphic tradition of performance in silence. Other theories are that it is a corruption of "raga"—Hindu classical music with which roga shares some philosophy in common—or of "ragtime," or of "reggae," or possibly even from "rock," itself. Some even theorize that the term derives somehow from Rogation Day, a Roman Catholic day of prayer—who am I to argue?

ROGA PLAYER: (I) A performer of ROGA.

ROLAND CHURCH: (I) A composer and performer of ROGA who is a superstar in the time of Joan Darris. Born in the UHURU habitats, with a given name in Swahili, he emigrated to the ST. CLIVE habitats, where he became interested in roga. His name is derived from an early-RENAISSANCE jazz performer named Roland Kirk whom he admired and, whose last name—in German—means "church."

ROPE: (A) LARIAT. See SQUATBALL.

RUBY THE RED-NOSED REINDEER: (I) A WICCEN rewording of the famous YULEtide song, with a female reindeer as protagonist this time.

SAINT CLIVE: (A) Future name of C(live) S(taples) Lewis (1898-1963) Oxford Don, poet, rationalist apologist for "mere" Christianity, radio lecturer, essayist, and bestselling author of nonfiction, science fiction, fantasy, and mythopoeic literature, member of the Inklings along with J.R.R. Tolkien, canonized by the First Cardinal of the MERE CHRISTIAN CHURCH the day before the christening of the space habitat named for him, and later that day declared the Kingdom of ST. CLIVE. In correct usage, Saint Clive (spelled out) refers to the man, and St. Clive (abbreviated) refers to the place.

SAMHAIN DAY: (A) WICCEN thanksgiving, a legal holiday in the Federation.

SATELLITE ANCHOR: (I) A news anchor on a broadcast to Earth relayed from a communications satellite.

SATELLITE CHESS: (I) An updated version of chess-by-mail, played by relaying moves in real time through a communications satellite.

SCANNER: (N) A small electronic device used for scanning brainprints, often worn on the wrist: wristscanner.

SCANNING: (N) Used by a MARNIE in TOUCHABLE hunting, and by the MONITORS in police work. It involves directional narrowcasting of a weak radio pulse on the universal frequency to which the receiving crystal of all IDENTITY TRANSPONDERs is tuned. The transponder is triggered by the pulse to read the PRIMARY NEURAL MODULATION of the person in which it's implanted, and to broadcast it an instant later on the universal frequency to which all SCANNERs are tuned. The scanner registers the direction of the incoming signal and records the just-received BRAINPRINT in a permanent memory. (The scanner's recorder is the part that's illegally adapted for use in PICKPOCKET TRANSPONDERS.) The scanner then telephones the just-received brainprint, via satellite, to the FEDERATION BUREAU OF IMMUNITY, which records the number of the scanner phoning in and the time-and-place of the status request, records the brainprint for which status is being requested, and matches the received brainprint to the registration in its computer files. Once matched, the Bureau returns to the scanner one of three answers: Citizen in Good Standing, Wanted by the Authorities—arrest if possible (this is the response for "no brainprint on file," or "double-reading") or TOUCHABLE. A Touchable who is scanned but—because he or she has no implanted transponder—does not show up at all by the long-distance scanning used in hunting can temporarily avoid detection; but automatic scanning is done periodically in public places such as SKYPORTs, and a person identified as not transponding a signal is—legally—a NONPERSON. To minimize the rare accidents caused by transponder failure, it is habitual in the Federation to scan one's own transponder before leaving home, and a person discovering transponder failure may call the Monitors for safe escort to the nearest office of the Federation Bureau of Immunity for correction of the problem. As well, if a Monitor scan discovers a citizen—otherwise in good standing—with no transponder signal, that person will be assumed innocent and likewise escorted to the FBI office for correction of the problem. However, if a Marnie should—by chance—scan someone close up and receive no transponded signal, this is a bounty indeed: the person being scanned has *no legal existence whatever* and—under the letter of Federation law, is legal game for *anything* including slavery for life, murder, or icaration.

SCANNING, LASEGRAPHIC: (A) Derived from LASERIUM. One of the three basic types of LASER image, along with LUMIA and DIFFRACTIONs. In LASEGRAPHY, the creation of solid-looking "written" laser images—RAW SCANS—by bouncing a pinpoint laser beam off a mirror which vibrates at high speed, "scanning" the beat toward a screen in a two-dimensional path. By controlling the frequency of the vibrations, the shape of the image can be changed. It is the ability to create discrete imagery through scanning that makes lasegraphy possible, since it is only through duplication of imagery—simultaneously and sequentially—that leitmotifs may be created and visual "chords" played. See also LUMIA and DIFFRACTIONS.

SCAT: (A) From the Greek word for excrement, *scata*, and from slang usage in the gay community today, where it refers to scatological sexual acts identified, in the gay-bar handkerchief color code, by wearing a brown handkerchief. In the Federation, scat has completely replaced the word "shit," and has the same vulgar usages and connotations. Since the scenes involving this practice are among the most controversial in the novel (at least one publisher declined reprint rights because of them), let me point out that writers ranging from Sigmund Freud to Desmond Morris to Robert Anton Wilson have pointed out the role of scatological "territory marking" and humiliation in the psychology of power, and it was for the emotional charge that excrement has in the human unconscious that I portrayed this practice in a work of literature intended for grown-ups.

SCATHEAD: (I) Shithead. Stupid.

SCHOLASTIC NOTATION: (I) Written lasegraphic notation, which standardizes the symbol system referring to laser-generated imagery as it is to appear in a dome, without reference to how that imagery is achieved. The precondition for lasegraphic performers to perform works composed by other lasegraphers with whom they haven't studied. Name derives both from its meaning as "formalist," and as an adjective referring to the proper surname of the first lasecologist (comb. laser + musicologist) to suggest that such notation was one of the preconditions for lasegraphy to develop: yours truly.

SCINTILLATOR: (N) No longer a misnomer for a Geiger Counter, but a device for reducing objects to scintilla: a nuclear incinerator.

SCREEN, THE: (N) A HOLOSCREEN. Also, used metaphorically to mean any writing surface: slate.

SECOND CORPORAL: (I) See CORPORAL.

SELF-OWNERSHIP: (A) The fundamental human right, from which all other rights derive. If one does not own oneself—thus being free to determine one's own actions, maintain self-control, and be responsible for one's actions— then one is not free, morally responsible, or fully human. If one does not own oneself, then one must be owned by another, and the usual claimant is the State. If one does not own oneself, then one has no right preventing one from being exploited as an involuntary servant to another person or group—whether that person or group wishes to make you give them part of your earnings (taxes), or your labor (community service), or your body (the Federation Peace Corps) or your life (the military draft).

SERVICE, THE: (N) In the Federation, refers to the Peace Corps.

SEX SELECTION: (A) The process by which the sex of a child can be selected before conception. Currently this requires clinical intervention before conception, but a pharmaceutical way to achieve this is undoubtedly in the offing (see ADAMINE and EVELINE). When this happens, there is the potential for political manipulation of the gender-ratio for a host of reasons, such as the seven-to-one ratio of males to females caused by military competition in the BRUSHFIRE WAR, and later made permanent by a female ruling class in the Federation to whom the trade of freedom for power was seductive.

SHOTS: (N) In the Federation, when used without further qualifier, means birth-control shots. If a male today asks a female with whom he wishes to engage in sex whether she's had her shots, it's likely not only that he will never engage in sex with her but also that she will inflict immediate physical damage upon him. In the Federation the question is merely a sensible precaution against unwanted pregnancy.

SINSEMILLA: (N) Agricultural area of northern PACIFICA (now California), named for its chief harvest: seedless marijuana.

SISTER: (N) ROGA slang for a female FRIAR.

SKY BELT, SKYBELTER: (A) FLYING BELT, and a user thereof.

SKY MARSHAL: (N) A MONITOR who uses a SKY BELT, a glamorous job equivalent to motorcycle cop.

SKYMOBILE: (N) Sky-automobile. A highly-maneuverable, high speed, characteristically Short-Take-Off-and-Landing jet flying craft that requires neither extended fixed wings nor extended rotors, but instead lifts itself by the pressure-differential created by its wing shape and control surfaces, impelled by the ample thrust produced by its thermonuclear-powered jet turbines. When taxiing, a skymobile deflects its thrust downward to create ground-surface effects like a hovercraft, and at full power can be a Vertical-Take-Off-and-Landing aircraft, though this is somewhat clumsy for it. In the Federation, skymobiles are about as expensive (in terms of percentage of income needed to buy and maintain one) as an automobile is now, and are just as common.

SKYPORT: (A) An airport serving suborbital and orbital shuttles.

SLINKY: (A) A trademarked coiled toy available today.

SLOPPY SECONDS: (A) Vulgar usage today, standard usage in the Federation: a woman available to a subsequent partner after a male has ejaculated into her.

SMOKE: (N) In the Federation, toke.

SMOKING SECTION: (N) A section designated for compulsory smoking. See NONSMOKING SECTION. Then think about how we customarily use language affects our approach to political issues.

SNAREMAN: (I) See SQUATBALL.

SNOW WHITE TALKING MIRROR: (I) A toy mirror programmed for replacing a reflected image with the image of Snow White when one asks "Who's the fairest in the land?" and arguing the point at length with the questioner.

SOAP OPERA: (N) Marathon stageplays adapted from early-RENAISSANCE television scripts, and considered high, classical drama suitable for an evening of highbrow entertainment.

SOLERI SKYPORT: (I) Skyport named for RENAISSANCE architect and habitat designer, Paolo Soleri.

SOLSTICE: (N) When used without being preceded by MIDSUMMER, refers to the Yule—winter—Solstice. See YULE SOLSTICE.

SOLSTICE TREE: (I) A tree decorated for display at the YULE SOLSTICE: in practice, identical to a Christmas tree.

SORORITY: (N) In Peace Corps, 1/5th TROOP, comprising 45 women segmented into five HAREMs.

SOUTH AMERICAN UNION: (I) A PROVINCE of the Federation, comprising all of the continent of South America and related islands.

SOUTH, THE: (N) In Concord political jargon, Mexico.

SPECTRAL: (A) Relating to the spectrum of light as seen in air. Consequently, both rainbows and ghosts are spectral.

SQUATBALL: (I) A popular contact sport—deriving elements from sumo, golf, miniature golf, baseball, rodeos, American football, basketball, soccer, chess, and hockey—played by two teams in opposition. Professional and College Squatball is Tackle Squatball, and Little League Squatball is Touch Squatball. Scoring is accomplished by placing the squatball (a flattened spheroid bladder stuffed with foam rubber) into a hole on a squatball course. A game is played on a boobytrapped turf course of eighteen holes (though in squatball the hole is about the size of a basket in basketball), for which each team is given a chance at offense, the team playing offense given five chances to score, called "downs." The team playing defense, of course, tries to stop them. The defensive goalie at each hole is the Netman, who uses nets reminiscent of fishing nets to entangle the offensive players to prevent them from scoring. The Netman is most often opposed by the offensive team's Snareman, who uses a lariat to rope the Netman and allow an offensive player to score or pass to another player. Other players include the Center Quarterback (one position) who provides offensive strategy, Endbacks, and the Hunchback—a player charged with carrying an offensive player over sand and water traps: the squatball is not allowed to touch ground or get wet. The team with the score closest to eighteen at the end of a game wins. In the event of a tie, the game is stalemated and not scored. The name of the game derives from the sumo squat in which opposing teams start each down. Professional Squatball is divided into two leagues—the Transmeridian League and the Federation League—and consists of thirty-eight teams per league, who work their way up to their League Cup and then face off in the yearly World Series. It's the most popular sport in the Federation, and players are worldwide celebrities who often become holovision stars as well. At least they do the majority of beer and deodorant commercials. Squatball courses exist in the habitats, but the sport just hasn't caught on there.

STATUTORY RAPE: (A) See RAPE, LEGAL DEFINITION OF IN THE FEDERATION.

ST. CLIVE: (I) Cluster of FREE-SPACE HABITATs, built in the asteroid belt after the passage of the Federation Universal Service Act, as a refuge for Christians wishing to raise daughters in equal number to sons and without having to worry about their being drafted into the Peace Corps. Population is one-quarter billion—the largest population center of any of the habitats. St. Clive is also the only constitutional monarchy in the habitats, with a hereditary Royal Family, however—in practice—the Constitution of St. Clive is little different than the AD ASTRAn LEASE, giving the Monarch largely ceremonial duties, and declaring the Monarch to be Commander-in-Chief of the Armed Forces and First Cardinal of the MERE CHRISTIAN CHURCH. Succession of the Crown is to the first born of either gender, starting with KING ELWIN. His reigning Queen is Lucy, but she is only the Acting Monarch in the event that the King is incapacitated or DEANIMATEd. See also SAINT CLIVE, QUEEN LUCY.

SUNDALE: (N) One of the valleys in NOVA PAULUS. A lot of sun-worshippers there. See SUNNY GLEN and VALLE DE SOL.

SUNNY GLEN: (N) One of the valleys in NOVA PAULUS. They really do have a lot of sun-worshippers there. See SUNDALE and VALLE DE SOL.

SUPREME MATRIARCH, THE: (I) Five-cross MATRIARCH, top rank in the Federation Peace Corps. The Minister of Peace is, under the ARTICLES OF FEDERATION, a higher office than the Supreme Matriarch, and theoretically the Supreme Matriarch could be inferior to a Minister of Peace, but in practice the offices are combined, making the Supreme Matriarch a CABINET minister and second only to the FIRST LADY in command of the Federation Peace Corps.

SURROGATE: (N) SURROGATE BODY.

SURROGATE BODY: (I) A specially grown body, essentially brainless after a CEREBRAL ABORTION, grown as the new home for a genetically identical, cryonically preserved brain after a brain transplant. See also CRYONIC SUSPENSION.

SYMBOLISM: (N) The lasegraphic period following the CHALDEAN and preceding the IMPRESSIONIST PERIOD, wherein lasegraphy attempted to portray explicit symbols, rather than merely suggest them. It was so heavy-handed that it almost led directly to an ACHROMATIC Period, and would have if Wolfgang Jaeger hadn't single-handedly won the artistic battle for Impressionism with his *Rainbow Vistata*.

TACTATA-AND-GENITATA: (I) Joan Darris's attempt to invent a form for sexual activity, which she correctly apprehends is a potential art form, since it relies on tension-and-release DIALECTICs.

TAILOR'S CLOSET: (I) A cabinet which, by low-powered LASER graphing, takes body measurements then given to a robot that tailors garments, to create a perfect fit.

TEAPOT DOME, THE: (N) A MOCHA HOUSE in Los Angeles, at the corner of Sunset Boulevard and Doheny Drive, and aptly named because a) it has a dome for ROGA performances; b) it serves COCA MOCHA, which looks a lot like crude oil; and c) Doheny was the man charged with bribing U.S. Interior Secretary Fall in the Teapot Dome "oil leasing" scandal of the 1920's, the biggest scandal in American politics before Watergate.

TELEVISION MUSEUM, THE: (I) The Metropolitan Television Museum of NEWER YORK, the largest repository of television kinescopes, films, and videotapes in the Federation. The reproduction rights of this are equivalent in value to the Louvre's art collection.

TENOR FORTISSIMO: (I) See FORTISSIMO.

THERMOCRAYONS: (I) Heat pens which, when applied to RAINBOW PAPER, cause them to change color. A child's toy.

THIRTY-SIX-COLOR SCALE: (I) In LASEGRAPHY, the DICHROIC SCALE as projected by a chromatic laser in a dome. It is divided into thirty-five colors, plus an ultraviolet used for phosphorescent SCANNING and LUMIA. The division into thirty-six colors is to project the scale in a color circle corresponding to thirty-six deca-degrees in the circular perimeter of a dome. If it had not been necessary to include the ultraviolet, it would have been simpler to divide the scale into six colors of six hues each, instead of the seven colors of five hues plus ultraviolet which is standard usage in lasegraphy.

THROW OUT: (A) In the habitats, slang for vomiting in zero-gee. The logic is that in free-fall there is no "up" or "down" so one can't throw "up"—one can only throw out.

TIGER PIT: (N) The pit in the center of a CATHEDRAL floor where the CHROMATIC LASER is placed and from where the LASEGRAPHER performs. It was named thus by Wolfgang Jaeger, who decided that lasegraphy, in its worst moments, was like stories he'd read of people being tortured and killed in a "tiger pit" during the American-Vietnam War.

TIGER, THE: (N) The artistic trauma found in the TIGER PIT and, by extension, any trauma. Compare with WOLF, THE.

TIGHT: (A) ROGA slang derived from current popular music: professional, rehearsed.

TOKE: (A) To inhale marijuana smoke.

TOLKIEN VALLEY: (I) In Cair Paravel, ST. CLIVE, a valley named for J.R.R. Tolkien (1892-1973), a friend of SAINT CLIVE.

TORCHSHIP: (A) See *ROBERT A. HEINLEIN, THE*

TOUCHABLE: (I) From reverse of "Untouchable" among Hindu castes in India. However, in the Federation, a Touchable is not born into a caste, but a person who, convicted of certain non-capital felonies, is given a life sentence to be state property hunted by MARNIEs as legal game and—when caught— "touchable for sexual satisfaction between sunset and sunrise, consent granted by the Federation." The most common of the felonies in the Federation for which one can be sentenced to touchability are first-offense rape (compounded by additional punishment if the offender is male; see PEOTOMY), willful non-compliance with the Universal Service Act, and desertion from the Peace Corps. Capital felonies such as homicide, kidnapping, terrorism, and treason are sentenced to death in the MICROWAVE OVENs, as are all further crimes by Touchables, and all offenses less serious than these, including crimes against property, are considered misdemeanors, punishable by restitution, fine, and/or compulsory community service. Touchables are forbidden to work in a profession or at a fixed location, to own property, or to appear in public not wearing their officially mandated garment: a RED cloak worn as a Scarlet Letter. The Sixth Amendment to the ARTICLES OF FEDERATION forbids Bills of

Attainder, so Touchable status is not hereditary: the children of Touchables are not Touchable. But if a Touchable parent has nowhere else to raise their children, the child might as well be. Female Touchables with small children are allowed to raise them in designated ghettos—the VAGINATOWN Ghetto in RAINBOROUGH being one—and such Touchables may retire into their ghetto at night, secure against hunting or rape. The Touchable punishment is considered "efficient justice" by Federation economists, inasmuch as Federation taxpayers no longer have to support felons in prisons, but instead get the "reparation" due to "society" for the felony, by having a convict available for sexual sport. Also, it is considered "punishment to fit the crime" for rapists, as well as draft-evaders and Peace Corps deserters unwilling to serve the cause of preserving the peace gladly—and a formidable deterrent to rape, draft-evasion, and desertion. All jurisdiction for Touchables falls to LEGOS, LIMITED, with final appeal to the FIRST LADY. It is customary, once a year at the YULE SOLSTICE, for the First Lady to grant conditional pardons to all female Touchables who, the previous year, have entered menopause.

TRANSPONDER: (N) IDENTITY TRANSPONDER. See also SCANNING.

TROOP: (N) In the Peace Corps, 1/2 of a DICTERIAT, comprising 225 women, segmented into five SORORITIES. The designation is used primarily for drilling and parades.

TSIOLKOVSKIIGRAD: (I) City-cylinder in the LENIN habitats, named for Konstantin Tsiolkovskii (1857–1935), Russian rocket experimenter who called Earth "the cradle of Mankind" and predicted that someday human beings would move into cities built in space itself.

TWIN: (N) In Federation usage, a female child identical to her mother, produced by PARTHENOGENESIS. Compare also with CLONE.

UNIVERSITY OF AD ASTRA AT NOVA PAULUS, THE, UAANP: (I) the main campus of a private university having campuses in each of Ad Astra's cities, with which the DRYER SCHOOL OF LASEGRAPHY is affiliated. Students of the Dryer School fulfill all Liberal Arts requirements at the UAANP, and the UAANP issues a Bachelor of Lasegraphy degree to Dryer students who fulfill the course requirements of both institutions.

U.H.I.: (I) United Holovision International: an all-news HOLOVISION service in the Federation.

UHURU: (N) From the Swahili word for "freedom." The FREE-SPACE HABITATS built by black African separatists after apartheid was ended in Africa.

UNIVERSAL SERVICE: (N) In the Federation, the draft. See CONSCRIPTION and MINISTRY OF UNIVERSAL SERVICE.

UPPER HUDSON: (N) The northern part of HUDSON PARISH.

UPPER MANOR: (N) The upper house in the Federation's bicameral legislature, the HOUSE OF GENTRY.

VAGINATOWN: (I) From assonance with "Chinatown," slang designation originating with MARNIEs for a TOUCHABLE ghetto where female Touchables with small children are allowed to live unmolested. The official name is the Rainborough Park Children's Reservation.

VALLE DE SOL: (N) Literally, "Sun Valley" in Spanish, a valley in NOVA PAULUS. See SUNDALE and SUNNY GLEN. I *told* you there are a lot of sun-worshippers there.

VELLEITY: (A) The lowest level of volition, wish, or inclination, and—by extension—psychokinesis (or precognition) in the game of VELLETROM.

VELLETROM: (I) Combination of vellity + trombone. A game played in a casino—either of gambling or betting, depending whether one believes in either psychokinesis or precognition—whereby players make bets on the probable hits of subatomic quanta shot out of a trombone-shaped particle accelerator at a numbered target. Since the house percentage is small, even the most minor psychic ability to influence or predict quantum-mechanical outcomes should produce consistent winning. However, the probabilities of a player actually having the ability to influence quantum probabilities is already figured into the house averages, so one would need to be a true psychic indeed in order to beat the probabilities and win consistently. In essence, velletrom is betting on one's ability to beat the house percentage through sheer willpower, a proposition on which gambling houses through history have always made a profit. Forget about bending spoons: if Uri Geller could consistently win at velletrom, Randi would have to pay up as well.

VENERY: (A) In the Federation, TOUCHABLE hunting. *Webster's Ninth Collegiate Dictionary* gives two separate definitions of venery: "the art, act, or practice of hunting," derived from *venari*, the Latin word for venison; and "the pursuit of indulgence in sexual pleasure," derived from the Latin root "vener–" from Venus, the Goddess of Love. These diverging Latin roots are combined in the Middle English *venerie*: to hunt. Makes one ponder what the tension of hunting and the release of killing animals is a substitute for, doesn't it? See DIALECTIC.

VETERAN: (N) A woman after she has completed her term of service in the Peace Corps.

VIDEO: (N) In the Federation, a videophone.

VIRGINIA STATION: (I) A habitat-sized, HOOP-DOG-shaped space city containing commercial areas and hotels, a military base of the FEDERATION SPACE CORPS, passenger, freight, and private torchship and shuttle docking facilities, and zero-gee manufacturing facilities, in a geosynchronous orbit above Earth's equator at the longitude of NEWER YORK—a longitude convenient from SOLERI and CANAVERAL SKYPORTs. The only space habitat under the jurisdiction of the Federation since the Colonial War, and the only source in the Federation of zero-gee manufacturing goods during the long trade embargo. Because of economies of scale and costs of lifting raw materials from Earth, zero-gee manufacturing here is not competitively priced with comparable goods from the habitats, which obtain their raw materials from the asteroid belt.

VISTATA: (I) A "visual sonata." A misnomer, actually, since—in Italian—*sonata* is the past participle of *sonare*: to sound. The correct past participle of the Italan *vedere*—to see—is *vista*. However, since the word "vista" had already made its way into English with a more commonplace meaning, early lasegraphers—wishing a discrete name for the form in which they were composing—used the three-syllable word "vistata" as a soundalike to "sonata." The term was accepted by common usage. The seven-movement standard form evolved largely in the IMPRESSIONIST PERIOD, following on Wolfgang Jaeger's use of COLORATURA in his *Rainbow Vistata*.

VIVARIUM: (N) Literally, House of Life or Quickening. In original usage, a terrarium or greenhouse used for raising plants or animals, the term evolved to refer to a hospice where cryonically-preserved persons could be stored and reanimated, as well as a facility for growing surrogate bodies for brains whose original bodies are damaged beyond repair. See CRYONIC SUSPENSION.

WARD: (N) The adopted mate of an ANDRO husband: direct counterpart to wife. The husband is considered the senior partner, the ward junior.

WAR, THE: (N) In the scarred memory of anyone who lived through it, the WAR OF COLONIAL SECESSION.

WAR OF COLONIAL SECESSION: (I) The Revolutionary War of Independence whereby the FREE-SPACE HABITATS severed political and economic dependency on Earth. After several ultimata back and forth, the O'NEILL habitat was destroyed by an off-course nuclear missile fired as a "warning shot" by the NORTH AMERICAN CONCORD, which unfortunately matched up with a malfunctioning laser-defense system in O'Neill; this was the first of the two major encounters in the War. The destroyed habitat's ally, AD ASTRA, was able to avoid further Federation attack by using the earth's moon as a shield and placing warning stations at strategic orbits, giving ample advance warning of any incoming attack. Using a strategy engineered by Robert A. Heinlein in his novel *The Moon is a Harsh Mistress*, Ad Astra used mass-drivers to launch a retaliatory attack of asteroids thrown as meteors against several Earth cities: the resulting "rains of terror" were about as devastating as nuclear attacks. Since the habitats could have laid waste to the entire planet this way, having no shortage of asteroids, the belligerent Earth nations, led by the North American Concord whose cities were destroyed, sued for a cease fire, agreed to by the habitats: the secession was successful. But Earth soon after formed the WORLD FEDERATION, originally a defense pact and an attempt to enforce a trade embargo against the habitats. This attempt succeeded, but the habitats' counter-embargo of Earth was far more damaging to Earth's economy than Earth's embargo was to the habitats. Two decades after the destruction of O'Neill and the RAIN OF TERROR, the RAINBOW COMPACT (the name taken from God's sign for agreeing never to destroy the Earth again) was signed in RAINBOROUGH PARK formally ending the War and ending the mutual embargoes.

WEST SIDEREAL STORY: (I) A later production of *West Side Story*, set in the habitats: an updating much as *West Side Story* was to *Romeo and Juliet*.

WHORE: (N) In the Peace Corps, a word honoring a CORPORAL. The connotation to prostitution has been lost.

WICCE, WICCEN: (A) The roots for "woman," "wisdom," "wicked," and "witch," all refer to the Old Religion—alternatively called the Craft—of which the three-fold GODDESS of MAIDEN, LADY, AND CRONE is worshipped in almost precisely the same way that the Christian Trinity is worshipped. There is some evidence that it is indeed the Old Religion, preceding even Judaism by quite a bit. For some reason, worshippers of God and worshippers of Goddess have been persecuting each other for all recorded history. God/dess only knows who started it. Because of its honor of female symbols above male symbols, and because it does not have the monogamous sexual code of the Judeo-Christian tradition, Wicce grew to be more popular than Christianity on Earth when sociological changes made monogamy an institution only for a chosen few. It became a politically powerful religion on Earth by the time of the Federation, and provides ritualistic support for the World Federation in exchange for having its feast days made legal holidays. Nevertheless, Wicce is not an official religion in the Federation, since the Third Amendment to the ARTICLES OF FEDERATION mandates separation of church and state. (Neither, by the way, is Christianity proscribed by law: the anti-Christian attitude on Earth is social, not legal.) Nevertheless, by the time of the Federation, Witches hunt Christian Touchables and burn them—when permitted—in MICROWAVE OVENs. An old Arabic saying is, "Revenge is a dish best eaten cold." The Wiccens in the Federation think it's best warmed in a microwave oven.

WICCENSTED: (I) New name, in the Federation for Christiansted, St. Croix, Virgin Islands. The name was changed to remove the reference to Christianity. See also ISLE OF ARTEMIS.

WIDDERSHINS: (A) Counterclockwise.

WINDFIELD: (I) An adjustable electrostatic field surrounding a FLYING BELT to reduce drag and prevent windburn.

WOLF: (A) In music, an imperfection in a musical instrument resulting in an unpleasant sound. Later in LASEGRAPHY an imperfect spectral line in a CHROMATIC LASER. The infrared "wolf" in the lowest red fire gem in Joan's LCAA MARK 800B laser is only deadly at ABSOLUTE POWER, which was never intended to be used in rehearsal or performance, so was not considered a reason for rejecting an otherwise acceptable FIRE GEM, considering how rare and valuable they are.

WOLF, THE: (N) In lasegrapher's jargon, the wolf-at-the-door—all the mundane problems that interfere with the artistic life and—by extension—external problems to be contrasted with the artistic ones in the TIGER PIT. See also TIGER, THE.

WOMEN: (A) One of three socio-political designations in the Federation, along with ANDROMEN and COMMEN. Women are the only one of the three subject to UNIVERSAL SERVICE, and may stand for office—or vote for—the PINK Seat in the HOUSE OF GENTRY. A woman—the FIRST LADY—is Head of State of the Federation, Chief Justice, and Commander in Chief of the Federation Peace Corps.

WORLD FEDERATION, THE: (I) Successor to the League of Nations and the United Nations, the long-sought World Republic—population circa 2,000,000,000—in which former independent nation-states are provinces. The Federation was enacted soon after—and as a direct result of—the hostilities of the Colonial War, the point at which nations on the planet had an external enemy to unite against. The Articles of Federation call for a bicameral legislature—called Congress or Parliament—consisting of a HOUSE OF GENTRY and a HOUSE OF COMMEN, to distribute power equally into three branches among the three official genders: WOMEN, ANDROMEN, and COMMEN. Legislation must pass both houses to become law, the Head of State and Chief Justice of the Federation is a woman called the FIRST LADY, the PRESIDENT (Chief Executive) and Provincial Governors (Gaylords) are andromen, and the Chairman of the Governing Cabinet (PRIME MINISTER) is a comman. The Federation is divided into PROVINCEs often consisting of the old nation-states which are administered by a GAYLORD (the provincial governor who's also the junior senator in the House of Gentry) with absolute free and open borders between provinces for Federation citizens and trade goods mandated by the Bill of Rights in the Articles of Federation. The Bill of Rights also mandates privacy protection, right of habeas corpus, protection of property rights, a republican form of government for each Province, freedom of expression and religion, hard money, separation of state and economics, emigration rights to outer space, and other civil liberties. In theory, the Articles of Federation promise—on a global scale—the liberty that the United States Constitution promises—and it is a debatable question which delivers more.

WORLD FEDERATION PEACE CORPS, THE: (I) The pseudo-military "sexual service" of the World Federation comprising 4,500,000 "CORPORALs" at any given time, women drafted into active duty for three years. It is under the jurisdiction of the HOUSE OF GENTRY, its Commander-in-Chief is the FIRST LADY of the Federation, and it operates the DICTERIA providing sexual services to COMMEN. Not only are corporals in the Peace Corps *not* regarded as lowly or immoral, they are considered the bravest and most moral members of society—not only by the commen who directly benefit from their service, but by the powerful women veterans of the Peace Corps, and their ANDROMEN political allies, who indirectly benefit from it. Being drafted to duty in the Peace Corps is the highest honor that can be bestowed upon a woman in the Federation: a prize which is given to a woman for being young and politically powerless.

YONI: (A) A stylized symbol of the female genitalia in Hindu culture—represented here— ( ) —by two opposing parentheses, later used as insigne of the ranks of CORPORAL in the Federation Peace Corps. Compares with the Hindu "lingham," but in practice the word "phallus" is considered more understandable.

YOUR LADYSHIP; (N) Except when addressing a LADY elected to the HOUSE OF GENTRY, ragging used on a woman to imply she's hoity-toity.

YULE: (A) The YULE SOLSTICE.

YULE SOLSTICE: (A) The winter solstice, the celebration of which by Druids and WICCE was later co-opted by the Christian celebration of the birth of Christ at Yuletide, for which there is no evidence whatsoever.

Christmas adopted most of the pagan Yule practices: decorating a Yule tree, hanging mistletoe, gift-giving, feast days, etc. The tables were later turned again in the Federation, where Wiccens adopted much culture associated with Christmas and reapplied it to the celebration of Yule.

YURI GAGARIN, THE: (N) A thermonuclear torchship named after the first man (1934–1968) to enter orbital space.

BIO OF A SPACE TYRANT
Piers Anthony

"Brilliant...a thoroughly original thinker and storyteller with a unique ability to posit really *alien* alien life, humanize it, and make it come out alive on the page." *The Los Angeles Times*

A COLOSSAL NEW FIVE VOLUME SPACE THRILLER—
BIO OF A SPACE TYRANT
The Epic Adventures and Galactic Conquests of Hope Hubris

VOLUME I: REFUGEE   84194-0/$3.50 US/$4.50 Can
Hubris and his family embark upon an ill-fated voyage through space, searching for sanctuary, after pirates blast them from their home on Callisto.

VOLUME II: MERCENARY   87221-8/$3.50 US/$4.50 Can
Hubris joins the Navy of Jupiter and commands a squadron loyal to the death and sworn to war against the pirate warlords of the Jupiter Ecliptic.

VOLUME III: POLITICIAN   89685-0/$3.50 US/$4.50 Can
Fueled by his own fury, Hubris rose to triumph obliterating his enemies and blazing a path of glory across the face of Jupiter. Military legend...people's champion...promising political candidate...he now awoke to find himself the prisoner of a nightmare that knew no past.

THE BEST-SELLING EPIC CONTINUES—
VOLUME IV: EXECUTIVE
89834-9/$3.50 US/$4.50 Can
Destined to become the most hated and feared man of an era, Hope would assume an alternate identify to fulfill his dreams ...and plunge headlong into madness.

VOLUME V: STATESMAN
89835-7/$3.50 US/$4.95 Can
the climactic conclusion of Hubris' epic adventures:

AVON Paperbacks